A MAD PASSION

"You are a handsome man, Louis. You make me wish I knew what it was like to be a woman," she whispered.

He drew his finger lower to trace her rain-slick lips. Sabine closed her eyes and allowed him to explore the curves of her face. Louis drew his finger gently down her chin, following a spidering trail of rain. Pools of water collected over her eyelids and spilled softly across her cheeks like so many tears.

"Kiss me, Louis."

Thinking he should only brush her lips gently and then pull back, Louis touched his mouth to Sabine's. But his burning need took him much further. He kissed her slowly, lazily, teasing himself to control his desirous urges. Her sigh was immediately captured by his mouth and Louis felt the released emotion surge straight to his heart. Blood pounded in his ear. Fairy glamour had never been more powerful.

Cupping her head in his hand, he deepened his kiss against her seeking lips. Pushing his hands up through her crown of hair, he couldn't help but think that this was most likely her first kiss.

And the first he would ever remember.

After a very long time Sabine opened her eyes and gave him a shy smile. Her voice took on a husky timbre, that of a woman who would tempt a man into her arms as Venus did Adonis year after tempestuous year. "I know what you think of me, Louis."

Did she really? Louis blushed. "Whatever do you mean?"

"You have in your presence a madwoman. . . ."

MY LADY MADNESS

MICHELE HAUF

Zebra Books
Kensington Publishing Corp.

http://www.zebrabooks.com

PART ONE

Tell me where is Fancy bred,
Or in the heart, or in the head?

—*The Merchant of Venice* Act III, Scene 2

PROLOGUE

1745

The air was humid and heavy with summer's seductive perfume. Meadow flowers bloomed full and bright in crimson, periwinkle, and saffron. Louis could smell the mist of their fragrance on his worn cotton frock coat. The brief touch of a dragonfly's wings across his hair sounded crisp against the surrounding symphony of insect hums.

The alley of trees that led up to the Bassange estate was badly in need of trimming. Twisting oak branches had grown to a great canopy of luscious emerald and olive foliage. Thin, snaking vines of a nature he knew not spiraled around thick bark and affixed themselves to every single branch.

Each step of his horse's hooves stirred up dandelion umbrellas in a thick cloud of whiteness. The coal-dust Andalusian bristled at the sight, but marched on at Louis's urging.

The narrow tree-lined aisle opened up before the crumbling, rough-cut fieldstones of an ancient castle. Two circular towers framed a stretch of wall that was once a fortified keep. The battlements had decayed, leaving straight lines where once were crenelated tooth marks. Here and there, great masses of tangled vinery clung to the walls as if they were peeling emerald paint. Infrequent dots of rose blossoms were the blood of battles long forgotten splashed during enemy raids. Yew hedges spotted with fleshy red berries grew wild about the castle base, and the grass shot as high as the stallion's knees. Within the scattered weeds and tall grasses were sprinkled wildflowers of fiery red, lemon yellow, and pink so vivid as to rival even a blushing maiden.

A plump bee buzzed past Louis's ear, causing him to smile at the fleeting scent of pollen. Everything was wild and carefree. A fantastical feeling enveloped Louis like a thick wool blanket on a cold winter's night. For a brief moment he was able to release his anxieties to the gentle winds that feathered through his dark hair.

Glancing up, Louis could not help but smile. Just slightly. Never in his wildest fantasies could he imagine so perfect a sight.

Whoever lived in this castle . . . surely they danced with the fairies by day and soared with the unicorns at night.

And then, as if in answer to his imaginings, a beautiful fairy danced into Louis's view. She appeared from the side of the crumbling left tower, her silken skirts of the softest peach shade flowing lightly across the grasses. Her arms, pale and lithe, twirled about her as guidance in her flight. A mane of sun-kissed gold danced across her shoulders and softly framed her delicate features as she spun closer.

Perhaps she was aware of his being there. Perhaps not. She danced as if in a world all her own, seemingly heedless of his presence, dipping to trace her fingertips across the tops of the grass blades. Twirling gracefully forward, she swooped widely and then pirouetted to a grand finale but a few feet from Louis.

She tiptoed up to his stallion and touched a fairy finger to its velvet-suede nose. Sweetness painted her smile. Her eyes danced upward and Louis felt his heart catch and freeze for a breathless moment.

He had been captured by two round pools of sparkling violet, so intense and lucid that should a jewel possess the very color, it would command a king's ransom. As she looked at him with such pure knowing, he swallowed the lump that lodged in his throat. He made to speak, but his thoughts would not collect properly. Instead, he made a sighing cough.

As she bowed before him, her long tangle of buttery tresses swept over the wild crimson poppies that sprouted in Louis's gray shadow.

"My lord," she said in an elegant voice, "we are most honored to welcome you to our humble home. I pray you dismount the unicorn and allow it free rein in our meadow."

CHAPTER ONE

Earlier that day . . .

A slash of sunlight guided Louis de Lavarac across the oak-wood floor worn to sloping waves by ancestors too far distant for him to recall. A slow trudge was all he could manage in his dejected state. He did not bother to curve his steps to avoid setting well-memorized boards to a creak. Let them whine and moan in complaint.

Nothing mattered anymore.

The unexpected brightness of the day held him back against the doorframe, cowering in the cool morning shadows. But much as his mind had fought good sense for the past two weeks, it had come time to peel himself from the twilight and enter the real world. He stuck a bare toe out into the sun-golden air. Warmth. Comfort. Strangely . . . welcome.

Louis walked across the second-floor veranda and leaned against the splintering pinewood railing, his back to the bur-geoning field of grapevines and surrounding forest that stretched leagues beyond the de Lavarac château. The grass, lush and green when he had returned from military duty just weeks before, was slowly becoming a patchwork of brown and burnt tan. The July heat stifled life with a smothering squeeze; the sun, unmerciful in its search for bare flesh and bed-rest–weakened eyes. Ah, but it was a blessing for the grapes, for they would drink heartily of the sun's precious elixir and sweeten to create the finest *vin rouge,* the de Lavaracs' signature vintage.

Louis touched the linen bindings wrapped tightly around his wrists, feeling his heartbeat lurch and sink. *No medal of honor for this act of cowardice.*

He closed his eyes, but incessant flashes of battle poured through screens of crimson in his mind. Not-so-distant memories revived the monotonous thump of battle drums. *Brum. Brum. Brum.* The sound of solid iron shot finding its mark in enemy flesh. *Thash.* It was sickening, the final death cry a man makes as he realizes his life is finished.

Dozens of those cries lived inside Louis's head. Screaming for vengeance, for mercy, for salvation. Reminding Louis of his cruelty. And finally, begging his compassion with a soft woman's voice he had never heard save in his nightmares.

There will be no redemption for you.

And her husband's dying words . . .

Tell her I love her, my Evangeline.

In desperation and despair for the destruction he had been a part of, Louis had tried to end his own life . . .

"So you've finally seen fit to return to the world of the living?"

At the sound of his older brother's voice, Louis jerked his gaze up from the partially unwound bandage. Henri's long midnight-blue hair was not fastened in its usual neat plait, nor was he shaved. The vineyards demanded relentless attention during the spring and summer months. Pruning and budding and insect control kept a man and six farmhands busy through the late hours of the night.

Louis compared his brother's condition to his own lack of care for his appearance. He did not even bother to smooth away the long, tangled strands of hair from his face as the breeze pushed them across his parched lips. Since returning home, he'd done little more than lie in his bed. Misery and guilt had pinned his bones to the feather mattress like lead weights. He'd become weak both in mind and body. And as for the spirit, well, Louis was not sure if that even existed anymore.

He had brought death to so many. Without so much as a by-your-leave. All for the French flag. *Vive le roi. I am your king! Kill for me and suffer endlessly after.*

It was not right! Or perhaps it was right and it was only Louis that wasn't right. Not right with himself or the world and its expectations, its desires, its dangerous traps of despair. He could not truthfully decide.

"Home a fortnight and all you do is mope, brother. By God's faith, when will this end? You are alive. Accept that and move on."

"Alive." Louis rolled the word around inside his tired mind. *I live, and yet so many have died at my hands. Ah, Evangeline, can you ever forgive me?* "I feel as if all life has left me, Henri." He gazed across the parallel rows of grapevines, thick and full with vivid green leaves, like billowing clouds bound of tightly napped wool.

"I cannot bear to watch you wallow in self-pity."

Self-pity. His relentless master as of late.

"Where is the proud young man I once knew?"

There had been a time when Louis would have used the word himself. But war works cruel menace on all participants. Pride is demented and twisted into a cruel lust to win and conquer no matter what the cost to human life.

"He died on the battlefield. Each thrust of my sword cut deep into my heart, and now I am but shreds. Do you not see?"

Henri strode over to him and took up Louis's bandaged wrists. The heat of another human being's life force beating a steady pulse against his own startled him.

"Fight the demons within, brother." Henri's dark eyes held Louis in an acquiescent silence. "War has its purpose, and the Lord forgives all men their sins. Your life has been spared for a reason. You must persevere. If I can, then you must also."

If I can . . .

A strong man, Henri. Strong enough to withstand the shock of losing his wife, Janette, and his only child. *My life lies beneath this ground,* he'd said a year earlier as he stood at the edge of their fresh graves, fingering a single white rose to an oily pulp. And yet with all his pain, he stood before Louis now, encouraging him.

"Will you walk the rows with me tonight?" Hands behind his back, Henri strode to the end of the veranda and scanned the rolling waves of vines. "I need to check the grapes, assure there are no insects or rot. Pray heaven above for the rains."

"Of course." Louis found it hard to show any more enthusiasm. He wasn't ready for life. To become a human being again. Redemption hung too far from his grasp. "Perhaps . . . after I've rested."

"No!" Henri pounded the pine railing with his fist. "You've made the first step. I won't allow you to burrow back into your protective nesting."

Louis crossed his arms over his chest and tucked his chin to his neck, closing his eyes to Henri's chiding words.

"There is something you can do. I haven't the time this month."

"What is it?" Louis said on a lackluster sigh. Below, an olive katydid chirped sharply and sprang from a grass spike to the cool depths of shaded foliage.

"I need you to ride to the Bassange estate. See that things are going well, carry along supplies. I've gone every month for years now. 'Tis time someone else took up the task."

"You are looking after a family?"

Henri nodded. "Tenants. I've looked after them since Father's death. It's not as if it will continue for much longer. The old man is rattling heaven's gates. Once he's gone, we can sell the land, for they owe years in rent."

Louis raised a brow.

"It is just the girl, Sabine, and her *grand-père*. They've lived alone for more than a decade in that dilapidated castle beyond the valley. I bring them food and supplies monthly and help around the grounds. The old man is blind, and the girl, well . . ."

Louis had completely unwrapped one wrist. He dangled the binding over his fingers. "The girl?"

"She is deranged."

"Deranged?" He squinted his eyes against the sunlight, but could not read Henri's stony expression.

"Touched in the head." Henri snapped a finger against his skull.

"Really? You jest."

"I do not. I've seen her only the one time. Screaming and flailing she was. Pulling at her hair and moaning. I've not seen her since. Figure the old man keeps her locked away." Henri rubbed thin, labor-roughened fingers along his wide jawbone, smoothing a thumb across his sunken cheek. "They say she's been that way since her mother and father were murdered before her eyes. She was but a child of nine or ten. Horrendous thing."

Horrendous things happen all the time. *War has its purpose?*

Perhaps so. But Louis had yet to determine exactly what.

"But surely someone must take care of the two?" Louis wondered aloud. "When you are not around?" He paced the patio in his lawn shirt and bare feet, following the edge of sunlight splashed across the pine boards. "If the old man is ailing, who cooks for him? And the girl, if she's mad, does she not require . . . special care?"

"No one dares work there," Henri said with an exhausted sigh. "The castle is said to be haunted by the girl's parents.

She has her lucid moments, I've been told by the old man himself. She cooks and tends to him. Though as for who cares for her, I haven't the faintest.''

Louis let the remaining bandage drop at his feet and pressed his forefinger to the scabbed wound snaking across his wrist. The cuts had been miserably shallow. Brandy had dulled his senses so much that he hadn't realized the knife had been duller than his wits.

Louis looked up through a mist of cloud and seared his gaze to the sun until teardrops spilled down his cheeks. Perhaps someone had been watching over him. Some *presence* had made sure it was the dull carving knife he'd taken up instead of the razor-sharp dagger he usually carried sheathed at his hip.

"I don't know." Louis spoke to the heavens and then lowered his gaze to Henri. "I cannot do it. I just . . . haven't the desire."

"You will do it." Henri's breath warmed the side of Louis's face as he was suddenly by his side. "I thought it good fortune, your return, but for weeks now you've been haunting the château like death's shadow. Your chores have gone undone, the hired hands have no respect for you. You will do this, brother.''

Louis's body fell against the railing, his head bowed to disguise his grimace. "It is as if life itself shall never again be the same. *I* can never be the same. Never become the man I once was. Young . . . carefree . . ." *Carefree? Had he actually said such a word? Been such a thing?* "There is nothing left in this world that can make life worth living. You will never understand, Henri.''

"Understand?" Henri's fingers pinched into Louis's shoulder. The veins at his temples pulsed and the sweat beaded on his forehead. *"I* will never understand? You know nothing, do you hear me? Nothing!''

Held captive by his brother's dark, raging eyes, Louis choked down a hasty retort. A fool he was for saying such a thing. Of course Henri had suffered far more than he. He had lost his own flesh and blood. A child who had never been given the chance to take its first breath. And his wife of only one year.

But Henri did not have the souls of hundreds haunting him. The two of them sheltered very different pains. Louis was ashamed for thinking himself the only one who knew suffering.

"Forgive me, brother." Louis looked to the sun, closing his eyes tight. "Forgive me."

Henri did not speak, though Louis could read the lost hope in his tired release of breath.

"Very well," Louis offered dispassionately. He had been spared for a reason. It was time to discover what that reason was. "I will go."

Never in all his imaginings had he thought madness would cloak itself in such a soft and elegant creature. With eyes as lucid and precious as flowing water and a grace that rose above all natural movement.

Struck deep to his heart, Louis clutched his hand to his chest. But the arrow, thrust mightily by Cupid, broke off at the surface; he could never retrieve it. Nor did he desire to.

Louis slid off his stallion and tossed the reins over the Andalusian's back. His knee-high jackboots trampled virgin grass and sent a scatter of billowing dandelion kites flying up about the two of them. The woman in fairy silks giggled and danced about, tracing their elusive flight with her slender fingers and blowing carefree kisses to send them on their way.

"My lady," Louis called to her as she skipped about, "if you would gift me with your name?"

The fairy child spun over to Louis and stopped. Standing perfectly still, she lifted her lips into a delightful smile and said so softly, as if a prayer whispered in church, "It is Sabine Bassange, my lord."

The bewitching spell she cast upon Louis dazzled in its intensity. Her presence seemed to spring forth in an invisible mass and enter his body as a shivering motion of warmth and joy.

Louis shook away his awe with an abrupt jerk of his neck. He was there simply to deliver supplies. It would not do to let his mind wander so. "Mademoiselle Bassange, it seems I find you well and happy." *And so very delightful.*

Madness? Louis searched his mind and retrieved images of screaming souls, forgotten by society, imprisoned behind the rusting bars of a rat-infested asylum. Not this woman. Henri had seen things all wrong.

"Might I inquire of your *grand-père?*"

Sabine turned her back to Louis. He followed her gaze up the crumbling walls of the far tower to an arrow-slit window, narrowly fashioned centuries ago so that enemy fire could not penetrate. Was that *Grand-père*'s room?

"He is silent as of late," Sabine said in a concerned manner. She started walking and indicated with a graceful splay of her hand that Louis follow. "Come. The unicorn will be safe. I shall bring you to *Grand-père*. He has not had much to say. Rather lost his appetite too."

"Do you prepare his meals?" Louis wondered as they entered the cool walls of the castle. But of course, she seemed perfectly able. Henri's descriptions of her madness were most definitely overblown.

"Not lately," she spirited out with a gay twirl on her toes and a balletic bow.

She seemed to float up the leaf-scattered spiral stairs, her silken skirts following like graceful birds on wing. Louis noticed she did not wear the confining dresses that the ladies of Paris stuffed themselves into. No tight stays or wide skirts. Just a simple gown that allowed her limbs to dance about. Almost a chemise, but not so thin as to betray her modesty.

Mindless of life's worries, Louis thought. Oh, to possess such a state for a precious moment. To have never experienced the horrors of war. To know the freedom that this woman embodied. To embrace this golden fairy in his arms . . .

A firm thump to the side of his head with his palm shook him back to reality. Where had that thought come from? To embrace this woman? Foolishness! His life was complicated enough without burdening another soul with his troubles.

But on the other hand . . .

Louis could not recall seeing a lovelier face, a more graceful figure. "Perhaps this is just what you need," he muttered to himself, smoothing his forefinger under his chin. "A fine wench to ease the pain. A warm body . . . Blast! If Henri is correct, she is not well. You've gone mad yourself, de Lavarac."

Though it did seem to Louis that Sabine Bassange was not so gone in the head that she could not hold a conversation. She understood all he had asked thus far. Perhaps a lonely life spent walled up with an ancient man and no friends or pastimes to occupy her mind had simply made her delicate. Wasn't madness so much more vile?

As Louis followed her up the steps inside the castle tower, he noticed that no one had swept since perhaps last fall, for along with scattered acorns that crunched and snapped beneath his boot heels, dried and crumbled leaves whispered soft death cries. Had Henri done so little in all the times he had been here? Surely any man would see that with a little work, this castle could be made more livable. A mere day's labor.

A surge of ambition lit through Louis's veins as he pushed back his sleeve. And it felt good. He would see to it the place was cleaned before he left today. Perhaps Henri was right. Work would keep his mind from more depressing thoughts.

And perhaps then he could forget about Evangeline. *Tell her I love her* . . .

"Do not be surprised if *Grand-père* chooses not to speak." Sabine was suddenly at Louis's side. Faint perfume of wild-flowers lingered near his nose as she whispered gaily in her breeze-kissed tone. Like an elusive moth, a wisp of her long hair brushed across Louis's cheek. He touched the spot. It held a hot, tingling vibration. He'd just been kissed by fairy wings.

"He is in there." She pointed to a great iron-banded door. And off she was in her twirling dance to some soundless symphony. "Go on," she prompted midtwirl. "You mustn't be afraid."

Afraid? Without thinking, Louis gave a guttural grunt. After all, he'd seen in the army. There was nothing that could scare Louis de Lavarac. Except—Louis stopped cold before the door—senseless death. Rubbing his thumb over the wound on his wrist, Louis eyed the door. *Fight the demon within, brother.*

Drawing in a breath of courage, Louis pushed against the dry, cracked wood, which responded with the icy creak of a hinge. The skittering feet of tiny insects restored a brief picture of the asylum to Louis's mind. *Do we not all possess some little scrap of madness? Deep within?*

Curiosity pulled Louis across the cleanly swept stone floor, but immediately his senses were suffused with the sickening stench of rot. Flies buzzed about the great waves of moth-eaten netting that had been firmly anchored over the bed and to the floor. Pinching his nostrils shut, Louis stepped forward and leaned cautiously over the bed. A fly buzzed past his ear.

Grand-père lay gray and rotting, the pallor of death long gone and replaced by the hideous mask of decay.

Gulping down the bile that curdled in his throat, Louis backed out of the room and saw Sabine still danced her mindless waltz. "He is dead!"

Sabine stopped suddenly. It seemed she considered the idea for a moment. Her lips pursed and her eyes took on a sparkling clarity. Lucidity. Until . . . "Yes, I know!" She bowed grandly and spirited away into her dance.

"This is lunacy!" Louis pushed past Sabine and marched down the stairs, twirling up a storm of leaves in his wake. The old man had to have died over a fortnight ago.

Louis pressed a finger to his aching brow. Did she not realize what dead meant? Had she tended that stinking body for weeks without so much as a clue to the old man's condition? What horrors had her mind endured to have taken leave?

She truly is mad, he thought. For a normal person would not have allowed such a . . . thing . . . to lie in this heat untended.

He pulled back the heavy wood door and inhaled the fresh meadow air, cleaning away the rot that had invaded his senses. Behind and above him the girl danced her senseless ballet. Perhaps it was a good thing that she wasn't rational. For surely such a sight could send any sane person over the edge.

In a few minutes, Sabine appeared by Louis's shoulder. She sat upon the bottom step, smoothing her pale peach skirts out over her legs, and politely folded her hands in her lap. Louis looked at her face. She blinked slowly and deep, golden lashes dusted the saffron-scented air. There was an utter gentleness about her, almost childlike in its innocence.

Unaware of his own actions, Louis reached down and touched the softness of her hair. It was clean and of the finest texture, the color like freshly churned butter. He'd never touched a woman's hair without the hindrance of pomades and oils and powders.

"We shall bury him," he said as he smoothed his palm over her head, inexplicably compelled to the velvet softness. "Immediately. I'll bring him down." He turned, and with a deep breath pulled in enough courage to go back up the stairs.

"Monsieur," Sabine said suddenly.

"Yes?"

"What will become of me?" Violet jewels sparkled with sunlight, precious gems set against a peaches-and-cream countenance. "Will you leave me here to rot as my *grand-père?*"

Louis stepped quickly back to her side and placed gentle hands on her shoulders. "Oh, no, no, mademoiselle."

He had expected perhaps a tear, perhaps a quivering lip. But there was nothing. No emotion in her jewel eyes; no curve, neither up nor down, to her delicate lips. She was clearly of this world at the moment. It seemed when she was rational, she possessed no emotion. Only when she was in her other world did her face take on the emotions of her soul. Her body dancing to the music within.

"Then what?" she said. "Will I be hauled away to Paris and left to die in chains in some filthy institution? I could not live like that, Monsieur de Lavarac. I just could not. I know I am . . . hmm . . . unable to grasp . . . things. Though . . ." Her voice returned to a singsong tone. "Sometimes I understand very well. 'Tis the fairies . . ." Vivid delight danced in her eyes. "They care for me. They see me through day after day. But if I should be taken to Paris, I fear they will leave me. I would be so very alone if they were to leave, monsieur. You must help me."

"A trapped soul," Louis whispered to himself as he gazed into her lovely eyes. He brushed the back of his hand across her cheek. More precious than the finest of silks, her flesh. Louis felt sure he'd never in his life touched something as soft. "What can I do to free you?"

She touched his hand. A fairy lighting upon his flesh. "Monsieur?"

Louis startled. *"Huh?* Oh, pardon, mademoiselle." He withdrew his hand and slid it inside his waistcoat. For a moment it had felt as though he held a rose in his palms, so delicate and velvety and alive with the fragrance of life. "I—it is only— that I was lost for a moment."

Sabine gave a soft chuckle. "I know that feeling. Where were you?"

"Where? Er . . ." Her sweet observation set his heart to a rapid pace. Yes, this one was of a species he had never encountered before. And to truly know her would be a delight. "I was lost in your eyes, my lady. I fear they possess powers of which you are quite unaware. It is truly a pleasure to lose oneself in them."

"Really?" she gasped breathlessly. A delighted smile captured her face.

Louis felt a warm satisfaction in knowing he'd pleased her. To have been the tool that generated such an exquisite smile. It had been far too long since he'd done anything so benevolent.

Mon Dieu, what am I doing?

A black-winged gnat buzzed past his nose, reminding Louis there were things that needed prompt attention. Like the fly-infested corpse lying above. It was with great reluctance that he stood and took another step. "If you'll excuse me, mademoiselle." He brushed his thumb over a smudge of dirt on her chin. "Perhaps you could select a fitting place in the meadow for your *grand-père*'s final rest?"

She curtsied grandly, lifting her skirts with the grace of a princess. "I should be honored, my lord."

CHAPTER TWO

"Insufferable Paris," Cristoforo muttered as he paced the length of his lavishly decorated apartment—courtesy of Marie Leczinska, Queen of France—on the newly developing Rue de Rivoli. Everything glinted in gold and silver and crystal. Champagne flowed like a raging river, and plush carpeting, imported from India he was told, cushioned his bare feet as he stomped. "Why in Saint Genarro's holy vows did I ever agree to this madness? Ha-oow!"

Sharp pain jerked him out of his pacing. Since arriving in Paris, the headaches had seeped out of remission. They lingered behind his temple, a slight tremor just beneath the flesh, then stronger . . . then an evil simmer. Until he was performing. Then they would attack with brutal force.

He pressed his fingertips to his forehead. The pain wasn't unbearable. It was just that it was always there!

Cristoforo allowed his body to slump onto the rose damask day-chaise, his gilt-embroidered robe fanning about his hosed legs. He gestured to his servant, Pietro, to bring water. The precious elixir. All too hard to obtain in Paris—unless you preferred it tainted with filth or stinking so badly, it could not be drunk.

"Another head pain, master?" Pietro questioned as he slipped a goblet into Cristoforo's spidery fingers. The boy knelt on the elaborately woven carpet and pressed his cheek against Cristoforo's thigh, fixing adoring eyes on his master as the man sipped his water with all the grandeur of a king.

Cristoforo absently spread his fingers through the boy's soft crown of hair. The water felt good as it trickled in diamond rivulets down his throat. A trifling reward for tonight's performance.

Ah, yes, the audience had adored him. They had risen to their feet and cheered for a full ten minutes after his aria bravura. Pietro had counted. Cristoforo had sung three encores and collected dozens of roses at his feet. Oh, how they always wanted him. The men had cheered loudly, clapping above their heads. And the women—overstuffed pincushions topped by powdered towers of rotting hair—how Cristoforo loved to see them swoon.

But it was the one woman who hadn't gone weak in the knees, had held her head defiantly, so that she above all others was noticed in the crowd, who had captured his attention.

The Countess de Morieux. Tragically widowed just last month. Seems the count had tripped on her skirts when exiting a carriage behind her. Snapped his neck like a twig. Tonight she waited for Cristoforo at her apartments on the Rue Vignon.

Another hot ache bit at his temple. Cristoforo pressed his palm to his grease-painted forehead, inwardly cursing the one uncontrollable force in his life. Tiny bursts of lightning surged through his temples in haphazard rhythm.

Damn the heavens and hell while they're at it!

Matters needed to be taken care of. And soon. He could not allow this pain, this insufferable torment, to interfere with his life any longer. Not now that he was finally becoming recognized as one of Italy's greatest operatic singers. In the past three years, he'd risen from virtual obscurity to one of Italy's finest and most sought after performers. He'd sung for kings and queens, even the Russian czar, and was now in Paris for three months at the invitation of King Louis XV. Quite a coup considering France had outlawed castratos from performing. Why, he was even being hailed as a greater singer than the illustrious Farinelli.

But now that he was in Paris, the headaches had worsened. Cristoforo had suspected such a thing would occur. He was so much closer, the connection only grown stronger. And he knew what he had to do to bring everything to its perfect order.

The ties that bind had to be severed.

"Did you dispatch the bravo?" Cristoforo questioned the ruby-lipped boy at his side.

"*Sì*, Cristoforo. His work will be complete by this evening."

They piled many stones upon *Grand-père* Bassange's grave, Sabine working as diligently as Louis to retrieve them from the field just behind the weeping branches of a silver-gilded willow. The rocks bordered a stream, where Louis had decided Sabine must wash her hair and bathe; else how could she be so clean?

Louis fashioned a makeshift cross of two elm branches, promising Sabine that he would come back with a fine cross of stone as soon as he could. Where and how he would find such a thing, he hadn't a notion.

He hadn't thought of much since arriving. Other than to lose himself in the strange fantasy of carefree madness that seduced with a virgin's innocent smile.

A storm of wispy dandelion heads swirled delicately through the air as Sabine knelt and Louis stood just over her shoulder, listening to her eulogy.

"May the angels watch over you, *Grand-père*. Their harps

will never cease playing you delightful songs. Dance upon their music and you shall be carried into the heavens.''

Louis looked up to the perfect blue sky, attempting to choke back a tear. So odd that the tears came now, for the first time since childhood.

''You mustn't worry, *Grand-père*,'' Sabine bent and whispered to the rock pile, ''the fairies will watch over you until the angels come.''

A thin oak branch lay at her feet. Sabine picked it up, wrapped her fingers around it, and then broke off the exposed ends on either side of her palm. She poked the small portion of stick into the mounded earth. ''Never farther than a heartbeat away.''

Louis wiped his eyes. For some reason he could not explain, he felt compelled to protect this innocent woman from all the evil in the world. As a young man of seventeen, he had not been prepared for a soldier's life and the horrors he had witnessed daily. Six years later his heart had hardened.

And here sat a precious, delicate child of sunshine who should never have to witness the same.

But he knew not how to protect her. Louis rubbed his wrist against his thigh, wincing as the wound grated across the seam running the length of his breeches. He felt sure that no matter what he might do to help Sabine Bassange, her scars would remain forever. As would his.

And who was he to even think he could help? Louis de Lavarac, the coward who had tried to end his own life? Ha! The devil must be having a laugh right about now, Louis thought grimly. To see him fumble about in an attempt to provide compassion, when the fount of his emotions had dried to dust long ago.

''We should be going,'' Louis offered, wishing to just get on with things.

Unfortunately—hard to think of fortune lately—he knew that she could not remain here.

''Going? But where, my lord? My home is here.''

He helped her up by the elbow. "I'll not leave you alone. Come home with me, mademoiselle. You can stay until I've notified the proper authorities. Perhaps your *grand-père* has arranged for you to be cared for by a relative?"

"Relative?" Her entire body shriveled into a noticeable sadness, collapsing her narrow shoulders to rounded slides. Then just as quickly her spine snapped straight, and the sparkle returned to Sabine's jewel eyes. "Oh!" Her face brightened as she slipped her fingers beneath the lace-rimmed neck of her dress and brought up a slender silver chain on which dangled a rusted key. *"Grand-père* always said this would protect my future."

"Perhaps it is the key to his will and other important things." Louis held his hand out for the key.

"But you must catch me first!" Sabine tiptoed across the gravestones and then fluttered into the meadow amid a snowstorm of dandelions.

"And catch you I shall."

He didn't even think. Couldn't even bother to worry that this was not what a grown man racked with guilt should be doing in the middle of the afternoon. Instead, he skipped through a flower-speckled meadow in pursuit of an elusive fairy child.

Louis grasped Sabine around the waist. Gay, childish laughter spilled from her lips as he twirled her off the ground and around in a half circle. So this was happiness!

"Have mercy, monsieur! I surrender!"

Too familiar with these words of defeat, Louis abruptly released his prisoner. He stumbled back and away from her, pushing his hands up in defense. "No, no, I did not mean it that way."

"Monsieur?"

Innocence sparkled in her violet eyes. She was not the enemy. *Not the enemy.* Louis dropped his hands and kicked a thicket of crimson poppies. "Forgive me."

The chain dangled from her fingertips, the key swinging before her skirts.

"Merci," Louis said as he yanked the key from her hand. A bit too abruptly, he knew. But the magic of the moment had been cursed by his memories.

"He's come! He's come! My knight!" Meadow poppies snapped at Sabine's ankles as she flitted about in skipping leaps. Twirling gracefully, she allowed her body to crumple and land with a pouf of dandelion heads in the long grasses.

She closed her eyes and smiled at the feel of the hot sun kissing her lids. Earth scents mixed with the flowers and fresh air to brew a blissful perfume. Her heart swelled and she felt very strange, different from anything she had ever experienced before. A burst of heat, like the rays of the sun, blossomed in her breast. An odd shiver flashed through her body, leaving chill bumps in its wake.

His face came to mind. Dark eyes and long, flowing hair. A thin trail of dark hairs above his lips, paralleled by a smudge of beard on his squarely chiseled chin. Her knight possessed the smile of a rogue, yet the eyes of a desolate soul.

The heavy head of a half-opened poppy hung over her face. Sabine plucked the flower and tried to divine its elusive scent. Methodically she folded back each of the outer crimson petals. "Fairy sweet, fairy bright, who shall be my love tonight?" She touched a petal, preparing to pull it off, when her memory suddenly clouded. An all-to-common occurrence. "Vex me to the bone! I can never remember the rest of the ritual. I thought eating burdock pods would help things stick in my mind. Oh! Now I shall never know the answer."

As if the darkness that shadowed her mind were seeping from her head, Sabine watched as a fat shadow fell over her lap and stopped just below her knees. She twisted at the waist and squinted to view better the tall figure looming above her.

*   *   *

Sure enough, the old man had locked away a thick stack of important-looking parchments. Some were sealed with a blue wax monogram bearing an ornate B. Others were tightly bound with twine. Louis did not take the time to read through any of them; he could do that later at home, with Henri's help. Life in the military did not require an expansive knowledge of letters, though he had picked up some ability here and there.

As he circled down the left tower's spiraling staircase, Louis felt a wicked chill curdle up his spine. Someone was singing. No . . . It was more like a yell. Sabine's manic screams echoed up from the meadow.

I've seen her . . . screaming and flailing . . .

Papers scattered to the ground as Louis sped out the castle tower and rushed toward Sabine's cries.

Bright sunlight blinded him until he rounded the tower wall. Then he saw someone else in the field. A man. Strangling Sabine.

CHAPTER THREE

Louis's hand moved to the dagger sheathed at his hip. as his feet took flight through the slashing meadow grass. Wispy dandelion sprigs caught on his eyelashes and in his mouth as he screamed, "No! Stop!"

The man, dressed from mask to boots in black, straightened at Louis's voice, dropping Sabine in a wilted heap amid a patch of muted blue cornflowers. He slipped a gloved hand inside his cape and a glint of steel harnessed the sunlight into a blinding beacon.

Louis unsheathed his own weapon, his soldier's instincts taking over. The sharp cry of a crow on wing echoed the terror gushing through his veins. *Kill the enemy or be killed yourself.* Louis felt only slight resistance as he ran the tip of his dagger through the man's heart.

"*Diavolo,*" choked the intruder. His eyes flashed wide as Louis had witnessed hundreds of times in battle. The shock of mortality. The man involuntarily released the pistol he'd pulled from his cape.

"Who are you?" Louis demanded. "Why are you doing this?"

Death curled a wicked smile onto the man's face and spit a gurgling trail of blood onto Louis's breeches. "Cristoforo," the man croaked hoarsely, and then dropped his head.

Blood gushed at Louis's fist. Supporting the man's entire weight on his short blade, Louis fought the regret that threatened to pull him to his knees.

And so you've murdered another. Without so much as a second thought.

Louis stepped back, tilting his dagger so the dead man slid off at his feet. Revulsion churned his gut. Again! He'd done it again!

But he'd had no choice. Darkness had visited the fairy's castle. And in its path lay the wreckage of innocence. But why? Who or what was this man dressed as the devil, wishing only to destroy innocence? Cristoforo?

A glance to the ground found Sabine motionless, angelic in her peace. Dead. By the saints, she was dead!

"Ooooh . . ."

"Sabine!" Louis plunged to her side. He wrapped her delicate frame into his arms. A rush of elation surged over the hideous tension that had corded his muscles. She was still alive.

"Is this heaven? 'Tis beautiful." Sabine pushed up, and with a hand from Louis was able to stand. She rolled her head from front and around to back, as if stretching out a kink. Or perhaps checking to see that her head was still attached. "So very much like my home," she marveled as she looked about.

Louis did not want to contradict her—for when had he ever stood in the presence of an angel such as she?—but he could not lie to her. If her mind was of another realm, then a lie would only further her madness.

"No, my lady, you're not in heaven. You are quite alive, praise God. But—"

"Oh!" She stared, openmouthed, at the dead man who had fallen on his back, a gushing fountain of scarlet creeping to an ooze from his breast.

Instantly Louis cursed himself for a fool. He reached to touch her, to turn her away, but she slipped through his fingers.

"The man is bleeding." Sabine knelt by the body and bravely touched the center of his chest. "Pretty though."

Louis winced.

"Sabine."

"So very much"—she leaned closer to the man's body, almost as if to smell it—"like summer roses, the color. Don't you agree?"

Did she not recall that the man had been strangling her? Had wanted her dead. And for what reason? Who would journey to a remote castle in the country and attempt to kill an innocent woman? The killer had appeared out of nowhere. Louis had been in the castle all of ten minutes. He hadn't even heard the man's arrival.

Louis looked around, but saw no mount or carriage. A line of elm and olive trees to the north of the castle blocked his sight. Possibly there, behind the wall of trees, stood a horse awaiting a rider.

"Sabine!" He tried to make eye contact with her, but she continued her exploration of the man's chest, dragging her fingers over the stained clothing. "Look at me!"

Whether it was the harshness of his words, or the loud tone that he used, Sabine suddenly stiffened, tilted her head, and turned to him. Her lips fell slack, her violet eyes peering wonderingly from beneath a fringe of long lashes.

"Sabine?"

"Yes, Monsieur?"

Her voice was once again of the here and now. Louis motioned with his hand that she stand. When she did, he pulled his shirt from his breeches and wiped the blood from her fingers. "You mustn't do such things. 'Tis . . . not right."

No reaction.

"He tried to kill you, Sabine. Do you remember? Your neck . . ." Daring a chance, Louis reached up and smoothed the pad of his thumb along the red bruises. Her flesh was hot and so very soft, softer than the fine silks and damasks that were used in such worshipful abundance at court. A fine canvas for a man's tongue to swirl his desirous picture upon. He felt her swallow at his touch, but she did not protest. It was enough, though, to jar Louis from his lustful thoughts.

Curse the man for bringing harm to such an innocent soul! Battle sparks fueled a fire in his heart. Louis vowed to discover why the intruder had come to this castle, to take the life of this child-woman.

"If it is the last thing I do," Louis whispered.

"Monsieur?"

"Are you all right, then? You're not in pain?"

A shrug set her hair into a shimmering slide across her back.

"And now you see I must bring you with me, Sabine. You cannot remain here by yourself. Not after what I have just witnessed. You understand?" He waited for her big, beautiful eyes to show some sign of comprehension. He knew she was hearing him. But did her tormented mind understand?

"As you wish, Monsieur." Her body became light, and with a gleeful smile Sabine dipped away and twirled through the knee-high grasses, her steps magically missing the dead man. The winds swirled her hair into a liquid stream, flowing teasingly just out of Louis's grasp.

"Oh!" Sabine raced back to Louis, stopping only when her slippered toes touched his boots, her face but inches from his.

Louis's hands froze before him, wanting to touch, to embrace, but not daring. Never had he been so cruelly tempted. She was the most seductive woman he had ever seen—and totally unaware of the power she had over him. Steeling himself against his body's desires, Louis drew in a deep breath, but that only filled his senses with her sweet, flowery scent.

"May I ride the unicorn?" came her sweet question.

A relieved smile broke Louis's concentration. "Of course, my lady of the fairies."

The sun had nearly set on the horizon. Narrow fingers of amber stretched from hillock to valley and much farther than the naked eye could see. Yvette had just come in from lighting the great torches along the road to ease Louis's way home. Henri had thought it best considering the late hour.

"A thousand devils!" Henri pointed down the pounded red-dirt road. "Look there!"

Yvette scanned the horizon in the direction Henri pointed. "What is it, my lord?"

" 'Tis my brother. And he's the girl with him."

She'd nervously clung to her knight until they'd cleared the narrow alley of trees and reached the open air. A feeling of utter freedom blasted upon her senses like a downpour of spring rain. Sabine let loose a chuckle that melted into a vivacious strain of song. She sang at the top of her lungs, first a happy, silly melody of fairies and toads and then—that most vexing of verses that always haunted her thoughts—a snatch of opera.

As the unicorn made its way down the packed dirt road, followed closely by the other unicorn that Louis had discovered tied behind the elm rows, Sabine marveled at the row of candles glittering a path up to what Louis had explained was his home. Luminaires stood as tall as a man's shoulders, held regal and erect by smooth wooden poles. They gave the night a magical glitter. 'Twas truly a path laid for heroes and knights home from rescuing their damsel.

Feeling like a great queen upon her mount, Sabine gave a

regal tip of her head to each and every candle in acknowledgment of their courtly duties.

" 'Tis a fine welcome you've assembled at your court, monsieur."

The sound of her knight's chuckle made Sabine feel warm and melty inside. Well, just about everything about him made her insides mushy. Besides his soft, deep voice that seemed to seep through her pores and flow with the rhythm of her blood, there were other intriguing things she'd noticed of him. Eyes of fine chocolate and hair the color of soft spring-fresh soil. Though his eyes possessed an inner darkness, the few times he'd stared directly into her own eyes, she'd felt a mystic connection. So very different from that *other* connection.

This man was The One. Deep inside, she knew. He had come to rescue her from the darkness.

Louis slipped from the unicorn and helped her down. Sabine placed her slender hand in his broad one, palm pressed tight to palm. It had been so long since she'd felt the warmth of human touch. *Grand-père* had always been so cold and distant, ignorant of her need for companionship or even simple conversation.

Sabine had no chance to thank Louis for rescuing her for another man burst through the door of the château, his dark, unbound hair batting the air violently. The Dragon Lord!

"What is the meaning of this?" Henri spat out. "I send you off on a simple errand and you don't return until nightfall, and with—with this!"

"There is no need to raise your voice, brother." Louis turned to Sabine. She hovered just behind him, eyes wide, obviously frightened by the gusto with which Henri burst upon them. "I had no choice."

"No choice? Taxes you've no choice. Death you've no

choice! But this! Where is your head, Louis? Has her madness become yours?"

"Silence," Louis reprimanded cautiously. "We will discuss this later. Mademoiselle Bassange is tired. She needs to rest. I'll take her upstairs to Yvette, and when I come down, I'll explain everything."

Louis bent his head so that he was eye level with Sabine. He did not mind the long moments it took for her dancing gaze to intersect with his, and finally snap into comprehension. "Come."

She stepped a wide circle around Henri and followed him inside.

"You cannot keep her here!" Henri barked as the château door closed.

Laying a firm hand against the door, Louis told himself again that he'd had no choice. But how could he watch over an invalid when he himself felt his connection to madness growing stronger day by day? No. He hadn't the time for such nonsense.

But it was too late now, wasn't it? He would have to figure something out.

Remembering his guest, Louis turned and gestured to the stairs. Sabine had not spoken a word since stepping down from the unicorn. Er, horse, that is. *You've already fallen under her spell, haven't you, you crazy man?*

Perhaps Henri was right. Her madness had become his own.

Louis noticed Sabine take in the grandeur of the house as she preceded him up the stairs. Her eyes missed not a thing, not the scar in the wooden banister, nor the dancing gold fleur-de-lis on the out-of-fashion English paper.

He watched her run graceful, curious fingers along the painted chair rail, and remembered with a wince the time he'd run head-on into the raised wood and knocked out a tooth. Memories of Mother's special party dress swirled inside Louis's head as Sabine lightly touched the English paper in softest periwinkle that covered the walls. But his heart was lost to the fairy princess as she twirled beneath the iron chandelier at the top of the stair.

The slam of the front door, followed by Henri's mumbling stomps, startled Sabine into a wide-eyed statue.

"Don't be frightened. Henri is my brother," Louis gently calmed. "Do you not remember him from his visits?"

"I do. The Dragon Lord has a fiery voice. I don't like it."

Louis smirked at her description. Yes, on his moody days Henri did have a tendency to breathe fire. No wonder his brother had seen Sabine only the one time. She'd probably been too fearful to show her face after that.

He directed Sabine toward the extra bedchamber. It was furnished only with a simple iron bed, armoire, and sitting table, but it was cool and comfortable. Far more comfortable than anything she could have slept on at the Bassange castle, he felt sure. "You can trust me, Sabine. You may remain in my home until I've found the proper care for you. Come."

Like a cautious feline carefully sniffing its surroundings before venturing farther, Sabine slowly stepped inside.

"You look tired," Louis offered quietly. "I'll have Yvette bring in clean clothes and a morsel from supper. Tomorrow is a new day."

Sabine laid her arm over her forehead in grand display. "I am so dreadfully fatigued. Would you be a good man and send my servants, posthaste?"

Suppressing a smile, Louis called for Yvette and within minutes had explained things to the maid. He trusted Yvette. She was old and wise, and had been with the family since his parents had wed.

Yvette laid a hand on Louis's arm. "A bit too much powder in her wig, eh?"

"Well, I wouldn't exactly—"

"Henri said she's touched," Yvette observed with a cautious eye across the room to where Sabine stood fingering the smooth black iron bed frame. The maid clutched the silver filigree cross that hung just above her generous breasts.

"Perhaps." Louis felt reluctant to make any sort of medical pronouncement. But there had been that odd reaction to the dead man . . . "Just be gentle with her."

"Worry not, my lord."

"Will you be comfortable for the evening, mademoiselle?" Louis called across the room.

Sabine tilted her head, silent for a moment, and then she suppressed a dramatic yawn. "Monsieur de Lavarac, you've been most kind. I shall send for you in the morning."

Reluctant to face the consequences of his spur-of-the-moment actions, Louis drew in a deep breath and stepped forward. The hearth fire blazing in vicious licks behind his brother was no match for the flames in Henri's eyes. Dragon Lord, indeed.

"I had to do it," Louis began to say immediately. "The old man was dead. The maggots had him nearly chewed to the bone."

"Dead." Henri raised a thoughtful finger to his chin and paced the floor.

Yes, grotesquely dead. Was there not a thing in this world that would not continually stir up memories of war? "Damn near a fortnight, I figure. The smell was so putrid—"

"Enough already," Henri intervened. "So he has finally passed on. Good. We could put to good use the profit from sale of the estate."

"Unless the old man has bequeathed it to someone else." Louis held out the sheaf of papers he'd taken from the grandfather's lemonwood chest.

"Yes, well, whatever the results, someone owes us money." Henri snapped the papers from Louis's grasp. "We shall bring the girl to Paris in the morn. I'm quite sure Salpêtrière will take her in.''

''No!'' Louis said, the rage tensing his hands in to fists. He froze. Why had he said that? Why the sudden defense of a woman he had known but hours? A woman who could never mean anything to him.

But he knew why. She was *his*. Well, at least, she was in his care. What was Henri thinking? Louis could not allow such an innocent creature to be taken to Salpêtrière. Never. The institution was notoriously dirty and creeping with filth. As with most Paris hospitals, patients went there to die, not to be cured. No one deserved such a fate.

''No?'' Henri's raised brows presented an all-too-knowing challenge. ''You don't expect that she'll stay here? She's mad, Louis. She needs proper care. Care that we cannot provide.''

''And what then?'' Louis paced away, anger pulling his jaw tight and clenching his fists to white balls. ''You'd condemn her to rot as her *grand-père* did? That is no life for such a lively, precious thing. She is too young. And besides''—his voice softened as his thoughts took him back to the sunlit meadow, brushed white by dandelion kites—''I don't think she's as far gone as you think. She spoke to me. Very plainly. She understood things I said, Henri. I don't agree with your assessment of her. She is not mad.''

''Precious, eh?''

Louis had to think back. Yes. He had called her precious, hadn't he? Hmm. Well, of course she was. Far more precious than any jewel or piece of enemy land gained by a French regiment.

''Seems my brother has been doing more than just digging graves this afternoon,'' Henri added slyly. ''You don't mean to say you've feelings for this ragamuffin?''

Feelings? ''I—er—she's not a ragamuffin.'' Meadow fairy

was a more exacting description. "Did you not see her with your own eyes? She is lovely. Did you look? She is sweet and gentle—"

"Do you mean to tell me that you did not see her raving? I've heard her screams, brother. She is of the devil! And I'll not have her disrupting our lives!"

"The devil? Bah! It is only that she needs to be around others. Others who care. Not a coldhearted institution. What can one expect after years of living alone in that secluded castle with only a blind old man her company? We cannot consign her to Salpêtrière to sit in chains among the rats until she rots!" Louis turned on his brother, wishing to impress the things he had seen with his own eyes into his brother's sight. He held out his fingers, cupped to receive or give aid, as he spoke. "She has her lucid moments. I've seen it. By the heavens, 'tis remarkable to behold."

Henri lifted an eyebrow.

"There's another thing." The entire ride home, Louis had been haunted by the horrifying image of the dark figure bent over Sabine's frail body. Had he been a moment later, he would have been digging her grave too. "There was a man. He tried to kill her."

"The girl?" The center of Henri's forehead arrowed downward. "What do you mean? Why? Who would—"

"I know not." Louis shrugged his fingers back through his hair. He was tired. And hungry. "I have no idea who he was or why he was there, nor do I care to think why any man should choose to harm such a—"

"Precious?"

Seething, Louis clenched his fist near his ear. Would he never see? Henri had already locked Sabine away and dangled the circle of rusted keys just out of Louis's grasp. Had Janette's death erased all of the man's compassion?

*And where was yours when you needed it most? Hiding
behind your musket? Deaf to your enemy's cries for mercy?*

He was unable to fight the screams of his own conscience.
Yes, who was he to speak? Compassion? He couldn't begin to
know the meaning of such a word. Perhaps the girl would be
better off in an institution.

With a surrendering sigh, Louis paced out of the room.

"She'll stay here until the old man's papers are sorted
through."

Louis stopped beneath the simple painted archway that led
from the hearth room to the pantry.

"Perhaps he has designated a caregiver for her," Henri
offered. He ran a fingernail along the blue wax seal on the
topmost paper in the pile Louis had given him. "I'll take a
look."

"Shouldn't we wait for a lawyer to look at them? It wouldn't
be right."

Henri paused. "Perhaps. But you promise you'll go along
with whatever these papers say? If she is to go to the asylum,
then that is where she will go."

A tangible lump formed in Louis's throat. He needed a drink.
Spirits, wine, anything to relax him and chase away the emotions he'd unintentionally allowed to emerge that day.

Consign Sabine to an asylum? If that is what the grandfather
had designated in his will, Louis could not go against his wishes.
Much as he feared that outcome, he acquiesced with a curt nod.
"Of course. But I'll not have you saying anything cruel to her
while she is in our company. She is a delicate creature—"

"Ahhhh!"

The brothers rushed to the stairs at the sound of Yvette's
voice. They found the robustly fleshed woman clinging to the
wall outside Sabine's room. From inside came the frantic chanting of a terrified child.

"I simply wanted to exchange her ragged dress for something

less tattered," Yvette pleaded, the refused item dangling from one sausage-roll hand.

Sabine stood in the corner, her hands to her forehead, chanting nonsense words and rocking from side to side so that with each return to the left she banged her shoulder into the wall.

"Such a delicate creature," Henri drawled from the doorway.

"Leave us!" Louis demanded, and slammed the door in his brother's smirking face. He rushed to Sabine. The shoulders of her dress were pulled down in preparation for undress. As she turned her head from side to side, her hair slipped up and down to reveal two silvery scars tracing faint parallel lines down her back. They were very fine, barely there.

"Your wings have been lost," Louis mumbled, not really aware of his own voice. "You truly are a fairy child." The urge to touch her, to trace the lines as one would trace the seam of a long-awaited love letter, was strong. But Louis pulled back.

No. He could not allow himself to believe in such nonsense.

Sabine's chanting became softer now that they were alone. Louis dared to touch her arm. She flinched but did not shriek or protest. Her flesh was warm and smooth. Carefully, ever so delicately, Louis ran his thumb over the smooth underside of her wrist, so soft . . . and no scars. "Sabine? It is Louis. Sabine? Look at me."

When she would not look up, Louis gently tilted her chin so that he could trap her eyes in his gaze. Her chanting stopped, her lips parted in silence as the glaze cleared from her expression.

"Sabine?" Her eyes were clear, so focused on his. That was the trick, wasn't it? Whenever Louis made eye contact with her, it was as if some misted veil lifted from her soul. Pulled her from the horrors that taunted her mind. " 'Tis all right now," he offered in a gentle whisper. "Yvette simply wanted to help you dress for the night."

"Cold hands," she whispered, a meek grin wriggling onto her lips.

Louis chuckled with relief. So that was it? Yes, the housemaid did have inordinately cold hands. For as much flesh as she carried on her rotund figure, the woman always complained that she was cold.

"Would it please you if I informed Yvette that she must warm her hands before touching you?"

A genuine smile graced her lips. "Very."

"Then so be it. Is there . . . something else?"

"She wanted to take my dress away."

Louis fingered the tattered silk over her elbow, thin, dirtied through time to a dull earth tone. He could almost count the individual strands of threading in some places. Worn for many years, he was sure. "You need a fine dress, one that fits you well."

"But this is Mama's."

"I see." Had she never owned a new dress? One made especially for her? Perhaps not if she had been without parents since a very early age. "We needn't dispose of it. You can save it. But wouldn't you like a dress of fine silk? Perhaps damask?"

Delicate fairy fingers pressed to Louis's waistcoat, exploring the fine weave with careful precision. He wondered if she could feel the beat of his heart, racing toward the edge of the ravine, ready to take the plunge should the fairy request. "Yes, I would like that, Monsieur."

"Please, you must call me Louis."

She did not flinch when he folded his battle-roughened hand over hers and brought it to his mouth. He pressed his lips to her knuckles, then her wrist, and held still, gauging the beats of her heart as they slowed beneath his mouth.

Why have you done this to me, God? Louis wondered. To tempt me with such an exquisite creature, when it could be dangerous to lose my heart to her?

But you have already lost, came the deep, chortling voice.

Sure that the devil himself had just laughed at him, Louis closed his eyes.

Let's see if you can resist this forbidden fruit, the voice teased.

But why must she be forbidden? Perhaps this is what she needs. Companionship. The warmth of another human's touch, a gentle word . . . love? Perhaps . . . could it be . . . what *he* needed?

Love is for fools. How can love fix your wounded soul? It can never erase your guilt.

"Perhaps not," Louis said.

"Monsieur? Er, Louis?"

"Forgive me, mademoiselle. My mind wanders."

Her laughter echoed through Louis's body, coating his heart in gilt. "You have that problem too?"

He smiled. "Sometimes, Sabine. It is only—" Dare he tell her? *If you bring her into your world, your confidence, your life, you may risk further harm.*

Louis closed his other hand over Sabine's and walked her to the window. From the second-story bedroom the entire estate was visible. The vineyards stretched in thick green lines down the side of a gently sloping hill and finished in a slight curve. His future had been planted decades ago; deep within the roots of the trees his life was nourished. But could he persevere as had the twisted and blackened trunks of the vines? They had not survived for so long without care and constant nurture.

"To be in your presence, Sabine, is as if a gift from the heavens. And I make this promise to you—I'll not let any harm come to you. I swear it. No one shall ever give you cause for grief or worry. I want you to stay as long as you wish. To get better, if possible. And to always know that you can trust me." He tilted her chin away from the window and smoothed a thick flow of her hair over her ear. "Do you know that you can trust me, Sabine?"

"I do."

Good, he thought. Now, if only he could trust himself.

She lingered by the open window after the cold-handed maid had left her to dress in a borrowed night shift and slippers. An odd shudder ran through her body, as strangely sudden as an eel that slips past a swimmer's legs in dark waters. She'd felt this sensation many a time, always brief, yet enticing. It was a pleasurable feeling, sizzling in her loins, surging a flash of heat across her chest and through her cheeks, making her wonder—was this a wicked feeling or a good one? A good one, she hoped, but she feared it might be more wicked than she could ever dream.

And always so elusive.

Imagined or real? She could never be sure.

My secret pleasure, she thought. *This, too, I must never tell.*

Quickly come, quickly forgotten for a more tangible interest.

From where Sabine stood, she could see as her knight walked down the row of luminaires, extinguishing them one by one. The smell of burnt wood and oil sweetened the air for moments after.

Do you know that you can trust me, Sabine?

Yes, she did. It was odd to realize, but she had already developed a complete trust for the man who had rescued her from that prison of memories. For he'd been so gentle with her. Had never once raised his voice or given her that odd, condescending shake of his head that Grandfather had so often given her. There was nothing to fear from Louis de Lavarac.

Though the nights, in all their darkness, had grown less threatening over the years, it was the darkness that shrouded her soul, clinging with long talons, that frightened her most. Grandfather had never understood. Finally, she had just given up on trying to communicate with him.

As the world had given up on her.

But now hope strode just outside her window. Louis paused by the last torch and looked up to her window. The intense frown left his face as she waved to him, and he returned the gesture.

Sabine stepped back, leaned against the papered wall, and pressed her cupped hands to her breast. Something splendid had begun today.

CHAPTER FOUR

Wine glistened on his stomach like a port stain marring a newborn's face. Slowly it was sucked away by the Countess de Morieux's eager lips. Cristoforo settled back into the sinking piles of overstuffed brocade pillows. Boredom engulfed him. What was it with these women that once was not enough for them? He'd already brought her to screaming fits of pleasure. Twice. Yet still the countess wanted more, more, and more.

More! Always the word on everyone's lips. Be it a wench in bed or the adoring admirers at the footlamps. More! More! *Viva il coltèllo!* Long live the knife!

Yes, and weren't the women who vied to get him into bed thankful for the knife. For they had no fear of conceiving and could wile away the entire night drinking of his naked flesh and demanding he gift them with one after another command performance. Not that the hags he tended to sleep with were still able to bear children. Cristoforo had learned long ago that when it came to a choice between the young, beautiful admirer or the wrinkled old crone, 'twas the crones who wielded the largest and most generous purses.

There came a quiet knock on the boudoir door, which startled the countess from her attentions to his stomach.

Thankful for the interruption, Cristoforo—much against the countess's protestations—called his valet in. "What is it, Pietro?"

Pietro did not seem to notice the countess, who huddled beneath the sheets in hope of hiding her nakedness from the servant. Cristoforo toed down the sheets, pulling them across the countess's goose-pimpled back. A satisfied smile revealed his straight row of pearly teeth. He prided himself on their whiteness, and spent a full fifteen minutes morning and night in their cleaning.

"It's . . ." The valet nodded to the countess, and when Cristoforo gestured with a hand that he continue, Pietro whispered, "The bravo, master."

"Ah, yes." Cristoforo threaded his fingers through the stiff red curls that fell over his bedmate's face and tilted her head back. "Countess, if you'll be so kind as to leave us?"

"Leave? This is my home, Cristoforo. I'll not leave my own bed at your valet's whim."

"Very well." Cristoforo threw back the sheets from his long, thin legs, revealing the countess huddling tight to his torso. She curled her legs up to her paunched gut and shrieked. With a devilish smirk he gestured to his valet to bring his shirt. "Then I shall leave."

"Oh, no, Cristoforo!" Forgetting her nakedness, the countess pawed at Cristoforo's waist. Her bare breasts hugged his thigh, two wilted market bags desperately in need of more fruit. "Please, you promised to stay through the morning."

"So I did. Well then, you'll be a good little countess and fetch me some water. I'm dreadfully parched. Run along."

Catching her defiant gaze in a silent staredown, Cristoforo

tapped his throat and the countess got the hint. She could not deprive the great Cristoforo of his magical elixir.

Both men watched with pained boredom as the miffed countess scrambled for her robe, wrapped it about her withered flesh, and with a haughty "humph" left them alone.

"I've asked you before what you see in those shriveled old purses," muttered Pietro. He hooked a toe under Cristoforo's abandoned shirt and lifted it from the floor.

Cristoforo slid an arm through the shirtsleeve. "And you just answered your own question, my love. Purses. Grand, full, and bursting purses, dangling from the ends of rotted old fingers eager to fill my cup."

Cristoforo held his arms out to his sides while Pietro buttoned him up and tied his jabot. The servant adjusted the gilded lace to perfection. This was as good excuse as any to leave the countess. Thankful for the diversion, Cristoforo tousled Pietro's short crop of Gypsy hair and pressed a devoted kiss to his dove-soft cheek. "As always, your timing is impeccable, Pietro. But now, what of the bravo? He has completed his task? Ah, but of course." He pressed a finger to his temple. No noticeable pain. "I feel that he has."

As Pietro pulled his master's breeches up and fastened them, Cristoforo's thoughts went back to the moments before this evening's concert. He'd clung to the stage scaffolding as the head pains had pounded with the most vicious cruelty. The heavy jeweled headdress he wore had fallen with a metallic clatter to the wooden stage. Flashes of brightness appeared before his reality-blinded eyes, clouded over by strange floating wisps, and finally covered with red streams of liquid. Blood. Then all was silent. The violent attack was gone as quickly as it had come. None had ever been so harsh. And none had ever felt so final.

"He did not." Pietro retrieved Cristoforo's silver-embroidered frock coat from the candelabrum mounted on the wall and held it up for his master, his face lowered in expectation of a tongue-lashing.

"Did. Not?" Cristoforo paused, his right arm halfway through the sleeve of his coat. "Did not *what?*"

"The bravo is dead, master. I sent another to follow up as you requested, and he returned to tell that the bravo was dead— stabbed through the heart—and the girl gone."

"Gone?"

"The *grand-père*—" Pietro wrestled with the bunched Belgian lace edging Cristoforo's shirt cuff, trying to pull it out of the heavily embroidered frock sleeve.

"What of the *grand-père?*" Cristoforo demanded impatiently.

"Dead also."

Cristoforo jerked his other arm through the remaining sleeve and shrugged away from Pietro's touch. This was insane! Impossible. The bravo dead? *And* the *grand-père?* But what of the girl?

"The old man was found in a shallow grave," Pietro explained. "No sign of the girl."

So it had not been the final attack.

"Curse the bitch!" Cristoforo stormed across the rose-and-blue Aubusson carpet, kicking his shoes over and hastily shuffling his long, oversized feet into them. The jabot circling his neck suddenly constricted in the most painful squeeze. He dug his fingers into the knot and struggled furiously.

"Allow me, master."

He allowed Pietro no more than a moment to free him of the bothersome necktie. "Dammit, dammit, dammit!"

Pietro scooped up Cristoforo's discarded wig and sheet music and followed his master down the impossibly long hallway. "Your wig, Cristoforo."

"Damn the wig," he fumed. "I think I've the lice again. Whether from that damned wig or from the countess's pussy, I do not know." He marched around a corner that led to the door. "Small wonder the vexing little nits would choose to nest in either place. Both are old and dusty. Ha! Of course they hold out long enough to attach themselves to me—bah! Something must be done."

Pietro scrambled down the marble steps behind Cristoforo to the waiting carriage. "About the lice, master?"

The carriage joggled upon its springs as it received Cristoforo's lanky frame. He slammed the door in Pietro's face, then whipped the damask curtain away from the window, sticking his forehead out. "No, fool! About the girl."

"Sst, sst, sst."

From his post at the window, Louis lingered on the sight of a young child splashing a tattered boot toe in the remainder of a mud puddle before pulling his gaze to Ambroise l'Argent sitting behind his desk, reading through the papers Louis had found in the Bassange estate. A lawyer's notation on one of them had led the brothers there.

"Sst, sst, sst."

Damn. Louis could not determine what the pox-scarred man was doing to make such a horrendous sound, but it was coming from his mouth. Probably sucking his saliva in through the gap between his lower teeth. Gave Louis the shivers. He checked the dagger at his hip, then crossed his arms over his chest.

Henri glanced over his shoulder at Louis, raising his gaze to the heavens and shaking his head. It seemed hours had passed since the *notaire* had said a single word. Louis paced behind Henri's chair. "So what does it say, Monsieur l'Argent?"

L'Argent ceased his slushy noises and set the papers down. He cleared the phlegm from his throat and narrowed his squinty gaze on the two brothers. "Mademoiselle Bassange is heir to half of the Vicomte Bassange's fortune."

"Vicomte?" Henri remarked. "I never knew. And all these

years the old coot had me believe he could barely afford clothes for his back!''

"Yes. The old man hoarded quite a mountain of coin over the years. Very nearly worth one million livres. Most in Italian coin.''

"Italian? That's odd,'' Louis said.

"One million?'' Henri gasped.

Louis did not return Henri's greedy lift of his brow. "You say the girl gets half? What of the rest?''

"Bequeathed to the other heir.''

"Other?'' Louis prompted.

"But who?'' Henri had suddenly gained an acute interest in Sabine. "She has no remaining family as far as I know. In the years we've been watching the estate, no one—one million, you say?''

Such an interesting position Sabine found herself in, Louis mused. And himself. "Who is the other heir?''

"I am not at liberty to reveal the other party.''

Louis's disgust for the man increased with his curt announcement. Not at liberty? Yet the man had just read through the entire will for him and Henri. Hadn't even questioned if they were relatives until well into the second page. Of course, circumstances as they were, he'd easily been able to persuade the lawyer to continue. Someone needed to know what was going on if they wished to help Sabine.

"It will take a few days to locate the other heir. Until then, things cannot be finalized. *Sst, sst.* The girl is staying with you?''

Louis nodded.

"She'll need to sign this preliminary document. Proof that she does exist, you understand.''

Louis hadn't even heard l'Argent's last words.

Numbness washed over his limbs. Other heir? That could mean only that there was a relative somewhere. Someone who would eventually lay claim to his Sabine.

His Sabine?

His heart fell to his gut. She was the loveliest creature he had ever seen, and her mere presence begged his undivided attention. But he was in no condition himself to even begin to provide her the help she needed. And as much as he hated to admit it, she did need help.

"How many days," Henri wondered sullenly, "for you to locate this missing heir?"

"Not sure," l'Argent said with a casual flip of his bony fingers. "No more than a week, I should hope."

"Perhaps we can bring her to Salpêtrière—"

"Absolutely not!" Louis slammed his open palm down on the desk before Henri. L'Argent dove to protect the Dresden figurine that toppled near the edge. "You heard as well as I that her grandfather does not want Mademoiselle Bassange to be institutionalized. He wishes her to stay with a good family, someone who can provide for her education—"

"A family," Henri stated firmly, "we are no longer. Certainly the vicomte wished her to be in a home where there is a mother and a father. And very possibly an entire crew of physicians."

"Salpêtrière?" l'Argent prompted curiously. *"Ssssst.* Does Mademoiselle Bassange suffer an ailment?"

"She is mad," Henri threw in before Louis could stop him.

"Slightly confused at times. A little melancholy perhaps." Louis could not allow himself to be so harsh when he was sure he might appear equally mad to others who should witness his own self-destruction. He could not deny that Sabine needed far more than he could offer. But something—some glimmer of the unknown, like fairy glamour—kept him from releasing her care to another. "She will stay with us until you can locate the other heir, Monsieur l'Argent. Perhaps then we can all sit down and decide what is best for her."

"Perhaps so," Henri drawled as he settled back against his chair. "An heiress, you say?"

"Enough, then." Louis nodded to his brother, who took his urging and stood. "Wait for me outside, Henri. I would like a word with l'Argent alone."

He expected the sly summation Henri gave him, as if the man now considered him a competitor for a cache of riches and he couldn't be too careful leaving him alone. But riches belonged to neither of them. And Henri understood that as well as Louis.

"Good day, Monsieur l'Argent."

Only when Henri had left and Louis watched him cross the cobblestones to the city well did Louis turn to l'Argent. He could fight the incessant nightmares no longer. For the sake of his own well-being—and perhaps to prevent his own imminent madness—he had to ask. "There is someone I wish you to locate."

"The missing heir."

"No. This does not concern Mademoiselle Bassange. I haven't much information for you to go on." He paused, wondering if he should really do this. Wouldn't it be wisest to leave well enough alone? *And risk your own madness? Dancing in flower-dotted meadows would not suit you.* "There is a woman . . . I must know if she is . . . well. If she needs funds, a home. She is a widow."

"Ah." L'Argent's chair squeaked as he adjusted his weight. "A fellow soldier who died alongside you? You wish to see his family secure? It happens often, monsieur. I can do that. The man's name?"

"I do not know." Louis glanced out the window. Henri's gaze was shadowed by his tricorn, but it was directed toward him, he could sense it. He spoke to l'Argent quickly and cautiously. "At least, I have not looked."

He dug inside his pocket and produced the folded and muddied parchment he'd stolen from his final victim. "I've his commission papers. You may read them after I have left. Most unfortunately, I do know his wife's name. Evangeline."

To speak the name to the air instead of chasing it in his dreams seemed to weight the horrors in heavy clay. It was reality now. The horrors. His horrors. Evangeline's horrors.

The *notaire* studied the folded paper, began to carefully pry it apart, looked ready to scream, then to run, and then, finally, to laugh. "These are English commission papers. You can't mean to tell me—"

"Find her," Louis ordered. "Her husband died on the night of May the fifteenth under the Fontaney rains. His regiment surrendered the following morning. You've all the information you should need to locate her. Find Evangeline for me, l'Argent."

Sabine kept right at her task of helping Yvette shell peas as Louis laid the parcel of legal papers down and sat astride the chair, one leg to either side. He pushed his fingers back through his hair and rested his chin on the chair back. For the first time in weeks he felt relaxation encompass his body like a long-awaited summer storm. It was being around Sabine that did it, he knew.

And as much as his conscience commanded he rise and find work, sweat away his sins and begin to strive for retribution, he first had to slay the man of his past. The man who once killed on command. A man he was suddenly determined to defeat forever.

Both Sabine and Yvette wore a string of tiny peas. Sabine's doing, certainly. Although . . . Yvette was notorious for her belief in spirits and monsters and creatures of the night that rose from their graves in search of innocent souls. Gentle and wise in her ways, she never ceased to amaze Louis with her eccentricity.

Sabine was so lovely dressed in the loose cotton peignoir Yvette had altered to make a suitable dress. Yvette agreed that Sabine should not be fastened into the restraining dresses the fashionable women of Paris wore. A comb of matching blue-painted wood was pulled through her sunlit hair, releasing gentle tumblets of curls across her narrow shoulders and down her back.

The urge to reach out and smooth the teasing waves between his fingers hit Louis like a musket ball to the chest. The softness of woman slipping over his palm . . . the anticipation of something more. Like a kiss. He looked across the table, smiling as Sabine chased a stray pea across the trestle boards with her pinching fingers. Her laughter placed the sun in his heart.

But there were things they had to discuss. He had to explain about the inheritance, and explain that she could not stay with him for long. For surely this unnamed heir would have his or her own designs for Sabine's future. A relative most likely, Louis figured. He hoped. Yes, he prayed it would be family. Someone she knew and trusted. He would not have it any other way.

"Sabine," he said gently, not caring whether she heeded him immediately. He could sit and watch her for hours, he felt sure.

Her fingers snapped the crisp green pods, then one long finger pushed the tiny beads out into a bowl. Her flesh had become stained with the sweet green juice. The thought of licking her fingers clean, sucking them into his mouth, nearly drove Louis to the edge of control. So succulent and ripe, like beads of flesh in the center of each breast that pressed against her bodice, a sign of readiness and womanliness.

"No," he whispered.

"Monsieur?" Yvette paused from her shelling, looking above the line her narrow spectacles created mideye.

"Er . . . excuse me, Yvette. Would you mind leaving the two of us for a few minutes?"

"Of course. I must start the evening meal. We'll be having peas tonight," she said as she dipped a flirtatious finger under her strand of jaded pearls.

"Merci, Yvette," Louis called after her.

Plink. A tiny jewel hit the inside of the pottery bowl on the table. Off in the pantry, the great iron kettle used for stews and soups *chunck*ed against the floor. And then began the carefree humming that always accompanied Yvette's culinary creations.

"Henri and I went to see a lawyer in Paris this morning. Sabine? Look at me, *chérie.*"

She tilted her head, the words to her quiet song slowly fading. Her steady rocking slowed as her mind began to connect to his through the contact of their eyes.

"I hope you are hungry." She spread her hand over the table to encompass the many bowls of bright green peas. The heat they'd been having had done no harm to the ground vegetables that were shaded by great elm boughs. Though the corn would have to be picked soon.

"That I am, Sabine." He caught a stray pea and quickly popped it into his mouth. Since returning home, his appetite had yet to return. Military rations forced a man's stomach to survive on very little. But now . . . now, for some reason, he could do with a grand and tasty meal. "Do you like Yvette?"

"She is wonderful. Merry and wise. You used to dance under and around her skirts when you were only in infant skirts yourself," she said with a secretive smile. "She told me you were a precocious child. And so adorable. Yes, I like Yvette." Sabine suddenly stopped snapping and settled her elbows upon the table. "But do you not fear her imminent death?"

"Death? Why would you ask such a thing?"

Sabine crossed her hands in her lap. "She is so very wrinkled. Just like *Grand-père.*" Her eyes held his steadily. "It won't be long for her, I am sure."

"Sabine, you mustn't worry. Yvette is young. Not fifty, I believe. She's a healthy woman. You mustn't dwell on death so."

"I saw it in her eyes," she interrupted, her posture still straight, her face emotionless. "It will come soon."

Louis dared not break eye contact. He could hardly believe she could think such a thing. But perhaps she could think nothing less when that was all she had been exposed to in her lifetime. He recalled Sabine's strange fascination with the dead man's blood. She had been compelled to touch death, to term it pretty, even. It was beyond him to understand what forces controlled her mind.

He rolled his arm over and eyed the scabbed wound on his wrist. Madness revealed itself in so many different ways.

"Louis?"

"Forgive me." He pushed a hand back through his hair and rested his cheek in his palm. "Lost once again, my lady."

"In need of rescue?" she wondered while carefully removing a row of peas from a pod with a push of her thumb.

"Perhaps. But I need to explain things to you now." He was determined to bring his thoughts back to business instead of the observation of Sabine.

He pushed the papers across the table. He didn't expect that she could read them—he himself could make out only a few words—but he wanted her to be a part of everything. Father had always made sure that Mama had understood all their lands and holdings. In the event that he should die first, he would always say. It hadn't happened that way. Fortunately for Mama, Louis thought.

"Your *grand-père*'s will was read to us this morning, Sabine. Sabine? Look at me, please."

He feared he had lost her for a moment, but she turned her gaze back on him and snapped a crisp pod over her bowl. "Go on, Louis."

"Your *grand-père*, er, the Vicomte Bassange, bequeathed half his estate to you. An amount totaling just over five hundred thousand livres."

"Is that very much?" *Snap. Pling.*

"That is *very* much." He could not resist a gentle chuckle. Never in his lifetime would he see such a fortune. With the vineyards, he and his brother toed the edge between bourgeois and upper middle class, but had no desire to begin to associate with the beau monde. Of which Sabine was now a member. "You shall never want for a thing, *chérie*. Your needs will be met for your lifetime, thanks to your *grand-père*."

Her expression smoothed to a serious somberness. "Am I to be locked up?"

"No. Oh, no, Sabine. That is not your grandfather's wish. I've volunteered to care for you. That is—well, I know I must ask your opinion first—but I wish for you to stay here until the other beneficiary is located. And when that time comes, we will then all discuss your future."

"Is my future not of my own making?"

Her insight startled him. Louis made a surrendering gesture with both hands. "Of course it is. I will do my best to ensure that your wishes are carried out. I will never permit you to be locked away. You must believe me, Sabine. I won't allow it."

Louis felt as though Sabine reached out through her eyes and grasped hold of his frock coat to pull him close and study him. The heat of her gaze was palpable.

"Very well. I do trust you, Louis."

"Good. I shall never give you reason not to. But now there is this other thing. It's quite confusing."

"What?"

"Your *grand-père* left you half his estate, as I said, and the other half, to someone else who was not named. At least, the *notaire* was not at liberty to reveal the name to us. Very odd really. Do you have any idea who the other person may be, Sabine? Have you any close relatives?"

"Relatives?" Her eyes glassed over so suddenly, like water strewn across a marble floor. Sabine dipped her head forward and began to hum softly. The two voices of Yvette and Sabine chased an eerie chill up Louis's spine. One was so full of life, the other so . . . vacant.

"Sabine? Is there something wrong? Do you know who this person is?"

"Lascialo, indegno . . ."

He had lost her. Something he said had pushed her over the edge and slammed the door in his face. Her singing increased in volume as her shelling became faster and faster. Peas plinked against the pottery bowl. Tiny jade pearls rolled off the table and across the fieldstone floor.

She knew who the other beneficiary was. He sensed it. There had been a brief spark, a knowing in her eyes before they had glazed over.

Louis resigned himself to press the matter later. He gathered the legal papers into a neat pile, carefully jogging the faded parchment sheets into order. If only it were as simple to gather a person's thoughts into order. To reach inside her mind and rearrange the clutter.

Louis focused his attention on the words she sang.

"Ah! Chi mi dice mai quel barbaro dov'e?"

Italian, he knew that much. Why was the vicomte's fortune in Italian currency?

He would learn. In time. Time provided answers and redemption to those worthy.

And to those unworthy . . . it tormented.

"I shall return later," he muttered beneath the melody of her music. "You must sign this paper."

"Where shall I sign?"

Louis's heart lodged in his throat. Contact. "Right here." He procured the writing quill and ink from the shelf above the hearth and dipped it for her, eager for the time he might have her attention. "You need only mark an X."

Sabine took the inked quill and touched it to paper. Slowly and with measured accuracy she drew out her entire name, Sabine Margot Bassange, in elegant, flowing script. With a satisfied smile she handed the quill and paper to Louis and then sprang to her feet, her pea necklace bouncing in soft taps against her collarbone.

"And what festivities are going on in here? The grand pea festival?"

Louis and Sabine both looked to the door, where Henri stood, glowering.

Louis sanded Sabine's signature carefully, trying his best not to break the sand glass, for his anger with Henri boiled his blood and tensed his fist about the fragile object.

In two graceful spins Sabine stood before Henri. Her flashing eyes matched his as she pronounced, "I have the riches of a queen. And you, sir"—Sabine tapped him on the nose with the pad of her forefinger—"will be the first I feed to the dragons." She gave a grand and graceful curtsy and twirled from the room.

Louis settled back in his chair, the satisfaction very evident in his ear-to-ear grin.

CHAPTER FIVE

A thin stream of dark hair flowed down each side of his mouth. A mouth that was relaxed in his rest. Lips that appeared as soft as the kiss of spring. The sun-darkened flesh that peeked out at the top of his disarrayed shirt beckoned to be touched. But she stayed her desires.

She'd watched him for the better part of an hour as he'd walked alongside the Dragon Lord, examining the rows and rows of grapevines. Had he been alone, she would have joined him. Instead, Yvette had called her to help with the sewing. There had been holes to mend, knees to reinforce, and seams to stitch up, a task Sabine quickly took to. She felt it a great joy to be useful.

He must have sat down to rest beneath the tree and fallen into enchantment. Careful not to disturb her knight's slumber, Sabine tiptoed between his spread legs and bent down for better observation. Warm summer wind dusted her borrowed skirts across his breeched knees.

"So perfect," she whispered. "Yet so troubled."

He could not hide his despair from her. The inability to concentrate, the dark, almost brooding gaze, his frequent sighs. She was familiar with it all. So dreadfully familiar.

"Not now," she said to the daisy-petal-capped fairy who appeared by his head. Climbed right down the tree bark and onto Louis's thick mass of dark hair. Such nerve. "You must be careful. He's not one of us," she reprimanded the fairy, whose gossamer wings twinkled a myriad of colors in the sunlight. "I so wish to become like him. But I cannot if you insist on continually following me about. Shoo!"

A flick to the air above Louis's head sent the tiny sprite fleeing into the dry, thirst-pulling air. Sabine's forefinger accidentally grazed across his hair. She examined the earth-toned strands. So soft. A little dry, almost torn at the ends, but dark and rich like his voice.

Gentle was her knight in shining armor. He did not even seem to realize his own gentleness. But she could see deep inside, beyond the desolation. This man needed her far more than she had ever felt need herself. He possessed troubles in need of untroubling.

"I will help," she whispered, and then blew a floaty kiss to his lips before carefully backing away and leaving him to his peaceful slumber.

Worn and splitting at the seams, but still good enough to serve their purpose. Louis nudged the discarded shoes aside with the toe of his boot. "You should see that Sabine wears shoes, Yvette. I shouldn't wish for her to injure herself."

"I try, my lord," Yvette huffed out a hearty sigh. "She sits patiently watching while I slip them on those wiggly little toes of hers, then she dashes away and kicks them into the air with all the care of a banshee. Just can't keep the things on her. She's a wood sprite, that one."

Louis pushed a hand back through his hair and smiled at the

abandoned footwear. "I'll speak with her, Yvette. Perhaps I can purchase her a new pair on my next trip to Paris."

He found Sabine sitting in the coveted shade of the twisting old oak that grew so wide at the base, three men could not join hands around it—the same he'd fallen asleep under earlier this afternoon. Her skirts, the color of sweet honeydew, were spread across the few green blades of grass that still existed, her attention rapt on the rustling leaves above her.

There had been a time in battle, Louis recalled, when all was quiet. Both sides had ceased fire for lack of ammunition, drive, or food. He'd settled beneath a battle-ravaged oak and pried his boots from his cramped and aching feet. A cool breeze had kissed his cheek as softly as a whisper, and for that brief moment, war did not exist.

If only it were that easy to erase the memories now.

Tell my wife I love her . . . Evangeline.

Squeezing his fists as tightly shut as his eyelids, Louis tried to chase away the haunting voice of death.

Animal! In his nightmares Evangeline always cried that word in a rage. She would fall to her knees, her neck tensing in thick cords as she screamed *Animal!*

"Monsieur?"

Louis jerked himself from his forlorn thoughts. Sabine stared up at him, a sparkle of sunlight dancing in her eyes. " 'Tis a lovely afternoon, is it not?"

"That it is." Made so much lovelier with her bright smile.

"Sit beside me in the shade." She tapped the ground with the short measure of stick she held. It was no wider than her fist. "You look a trifle hot."

She tucked her skirts beneath her leg as Louis sat beside her and leaned against the rough tree trunk. "I've brought your shoes." He set the leather clogs beside her in the grass, and noticed her bare toes quirked and wiggled with distaste. "You should wear them around the estate, Sabine. I shouldn't wish for you to hurt yourself. There are rocks and sharp branches lying all about."

"That is very thoughtful of you," she said as she drew a careful finger along the leather stitches diving in and out of the left shoe. "But I must refuse."

"Why?"

"Why not?" She bent forward and rested her elbows upon her knees. "If I were to cover my feet with leather and wood, then I should never know the delight of the grass cushioning them, or the funny tickle of an insect lighting upon my largest toe." She glanced to Louis, and the sudden flight of a grasshopper across her vision made her exclaim brightly, "Oh!" The insect, a dull brown from the lack of water, lighted upon her skirts, its filament antennae flicking cautiously. Sabine's voice took on a secretive edge. "Do you know they transport the fairies from fête to fête?"

Louis leaned close to examine the grasshopper. Its large oval eyes were muted jade jewels, much like Sabine's pea necklace. "How many at a time?"

"Only one," Sabine explained. "Otherwise 'twould be much too crowded. The poor insect would never be able to leap. Oh! He's off. Another fête, another fairy waits."

Louis was caught up in Sabine's delight as she watched the tiny beast spring away in search of passengers to some garden ball of firefly lights and cocklebell music. The urge to lean forward and kiss her struck him deep in his gut. If only to divine a portion of her soul, to draw from her kiss the childlike wonder and taste of her sweetness. He could not stop himself from leaning closer.

"He's headed for the dark forest," Sabine said.

"Huh?" Caught with his head in the clouds again. Inches away from a kiss. Louis looked off across the grass in search of the bouncing creature. "The dark forest?"

Sabine pointed to the vineyard.

"Ah, the vines. 'Tis not an evil place, Sabine. The vines

yield the most delicious of wines, which in turn yield a profit to provide food for our plates. Rather lovely, I think.''

''But won't this wretched heat suck the life from the grapes? I don't see how anything can grow. The grass is dying and it crunches when I walk in it.''

''True, we've had no rain for weeks. But the grapes thrive in this heat, they suck up sunlight like a baby at its mother's breast. Of course, a good rain would help to plump them up. We'll need it before the harvest. The irrigation system needs major repair after last winter's freezing temperatures.'' If they didn't see rain soon, the sugar levels would be low, which in turn would yield a dry and acid wine.

''But I can help.'' Sabine sprang to her feet and spun in a circle. ''I shall do a rain dance for your grapes and plump them up in no time.''

Before Louis could stand, Sabine was off, skipping toward the vineyard. He opened his mouth to call her back, but hesitated.

She began to spin through the narrow aisles of vines, twirling and singing a wordless tune. As if offering a prayer to the heavens, she raised her arms and tapped the air with lithe fingers. Sunshine washed over her face, coloring her with an ethereal radiance. Grace worked every bone of her body into an elegant and swaying dance.

Louis glanced around. It was the Lord's day, no hired hands were about. She would do no one harm. And the thought of spoiling Sabine's enjoyment did not sit well with Louis. She was a woman trapped in a child's mind. Her strange innocence protected her from the horrors she had witnessed as a child. Would she remain forever trapped in this spell?

It was hard to decide whether he wished it so.

''And what is your lunatic up to now?''

Henri's deep voice caught Louis off guard, but he did not turn around. ''She's doing a rain dance,'' he said matter-of-factly.

Henri gave a grunt which, Louis knew without looking, was accompanied by a smirk.

"She is harming no one." Louis stood and trussed his arms across his chest. "Leave her be, Dragon Lord."

"Dragon Lord?"

Louis chuckled. " 'Tis what she calls you behind your back. Most fitting as of late, I must admit."

Evangeline.

Her voice, floaty and distant, cried for vengeance.

"Animal! You have wronged me! My children cry into their pillows at night. The days are all of sadness. I loved him. Redemption?" She sneered. "You will never have it! It seeps through your clenched fingers, tainted to a foul ooze. You cannot be redeemed. Cannot!"

Louis sprang upright with a start. "Evangeline." He pressed a hand to his neck, catching sweat beads on his wrist. His breaths gasped dry air.

Another damned dream. She had haunted him for weeks. Her pleas for vengeance relentless, her refusal of redemption a truth that Louis knew all too well.

Flopping back into his pillow, Louis stared up at the ceiling, knowing that he must accept these nightmares as penance for his sins. Death would have been too easy. To suffer endless years of regret would be his fitting punishment.

It was then that he heard the soft singing of raindrops spattering against his windowpane. Louis closed his eyes, squeezing tight to stretch out the sleep that coaxed him. *Plink, ping, plop.* Like peas rebounding against the side of a glass bowl. When he opened his eyes, he knew he was not still dreaming.

It had to be well after midnight. Wearily he climbed from bed and padded down the hallway, rubbing his eyes, yet strangely compelled by the sound of the rain. He stood just beyond reach of the weather, beneath the slatted-wood awning of the veranda.

Louis smiled as the cool water moistened his feet and misted against his bare chest. A welcome shiver traced across his flesh. "Blessed rain, we've a sorceress in our midst. The girl has enchanted the heavens."

Heedless of getting wet, Louis braced his hands on the railing and closed his eyes. He wished only to revel in the moment. Salvation had come in the form of glistening warm droplets. The vines would drink heartily and the grapes would create the sweetest of wines. Henri would be pleased. No more Dragon Lord.

And perhaps . . . yes. Louis realized that he, too, was feeling happy. So easily. Like magic.

Had she done it? Was it because of Sabine that the heavens had opened this night and spilled luscious salvation across the land?

No. But the thought that she might have a mystical connection to the heavens was easy enough to comprehend.

Satisfied, Louis opened his eyes to see a water fairy sitting in the grass below the veranda, her thin night chemise soaked completely, her head tilted back and her mouth open wide to drink in the redemptive elixir. Quickly, he rushed downstairs.

The ground slipped and squished between his toes as Louis trotted over to Sabine. She made no move to acknowledge that he was there. Hands on his hips, Louis opened his mouth to chastise her, but the words did not come. Her thin lawn chemise was dangerously close to becoming translucent. The material flowed like the rain over Sabine's body, cupping snugly the enticing circles of her breasts and puckering in concealing folds between her legs. Her hair, colored a deep dirty gold, lay limply over her right shoulder, hiding the one breast, while the other sprang cheerfully upright, as if to drink in the falling mead.

Louis gripped the fingers of his right hand with his left. She does not understand, he reasoned with his conscience. She does not know how the sight of her body stirred such desire within him; within any man. Louis glanced toward the house. No one in sight.

"Sabine." He plunged to the ground, taking her hand up in his. The back of his wrist inadvertently brushed across her nipple, which might have been what brought Sabine out of her spell.

"Louis!" She smiled. "You see, I danced for the rain and it has come. Isn't it refreshing and sweet? Taste it, Louis. Stick your tongue out. 'Tis the most incredible flavor."

"Sabine, I—"

"Oh, please, Louis. For me?"

She had no idea of the power of her innocent gaze, the lucid violet sparkle of temptation. It pierced his resolve and stirred in his gut, welling his loins into aching anticipation.

A battle cry screamed inside Louis's head, forced there by his own desperation to control his desires. Memory of his dying enemy's last breaths squelched all lust. *Yes, Henri, war does serve its purpose.*

"Louis," Sabine wheedled softly. "Try it, please?"

"Very well." He tilted his head back, wincing as a few raindrops speared his eyes. Anything to make her happy. It was just water, after all. Water had no flavor.

He swallowed tiny wet rain-kisses, straining to divine the taste, to sense a hint of the magic that colored Sabine's life into a fantastical wonderland. "Tastes like water," he sighed. "I'm sorry, Sabine, I just don't see things the way you do."

"You will," she reassured him with a squeeze of his hand. "Your soul is shadowed, Louis. I see that."

He turned in surprise.

"I see struggle and pain in your eyes," she whispered, oblivious of the steady droplets that splattered her eyelids, her nose, her lips. "But I also see redemption."

"Redemption." Louis gave a soft chuckle. She could even see his deepest desire. "I fear not, Mademoiselle. Once the soul is darkened, there is no salvation."

"You are wrong, Louis. There is always hope."

He met her gaze and had to choke back the rising emotion that pooled at the back of his throat. Hope? If there was to be any salvation, he wished only that it would focus on this fairy angel. For in her innocence she was far more deserving.

Louis tilted his head to the side. "What are you looking at, Sabine?"

"I like the way your eyes breathe me, Louis. 'Tis as if you are reaching out and trying to pull me in. So much—" She perked suddenly and moved to her knees. "Like Papa and Mama." Sabine closed her eyes and reached up with one hand, bending her fingers slightly as if to gently smooth over an unseeable object. "I remember watching them one night long ago. The moon was full and white. Cherry blossoms perfumed the air with a scent that Mama used to say made her drunk." Sabine smiled at her recollection, her face like porcelain splashed with water droplets.

Enchanted by her fairy glamour, Louis caught his chin in his palm.

"They stood in each other's arms. Papa smoothed the back of his hand across Mama's cheek. So gently . . ." Her own hand emulated the motion. "Like a whisper. He trailed his fingers down Mama's neck, moving so slowly until he reached her bosom. Mama twined her long, beautiful fingers through the golden silk of Papa's hair—" Sabine's smile grew wide. "I used to do the same, telling him that surely the silkworms lived in his tresses. Oh—"

Louis jerked his head up at Sabine's sudden silence. Her eyes had clouded; she stared blindly over his shoulder as droplets splinked upon her long lashes. Not yet, he thought. *Don't retreat into the dark shelter of your mind yet. More, give me more.* "Sabine." He touched her cheek with the back of his hand and she tilted her head against it.

"You are a handsome man, Louis. You make me wish I knew what it is like to be a woman," she whispered, her eyes still focusing beyond, as if searching for stars in the raindrops. She turned and seared her gaze onto his. "The looks you give me, they remind me of how Papa used to look at Mama."

Louis felt her knowledge. The woman resided inside the child. Somewhere. Not so much raging as *pining* for release. He drew his finger lower to trace the rain-slick mounds of her lips. Sabine closed her eyes and allowed him to explore the curves of her face. From her lips, Louis drew his finger gently down her chin, following a spidering trail of rain. Her jawline was fine and delicate, as if fashioned of paper. Pools of water collected over her eyelids and spilled softly across her cheeks like so many tears.

"Kiss me, Louis."

Such a simple request. One that immediately enflamed Louis's physical desire. It had been many, many months since he'd lain with a woman. So many more since he actually remembered enjoying himself in the act.

Thinking he should only brush her lips gently and then pull back, Louis touched his mouth to Sabine's. But his burning need took him much further. He kissed her slowly, lazily, teasing himself to control his desirous urges. So soft were her lips, like nothing he had ever possessed in his harsh lifetime. Her sigh was immediately captured in his mouth, and Louis felt the released emotion surge straight to his heart. Such sweet wine, her mouth. Peach wine, a rare and treasured thing. Blood pounded in his ear. A groan crossed his lips. Fairy glamour had never been more powerful.

Cupping her head in his hand, he deepened his kiss against her seeking lips. Pushing his hands up through her saturated crown of hair, he couldn't help but think that this was most likely her first kiss.

And the first he would ever remember.

It was a very long time after he finally pulled away that Sabine opened her eyes and whispered, "You are my knight in shining armor, Louis. I feel you would slay dragons for me."

"That I would, my lady of the fairies. Should I stumble upon one, I will slay it for you and bring you a fine crown of bejeweled dragon scales."

She smiled and clasped her hands to her breast. "And will we eat roast dragon for our wedding feast?"

"Yes, my lady. Yes."

CHAPTER SIX

It had taken two hours since leaving the gates of Paris to traverse the ill-trodden country road. Along the way, a carriage wheel broke upon a large, jagged stone and had to be replaced while the passengers waited beneath the horrendous sun. A flock of hell-winged crows covered the carriage windows with their slimy droppings, and Pietro had fallen physically ill from the heat and the joggling motion.

As they drew to a wobbling stop, the coachman navigated a low tree limb, causing a sharp splinter from the branch to tear across the cloth ceiling.

"What more?" Cristoforo declared with his fist raised to the slash of crystal-white sky that blasted through the torn roof.

Pietro, still a foggy pea color, placed a cushioned prie-dieu on the ground below the guano-streaked door, and Cristoforo stepped out. The summer heat was nearly unbearable in the silver brocade and Belgian lace frock coat. Blowing back the strands of hair that had loosened from its queue, Cristoforo patted a lace-edged handkerchief across his brow, which Pietro dutifully—yet a trifle queasily—retrieved and replaced with a fresh lemon-scented one.

"Head up, Pietro," Cristoforo snapped. "If I can endure this foul wretchedness, certainly you can."

"Yes, master," Pietro muttered.

His first sight of the Bassange castle did not unsettle Cristoforo as he'd suspected it might. All the better. Memories did nothing but torment.

A great cloud of dandelion fluff rose about Cristoforo's body as each unsure step of his red-heeled shoes took him up to the dilapidated castle door. He kicked the ungiving door, then pranced back and forth across the pounded red dirt that served as collector of dried leaves and sharp brambles. "Could anything be more of a bother!"

Pietro scrambled across the field, a lace fan in his right hand, a chalice of splashing water in his other. "Master, let the coachman help you," he said of the thick brute of a man who rumbled up behind him.

Cristoforo pulled Pietro's hand up so that the fan swished directly before his face. "If the bravo would have done his job, there would be no need for me to be out on such a dreadful day."

"Yes . . . master," Pietro acquiesced weakly.

Cristoforo squinted up at the sun. "Ghastly, this weather. I've gone beyond wilting. I feel as though I may begin to ooze out the bottoms of my breeches quite soon. And this Asian silk does not take well to body perspiration," he said of the fine waistcoat he wore.

With a grunt the coachman succeeded in pushing open the iron-banded door. A gush of dried leaves swept out across the men's feet, bringing with it a moist, rotting breath of air.

After a thorough yet delicate search of the lower rooms, Cristoforo came to a few conclusions. The castle was a shambles. Who could even think to visit, let alone live in such an ill-furnished, unclean place? Why, there were but two beds here, two wobbly chairs, and a blackened hearth. A small trestle table gouged deep by knife wounds and topped with a few bent pots made up the end of the list. Poverty.

An odd thing, knowing what he knew.

Cristoforo smoothed the pad of his finger over a circle carved deep into the wood door of the kitchen; its outline tore through the curved arc of another circle, joining the two. It had taken three different occasions to carve the entire thing, for it had to be done in secret.

Finally Cristoforo progressed to the far left tower, a room strangely bare of memories. This had been *his* room.

"The girl is nowhere to be found, master." Pietro trundled up the spiral stairs, where Cristoforo stood at the end of the cobweb-laced bed.

"I can see that, idiot. What of the *grand-père?* Did you find his body?"

"Er—yes, master. Outside. See there?"

Waiting first for Pietro to brush away the dust and spider-webbing from the sill, Cristoforo looked down across the weed-ridden stretch of land to the pile of rocks Pietro pointed to. A makeshift cross of twisted elm branches, wedged between head-sized fieldstones, marked what might have been a pauper's grave.

Again, impossible for Cristoforo to believe.

"Pietro." Cristoforo had only to hold out a graceful hand to have Pietro place his handkerchief in it. The boy had been well trained. He didn't know what he'd do without him. Even if he did smell worse than spoiled pâté at the moment.

So, the old man was dead. Cristoforo allowed himself a satisfied smile. But it lasted only a moment.

There was still the girl. Where could she have gotten her crazy little head off to? Maybe the bravo really did do away with her? Did he hide her? Was there another grave somewhere about?

"We found no other graves," Pietro added.

"You're sure?"

"Positive."

"The bravo?"

"Tossed off beyond that copse of trees. Not even given a proper burial."

"I see." Cristoforo let his gaze rise from the ruffled treetops to the clear wash of pale turquoise sky.

He had known before coming that she still lived. Felt that niggling streak of impending pain just behind his left eyeball. But where could she be? Had she walked somewhere? There were no homes close by. Paris was a good six leagues away. Perhaps she had wandered off into the forest and had gotten lost. He night never find her.

But it was imperative. The death of the lunatic was as essential as the air he breathed. For only then would the maddening pain cease.

And then, too, there was the other matter. Now that the vicomte had passed on, all sorts of financial matters had to be put in order. And Cristoforo's finances would undergo a drastic change.

He glanced down at the grave once more. It was not a pauper who lay beneath the heavy stones. He knew that much.

He must speak to l'Argent immediately.

She hopped about on one foot, her ample flesh jiggling with each bouncing step. She mumbled nonsense quietly, but loud enough for Louis to take notice as he passed by the hearth room. In her hands hung a freshly plucked chicken, its flesh all loose and pale, its head lolling to and fro in opposite rhythm to her steps.

Louis could not stop his curiosity; the words just rushed out. "What are you doing, Yvette?"

She stopped abruptly, the chicken head dangling over her

thick fingers. Her wide eyes settled to calmness upon seeing it was only him. "Blessing this meal, my lord. And—"

"No!" He threw up a defensive hand. "Don't tell me. I don't think I want to know."

"As you choose." She stood waiting for him to leave.

Louis knew she would begin as soon as he disappeared. Why or how she was compelled to her strange habits, he did not care. Yvette was a good servant, more a family member, than employee. Her religious beliefs were of no concern to him as long as they brought no harm to him or his family. And she did have a way with poultry. Finer than the court cuisine he'd once sampled.

He made to leave.

"My lord?"

He peeked back into the room. "Yes?"

" 'Tis good to see the smile has returned to your face."

Like an unstoppable rain, he could not help the wide grin that spread across his face. Yes, something had happened. A something whose kisses tasted of peach wine. "It feels good, Yvette."

Louis's boots barely touched the newly resurrected grass outside the château before he heard Henri's voice.

"I need your help. The press needs repair. It'll take two hands at least."

He'd planned on finding Sabine. Spending the afternoon with her sitting in the grass and watching the sky and the birds sounded very relaxing. But the time had come to take his place in the family once again. He was no longer the dead man who had lain for weeks in his bed. And damn if he didn't really desire the work too. To flex his muscles and repair his soul with good hard sweat and labor. "Of course."

The brothers' long strides took them across the yard and to the pressing house half coved in creeping vines that kept the house cool in the late summer months. The outer walls were frothed with clematis, their spiraling new shoots like curly mice tails.

"I saw you last night," Henri said as he rolled up his sleeves and sat on a three-legged stool at the base of the wood press.

"Saw—" Louis propped the door open with a fieldstone and tried not to show his dismay as he scanned the semidarkened room for the oil lamp. Damn, Louis thought. Henri had seen him out in the rain. He must have seen him kiss Sabine.

"What were you thinking?"

"I—I could not stop myself. I—"

"I, too, had the urge to rise and stand in the rain. Blessed rain. Thank the Lord," Henri yelled to the ceiling rafters.

Nothing but the rain. Henri had not seen the girl. Relieved, Louis blew out a breath and reached for the tinderbox that rested high upon a horizontal beam.

"Perhaps it was your lunatic?"

Flame flashed blue in the lamp base. Louis jerked a questioning gaze to Henri.

"She did do her little rain dance," Henri added as he fingered the iron workings of the press, his fingers already coated with heavy black grease.

"You're not saying you believe in such nonsense?" Louis said with new wonder.

"You believe that you can cure the lunatic," Henri growled sarcastically. "Then I suppose I can believe in her black magic."

" 'Tis not black, her magic." Louis kicked a stray pebble, and it rebounded against the north wall of the pressing house. " 'Tis of a color I've never yet seen. Perhaps all the colors of the rainbow."

* * *

"L'uttima pròva Dell'amor mio Ancora voglio
"Fare con te . . ."

Following the eerie strains of music that lingered like fine Parisian perfume in the heavy evening air, Louis carefully slipped onto the second-floor veranda and padded barefoot across the warped pinewood boards.

"Mi manca, O Dei, la lena."

Sabine's eyes were closed as her song hushed to near silence, the clear, high notes barely whispering over her lips. Moonlight—nearly full—settled in gleaming silver streaks upon her loose hair. Louis leaned against the railing, setting the sun-tortured wood to a dry creak.

Sabine stopped abruptly.

Silently cursing his carelessness, Louis offered her an apologetic shrug, then sat next to her on the swinging bench held secure by thick hemp ropes. The old wood also creaked to accept his weight. It had been a long time since two had shared this swing. Far too long.

"I didn't mean to disturb you. It was lovely. I had no idea you speak Italian."

"Italian?" A rueful little smile crinkled her lips. "So that is what it is. How curious. I do not speak any language other than my own."

"Then I'm amazed. Where did you learn to sing opera? And in a language unfamiliar to you?"

Blush-colored lids blinked softly against the moonlight as Sabine tilted her head back to admire the star-dusted sky. "It just comes to me. There are times the music fills my head, pushing and crowding out all thoughts, until I'm sure my mind will burst." She played with a portion of her cotton skirts. "The only way to alleviate the overcrowding is to let it flow out through my mouth."

"Fascinating."

She turned to Louis and gave him a shy smile. A smile that transformed into something very intriguing. He knew not what it was, but suddenly she seemed to possess some secret knowledge.

In proof, her voice took on a husky timbre, that of a wise and daring woman who would tempt a man into her arms as Venus did to Adonis year after tempestuous year. "I know what you think of me, Louis."

Did she really?

"Whatever do you mean?"

"You have in your presence a madwoman. One who is not in control of her mind."

"Oh, no, Sabine—" Not what he'd expected. No. He'd been thinking more of his desire for her.

"Yes, Louis." She laid a delicate hand upon his knee, while her smile remained that of a vixen.

Louis jerked his gaze to her action. Every touch, every simple brush of their bodies, had become such a maddening temptation. Oh, he could have done so much more than just kiss her last evening!

"You mustn't think I'm so far gone that I cannot see myself from the perspective of others. I can be quite lucid at times. More often than not."

"Yes, I know." She challenged his every theory of her. As soon as Louis felt he was beginning to form an understanding of this enigma, she shattered it like an illusion of water and lights.

"But the madness is a dark shadow that clings like a beast to the light within my soul."

The pleading conviction of her words tore at Louis's heart. He wanted so to understand this lovely creature of the fairy realm. To know how to comfort her, make her whole and normal and right. But how could he even begin to know what to do, when he himself was not whole?

"It is a darkness I fight daily," she continued in a desperate whisper. "Sometimes I feel as if I'm drowning, being sucked into the belly of this beast. My light is extinguished more frequently. Without warning. But you, Louis"—she spread her palm across his cheek, sending an alarmingly sensual tingle across his scalp—"you are the light that I can reach for. A beacon that blocks the darkness, chokes it out."

"Yes, but—"

He silenced at the press of her finger to his lips and instead kissed the tender digit. Ah, she tasted of sweetness and summer-fresh grass. Louis inhaled. He could read her flesh like he could read the wines in the family cellar. All the elements of the earth went into the creation of a superb elixir. And she was of the earth, the flowers, the sun's warmth, and the rain's sweet tears.

"You are surprised I can speak of my madness so?"

He nodded.

"I try to fight it, Louis. And it has become so much easier now that I am with you. You've given me a light to guide me to the surface. I'm just afraid sometimes . . . afraid that I will lose the fight."

"Never . . ."

"No, Louis. Certain things set me off. I am not myself when I am alone. The darkness crowds over the light. I see horrible things. Fantastical things. These visions come to me. . . . And the music—this strange language I do not know—it is so odd, Louis. Frightening. I do not understand it."

"No, no, Sabine. You must never be afraid." He pulled her fingers to his lips and pressed a kiss to them, holding firm so that he felt the pulse of her blood against his mouth. How to inject courage into her heart from his own diminished stores, he knew not.

"Louis, you are my salvation. I need you." Her features

smoothed as she began to trail the tip of her finger over his lips. Slowly and tenderly she explored his mouth, her expression fascinated. "You so remind me of Papa. So gentle and loving. You could never harm a soul, I feel that."

Bitter black regret stabbed at Louis's heart as he felt Sabine's touch journey across the stubble that darkened his jaw. *You could never harm a soul.* If she only knew of the death and destruction he had caused. He'd walked the trenches with hate in his soul, the enemy colors burning in his eyes. The battle cry had come to him like laughter to a child, so easy, so thoughtless. Lighting his musket and dropping the cock was as natural as a bodily function. Enemy. Kill. Not a second thought. Until the victory flag had been raised and the blood ceased to flow . . .

Tell my wife I love her . . . Evangeline.

Animal!

Louis wanted to push Sabine away, to run and bury his face in his murderous hands, but he could not bring himself to sever the connection she had instigated. He treasured her touch. Craved it. Perhaps . . . needed it.

Sabine's hand moved slowly over his hair, lingering in the curled ends, so innocent of her effect on him. Her touch was maddening, enticing, and healing all at once. He wanted to pull away and run. Run from the emotions she was forcing him to confront. He wanted to melt in her embrace, a small child in search of comfort. He wanted to take her in his arms and satisfy his screaming lusts. She knew not the temptation her closeness caused him. The need to lose himself in her, to take her, to have her in the ways he desperately needed a woman grew stronger as the days passed.

Control! He must harness his emotions, curb his desire.

Unaware of his inner torment, Sabine turned his hand over to trace the lines of his palm. Louis jerked away.

''What is this?'' She pulled his hand back to her lap and pushed the frayed and wine-stained edges of his sleeve away.

The coolness of her finger tracing the jagged scar that trailed across Louis's wrist almost sickened him. Instantly he knew he'd betrayed her trust. She thought him a gentle and kind man. Her knight in shining armor come in rescue of her darkened soul. ''It is nothing, Sabine. You would not understand. I have lived a life that no man wishes to live.''

Her eyes searched his while her fingers curled tight around his wrist.

''You tried to take your own life,'' she said in hushed amazement.

He nodded curtly and pulled his hand away, tucking it under his opposite arm.

''Tell me.'' Her soft whisper circled Louis's mind, seeking out the hidden well of fear and anxiety he closeted deep inside.

He could not. Could not reveal his greatest defeat, the weakness that had fused deep within his soul, planting roots that snaked and curled and strangled his courage, his confidence, his pride.

No redemption. Not ever.

''Release your pain to me, Louis.''

Release your pain. . . . The phrase wavered over and over in Louis's mind. A haunting, a tempting . . .

An invitation.

Inexplicably compelled by the gentleness of her request, Louis sighed. A sigh that worked to release his heartfelt fears. And he began to explain.

''For six years I was a soldier, Sabine. Soldiers are trained to kill or be killed. I . . . did my job well.''

He felt her fingers push up under his crossed arms. He loosened his strong clutch and allowed her to join hands with him. The beat of her pulse drummed against his palm.

"The fighting at Fontenay was terrible. Rain had been falling for days. I was muddy, tired, starving, and beyond true comprehension. An enemy pikeman surprised me from behind, but I was too quick. My dagger was like a part of me, finding its victims far easier than my mind will allow. I fell to my knees, exhaustion pulling me down, and stared coldly as the rain washed the life from my enemy's breast. The rain turned heavy, sharp in its touch. It was then I realized that the man had wounded me with his pike. I touched the open wound on my shoulder, covering my hand with a swirl of blood."

Louis paused, gauging Sabine's reaction to his brutal description of battle. She squeezed his hand. She had witnessed far worse.

" 'Tell my wife I love her' were the man's dying words.

"Evangeline." Louis's thoughts carried him to the faceless woman who mourned her husband in his tormented nightmares. *Animal! There is no redemption for you!*

"Evangeline," Sabine whispered.

The sound of that name, spoken by someone else, worked an odd twist within Louis's mind. "What?"

"The name," she said. "I heard you call it out in your sleep the other night. Why does it torment you so?"

"Why?" Louis continued. "She is a widow because of me. As I knelt over my dying enemy, he raised a bloody hand into the air, and for some strange reason I clasped it with mine. Our blood flowed together, mixing with the rain, and I saw things so clearly. *Our* blood. We were the same beneath the surface. All men are equal beneath the flesh. Enemy colors and battle drums separate us for reasons unknown to us. Insanity, I thought. I had been on a killing spree for years, without so much as a thought for my enemy. The enemy was myself. I could have just as easily been him lying there, waiting death's grasp.

"It sickened me. I felt my stomach rise to my throat, but I

hadn't eaten for days, so I only coughed and choked. For that one instant, as I knelt there by this man who had suddenly become my brother in blood, I felt the deepest regret. Evangeline, his wife, her tears and screams entered my head. Her life would be forever changed because of a quick flick of my wrist. And I knew there would be no redemption for me.

"I mustered out. Decorated with honors. For bravery. Bah! I felt such despair, I did nothing but drink. Henri left me to myself. Until the night I attempted this."

Louis felt Sabine's thumb smooth over his wrist. He inhaled. "If I hadn't been soused, perhaps I'd have used my dagger and done the job right. As it was, I botched my own death."

"But perhaps . . ." Sabine said softly.

Louis stared hard into the lucid gaze of the woman he held, waiting for her to continue. She understood everything. He knew that she did. For she lived in her own personal battleground, and fought far worse enemies.

"Perhaps it was for the best."

"For the best?" He chuffed a breath out through his nose. "Tell that to Evangeline."

Sabine's gaze faltered and trailed off across the sky, and just when Louis felt sure she had retreated to the sanctuary of her own world, she turned back to him.

"Come to me," she beckoned, holding her arms out to embrace him. "You need me as much as I need you. Please, Louis, come."

Giving in to his pain was far easier than he'd ever thought. Louis bent forward and cradled his body against Sabine's, slipping his arms around her waist and pressing the side of his face against her exposed décolletage. She held him as a mother would a frightened child. Soft caresses hugged him closer. He closed his eyes against the light press of her lips to the crown of his head.

Powerless. A lost soul, himself.

An overwhelming feeling embraced Louis. And it felt too

wonderful to describe. This was a good feeling of surrender.
He could lose his fears and anxieties in the arms of this woman.
Salvation wore a fairy smile and sang Italian opera.

For the best? Yes, perhaps. For if he'd drawn his dagger
across his wrists that night, he would never have lived to find
Sabine Bassange. Never known the blessing of her embrace.

Gentle whispers slipped down to his ears. "This feels so
very right, Louis."

Louis tightened his grip, pushing his palms up the smooth
fabric that covered her back. He closed his eyes. "That is does,
my fairy angel. That it does."

"You know . . ." Her fingers worked lazily in the thickness
of his hair, each trace of her nails sending delightful shivers
across his scalp. "You make it so very easy, Louis."

"Easy?" He curled a stray wisp of her golden hair about
his forefinger and pressed it to his mouth. "What is easy,
Sabine?"

She hugged him tightly. "Just . . . being."

"So you know where she is," Cristoforo said, trying to
remain calm.

"*Sst, sst. Oui,* Signore, I spoke to the two gentlemen yesterday morning. Messieurs Louis and Henri de Lavarac."

Pacing across the worn tufts of Persian wool carpeting, Cristoforo commanded the room dressed in a long robe of red
damask edged in silver tassels, and still wearing the massive
feather headdress that he was fitting for that night's performance.

"And these men plan to keep her?"

"Until the other heir can be located."

"Yes, the other heir."

"*Sst, sst.*"

Cristoforo jerked his neck and smoothed his palm along the
right side. That irritating noise. Was the man not aware of the

distraction? "How long did you say it would take to locate the . . . heir?"

"I told them it could be a week." L'Argent's narrow gaze sought out Cristoforo's approval. "That is what you wanted?"

"Yes. Excellent."

"There was mention of her madness."

"Really." Cristoforo wasn't the least surprised. He knew far better than anyone the girl's condition. "What did they say?"

"The eldest, Monsieur Henri, wanted to be rid of her, it seemed. The other would not allow it. It was almost as if he cared for her."

Cristoforo couldn't stop the laughter from exploding in a short burst. "Care?" he ground out between his teeth. "For a lunatic?"

L'Argent shrugged.

Care? Cristoforo felt the muscles pinch together at the back of his neck. Oh, he would show her the meaning of *care*. "I am quite sure his *care* began the instant there was mention of an inheritance. You know where they live?"

"*Oui.* I've all the information written down for you."

"Excellent."

"There is one other thing."

Cristoforo paced past the *notaire* and paused before the mirror that stretched from floor to ceiling. He adjusted the papier-mâché headpiece designed in the shape of a swan's body, and pursed his lips. Blood-red carmine for his lips tonight, he thought. That way his face would not be entirely lost beneath the great sprays of white ostrich feathers. "Spit it out already."

"*Sst, sst.* The younger of the brothers, Louis, he requested I locate an Englishwoman. I don't believe it has any bearing on the matters involving the, er, Mademoiselle Bassange, but you should know he was adamant about finding her."

"Have you found her?"

"I have connections in the military. I'm sure I'll turn her up. Nevertheless, I'll keep you informed."

"You do that."

"Sst, sssst."

Cristoforo spun about and slapped his hand over the lawyer's mouth. "Enough," he spat out. "You sound like a dying rat."

CHAPTER SEVEN

Cristoforo counted approximately half the audience applauding his appearance onstage. He stood, quiet and composed, scanning the crowd, drawing in the conflicting vibrations of the people in the pit. Most were engaged in conversation, drinking and laughing, women exchanging seductive glances with a wanton cad, and more than a few were even involved in a round of cards. Not unusual, Cristoforo knew. He was in Paris, after all. And although the audiences were much the same in Italy, Italians appreciated their singers far more than the arrogant French did.

But not for long. He would have the demoiselles and the simpering rogues swooning in the aisles and begging his eternal affections within seconds.

While he normally did not employ this little trick until an encore—or not at all—it was necessary to put these Parisians in their place immediately. Show them just what sort of a presence they were dealing with.

Ignoring the hopeful face of the conductor, who awaited

Cristoforo's winking signal to begin the music, Cristoforo set his voice free. A high A note, honed over the years to perfection, traveled across the garbled din, drowning it out and filling the entire room in an amazing feat of acoustics. Twisting his left hand into a loose grip, Cristoforo clutched the air as he drew out the note, not reaching for a breath—for he did not require one; he could carry this note for a full minute if needed.

Conversations were abruptly cut off with a gasp. Within seconds the games ceased, the players turning to see what the commotion was. Women who had initially clapped and waited raptly for Cristoforo's voice sighed. The entire room settled to complete silence in the period of—count them—yes, nine seconds.

Expanding the note to a great crescendo, then ornamenting it into a birdlike trill, and then, with the silence of the room, bringing it to pianissimo, barely a whisper, Cristoforo smiled inwardly. He had gained control.

The devil take the haughty Parisians! Cristoforo had arrived.

As the note began to fade in his throat, Cristoforo signaled to the maestro and six violins carefully joined, followed by the deep bellow of a bass violin. He seguéd into the aria bravura, his signature piece, the audience chained to his voice, his voice master over all.

It was at such times that Cristoforo thanked the heavens for the gift he'd been given. To be able to command a room to silence, and more often than not to tears. To be able to create smiles, and force a sigh from a staunch man's lips. To be revered and worshipped. To be so close to God that some had trouble telling the two of them apart.

How quickly triumph is overcome by adversity.

He could not see the pitchfork, but the pain felt all too real. Cristoforo clutched his forehead, trying vainly to maintain his composure. Pain streaked through his temple, threatening to cloud his concentration and mar the notes that wavered high above the wigged and powdered heads. The plumed headpiece went askew, sliding dangerously close to his left ear.

Not now, he thought as he reached for a lingering C. A dashing obligato followed, which needed a great breath of air, but as Cristoforo began to draw in the elixir of his trade, he could no longer control the forces straining to bring him down.

The C note ended in a frightened squawk. Cristoforo fell to his knees, gluing both palms to his forehead. The swan helmet fell to the stage with a crash and wobbled awkwardly to the edge, where a flame from one of the footlights singed a white feather. He did not hear the gasps and startled cries. His entire brain hummed and vibrated in squeezing clenches. Dammit, he should have expected this! A full moon hung in the sky!

"Pietro," he managed to gasp.

Already by his master's side, Pietro bent over him and levered him to his feet. A burst of amber flame flashed in Cristoforo's peripheral view as the headpiece was devoured. With Pietro's assistance, Cristoforo staggered off the stage while the orchestra attempted to fend off his many fans.

Once backstage, surrounded by bustling stagehands and actors, and the beautiful young contralto all trying to steal a look, Cristoforo allowed his knees to buckle. Protected from the crowd by Pietro's feeble, spread-limbed blockade, Cristoforo pressed his forehead to his knees and screamed into his legs.

Startled out of sleep by an odd pressure on his shoulder, Louis rolled over in bed and opened his eyes to his brother's sleep-lined face. His expression was enough to scare any man out of his dreams.

"Your wench is outside, baying at the moon," Henri hissed, and stomped out of the room.

Fighting off the clinging remainders of sleep, Louis stumbled out of bed, groping about the tangled sheets and coverlet for his discarded dressing gown. He pulled the worn embroidered cotton over his thin lawn nightshirt, repeating the words his brother had just spoken. "Baying at the moon . . . Your wench . . . What? No!" Louis burst down the stairs to where Henri held the door open to the grounds.

"You do not think her mad?" he said as Louis paused, clenching the doorframe to summon the courage to move. Henri nodded toward the yard where Sabine's maniacal screams echoed up to the moon. "Look there."

Frozen in place, Louis watched as his beautiful golden fairy went through the most hideous contortions. She wore only the thin gown that Yvette had loaned her. Moonlight streamed through the fine material, defining her narrow legs and the curves of her breasts. She carried a scream out to an endless moan as she pantomimed an action of pulling. No. Pushing? It appeared as though she were attempting to pull something free. Or maybe push it away. Though she held nothing in her grasping hands. Soon she fell to the ground and her body curled over her knees as her screams became sobs.

"It will begin again," Henri said. "She goes through this scenario over and over."

"You've been watching her? For how long? Why did you not try to help?"

Henri's mouth drew into an irregular grimace as he nodded his head disdainfully.

Louis turned back to Sabine. It was then he noticed the field hands stood watching. Their mouths open wide. Laughing. Their eyes ogling the frail creature writhing in the grass.

"Get away!" Louis ran toward the men. "There is nothing to see here. Go back to your beds." He veered toward Sabine, but a flashing thought that he might frighten her stayed him.

"Sabine!" She did not seem to notice as her ritual began anew. Screams, along with the pulling or pushing. She spread her fingers through her hair and pulled hard.

"Sabine, no, please." Louis approached her cautiously. She turned in his direction, but though it seemed she looked right at him, he knew that she was not seeing beyond the torturous nightmares that haunted her mind. *The darkness.* He recalled her own explanation of her madness. It had clouded her light.

Not one of the field hands had made a move to leave. Henri stood with his back against the bougainvillea-laced château wall, the expression on his face almost of satisfaction.

So she is mad, Louis thought. Tormented by some unseen presence. Deranged by a life lived in seclusion and silence. Mad. But not of her own choosing.

You can be my salvation, Louis. You are my light.

Carefully, Louis approached Sabine. On the ground again, she sobbed into her palms. He could see the side of her face drenched in tears, could smell her pain in the salted wash that stained the diaphanous chemise. He had to help her, to let her know that she was not alone. To hold her as she had done for him.

Louis dove forward and clasped his arms about Sabine's body. She sprang upright, knocking her head against his shoulder, and began to scream. He struggled to maintain hold by pinning her arms to her sides, yet her screams turned into one word.

"Murderer! Murderer!"

"No, Sabine, it is Louis. Louis!" he yelled. Unmindful of his audience, Louis fought the demon that possessed this fairy child. He did not want to harm her, but she seemed to have the strength of a man his size. Her heel stabbed into his calf. Louis spread his legs wide. "Louis," he repeated. "Look at me, Sabine. It is safe! I am here."

Seeing that her struggles would only continue and possibly become so frenzied she risked harming herself, Louis buckled his knees and fell to the ground, bringing Sabine with him. He pushed her to the grass and secured her arms at her sides while sitting on her thighs to prevent her from kicking him.

"Look at me," he cooed over and over, trying to make eye contact with her. She wrenched her head from side to side, still proclaiming him a murderer. "It is Louis." He knew not what to do, what to say . . . when he recalled her magical words in the meadow. "Your knight?"

Her jerking struggles began to subside. When she drew in a sobbing gasp, perhaps to renew her scream, Louis said forcefully, "Sabine, it is Louis."

He felt her body tense to rigidity and then weaken like marsh grass in a rainstorm. Her screams silenced. Violet eyes searched his. He'd made contact.

"Sabine, 'tis all right. I will protect you. There is no one here who wishes you harm. You are safe, Sabine. Safe."

He felt the blood pump in his fist and realized he still had a firm hold on her frail arms. Louis released her from his grasp, but not from his gaze.

"Louis," she whispered, her voice hoarse and weak.

He nodded and offered a tentative smile.

She pushed up from the dew-kissed grass and wrapped her arms about his shoulders, pressing her body tight to his, clinging, hoping, seeking comfort. "Save me," she whispered.

"I will," he said as he began to rock her gently. "I will, my lady madness."

It took less than a robin's breath for Sabine to fall into a peaceful sleep. Amazing, Louis observed as he slowly padded to her chamber door. Yvette smoothed a hand across Sabine's forehead, lingering, Louis knew, on the fine silken softness of her hair. Divining the rich vibration of peace.

The way the moonlight played across the bed highlighted the curve of Sabine's leg, the slight arch of her back, the fullness of her breast. As much as he wished to deny his attraction to her, Louis could not. No matter that she was not whole and well.

Murderer!

She had been trapped in a mad replay of her parents' murders.

Though Sabine would not say exactly and Louis hadn't dared broach the subject, still, he knew.

He glanced over the plain oak armoire and out the window. Full and gorgeous, the moon seared a white beam across Sabine's motionless body. For all the tales Louis had heard of moonlight madness and the powers that mystical orb possessed, he'd never believed them. Until now.

"She's resting well," Yvette said as she laid a hand on Louis's arm.

"Yes." He closed the door behind them and stood waiting as Yvette readjusted the hand-sewn shawl around her shoulders. "Was it the moon?" he couldn't help asking.

A serene smoothness pulled across the old woman's face. She pressed both hands to either side of Louis's face. Wise warmth. Sabine was wrong about Yvette. She could live a long life. "I cannot say. But it was you who rescued her from the demon's clutches tonight, Louis. You've something special in your heart, child. It flows freely when you are with Sabine. Do you still believe that you were not meant for this life?"

He curled his fingers around her wrist and pulled her knuckles to his lips for a gentle kiss. "I haven't given it much thought lately. I've been too busy."

She gave a knowing nod. "Bless the heavens for bringing Sabine Bassange into our home."

CHAPTER EIGHT

"Grace?"

Henri could not have repeated the word with more distaste.

Louis looked up from his supper plate. "Yes, we should thank the Lord for this food before eating. Is something wrong?"

"Are you the same Louis de Lavarac who proclaimed war against the Church by pulling a knife across his own lifeline?"

Mention of his blasphemy always made the wounds at the base of his palms pulse.

"Perhaps not. I guess I'm seeing things differently lately. Parts of me have"—he recalled his conversation with Yvette late last night—"changed. I duly regret my actions, Henri. I ask your forgiveness for the pain I've caused you. You've been through far too much as it is to have to worry about me."

A rare smile lifted the left side of Henri's thin lips and drew a deep line from the corners of his dark eyes up toward his temples. " 'Tis about time you came around. Go on."

Louis said a quick, mindless prayer. Somewhere between

storming enemy lines and striking dead yet another redcoat, he'd given up on the belief that a supreme power watched over him. Given up on redemption and salvation, and all that religious babble. But the Lord had not given up on Louis. That was obvious by his very presence at this table. And so, he could at least begin to practice a faith that still believed in him.

"Amen," the brothers mumbled in unison.

The pleasant aroma of herbed chicken gravy would wait no longer. Tonight Louis planned to savor each and every mouthful. He'd put in a long day of work alongside Henri. He'd helped scythe the grasses bordering the vineyards, had pruned the lower vines and repaired the press. Appetite had returned.

And then, of course, if he must be truthful to himself, it might prove one way to curb his ever-present lust for the sensual delights that Sabine's body promised. Madness or not, he found his mind fixed on thoughts of her moonlight-haloed body and her heady kisses.

He took a small globe of fresh rye bread from the silver platter and dipped his knife into the gravy pooled on his plate in preparation for spreading it inside the bun. But the feel of the round, smooth loaf cupped against his palm startled him. Tipping his hand from side to side, Louis surmised that the bread was about the same size as a . . . a woman's breast. And equally as warm.

He cast a glance to Henri, who was busy with his own food, ravenous as always.

A stray drop of gravy slid over the oat-brown surface in Louis's hand, hinting to the slow trail he'd like his tongue to make across Sabine's breast. Ah, to nestle his head against her breast and inhale her scent, taste her sweetness and the salty flavor of her body.

"The lunatic dining in her quarters tonight?"

Louis's fingers locked, and the dinner roll toppled across the table, coming to rest a finger's width from the edge. "I will not stand for you to call her that."

"And just what should the Dragon Lord call her? Precious? Her mad majesty?"

Louis crossed the space between them in a breath. He lifted Henri from his chair, toppling his goblet of wine across the woven tablecloth.

Wrenching his shirt out of his brother's grip, Henri stumbled back, nearly tripping over the leg of his chair. "Her madness has begun to wear off on you!"

"No!" Louis yelled. "You are the madman for wanting to dump this poor girl on the steps of some rotting asylum and turn away without so much as an adieu."

"She does not belong here. You know that. She needs help. Someone who knows how to deal with her unbalanced mind. You have allowed yourself to be seduced by her beauty!"

"No!"

"Yes!" Henri lowered his voice to a hiss. "But this lunatic's beauty is truly only skin deep. Beneath the facade lies a vicious demon, a creature who howls at the moon—"

"How dare you judge her so? What of me, Henri? Did you cart me off to Salpêtrière the night I did this?" Louis held his wrists before him, displaying the scars to his brother.

Henri's wince did not go unnoticed. "That is different."

"How? Is it not madness to let one's own blood? To sin against your Church so grievously?"

"It is your Church too!"

"I'm not so sure. How could a loving, caring God allow me to perpetrate such vile acts upon so many innocent men?"

"War is sanctioned by the Church. Do not question the Lord's work! Only accept that in the end your faith will guide you to the light."

"The light. Bah! And what of the light he has stolen from Sabine Bassange?"

"You are my brother, Louis," Henri said in a firm, low tone. "I know not of the girl. But I do know you are not mad. Only . . . melancholy."

"Ha! Melancholy. Mad." Louis turned and walked away, dancing his fingers in the air in comical display as he turned back on his brother. "Are you sure you know which is which?" he drew out. "We know so little about Sabine. We have no idea what torments her mind has suffered over the years. You say her family was murdered before her very eyes."

"And that drove her to madness."

Louis thrust a staying hand toward Henri. "No. Surely what we witnessed last night was only a vicious memory."

"An uncontrollable memory that had her acting the lunatic," Henri reiterated with a forceful stomp of his foot. "She will remain forever insane, brother. There is no cure for madness. Get that into your thick head!"

"Then why confine her to an institution?"

"They have restraining devices that will keep her tamed—"

"Restraints? Damnation! What of love, Henri?"

"Love?"

"Yes, love!" Louis paced away from his brother. The fire in the hearth had fizzled to a red glow, dusted with gray ash, much like the fire that had once ruled his life. But the spark had not gone out. In fact, it had been renewed. "Love heals all wounds, does it not?"

Behind him his brother righted the toppled goblet. "You quote nonsense. Romantic babble designed by women for women."

Louis turned to his brother, his forefinger to his chin in thought. "You do not see her, Henri. You look right through her. Your eyes miss the soul within, the fire that burns for freedom. You know ... I can see Janette when I look at Sabine."

"What?" And now the blaze leapt to Henri's dark stare. "How dare you mention my wife's name in the same breath! God rest her soul, she is not like that lunatic who bays at the moon."

"Sabine is exactly like Janette." Louis stood toe to toe with

Henri, his brother's angry breaths heating his neck. "Janette was the strongest woman I have ever known. She suffered so trying to bring your child into the world—"

"I do not want to hear this!"

"You will!" Louis followed his brother, speaking louder when the man covered his ears with his hands. "Janette held strong to her faith and to her belief in your love for her. She did not give up. Never! She would not give up on her child. And even though God saw fit to end both their lives, she died with your name on her lips. She pleaded for you to go on. 'Do not suffer my loss, Henri, celebrate my unity with our child in heaven.' "

Henri clenched his fist near his face.

"Sabine is the same. She has great strength within. She will not give up, Henri. I sense it. She fights this demon daily. She has not yet lost. Triumph is attainable. You have seen with your own eyes that she is lucid more often than not."

Henri grunted a breath through his nostrils.

"When I hold her . . ." Louis clutched his closed fists to his chest and searched his memory for a fitting description, an image Henri could understand. "When our eyes meet . . . a part of her . . . *connects*. Things become so right. It is as though she is normal. So sane. Untouched by disaster."

"When you hold her." Henri gave a snorting chuckle. He walked around behind Louis, slamming his arms tightly across his chest, and came up close to whisper in his brother's ear. "And when you hold her, brother, do you fantasize what it will feel like to debauch her naked body?"

The only discernible sound, a flicker of candlelight. Louis's gaze fell inexplicably to the gravy-smeared roll that had fallen to the floor. "How dare you?"

"You cannot tell me you do not think such thoughts. Do you spill your seed when all are quiet and gone to sleep? Is that how you slake your lust, brother?"

Pulling back, Louis prepared to let his fist connect with his brother's face. But something stopped him. A breeze from the window. A silent whisper inside his head.

Tell my wife I love her. Evangeline.

Violence solved nothing. It only bred more violence. He would not allow himself to revert to his former self. No, he had a reason now to try to better himself.

Louis turned and stormed outside.

"Where is Louis?"

Henri found Sabine standing in the doorway to her room, Yvette's tattered wool night robe wrapped about her shoulders.

"He usually bids me good night," she explained.

Henri walked carefully over to the girl, sensing her need to step back from him, but slowing his pace so she would not. Dragon Lord, indeed. He'd give her reason to fear him if she so much as spoke those words aloud to him.

He stopped before her. A flare of his nostrils found the scent of fresh air and musk seeping from her pores. Very well. Perhaps a *little* like Janette. She carried the indelible mark of woman. Soft and sweet-smelling. Delicate. Except Janette had been whole and beautiful. Of course, Sabine was beautiful. In the physical sense. But she was not whole. Damaged, she was.

Henri clenched a fist near his thigh and lowered his voice. "Seems my brother does not trust himself around you tonight. Louis is in the vineyards . . . spilling his seed." He cracked a grin and paced away. "Good night, lunatic."

Flaky sheets of birchwood paper fluttered to the ground at the toes of Louis's suede boots. He unconsciously worked at the tree bark, peeling and tearing. His anger had lessened. He no longer fought the urge to bash Henri's face into this very tree. But the realization that Henri's taunts were true—so true—

tortured Louis more than thirty-six hours in the trenches firing
round after round at enemy lines.

Her naked body . . . Debauch her . . .

He could not deny his nights and days had been filled with
wicked fantasies of the delicate beauty that now shared his
home. Dreams that always began with Sabine dancing toward
him in the meadow, her golden hair flowing like honey behind
her as her steps stirred up a cloud of white thistle umbrellas.
They would fall to the ground in each other's embrace. Warm
earth and fresh meadow grass scented their lover's bed. In his
arms Sabine's body was as delicate and elegant as her mind.
She'd laugh gaily as Louis would strip her of her clothes and
take her beneath the shadow of the looming old castle. She
was perfectly sane. Completely understanding the act of love
and shying from nothing he should request of her.

Ah, but those were his dreams. Was it too much to hope that
she should be so lucid in reality? His desire was becoming
obsession, gnawing at his insides like a cutworm working a
rose petal to shreds. Louis felt the compulsion to know Sabine
in every way. Dive deep into the soul of the one woman—the
only woman—who had ever had a grasp on his heart. He
wanted to make her his in every respect: mind, body, and soul.
If only so that no one wielding chains could take her away
from him. Sabine was *his* fairy angel. No one else could ever
care for her as he did. He needed her like the vines that grew
up around him needed the sun.

"Louis?"

"Sabine?" A thin sheet of birch paper fluttered to the ground.
"What are you doing out here?"

"I've come to help. Henri said you had spilled some seed."

"Seed?" Why would Henri say such a thing? All the crops
had been sown long ago—wait. Flashes of their earlier confron-
tation came back to him with such a rage, Louis had to turn
away from Sabine so she could not see him punch his fist into

his palm. *Do you spill your seed when all are quiet and gone to sleep?* The bastard.

"Louis? What is wrong? Where is this seed? I do not understand why you would be planting so late."

"Ignore Henri, Sabine. He was being sarcastic."

"Sarcastic? I do not understand. What did he mean by—"

"It was a ..." Innocence shone in her eyes. Innocence shadowed by darkness. She did not need to hear the words that hung on the tip of Louis's tongue. But yet he had the urge to tell them.

"Louis? Are you lost?"

He shook his head. Lost. Yes, always in her eyes. "No, my lady. What Henri said to you was, well, it was a lewd reference to ..." No. He could not say that. He cleared his throat. "Do you know what is meant by carnal relations?"

"Carnal relations?"

It seemed the world became very still. Leaves did not even flutter in the midnight air. Louis could not fight Sabine's waiting, always-inquiring gaze. "Yes," he began slowly, uncertain where he should go with this thread of conversation. But he could not stop himself from saying the things he wished her to know. "It is an act of love shared by a man and a woman."

Louis hopefully searched her expression for a hint of comprehension.

"Oh, like kissing?"

He smiled at her simple understanding. "Yes. But so much more."

"Really? Oh, you must teach me, Louis."

The touch of her finger to his chin shocked and enticed.

"I want to learn everything. We are a man and a woman, so we can share these carnal relations as you've said?"

"No, Sabine, I—"

"You do love me, do you not?"

Trapped once again by her innocent logic, Louis wished only for rescue this time. How could he explain to her how much he wanted to take her, to have her, to share his body with her? That he wanted to teach her of the pleasures a man and woman could indulge. That he wanted her hot, naked flesh feeding his desires, pulsing around his member. . . . No!

He was afraid, so very afraid of doing her more harm than good.

But, damnation, if he didn't want—no—*need* her.

"Louis?" Golden hair slipped over one eye with the tilt of her head. Brushed away by fairy fingers. "Do you love me?"

She waited for a simple yes. A nod of his head. But he could not give it to her yet. Love was so very different from the lust that coursed through his body. He hadn't sorted the two out yet. Hadn't had a chance to wonder if his emotions were guided by his body or his mind.

Love? That would mean sacrificing the regret and terror and utter loss of humanity he had clung to for weeks. That would mean admitting that he was a caring creature, that he, too, hid behind a mask in order to escape reality. That would mean giving up his own torment for the normalcy of life.

More fearful than if he were standing down an enemy pike, Louis touched the curve of Sabine's jaw. Untouched treasure. Hidden for years by the world's strange cruelty. But oh, so precious. Not easy to resist the enchantment she worked. But he must. For now. "I cannot give you that answer just yet, Sabine."

She tilted her head in his palm, her eyes pooling with hurt.

"Forgive me." Louis jerked his hand away from the warmth of his salvation and stuffed it inside his waistcoat. Not yet. He still needed more time.

Turning, he swiftly paced away.

CHAPTER NINE

"No, no, not that one. That's my lucky wig." Cristoforo sighted Pietro over the end of his Spanish pistol. Italians made for the best singers, but the Spanish most certainly reigned supreme when it came to weaponry. He treasured the gold overlaid flintlock, a gift from Philip of Spain. Ha! If Farinelli, the Spanish king's little pet, only knew.

Pietro dug within the paperboard box that contained the dozens of periwigs and tangled hair attachments Cristoforo used onstage.

"Yes, that hideous pink one. Perfect. Don't be so jittery, Pietro, I'm not aiming for you."

Pietro snapped his eyes toward his master, as if he'd not even thought of the notion until then. "M-me?"

An impatient wave of his pistol sent Pietro fleeing for cover behind a carved Jacob chair. Cristoforo closed his left eye and held the pistol steady. An empty wine bottle, capped by the frizzy pink wig, sat on the table before an etched mirror, doubling itself, giving Cristoforo two targets. "If the bravo could not handle the slippery little wench . . ."

He dropped the cock. A spray of golden sparks showered his silk-breached legs. Glass exploded and sent silvery shards of mirror singing through the room. Pink fuzz fluttered like wine-tinted snowflakes. The bottle remained intact.

Cristoforo smiled. "Then I shall tend to matters myself."

It was nearing morning when Louis finally returned to the château. Two more hours would see the sun rise. A discreet check found Sabine sleeping soundly. Henri and Yvette were also sound asleep, though Yvette's snoring gave Louis some wonder as to how soundly she could possibly rest. If the garlic didn't work, surely the noise alone would keep the creatures of the night away.

He paced the hallway back and forth past his chamber door, his bare feet tracing his footsteps in the woven rag rug over and over.

The door to the small chapel Janette had requested Henri build was open. Each time Louis walked past, he could see out of his peripheral vision the rosewood cross that hung on the wall inside, the crucified Christ hanging in silent suffering.

The lingering scent of roasted fowl haunted Louis. Yvette had been creating such elegant meals as of late. Ever since Sabine had come to stay with them. And the hired hands, wasn't it odd how they'd begun to look so much fresher in the mornings? As though they had actually washed and combed through their hair before beginning their day, perhaps even patched a few holes on their breeches and washed their shirts.

Dammit, if even the vines hadn't perked since her arrival. Of course, that had been courtesy of the rain. A rain that might not have come had it not been for Sabine.

No! Louis pushed his hand roughly through his hair, rubbing bruising fingers across his temple. It was nonsense to think like that. Sabine possessed no magical powers. She could chant the rain no more than he could make flowers grow in midair.

And what of her real powers? The power to steal your heart?

Stopping abruptly, Louis turned to eye the cross.

Yes, she really had done that, hadn't she? Stolen his heart. How could he have let such a thing happen? He was a soldier, trained to hear and sense the enemy before it even began to think of attack.

"Why?" he asked of the wooden Christ.

Compelled to seek answers from a God he thought he had rejected, Louis stepped inside the room and plunged to his knees, pressing his forehead to the wall below the cross. "Why have you done this to me, Lord?" He looked up at the silent Jesus. "Is this the punishment I receive for trying to take my own life? You tempt me with fruit I may not have? Am I to be the Adam to this woman's Eve?"

Louis turned and sat on the floor, his back pressed to the wall, his head tilted back so his gaze studied the carved toes of the statue. The rosewood gave off a pungent, musty scent in the humid weather. A trickle of sweat sashayed down his neck and stopped to soak into the underturned neckline of his shirt. Louis pulled the drawstring free around his neck and closed his eyes.

So afraid he'd been of Sabine's simple question. Do you love me?

Standing alone out in the field after his refusal to answer her innocent question, he had searched for an answer. But it had not come.

And now, as he tried again, his thoughts cleared, his breathing slowed, and he concentrated on the raspy release of his exhausted breath. He had thought he was finished with life, with hope. *Was slitting your wrists not the final step?*

But God had not allowed that leap. And so now, he would try again. To give in, to release his soul to the hands of the only one who could help him. Without violence. Without the blood flowing from his veins.

"Are you testing me?" he murmured. "At first I thought that she was the reason you had spared me. That I was alive to find this beautiful and helpless soul and rescue her. But now . . . now I have fallen . . . in love," he pleaded to the darkness and the toes of the statue and to anyone who would listen. "Yes. Love! I love her and yet I do not think it right. How can that be?"

Images of Sabine dancing across the meadow, of her mindless spells when all was gay and the real world did not exist, flooded Louis's mind. Of another realm, she was. Truly the fairy he thought her to be. He'd never in all his life believed in such childhood myths.

But maybe . . .

Louis recalled the fine parallel scars he'd seen tracing down her back on the first day he had brought her there. Who had stolen her wings? What horrors held her mind captive? And how could he help her?

"She does not understand. Henri is right. I am only a character in her imaginary world."

Yet even as he said it, Louis knew that was not true. Would not allow himself to believe that. She had lucid moments. More so now and more with each passing day. She spoke to him, held conversations. *She understood.* Most of the time. Yes, the woman buried deep within the child was there. She just needed help to rise to the surface. She needed his light.

"I want to help her," Louis whispered. "But I need your guidance." He turned on his knees and pressed his palms together before his nose. "I will care for her. I will not let her down. But I must know from you what is right. I don't wish to cross the line that will leave her forever captive of her madness. But it is so hard." He pressed his head to the wall, feeling the tip of the cross dig into his forehead. "She—she tempts me so."

Feeling no answer, receiving no sign, Louis collapsed to the floor, the weight of this confusion of right and wrong too much for him to bear. How much longer could he fend off desire?

"Yes," Louis murmured seductively.

She dipped her cheek into his palm as he smoothed his hand along her jaw. But she wasn't sure why he'd said yes out of the blue like that. "Yes what?"

As he placed his cheek alongside hers, the aroma of chopped pine and hard labor filled her senses. "Yes," he whispered, his lips tracing the curve of her ear. "I do love you. And I must have you, Sabine. Will you be mine?"

Words she had pined to hear now slipped from her lover's lips and skimmed down the side of her neck, drawing up sweet, scintillating prickles along her flesh as they skated lower and disappeared beneath the loose lawn nightgown.

"Oh, Louis, I am yours. Teach me all that I must know to become the woman you need, the woman you desire."

"I already desire you." A kiss to her earlobe, then another to her mouth. Hard. Searching. A signal to surrender.

Tonight would be the night she stepped from the innocence of maidenhood into the arms of passion. For surely what she felt right now, as her body danced seemingly on air and her every nerve ending hissed with desire at Louis's touch, was the definition of passion.

"And do you need me, Louis?" she gasped as his hands roamed up and over her breasts, squeezing softly, and his fingers pulled free the opening of her gown.

"More than food and wine." His kisses began to step down her chin and taste her neck, her shoulders. . . . "More than the air I breathe." Her nipples hardened to tiny stones beneath his massaging fingers. "More than life, Sabine Bassange. I want to possess you—"

Creak.

Sabine started at the sound of a wooden floorboard whining in protest. She shook off the layer of dreamsleep cloaking her thoughts. But to recall the visions of her nocturnal desires!

Such odd feelings roiled just beneath the surface of her flesh. She *desired.* The taste of Louis's kiss. The touch of his hands exploring her body. Ah! These new emotions, these feelings, were exquisite. But perhaps not so new. For she felt much the same as when . . . *My secret pleasure.* Could it be? How curious.

This can only mean the feelings I have had are good, Sabine thought. *I hope.* Surely, Louis could never make her feel anything but.

Lying on the feather mattress, covered by a thin blanket, she closed her eyes and listened as Louis's creaking steps paced past her room until finally they came to a stop.

With her eyes closed her other senses were more acute. The sound of fabric sliding across flesh and then crumpling on the floor reached her. Water splashed. *He's washing his hands. Those big, rough hands that always hold me with such care.* Dull swishing. *Running them back through his hair. So soft and messily pretty.* And finally the creak of the ropes beneath his own mattress.

It was easy enough to envision her knight lying upon the bed, his dark hair splayed carelessly across the understuffed pillow. Careless, for he did not really seem concerned of his appearance. Not that he needed to. Tousled or not, his hair was only a part of the exquisite enchantment his appearance worked on Sabine. She'd come to pine for sight of his dark, brooding eyes. She no longer troubled over what they hid. The secrets his eyes possessed were slowly being revealed.

And tonight, as she stood at the edge of the vineyards with him, she'd suddenly realized how the rest of his features affected her. His narrow nose was a match to the Dragon Lord's. But beneath that, the thin mustache enticed her every time. It was soft and fine. And his lips. Never once had she even thought that a kiss could be anything more than two mouths pressing together. Not so with Louis de Lavarac. The one kiss he had gifted her with had erupted like fire within her body. Her heart had beat as if in fear, but she knew it was not. It was anticipation he created in her. Almost a need.

But her dreams had been only hopeful desires.

"You do not love me, Louis."

His running away from her had pushed the beating of her wanting heart to a torturous pace. No longer was she sure about these strange feelings. She was confused. Did the knight not kiss the princess when he loved her? If Louis did not love her, then why had he kissed her? And what of these "carnal relations" he had mentioned?

Days ago she had thought it was this Evangeline that held his heart. Why else would he call out her name in the midst of sleep? But now she knew otherwise, that it was only a haunting in his mind. An experience she was quite familiar with.

Life with Louis had become suddenly confusing. But in an odd way this worked to her advantage. For with so many conflicting emotions inside her, the darkness had little time to emerge.

Thank God, the full moon had passed.

For the visions, the memories, were at their worst during the full moon. It had happened beneath the ghostly white glow of a full moon. That terrible night of all nights.

Sabine released a relieved breath. She was safe for another month.

Sabine was not so preoccupied with the cornflower fairy that she did not hear the careful swish of Yvette's skirts sauntering beneath the sheltering willow. "You should go now," she whispered carefully. She tucked the palm-sized portion of stick inside the loose stays of her dress and flicked a stray piece of grass from her skirts.

"Talkin' to the fairies again," she heard Yvette mumble in her usual nervous tone as she came upon her. "Poor child."

"Yvette."

"Afternoon, mademoiselle. Might I join you?" Yvette looked about Sabine, as if searching the grasses for insects or a snake. "That is, if you're not already occupied."

"Of course not, Yvette. Sit beside me." Sabine held her finger out and the slender fairy dressed in blue cornflower-petal skirts and an acorn cap stepped onto it. She sat up, leaning against the trunk of the tree.

"So what's on your pretty little mind, child? Or are you just talking to yourself?"

Yvette could not see her tiny friend, Sabine knew that. And now that she'd been joined by the lady, she didn't really care for the creature's company anymore. And she knew just what to do to make her flee.

"Tell me of love, Yvette."

The fairy pressed her miniature fists to her hips and wrinkled her nose at Sabine. Hmmph, she seemed to say. What is love? Not fun and mischievous like fairy dust!

Perfect, Sabine thought.

"Love?"

"Yes, love." Sabine drew out the word as if she could almost taste its sweet flavor.

That was all that was needed. The fairy took to flight, having no desire to listen to what it thought frivolous conversation.

"Are we speaking family love here?" The hefty maid tucked one leg under the other and readjusted her weight to relax against the same trunk that Sabine leant against. "Or romantic love?"

"Oh, romantic love. I already know what family love is like."

"Do you really?"

Sabine nodded enthusiastically. And then Yvette's saddened expression worked to cloud her own heart. She did have good and wonderful memories of family. Somewhere. It was just rather hard to find them most of the time. But she knew she possessed them.

Somewhere.

"But I'm more eager to learn of romantic love, Yvette. You see, I believe my perception of what it might be must be incorrect. Or else . . ."

"Or else?" Yvette raised a brow. "You've an eye for young master Louis, haven't you?"

Sabine nodded. She ran her hands over her arms, startling her flesh to delicious shivers, much like the ones she felt each and every time Louis gazed at her with his faraway look. "I feel so very different when he is with me. Not so . . . confused. More myself. Like a . . . a . . ." Now, what was the word to describe the incredible feeling of *being* she felt when around Louis?

Yvette waited patiently, her thick fingers folded into sausage links upon her lap.

"A woman!" Sabine recited the word as it sprang to mind, surprised at her own realization. "Yes, that's it! Louis makes me feel like a woman, Yvette. And this feeling, it's simply marvelous and splendid and—"

"Too good to be true?" Yvette broke in. The kindness in her pale hazel eyes never wavered. Her soft, fleshy cheeks held a rosy glow. There were times Sabine wanted to simply hug her and call her mother.

"Yes. Too good to be true. I know these feelings I have for Louis are very different from the family sort of love. I want him to kiss me, Yvette. Every time I see him!"

"Ooh!" Yvette pressed a hand to her cheek.

"Is that so terrible? Oh, please you must tell me. I asked him if he loved me—"

"You did?"

"Why, yes." Worry worked Yvette's jaw. But Sabine could not understand the woman's dismay. "The knight never comes to rescue the princess unless he's in love with her. That's the way it always is. Tell me it's true, Yvette. Louis must love me. He's kissed me, and—''

Before Sabine could continue, Yvette laid a hand across her own hands. "Sometimes . . .'' She waited until Sabine looked into her eyes. Wisdom and trust held Sabine transfixed. "Sometimes the knight comes because he's been ordered. Or perhaps he's on a mission of his own—a search for self—and he merely stumbles upon the captive princess.''

"Oh." A search for self? But Louis knew who he was. A soldier, he'd told her that much himself. "I don't understand.''

"Now, I don't want to be wilting your sails, child, but you must think. Louis is a very troubled man. He's been through rough times. You can see that yourself. He doesn't need any more grief. *Mon Dieu,* if both the de Lavarac boys don't have a mountain of it to support upon their shoulders. And you, my lovely one . . .''

"Me?" Of course Yvette did not need to say more. Sabine knew exactly what the woman wanted to say. *You speak to the fairies and cannot control yourself in the full moonlight. You are different from us all. Not right.*

A throbbing ache pierced Sabine's breast, so very unlike any pain she had ever felt. It was numbing and squeezing, as though her heart were being strangled by Yvette's fingers.

How foolish she had been. Of course Louis could not love someone who was not even capable of telling fantasy from reality. It had seemed to her that his presence had begun to drag her up from the murky darkness of her soul. But perhaps Yvette was right. She was simply . . . not right.

"I understand, Yvette.''

The mischievous sprite suddenly flitted down on Yvette's shoulder and stuck her tongue out at Sabine as if to say "See?''

No. I do not see you, Sabine coached inwardly. I cannot if I am ever to have anyone think of me as *right.* If I am to have a man's love. She squeezed her eyelids tight.

"Sabine?"

Opening her eyes, Sabine saw Yvette worriedly peering at her. And . . . the cornflower fairy.

"Oh, go away!" She slapped at the fairy on Yvette's shoulder, much to Yvette's confusion. Too ashamed of her visions, of her failing struggle to defeat her own madness, Sabine sprang to her feet and dashed out from under the showering branches of the willow.

A crack. Like twigs snapping.

Louis pushed himself up in bed. Tension corded his arms. Someone was about. Close by. Perhaps just outside the château. He knew it. His soldier's senses were never wrong.

Snap.

Enemy.

Louis shuffled his breeches up his legs and carefully, silently, pulled his pistol from the wooden chest beneath his bed. Damn. No powder. *Crunch.* Louis's ears pricked like a dog honing in on his prey. He reached for his discarded clothes and slipped his dagger from the leather sheath.

From boyhood he knew each position on the stairs that would creak at his touch and easily avoided them. A surprisingly cool breeze sifted through the doorway as he slowly pulled it open. He listened. No voices. Who or what was about, he had no clue. But he was ready. Always.

Sniffing the air, Louis smelled nothing other than the fresh wind and peat.

Thrush.

He stiffened. Whatever it was was right around the corner. Moving slowly, almost with calculation.

Pressing his dagger lengthwise to his forehead, Louis closed his eyes, steadying himself. Concentrate. No sound. No motion. Wait until the enemy is upon you. . . .

Now!

Louis swung around the corner, bringing the point of his dagger in contact with the smooth silken skin of Sabine's neck.

She did not scream. Did not have to say a single word for Louis to read the pure terror in her eyes. Instantly his senses cleared. Fool! He'd been walking the trenches in a dream!

The stick Sabine had broken to fit her hand fell at her feet. Louis quickly snapped the dagger away from her. But it was too late.

"Sabine, no! I did not know—"

She seemed to have Achilles wings sprouting from her ankles for the speed with which she fled. Her footsteps silently carried her across the lawn and into the dark tangle of vines that she had called the Dark Forest.

"No, not this," he huffed as he scampered across the grounds. His steps wobbled in the freshly moistened soil, nearly pulling him off balance. With the moon hidden behind the clouds, he had to use his soldier's senses to blindly track Sabine's light footsteps. He finally found her beyond the fencing line of olive trees, huddled down by a huge trunk.

Gentle sobs filled the cup of her palms as she held them to her face and rocked back and forth. Heaving and breathless, Louis gulped back a choke. Having a knife pressed to your throat would be enough to scare the blood out of anyone. But Sabine was not anyone.

He knelt near her, gauging carefully whether or not he dare touch her. "Forgive me," he whispered over her sobs. If she did not hear him, the least he could do was try to appease his own breaking heart. "It was the soldier in me. I heard a noise. I did not think—"

"How many men did you do the same to on the battlefield?" she forced out through her sobs.

Louis drew in his lower lip and bit down. Madness danced in Sabine's eyes, but it was anger, not insanity, that clawed through her words.

"Many," he replied softly. "I regret—"

"Regret does not bring back the dead," she said in a voice so steady and strong that Louis flinched. "This"—she grabbed his wrist and held it before his eyes so that the sparkle of hundreds of stars flicked across the scar—"does not bring them back either!"

"And what will?"

"You cannot, Louis. I . . ." She faltered, dropping his wrist. "So much blood. Gushing . . . and gushing . . . I cannot . . . bring them back. Ever." The passion in her eyes drained away. Sabine's body fell limp into Louis's arms, and she pressed her head against his chest. "I cannot bring them back. Cannot . . ."

I cannot bring them back. Words spoken by a child who lost her parents to a most hideous crime.

Her chest pulsed against his own with each sniffling breath she drew through her nose. Louis spread his hand over her hair, thinking the tresses like shards of gold come to liquid life between his fingers. Fingers that had done the most hideous things to innocent men. Fingers that he'd once thought capable of only the most damaging touch or the final death blow. But now, as he smoothed them over Sabine's head, he felt the dam he'd built up inside him fissure and break. He tucked himself over Sabine's body and cradled her tight, and she began to rock.

"If only I could bring them back, Sabine," he whispered into the softness of her hair. Bring back the dead soldiers. Bring back Henri's wife and newborn child. And bring back the parents who had once held his fairy angel dear. "If only."

She squeezed her arms about his legs. "I used to say that all the time."

"If only?"

She nodded. With all the grace of her dances, she then appeared to pull herself into order, calmness, a resolute acceptance. "You must learn to live with it, Louis. There will always be regret, but you cannot allow it to torture you until you remain but a shell of your former self." She pushed up in his arms and touched the tip of his chin. "You are far too strong to be defeated by the darkness, Louis."

So wise and complex, this frail and mysterious woman. Speaking words that would heal her own hurt yet heeding them not. She spoke these healing words to him, for him.

Louis felt her strength enter his body like rain soaking through his clothes. She fed the emptiness within him. He, her salvation? No. It was the reverse. Sabine Bassange had rescued him.

CHAPTER TEN

Yvette clutched at the starched linen apron over her chest. She did not gasp nor did she cry out. Her eyes widened and her mouth dropped open. With a great choking heave she fell to the floor and lay still.

Having just entered the kitchen in search of Sabine, Louis dove to the maid's side and looked her over. "Henri!"

His brother was quickly at his side. Henri slapped Yvette's cheek gently, but she did not react. "What is it?"

"She's not breathing," Louis observed. He pressed two fingers to the vein in her neck. No pulse. "I fear she is dead."

"Impossible." Henri lifted the maid in his arms, grunting to contain her limbs without dropping her. "She's simply fainted. I'll lay her on the chaise. Send for a surgeon."

"It's too late," Louis said weakly. "She does not breathe!"

"We can at least try!"

But long minutes passed as the brothers attended the woman who had watched over them since they skipped in infant's skirts. No movement, no breath, no pulse.

"But how? Why?" Henri muttered.

Louis pushed his hand over his sweat-dripping brow. With this motion he happened to look up the stairs. There stood Sabine. When their eyes met, he discovered an odd luminescence to her stare. She had predicted this days before, when she had sat shelling peas. *Do you not fear her imminent death?*

Sabine spirited away. Louis dashed up the stairs and found her in her room. Silent and unmoving, she stood with her forehead pressed to the wall beneath a simple wooden cross.

"Sabine!" He crossed the room and stood just behind her. "Sabine," he said again, trying to rein in his voice, "how did you know? The woman has died and you told me yourself it would happen. Sabine!" He pulled her around, sliding his palms up the satin that circled her thin arms and held firm to her shoulders. "Talk to me."

"I saw it in her eyes," she offered as innocently as a child.

"Saw what? What did you see? How do you know these things?"

"I saw the death, Louis. I saw the darkness curling about Yvette's soul. Her eyes were clouded with a murky gloom. I told you but you did not believe me."

She spoke matter-of-factly of witchery and fantastical things that only a soul such as she could know. It frightened him that she had such powers. No, that was impossible, it was merely speculation, but . . .

Louis gripped her wrist fiercely. "And what do you see in my eyes?"

She tried to pull away. Her expression grew fearful, as if he might hurt her, squeeze his hands too tightly and snap her wrists.

But his desire for knowledge led him to ignore his conscience.

"Tell me," Louis demanded, and with a shake of her shoulder forced her gaze to meet his.

"Rage," she said in her wizened woman's voice. "I see rage and terror. And fear of the unknown. You fear me, Louis.

I see it! You say that you care for me, but it cannot be true, because I frighten you.''

"You do not!'' He released her and paced away, his hands on his hips. He feared nothing but his own mortality. His own life was a force he could not understand. Who was the mad one of the two of them? It was he who had tried to take his own life. And she was strangely aware of all that went on within himself. Lunacy was not her master, it was her protector.

Louis turned and marched back to her. He pulled both her hands up in his. "Do you want to know what I see in your eyes, my lady of the fairies?''

She shook her head, setting a forlorn gaze to match his own.

"I see true understanding.'' He released her and squeezed a fist between the two of them, before Sabine's wide eyes. "I see a passion bound tightly and shut up. I see a madness that has become your sustenance. You hide behind it for fear of stepping into the real world. Sabine, throw away your crutch. Release yourself to me.''

"But I don't know how.''

"We will teach one another.''

Louis divined the sweet sadness from her body with a kiss of urgent, fierce passion. He felt her protest as she struggled and pressed her body against his. Her hips were narrow and delicate against his thighs. He grew hard instantly. Her protests turned to a sigh and then to the same vigorous want that he felt. Her fingers clutched tight to his upper arms, pulling him close. She drank from him as a milk-starved calf did its mother. So wanting and greedy. Like him.

No. Not yet.

Louis stepped back, releasing her.

Sabine touched her fingers to her lips and then examined the delicate fingertips. Unable to look upon her innocent action, Louis turned away and strode to leave the room. He centered himself in the doorway, his palms pressed to the oak casing.

Why not turn and take her body and soul? Why torture

himself? Soon the heir would be found and she would be taken
from him forever. And without his ever loving her, holding
her, tasting her, taking her, plunging himself deep within her.

Louis turned to find Sabine had silently gained his side. He
could not help himself from pushing his fingers through her
hair and pulling it away from her face. *Take her. Satisfy your
needs. She is mad, she will not know to fight you or protest.*

She was a child harbored within the body of a woman. A
body that had grown into a delectable and enticing temptation.
A body that emanated a need for love and touch and life . . .

Louis abruptly snapped his fingers out of Sabine's hair. She
jerked a questioning gaze up toward his face.

"In time," Louis said in a whisper, speaking more to himself
than to the waif who waited his wisdom. "All things take
time."

"You will build her a cross as you did my grandfather?"
she called as Louis strode toward the stairs.

"Of course." He clenched the stair rail with both fists. Damn!
What was he doing? A woman who had cared for him all his
life had just died and he could think only of debauching the
woman above. "It is madness," he said to himself. "But it is
yours, not hers."

Yvette's funeral was held that evening. All the farmhands
attended, some with their wives. Yvette had been kind and wise
and loved by all. Sabine watched from her bedroom window,
which Louis thought best considering her macabre fascination
with death.

After all had left, Louis walked the road leading up to the
château, lighting the torches in honor of Yvette. He and Henri
were on their own now. Yvette had become a member of the
family over the years. Almost a mother with her gentle wisdom
and way of chastising that never seemed harsh, only loving

and right. He would miss her far more than the mother he had never known.

Ah, but so much had happened in this last week! Beginnings and endings and a scatter of madness swirled into the pot to top it all off. He needed a rest, perhaps to get away for a few days and sort through all that occupied his mind.

After spying Sabine watching the funeral from her window, Henri had reminded Louis it was imperative they discover the nameless beneficiary. For Sabine's inheritance would not be granted until both parties had signed the legal papers. A trip to Paris at this very moment might be just the thing Louis needed. Henri had suggested they post billets in the city and in the local villages, requesting the other heir to come forward, for l'Argent seemed to be of no use. Louis only prayed the man would spend more of his energy locating Evangeline. Of course, by announcing to the world their search, they would risk the possibility of fraud. How many would not try a chance at half a million livres?

And for the first time the thought finally occurred to Louis. He set the oiled torch-lighter on the ground at his boot. Why did *he* not care about this inheritance? It would be so easy to insinuate himself into the Bassange family. He need only marry Sabine. . . .

Marry?

The thought had not come to him until then. No, he would never marry Sabine to inherit her riches. Only for love. He'd come too far from the brink of death and was finally clinging to the edges of redemption. He would never marry Sabine for her money. Though he was sure Henri would not mind.

Ah, but all these thoughts meant little when the missing heir still remained at large.

There had to be another way of discovering the identity of this nameless, faceless person, Louis thought. There was one way. . . . Louis felt sure that Sabine knew the name of the other beneficiary. Locked away in her tormented mind. Perhaps she herself was not aware that she possessed the answer. She had had a moment of recognition the other day when he'd asked if she had a relative.

Louis was confident that with a little patience, and some delicate sleuthing, he could discover the answer to the riddle. All it would take was time. Time that could mean only that he would be allowed another, and possibly yet another, day with the meadow fairy who had stolen his heart.

Night dusted the sky with a hazy shade of lavender and the field hands had returned home to their wives and children. The grounds about the de Lavarac château were ablaze with a galaxy of glittering candles. Yvette always lit the yard as a signal of sorts that the work was done for the day and supper lay ready on the table. She let them burn until close to midnight, much against Henri's constant protests that she wasted precious candles. All she need do was begin to explain how it chased away the evil spirits, and Henri, wanting nothing to do with her superstitious nonsense, would wave her off and the candles would remain. It was a fitting tribute to her memory.

Not yet ready to call it a night, Louis stepped across the mounded land and headed for a tiny pond far away from the château. As he neared his favorite childhood play-spot, he heard Sabine calling softly.

When her goldenrod skirts came into view, Louis stepped back, hugging his shoulder to the thick oak tree whose twisting branches hung over the algae-sprinkled pond. A fat bullfrog croaked, startling a tiny swarm of fireflies across the black-mirrored surface of the water.

Sabine tiptoed along the edge of the ankle-deep lawn, peering curiously into the tall, thick reeds that circled the pond. The candlelight barely stretched to this quiet little corner of the grounds, but along with the starlight, there was enough illumination to see shadowed images. Her slippers lay perfectly placed

near Louis's feet. So tiny and delicate, fit for a princess. She
had given a squeal of delight when Yvette, after digging through
the ancient trunk she'd brought with her upon first arriving at
the château decades before, had presented them to her.

Reluctant to reveal himself and spoil her peaceful explora-
tions, Louis held back.

A parchment-petaled poppy grew high at Sabine's knee. She
bent to sniff the crimson bloom, running her lips over the crepe
as if using the sense of taste to determine its texture and smell.
Louis felt his flesh prickle in a hot flush, and his heart picked
up its pace. Soft lips parted in silent exultation as she sniffed
the delicate flower. A burning urgency flooded Louis's torso,
awakening his desires to an alertness that betrayed his longings.

To touch her smooth cheek, run the back of his hand down
under her chin, was such a blessed torture. She seemed quite
satisfied with the simplest contact. Touching, holding, kissing.
Until she'd innocently requested he teach her of carnal relations.
Do you not love me?

Yes, he did. But she did not understand that sometimes a
man could take a woman without love. As he had been so
tempted earlier that day after following her up to her room.
But now that he'd had time to relax, to accept the day's events
and to reason with his own inner torments, he realized he
wanted Sabine to know that he loved her before that ever
happened. But he could not deny it; he wanted more. He wanted
her in all the ways a man could have a woman. Her kisses
tempted and teased, allowing a mere taste of her glory.

Ah, but what if?

Dare he think of her in the way a man thought of a woman?
Would she understand? With her mind in such a fragile state,
Louis dared not press her. What would be the results should
he make love to her? Could her childlike mind fathom all that
could be between the two of them? Did she even have desires
that went beyond the basic human need for food and shelter?

The only reason she had asked him to teach her more was

because he had mentioned it. *Mon Dieu,* she'd thought he was planting seed.

Yet she was not helpless.

Could she remain lucid long enough for him to love her? Could he do for her what she had done for him? Return the wonder, the love, the hope that life once held. For she had done that for him. Returned his innocence. Given back to him his passion for life.

Only the one question remained. Could his love cure her madness?

"You're in over your head, de Lavarac," he muttered.

"Louis!" She lightened as he stepped down the hill to her side. "It was beautiful, Yvette's funeral. I know she dances with the angels now. Thank you, Louis."

"I've lit the torches for her this evening."

"I thought that might have been the reason." She touched his cheek with the back of her hand. "I've been thinking of you, Louis." Her features suddenly slipped into a worried sadness, and her fingers trembled as they slipped from his face. "You never answered me," she said in the softest, almost frightened voice.

"Answer? I fear I've forgotten the question, my precious one. So much has gone on today."

"Remember what I asked you the other night? About loving me?"

Do you love me? If only it were as easy for him to forget the bad things and direct his thoughts to completely unrelated subjects with a simple blink of the eye. But he did owe her an answer. Louis nodded and sighed. "I was afraid."

"Afraid? Of me?"

"No, fairy angel. Afraid of myself, I should say."

"Why would you be frightened of yourself, Louis?"

Her eyes teared, and Louis smoothed both palms along her cheeks, bracketing her face gently. "I was afraid that if I told you the truth, I would have to face that truth myself. But no more. I do love you, Sabine. There. I've said it.'' He released a breath, and with it, the day's burdens. "Ah, that felt good. I love you, Sabine.''

"It feels very good, Louis.'' She closed her eyes, seeming to wish upon a star. "Say it again.''

Louis pressed a kiss to her closed eyelid. The fragileness of a fairy wing mixed with the sweetness of a fine cream dessert. He lingered against her cheek, feeling the warm pulse of her life against his lips. "I love you, Sabine. I love you.''

He covered her mouth with his and stole her breath away. Mining deeper and deeper with his tongue, he vied for her soul. And it was as if her wishing star burned hot and bright in his breast. The taste of her was sweet and soft, promising to drown out all the ugliness in the world, make him forget his troubles.

Sabine teetered backward from his kiss, her cheeks flushed in rosy circles. "Louis, your kisses are so powerful. I fear I shall faint dead away one of these times.''

He laughed. "And I shall be there to catch you.''

"Promise?''

"Always and forever, fairy angel. Now, what is it that has you out here all by yourself? I thought you might have gone to sleep after everyone had left. It is very late.''

"Louis.'' She was all seriousness as she led him to the edge of the shaved lawn and spread her hand over the tall grasses that bordered the pond. "I thought I saw them from my window. But I've searched all evening. There are no fairies here.''

So she had been searching for her imaginary fairies, the lifeline that had served to soften the hideous memories. Small wonder she could not find them now, Louis thought. For she had come to depend less and less on her fantasies since coming to him.

"Ah, Sabine.'' He hugged her to his chest. "You do not need the fairies.''

"But—''

"You have me," he said in a whispery hush. "Besides, the

fairies are jealous of your beauty. They flee when they see you come.''

''My-my beauty?'' She curled her long fingers about his and kissed his knuckles. ''You think me beautiful, Louis?''

Her gentle amazement set his body afire with the longing to fulfill his desires.

''Beauty is too simple a word to describe you, Sabine.''

''Tell me more.''

More? He could fill the night with more. Louis led Sabine to the edge of the pond and pulled her down to sit near a thicket of soft rushes facing the shimmering water. Dragonflies buzzed zigzags across the water's surface. A broken sliver of marsh grass stirred its tip in the fathomless depths.

''Your beauty is like the silvery rays of the moon dancing across the rippling waves of a summer pond.''

''Oh.'' She sank into his embrace, pressing her back against his chest. ''You make my heart nervous, Louis.''

''Would you like me to stop?''

''No! I want to hear more. Please?''

He slid his hands down along her arms, wanting desperately to hold her tight, but hesitating.

Sabine touched his hands and wrapped them about her. '' 'Tis all right,'' she whispered. ''I am safe with you. I know now you love me.''

All the riches in the world could not compete with the satisfaction Louis felt at her words. She trusted him. Felt safe with him. And so he hugged her, relishing for the first time the relaxed permission her body silently gave.

''You want to hear more,'' he whispered, and pressed his cheek against hers. ''Sabine is like the poppy over there, swaying in the breeze, its petals so very frail that one could easily break them with a simple nudge of their finger. And yet they possess such inner strength as to stand up to even the most treacherous winds and rains. And after the storm the bloom is even more stunning and bright, unable to be defeated.

"You are strong, Sabine. I know that now."

"Yes, " she murmured. She turned around in his lap. "You are my salvation, Louis." She covered his mouth with a wanting, urgent kiss. He dared not protest, nor did he wish to end the moment.

Imitating his previous actions, she dove deep inside his kiss and searched out the pleasures she craved. And when she withdrew, Louis had to restrain himself from pulling her down on top of him.

"Your kisses save me, Louis." She jumped up and spread her arms to the moonlight. "Oh, 'tis more than just that." Eager vivacity lightened her words. "It is your presence, Louis, and your touch, and your voice, everything about you! When you are around, I am free. Free of this madness that has a fix upon my soul. Your kisses are the rope that pulls me free."

"My promise is good. I shall never leave you, I swear. I know I could not live without you. There is so much I want to do with you. To teach you things—"

"About the carnal relations?"

"The . . . carnal . . . relations?" The pulsing heat within his groin reminded Louis that his body was on the same track as Sabine's mind. "Er . . . yes." Her memory was certainly undaunted by her madness. He eased his palm over his breeches, hoping to hide his blatant desire from her questioning gaze. "Yes. That will come, Sabine. I want to teach you the things you request." He tousled a wave of hair on top of her forehead. "I want to fulfill your dreams."

"My dreams?" Her eyes lit, waiting his explanation.

"Yes, you've dreams, haven't you, Sabine?"

"You mean like the ones that come to me in the night? The horrid, wretched—"

Louis jumped to his feet and clasped her into his embrace. "No, no. Nothing bad. Never. Do you not have dreams of your future, Sabine? Goals, wishes, desires?"

"Like wearing fine dresses?"

"Yes, like that. Is that what you dream of? Would you like a fine dress?"

She smoothed a hand across the dull cotton skirt she wore, a makeshift donation from Yvette's armoire. "I once owned beautiful dresses. Oh, not of silk and damask, but they were quite pretty."

"Then you shall have one. No"—Louis lifted her chin, finding the sparkle in her eyes matched his own excitement— "many! What more? Tell me the rest of your dreams, my fairy angel."

"Well, I have always wanted to return to Paris. I went there many times as a child. The city is so lovely. The palace and the Tuileries."

"Then it is settled. Come with me to Paris, Sabine."

"Really?"

"Yes, I ride to Paris tomorrow." To search for the other heir and to see if l'Argent had news of Evangeline. But Louis couldn't bring himself to tell her that. As long as he did not speak it, then he would not have to believe it.

"I'd like you to come along. Perhaps it is what we both need. A vacation in the city to wash away our cares. We shall spend the day purchasing you new things. New dresses. New shoes."

"Oh, yes," she said between fervent kisses to his face.

"And hats. A lady must have hats."

"Yes, Louis, everything." Sabine pulled out of his arms and spun across the lawn, her arms spread wide. "I want everything! I've never been so happy."

Louis delighted in watching her. "You have made me so very happy, Sabine. You have made me see things differently. To believe that I can live again. You can't imagine."

She spun to a halt, her hair swishing across her eyes. "But I think I can. If it's anything like the way I'm feeling, you must be absolutely bursting within, your insides pouring out all over in a sparkling river of joy."

"Exactly," he said.

"Kiss me, Louis. Give me your happiness."

She melted under his kiss, as did Louis's restraint. Cradling Sabine in his arms, he pushed her mouth open and slid his tongue deep inside. Hearing her excited moans, Louis cupped his hand beneath Sabine's breast, lifting the soft mound and pressing it between his fingers.

"Oh, Louis, yes, you mustn't stop," she gasped. "I want to know the things that all women know. Make me yours, Louis."

Louis bent to kiss the tempting mound of flesh he held. Her skin smelled of summer breeze and the lilac soap Yvette made each autumn. The bud of her breast hardened between his fingers, and he kissed her roughly through the soft cotton material. He could take her now. So easily. And she so willing.

"Sabine, I wish to make you mine," he whispered in heated breaths. "But we must go slowly. This kind of love was not meant to be rushed."

"Louis—"

"No, Sabine, listen. It must be savored. You are a maiden, and I wish to do right by you. I know that in my arms you are whole. You are my Sabine. But trust me, if we take things slowly, the fruits of our torment will be rewarded tenfold. Will you allow me to set the pace?"

"Yes, but you must stop talking and kiss me before I cannot bear it!"

Her laughter scattered across the moonlit pond and took flight over the flitting tops of the meadow grasses. It bounced from tree branch to rooftop and wavered atop the wind, catching a burst of speed from the sails of a windmill and finally fluttering softly to rest over the smoking chimneys of Paris.

It was in the middle of a note that he had swelled to nearly a minute's length when the unbounded presence of happiness entered his spirit and burst within. Cristoforo's voice fell abruptly silent, his left hand poised in a lax wave before his chest.

"*Mio Dio.*" He fell to his knees, the loose hardwood stage of the theater creaking beneath him. The theater was empty, this being merely a practice session.

This feeling, so overwhelming in its strength, so wonderful and whole, expanded within him, filling his great barrel chest with more air than his unnaturally large lungs could ever hold. It circled about and spiraled up above his head, setting everything around him to glittering.

And when he opened his mouth and drew upon this new energy, Cristoforo finally hit that elusive note that had been tormenting him for years.

PART TWO

Your soul is as a moonlit landscape fair,
Peopled with maskers delicate and dim,
That play on lutes and dance and have an air
Or being sad in their fantastic trim

—Paul Verlaine, "Moonlight"

CHAPTER ELEVEN

The Palais Royal grew in gothic splendor to their right. Louis gripped Sabine's hand as the sedan carriage wobbled down the sunlit cobblestones of Paris. More out of his own worry than hers, he was sure.

Though the Rue St. Honoré crossed before the most elegant buildings in all of Paris, still the streets seemed to seethe and writhe with a wild calamity of life, from the dirtiest beggars to the most elegant couples out for promenade. And promenade was not easy considering the condition of the streets.

Never in his life had Louis enjoyed an excursion to Paris. He'd spent years at the Louvre drilling and preparing for war. Brief interludes between battle found him struggling to pay rent for a louse-infested second-floor apartment above a tannery. He didn't even want to recall how many times he'd thought he'd die of starvation. He hadn't been able to afford a valet, for he valued the occasional semifull stomach above assistance in dressing. Henri had offered to send funds, but Louis refused, thinking he could tough it out. He was a soldier, after all.

Two years before, while on brief leave, his purse had been cut from beneath the cover of his frock coat and pilfered away without his even being aware until he'd thought to purchase a plump apple for his dinner and found it missing.

Evil snaked in and about the streets, there was no doubt of that.

"Paris can be a dangerous city," he warned, partially regretting that he had taken her with him.

"I will be fine, Louis." She squeezed his hand. "As long as you are by my side, holding my hand."

Louis drew his eyes to Sabine's. What he wouldn't do to ensure her hand was always in his. Forever. "I shall never let go."

The woman had emerged from within the child. In his care, Sabine had the chance to become whole again. And he wasn't about to forego her that pleasure.

Sabine hadn't closed her mouth since passing through the Porte de Vincennes. Her eyes took in everything.

This time Paris greeted Louis with a bittersweet kiss. The meager soldier's wages he'd saved during his final months rested in his pocket. It was enough to treat Sabine to a night at a fine inn and to purchase her the dress of her dreams. And there would be more, Louis promised himself. As soon as he returned to the château he'd start taking his responsibilities seriously. After their father's death, Henri had toiled three years alone while Louis was at war. Henri had run the vineyard by himself for far too long.

Louis had seen the ravages of hard work and grief in the lines on Henri's face and the lost smile that had once been so easy. Yes, it was time he looked beyond his own miseries and stood by his brother's side.

"I imagine Paris is not so very intriguing to you," Sabine said as she scanned the high stone walls that bordered the Tuileries. "Did you not say you spent many years here as a soldier?"

"Indeed, I quartered just down the way above a tannery. But I've not really seen Paris other than to march through her streets en route to battle, or to settle into her dark clutches with a cheap jug of wine and a wench—er, I mean—"

Her giggles only increased the heat that flushed Louis's neck. He hadn't meant to say quite that much.

" 'Twas good you were not alone," she said in a voice suddenly devoid of emotion. "Loneliness can be the devil's greatest triumph. A fine prize for his collection of souls."

"You'll never be alone." Louis pulled her tense fist to his mouth and gently kissed her palm. "I promise."

A sheaf of music, an inkwell and pen, a sand-filled velvet lap pad on which to write, a small treasury of rings and ribbons and delicate laces, an extra pair of shoes with paste buckles and red heels (mustn't bring the diamond buckles for fear of highwaymen), an assortment of feathered fans, a lavender-scented handkerchief and the lemon-scented one (should Cristoforo be in a mellow mood or perhaps prefer the spark of citrus to refresh his senses), and a porcelain pitcher of water which will have to be balanced upon one's lap so it does not splash during the ride (for porcelain retains the purity of water far beyond a metal or pottery receptacle).

"That should be all," Pietro muttered as he looked over the gathering of articles laid before him. Upon hearing the girl was staying with the de Lavarac brothers, Cristoforo insisted they leave posthaste for the country, much as he abhorred the idea of setting foot in the "sticks" again in less than a week's time since his last adventure.

With a smile and spring to his pace, Pietro hefted half the items into his arms and headed for the waiting carriage. Cristoforo insisted on not being woken until the very last moment. According to his private physician who attended him in Naples, the singer needed his rest in order to keep the various humors in balance. And so Pietro was careful that the door-lock mechanisms did not click as he left the apartment.

Such a lovely day! The sun was high and bright. And while the stench of some indescribable rot coated Pietro's throat with every breath he took, still the smile remained on his face. He adored the country for its peace and simplicity.

It was a pity he wasn't able to convince his master to take up residence in the country. The air would do his voice good, providing much-needed rest from the city pollution that forced Cristoforo to hole up in his apartments and spare his voice for all but the most important demands.

Ah, but Pietro had come to learn his master's every idiosyncrasy, his every desire, be it a whispered word or even a simple splay of his lace-encircled hand. He knew and loved Cristoforo and would serve him forever for the kindness granted in return. For Cristoforo had been the one to rescue Pietro from the humiliation of returning home to his parents after the knife was discovered to have failed in its task.

Oh, yes, there were those that *the cut* did not bless with the divinity of voice. Suddenly one day a perfect scale would be rendered a cacophony of hideous croaks and screeches impossible to direct into what had once been. Hair would sprout on the chin and cheeks, in the nose and on the chest. And the voice, after struggling between frog-speak and wounded hummingbird chatter, finally settled to a deep and manly tone, abandoning the high range of song forever. Utterly devastating.

What had once been. And what would never be.

Pietro paused for a moment laying the lap pad and shoes on the floor of the carriage. He would never be. But it mattered not. For the love he received from Cristoforo exceeded the dreams of fame he once had. The vicarious thrill of watching his master perform and the veneration heaped upon him satisfied

Pietro completely. He loved Cristoforo unconditionally and would do anything and everything to ensure that he knew it, every day of his life.

Sabine's heart danced and her whole body lit up as the shopkeepers in the Place Royale proudly displayed their wares before her. The seamstress in the dress shop had just what she needed when Louis mentioned Sabine did not like the binding stays and constrictive dresses that were the fashion.

How perfectly sweet of him to have noticed.

"And no pins, please," Sabine added, explaining that once she had worn the most hideous of dresses with pins that had poked at her sides. Where and when, she wasn't sure. Sometimes memories just slipped from her grasp.

"I can do that!" the seamstress proudly exclaimed.

Hours later Sabine was outfitted in a sack-style dress fashioned of peach silk—Louis's suggestion—whose back flowed in generous yardage behind her, and the whalebones had been removed, providing a comfortably stylish fit. She liked the squared low-cut neckline. It exposed more of her décolletage than she'd ever thought possible. Felt a little drafty, but it also felt different. A good different. All the women she had noticed while riding the streets of Paris had worn the same fashion. And so Sabine felt like one of them. Pretty even.

As she turned before the long mirror set on velvet-rimmed wheels, Sabine caught Louis's avid interest. *He's looking at me as if he wants to taste me.* The thought made her insides jittery. It made her cheeks and her newly exposed bosom flush hot.

But then she recalled Yvette's words. *Sometimes the knight is only doing what he's been told.*

This trip could be nothing more than a means to complete his business. Sabine had overheard Henri and Louis talking in hushed tones the other evening. Louis had plans to check with the *notaire* to see if the missing heir had been found. And if not, Henri suggested they post billets seeking this elusive personage.

She focused back on her reflection, allowing Louis's image to blur behind her. As much as he claimed to love her—he could not. He is not doing this for me, she thought. He wishes only to be rid of me. Dress her up and make her look nice so that someone will claim her. Chivalry is his disguise. But her knight had no intention of slaying dragons for her.

"We'll take it," Louis said to the dressmaker.

With a heavy-hearted sigh Sabine followed Louis along the odiferous streets of Paris. She hadn't worn her new dress, for it would surely be ruined in the mud and other clinging substances that made her footing slippery.

It was hard to hold on to the sadness in her heart when excitement vied for release at the same time. There were just too many wonderful things to see and do and touch! Deciding she would not give her worries another thought, Sabine erased her frown and smiled as Louis squeezed her hand and pressed close to her side.

Another hour was occupied at the millinery. Sabine found two hats she liked, both with dancing fringe around the brim and great fluffy feathers that reminded her of a fairy stage.

"Our carriage awaits," Louis grandly announced as he stood in the doorway, arms loaded with hatboxes.

Sabine reluctantly pulled her eyes from the counter and inclined her head graciously to the shopkeeper.

"Did you get everything you wished?" Louis wondered from behind the wide boxes.

Sabine glanced back to the counter where the milliner wound a bright red ribbon about his hand. A memory surfaced. Sweet summer rain had refreshed the city and painted a rainbow over the pointed spire of Nôtre-Dame. The morning had been spent purchasing plain muslins and lawn for dresses and new leather boots for Papa. An intense yearning, a child's only desire, rebirthed in Sabine's throat.

"The only thing I had ever wished for as a child was a ribbon for my hair," she said in a dreamy voice. "Father called it vanity." When she turned around and swept her eyes over the array of packages in Louis's arms, the desire sunk to her stomach and formed a hunk of leaden guilt. "Yes, Louis. I have more than enough. You have gifted me with too many fine things already."

Tinkling bells sounded from the waiting carriage, the coachman Louis had called out obviously disgruntled at the wait.

"We should hurry. I know you've the *notaire*'s office to visit," Sabine offered, and stepped through the doorway. "Are you coming, Louis?"

"Er, yes." He hiked an awkward hatbox up in the air, and the coachman directed it on top of the carriage with the end of his horse whip. "I shall return, posthaste. There's another box inside."

Nestled inside the softly padded carriage, Sabine lifted the cover of the dress box and smoothed her hand over the fine peach silk. "My knight," she whispered as she watched Louis's back disappear inside the shop. "How might I ever win you?"

There were just too many sights to visit in Paris to fit into one day. And the idea of having his fairy princess alone with him for another day easily justified Louis's decision to stay the night. Though upon checking inns and taverns, Louis found the city's offering of rooms bleak. Seems there was a royal to-do at Versailles in two days' time, and visiting dignitaries and royals, and, well, just about anybody who considered themselves somebody, was in Paris en route to the king's fête.

A room at l'Hôtel du Sens would not be available until tomorrow eve, when the Duchess de Gaulle's party departed for Versailles. After learning of their prices, Louis thought it best that he and Sabine spend their first night in Paris in a more reasonably priced inn, in any case. And after another hour of scouring the city, he finally settled on what he deemed to be the last and only room available.

Though it wasn't as fine as Sabine deserved, he placated himself with the knowledge that she had spent the day well. Two dresses with matching hats, and then there were shoes. *Mon Dieu,* but the woman did know how to shop! And with every squeal of delight that Sabine let out, Louis's heart only melted more and more. He was now quite sure that it was a slippery puddle jiggling inside his chest.

From hardened armor to a puddle.

Hmm. Must have breathed a bit too much fairy dust.

But now to solve the problem of sleeping arrangements. Paris's last room offered only one bed. A narrow trundle bed boasting thin sheets and a torn coverlet. Louis sat in the hard-backed chair near the small bedside table and watched as Sabine went through the motions of smoothing out the skirts of her new dresses, making them perfect, almost like two headless women lying on the bed.

One of the spindles in the chairback squeaked when Louis adjusted his weight. It was far from comfortable. And by all rights he should have taken up in the stables behind the inn. But ten horses already occupied six stalls, and the idea of trying to squeeze in there . . . He shifted on the unsteady chair again.

"You take the bed, Sabine."

Her eyes widened almost to fright. "But what of you? I cannot allow you to sit in that stiff chair all night while I lie in comfort. You must take the bed, I'll just lie on the floor. I've done it before—"

"Nonsense." Louis stood and had her in his arms before she could utter another word. The reeking Parisian mud that had clotted the heels of his boots was overpowered by Sabine's heavenly fragrance. It was as if she blinked the dewdrops of a thousand flowers and spoke the breeze of meadow winds. "You, my lady, will not sleep on the floor. I am the man, let me do what is right. Besides, what if I should lie on the bed and you on the floor, and then suddenly I need to get up mid-night? I might step on you!"

"Oh!" Her giggles shook her gently within his arms. Louis was duly aware of his increasing desires, his own rising body heat. "Well, if you insist."

"I do." He was about to release her, but she held him tight.

She sprouted a knowing grin. "Do you like holding me, Louis?"

Confound his dastardly male urges. If she pressed much closer to him, she'd know soon enough just how much he liked holding her. But he could not pull away after her innocent question.

"You know I do." His voice bordered on a groan, but he could not help that either. "When I hold you, it is like I've my own piece of heaven in my arms."

When she pressed her cheek to his shoulder, her hair tickled his chin. Soft as an angel's kiss.

"Hold me forever, Louis."

It was then he noticed the fervent beating of her heart against his chest. As fast as his own. Perhaps equally as desirous.

"Forever and always, Sabine." He pressed his lips to her hair and closed his eyes.

"Something is . . . not right."

Cristoforo pulled the ruby damask curtains aside to look out of the carriage. Long reeds of emerald grass grew nearly as high as a man's knee. The sky was of a shade of blue similar to the fresco on the ceiling of Sant'Onofre. The occasional splotch of red from a field poppy. More grass. And yet more grass.

Dreadfully boring.

Since leaving the gates of Paris, a strange wave of calm had swept over him, almost religious in its purity. A fantastic tease that promised hideous results. Results that could be stopped or changed only with the elimination of that—thing!

Pietro shook himself awake, smacking his lips once. "What is not right, master?"

"This peace," Cristoforo said as he drew the end of his feathered fan slowly beneath his chin. The passing landscape, combined with the bright sky, began to make him dizzy. Dropping the curtain, Cristoforo slumped back against the padded cushions.

"It is the quiet of the country," Pietro offered with a sensory-drunken smile. "Is it not beautiful?"

"You've the most naive and juvenile attitude toward everything, Pietro."

Not a complete set of dice in that boy's head. Of course, he was only fourteen, but that meant nothing. Cristoforo had befriended him after finding him whimpering in the shadows of Sant'Onofre's attic rafters. He'd been beaten for not learning his lessons. Poor boy, his voice had not been saved by the knife. Instead, it had developed into a symphony of bullfrogs. Pity.

Ah, but pity for pity's sake was just that. A sorrowful mess of woe and otherwise useless emotion.

"I abhor the country," Cristoforo said, pleased when he saw Pietro's eager grin slip. He fussed with the Italian lace that whispered across his wrist. "It offers nothing more than dirt and insects and menial living fit more for animals than man. Do you not like the fine things I've given you, Pietro?"

"Oh, yes, master. I cherish them. And the city too. You are right, always right."

"Of course I am. How do you feel this time around? No urge to expel the contents of your stomach at my feet?"

Pietro bowed his head, shamed. "Forgive me, master."

"No worry, Pietro. You do look a much healthier shade today. Perhaps the country is the place for you after all."

A look of pure, genuine fear widened the boy's black eyes to perfect circles.

"You take my words too literally." Cristoforo offered with a sweep of his fan. "I would never part with you, my beloved. Never."

Receiving the boy's head under his arm, Cristoforo hugged him tight. He cherished the bond he had formed with this young man. Pietro had become more than an amusement, he was a thing of value to Cristoforo now. A precious little pet.

But that other bond . . .

Now, that had to be dealt with.

Forever and always.

Sabine's soft, kittenish purrs rose from her pillow. The street-lamps were lit, for the moon was still a narrow arc in the sky. One such lamp shone through the streaked window that was just above the bed. It splayed across Sabine's body, showing Louis, as if on display, the curve of her waist that sloped up to a soft, rounded hip.

The last time he had slept in the same room with a woman—without sleeping beside her—was . . . never.

He hadn't thought straight since riding up the overgrown alley of trees to the Bassange estate and catching Cupid's arrow with his heart. For if he had, Louis would never have been so foolish as to believe that he could travel to Paris with Sabine and share a room with her and still keep their relationship chaste.

As it should remain.

But Louis could not deny the changes within him. Sparks

had ignited. The heavy guilt that had almost ended his life had by some touch of a sorceress's wand, been transformed to love and desire. He was eager, willing, and ready. Ready to begin a journey of trust and responsibility and promises that must never be broken.

CHAPTER TWELVE

After they had broken their fast on fresh rye bread, cheese, and mulberry wine, Sabine dressed in the new peach silk, swept her hair up into a chignon, and donned her fringed hat. Together they picked their way across the haphazard Rue St. Honoré to the gardens behind the Palais des Tuileries.

Louis pulled Sabine across the crushed stone walk toward a cove just outside one of many fountains that dotted the gardens. He seemed as eager as she to devour the garden's sights and smells and interesting textures. An entire day could be spent lingering in these heady surroundings, Sabine felt sure. And with Louis by her side, that completed her dreams of perfection.

Sabine snuggled in Louis's embrace on a marble bench. Water fell in streams of diamonds, splinking and plopping into the shell-edged basins. A creaking sedan pulled by two turbaned young boys in long, loose, brightly colored pants passed by, carrying two young lovers, their hands entwined upon the woman's striped skirts. All about were soft murmurs of adoration,

the gay cries of children playing, and the screech of birds on
wing.

"It really is as marvelous as I remember," Sabine said.
"Close your eyes, Louis. Feel the magic."

He did. And Sabine joined him. The deep piney aroma of
the yews permeated her senses, mingling with the scent of the
tumescent ripe berries that dotted their blue-green needles with
splashes of crimson. Wet bark on the nearby chestnut tree was
a soft undertone to the deep fruity scent of freesia sprouting
near her feet. There floated a hint of spice, from what she knew
not.

It was surprising to realize how closely the laughter of children resembled the carefree babbling of a brook. Or how a
passing whispered adieu enveloped her heart in a knowing
warmth.

"There are fairies here," Sabine whispered.

Without opening his eyes, Louis nodded. "Yes, I believe
there are." He reached for her hand, and Sabine giggled to see
him grope about the empty bench beside him. Louis opened
his eyes. Sabine waved and then twirled before him, losing
herself in the brightness of the day and the enchantment that
filled the garden. Today was not a day to sit and adore, but to
stand and dance and draw in the very essence of life that
surrounded her in canopies of green and walls of vivid color.
She wanted the whole world to feel her happiness.

As she spun, she saw Louis spring to his feet. He circled her
in the opposite direction of her whirls, his boot spurs clicking
deliciously as he stepped on the crushed-shell walk. He adjusted
his frock coat, lifting it so it settled comfortably on his shoulders. A gentleman's sword peeked out from the left hip-vent
in his coat. No longer a soldier, Louis had explained he wore
it now only for show. Though perhaps part of him still needed
to feel the power of the weapon. Was there any man who did
not relish the feeling of power?

If they only knew the power of happiness. Ah, but her soldier was learning. And that made her even more joyous.

Louis bowed and asked, "Might I have the next dance, mademoiselle?"

She giggled from beneath the fringed shade of her hat. "You make me so happy, Louis. Yes, teach me to dance like a princess."

"Very well." He circled her waist with his arm and spun her about, being careful so the sword at his hip would not poke her.

"But there is no music."

"Just follow me. Feel the music in my heart, love. You should know the melody, it was composed by you."

"I have never danced with a man before," she said in an exhilarated breath as they circled beneath the arched green shadows of a spiraling geometric topiary.

"I've never danced with a woman before."

"I don't believe it. Surely a man as handsome as you has danced with all the women in Paris."

Louis chuckled and spun her close so he could enclose her in his embrace. "That would leave me quite tired. But no, I haven't. I spent my youth at war. There has never been a woman in my life, Sabine." She pressed her back to Louis's chest, her steady breaths making her breasts rise and fall above his arm. She automatically bent into his cupped palm when he touched it to her cheek loving the flesh-to-flesh contact. "Until you. I love you, Sabine."

Such sweet words. The only words she had pined to hear from Louis since first meeting him. But with the knowledge she possessed, a sudden sadness threatened. "Do you really mean that?

"How could you possibly think otherwise?"

She turned in his arms and drew a long finger across his cheek and down his chin. "Forgive me. I thought perhaps you wished to be rid of me."

"Rid of you?"

"You have come to Paris to seek out my grandfather's heir, have you not?"

"Yes." He hesitated. "But . . . not by my choice, you must understand. I don't want to lose you, Sabine. But we must follow the rules of your grandfather's will."

"That doesn't mean that I must become the property of some long-lost relative. I want to stay with you, Louis."

"I want that too."

"Just because half the Bassange estate has been bequeathed to someone else does not mean that I go along with it. Does it?"

"Why, no. Not a single mention of that was ever made. Yes, you mustn't worry, Sabine. I will ensure all is right by you. I promise."

A promise from Louis was all she needed. The sadness left as quickly as it had come.

"Oh, Louis!" She turned and spun out into a pirouette. "You've made me so happy. I really am a fairy princess today."

"That you are, my love. That you are."

He hung back, allowing her center stage as she twirled gracefully beneath the shadows of a carved lime tree.

"What is that?"

Sabine spun around and eyed the tall creature he pointed to. "A dragon!"

He stepped in front of Sabine, gently coaxing her back with his left hand while he drew his sword on the shrub. "Fear not, my lady, I shall slay this beast for you." He went at the massive topiary dragon with his sword, dancing gracefully before it as he stabbed into the thick, frothy greens. He gave it an underhanded lunge, jumped back to avoid its return of vicious flames, and then spun about to deliver a quick, punishing thrust.

Sabine giggled and laid a dramatic hand over her forehead to feint a swoon.

"Take that, you beast!" He thrust a coup de grâce deep within the shrub's emerald breast.

Cheers and applause startled Louis from his dramatics, and he turned to find he had observers as delighted as Sabine. He gave a shy bow and sheathed his sword beneath the wide hem of his frock coat.

"My knight in shining armor," she declared to all. "He's killed the beast!"

"Bravo!" a plump, rosy-cheeked woman yelled, and tossed a soft pink rose at the couple's feet.

Caught up in the moment, Louis swept Sabine into his arms and kissed her. The crowd whistled with hearty approval. Louis bowed once more to the crowd, and then went in search of privacy. Finding a grotto cascading with ivy and white flowers that dripped of sweet fragrance, he gently set Sabine upon the marble bench and knelt on the ground before her. The rapid pace of her heart would not allow her to sit still. He had done it! Her knight had slain a dragon for her in front of all Paris!

But now, as he knelt before her, he seemed apprehensive, as if searching for the right words.

She pushed away a rogue strand of hair from his eye. "What is it, Louis?"

"Marry me, Sabine."

Glee tickled her smile into a generous curve.

"I love you. And I cannot imagine a life lived without you." He pulled her clasped hands to his mouth and kissed them. Once, twice, a half dozen sweet kisses. "Be my wife and let me love you forever?"

The sadness reemerged.

"You really want me forever?" she couldn't help but ask. After all, he knew that she wasn't . . . exactly—

"I should die without you."

"But—"

He pressed a finger to her crimson lips. "There are no buts in the life I promise you. Do you trust me Sabine?"

She nodded.

"Do you trust that I will care for you? That I shall always be there for you? Always."

Again she nodded.

"Then why should I see worry cloud your eyes?"

"Because I am not like other women, Louis. They are normal and whole and—"

"I do not want any other woman," he hurriedly said. "I do not want an ordinary woman. One who sees things only on the surface, flat and dull and lifeless. I want you, Sabine. I want the magic within you. I want to be your knight in shining armor and I want you to be my lady of the fairies. I want you to shower me with your fairy dust and dance the rains every day. You have stolen my heart, precious one. And I do not wish it returned."

Her smile pushed away all doubt. "Never?"

"Not in a fairy's lifetime."

"Oh, and that can be a very long time. Fairies live for centuries."

"Good. Then that ensures our love will last. Tell me, Sabine. Tell me you'll have me as your husband."

"Yes." Her voice was deep and confident. "I will be your wife, Louis. And you shall be my knight."

"We shall marry today," he said, the mood taking his heart to new and free-spirited heights. "Would you like that?"

"Oh, yes, right here in the gardens! I want to begin our life surrounded by the beauty that I find here. Please, Louis, could we do that?"

"Of course. And later"—he turned and gestured toward the slain topiary—"we shall feast on the dragon."

To say Henri was shocked was putting it lightly. What would bring Cristoforo, the famous opera singer, to his home?

He waited patiently while Cristoforo downed his second

tankard of water. The man's fingers curved daintily about the smooth pewter, Henri observed. And his face was a picture of beauty. He could easily see how the man could play female roles onstage. For he was sure that with a wig and a little face rouge, even the most virile of men could be fooled.

Not he, of course, but . . .

Just behind the singer stood a skinny young boy dressed in equally elegant attire. His wide eyes watched Cristoforo's every move, and he quickly jumped when the man waved a hand or jerked his head.

There was something remarkably familiar about Cristoforo's graceful gesture for all to sit, and in the sparkle of intelligence in his lavender eyes. A resemblance, a similarity. But what it was, Henri could not place.

"Forgive me for coming unannounced, Monsieur de Lavarac," Cristoforo began grandly, pacing the length of the hearth with such attention, as if he were measuring for a marriage bed. The diamonds on his shoes glittered and clicked with each long stride. "I realized you do not know me."

As much as Henri hated Paris and all its trappings of wealth and decadence, Janette had been a great fan of opera. Though he'd taken her only once, she had told him of the illustrious castrato Cristoforo. "Your artistry is known to all," Henri quickly offered.

Cristoforo smirked and shrugged. "I seek your brother, Louis de Lavarac. It seems he and I have something, er—rather, *someone*—in common."

"Louis is in Paris," Henri somberly offered. With Sabine. He hadn't liked that his brother had taken the lunatic along, but a least he would not be bothered with her for a few days. Yvette's death had been such a surprise. One of his laborers had sent his daughter to stay a few days—to cook and clean.

Henri settled into the chair beside the hearth and clasped his hands beneath his chin, leaning forward to examine better the interesting face of the man asking the questions. "Why Louis? I had no idea he kept such illustrious company."

"Monsieur." Cristoforo waved a dramatic hand. "You flatter me. But it is not your brother exactly. It is the girl he seems to have taken under his wing. Sabine Bassange?"

"Sabine?" Henri replied, then added under his breath, *"Mon Dieu,* the lunatic attracts them far and wide."

"How do you know Sabine, Monsieur de Lavarac? Is she . . . a relative?"

"No. No relation. Though . . ."

"Yes?"

"We are in search of a missing relative. Her grandfather mentioned such a person in his will."

Cristoforo's left brow arched regally, his crimson lips pursing into a question. So feminine, Henri thought.

"Why is it you seek the girl? Do you have information regarding this person?"

Cristoforo splayed his hand before him in a brief fan. "I believe so."

That was the reason for the haunting resemblance! Sabine's eyes were such an unusual color, and yet, here was another pair the exact shade of lavender. "You are the missing heir, then?"

"I am. I was just informed of the vicomte's death today actually." Cristoforo touched his hand to his chest and made a hasty sign of the cross, almost as if a bother. Behind him, the boy matched his movements. "I came as soon as I could. So . . . she is here?"

"I'm afraid she's accompanied my brother to Paris. You say you are a relation?" Henri pressed. He was sure of it now. The butter-blond hair, the frail features, and wide, expressive eyes.

"Not here," Cristoforo muttered, ignoring Henri's question. "Damn, this is most vexing. And after a horrendous afternoon traveling those blasted, ill-repaired high roads."

"You do know that she is . . . how shall I say . . ." Henri studied the intent attention in Cristoforo's eyes.

"Touched?" Cristoforo offered with a tap to his skull. "In the head?" His chuckle broke the tension. "Yes." Cristoforo smoothed a long finger along his temple. "That fact has been apparent to me for years."

"I know it may not be my place to ask, but if you have known Mademoiselle Bassange for quite some time, why have you not seen to the family? They lived appallingly. The girl needs help. She is not well. And you—"

"I—" Cristoforo struggled to modify his harsh tone. "Normally reside in Naples. And you are correct to assume that it is no business of yours. You need know only that I am the beneficiary of the vicomte's will and do not wish to waste any more time than necessary resolving the finances. So if I may wait here? Until the girl returns?"

"Oh, of course. I would be honored. May I offer you a meal? We were just preparing to dine."

"Lovely," Cristoforo drawled, motioning to Pietro for his stein of water. "What is on the menu this evening?"

Henri swallowed. Well, there was no way of putting this one delicately. "Er . . . capon."

CHAPTER THIRTEEN

"What God hath joined together, let no man put asunder."

Sabine's giggles filled the heavily scented air as a slender, apple-cheeked boy tossed a confetti of rose petals over their heads. Louis nodded thanks to the young man, a passerby caught up in the excitement after hearing of their wedding plans.

The priest blew a bothersome petal from the tip of his bulbous nose before gesturing that Louis could now kiss his bride.

"Make a wish," Sabine whispered as Louis bent to her mouth.

He paused, her breath dusting his lips. "That works only with stars and chicken bones."

"There's a star blazing in my breast for the happiness I feel right now, Louis. Go on, wish for our future. But silently. You mustn't spoil the magic."

"Very well." Louis closed his eyes and imagined he could feel the heat from Sabine's star radiating outward, encompassing him in its warmth. *To fairy magic,* he wished, *may it always grace our lives.* "Done. Now may I kiss you, Madame de Lavarac?"

"Yes, my love."

Starflash permeated Louis's entire body, this sorceress's wand sending intoxicating energy directly to his soul. It felt splendid and rapturous. The devil take his grief and regret. Wrapped within his wife's embrace, Louis now knew that he had been redeemed. Saved by the soul of his fairy child. Given another chance at life.

Nearly a quarter of Paris was now en route for Versailles, freeing up a much nicer selection of rooms. Louis loosened his boots from his heels and allowed them to slide off to rest on the ornate Chinese carpeting. L'Hôtel du Sens was a riot of ornamentation; thick gold filigree covered everything in the room save the carpeted floors and the hand-embroidered bedding. Boiseries of sculpted alder were set every five feet along lushly papered walls. Even the small looking glass had been embellished with heavy gold ornament.

But the design paled next to Sabine's reflection.

Long folds of watered-peach silk floated down from her slender shoulders and over the backless Queen Anne vanity chaise. But not a single rustle of material could be heard. Only the sharp snaps of the fire crackling in the hearth punctuated the silence. Sabine had discovered the mirror only moments after their arrival in the room. She hadn't seen her reflection since childhood, she'd declared. The dressmaker's shop had given her the first view of her face in years.

Louis couldn't believe it. But then, he could not recall many material belongings at the Bassange castle. Why had the vicomte not used some of his wealth to care for his granddaughter? To dress and feed her well? Those questions would forever remain buried beneath the dandelion-filled meadow, Louis feared. Perhaps somewhere in a dusty corner of the abandoned castle lay a shard of silvered glass, once cherished by the child who was now his cherished wife.

And as for the de Lavarac château, there was only the broken sliver of mirror that Henri retained in his bureau drawer—a precious remainder of Janette's presence. Louis himself had never known the need for a mirror. Hair was combed and forgotten, his face washed and shaved by either a fellow soldier or Yvette when he had that luxury. Who needed to pretty themselves up to go to battle? Besides, it was a near impossibility to keep up with Parisian fashion. One day it was two curls on either side of the head, the next it would be scandalous to be seen with any less than four. And to even begin to guess whether a queue was fashionable this season!

"You like what you see?" he wondered from his chair.

Sabine's reflection smiled gently at him. "I was always so pudgy." She pressed a finger to the underside of her defined cheekbone. "The years whittle away your defenses, do they not?"

"The years have carved a lovely woman from the cherubic beginnings of the child." Louis stood and went to her side. In the mirror his frock coat made a brilliant periwinkle background against Sabine's pale tresses. He suddenly found himself reminiscing. "Did you ever watch your mother comb her hair during her toilette?"

She nodded.

"I did too. My mother's hair was dark as midnight. I used to love to touch it. 'Be gentle. You mustn't pull,' Mama would always say."

Sabine reached back and directed Louis's hand to her shoulder, where his fingers slipped through a wash of her hair. "Born of the angels, Papa would say of the two of us. So alike . . ." Her thoughts seemed to drift, stepping beyond the room and diving into the mirrored reflection. "Yes, always alike."

So she did have memories of her family, Louis thought. And good ones, it seemed from her smiling expression.

"You are my mirror, my soul," Sabine singsonged in a lost voice to her reflection. "Never further than a heartbeat away. Don't tell Mama and Papa . . . never tell."

Memories had captured his wife's mind. Louis could not begin to understand the confusing mix of thoughts. Did she balance on the line between darkness and light at this very moment? Not tonight, he prayed. Tonight must be perfect. For tonight they would begin a new life as husband and wife.

"Sabine." He squeezed her shoulders gently.

She looked up at him in the mirror, startled. "Louis. Forgive me. I know not where I was just now."

"Think not another moment on it." He bent to kiss the soft flesh on her temple and was gifted with the fragrance of the thick, lush yews in the Tuileries. "I've something for you."

"What is it?"

"Close your eyes."

Slipping his hand inside his waistcoat pocket, Louis pulled free the long ribbon of scarlet moiré. Yesterday he'd told Sabine there was still a box inside the shop he had to retrieve before allowing the carriage to leave. He had seen in her eyes the desire for the simple treasure. He'd almost forgotten he'd purchased it until now.

Holding the ribbon in his right hand, he dipped the fingers of his left into the thick waves of honeyed cream. Yes, so soft. Just like Mama's. But this was a luxury he could indulge whenever he chose. He no longer had to wait for his mother to attend her toilette and invite him in on a cold winter night to sit beside the fire and watch her.

Here sat his wife. Always and forever.

Slipping the ribbon through her tresses, Louis pulled gently.

"What is it, Louis? May I look?"

"Yes, my love."

She gasped at first sight of the ribbon, woven somewhat crookedly through her hair. She touched one end. "Oh, Louis.

From the hat shop? This is the most lovely gift you have given me. It's simply . . . splendid.'' The last word fell out on a hush.

"I'm not so graceful when it comes to arranging a woman's hair. Will you tie it prettily so I can admire it? And then, of course . . ."

"Of course what?"

"Later, I should wish to remove it in our marriage bed."

He ordered extra candles brought to their room. The additional charge did not dissuade Louis. Though he'd spent all he had to please his wife, every last sou was worth it. Sabine lit the long-stemmed columns, and when she had finished, the entire room glowed like the inside of a treasure-filled jewelry cache. Crimson damask lambrequins became weeping trails of rubies. Deep red Pinot Noir, sparkled inside the crystal goblets. A warm aura of comfort and satisfaction surrounded them.

"Mmm, now, let me decide." Louis pressed the soft, juicy bite of fruit between his tongue and the roof of his mouth, allowing the faint flavors to slide over his taste buds, tickling them with a tantalizing burst of coolness. His sight was darkened by the black band of satin he'd allowed Sabine to tie over his eyes. "I know what it is."

"Oh, this one is too easy," Sabine pouted.

"One more taste." Louis pulled Sabine's fingers to his mouth and found the tiny portion of fleshy fruit she still held. Sucking the entire piece across his lips, he then licked her fingers, holding firm when she giggled and tried to pull away.

"I believe that is cheating," she argued playfully.

"Very well." He swallowed. " 'Tis cool and mellow, much like melon. But," he quickly said as he heard Sabine begin, "there's the barest hint of spice. Cinnamon. Sweet and soft." He paused, sensing Sabine's gaze on him. "Like you. And deep and gold in color, the color of your soul."

"Flirting with the judge will not help you either."

"Persimmon," he announced, and lifted the bottom of his blindfold away from his face. "Correct?"

"Correct. Now me, Louis. Blindfold me."

"With great pleasure." He slipped the silk from his head and proceeded to fasten it carefully over his wife's eyes. Her hair was so soft and satiny that the silk kept slipping down over her ears.

"Lie back," Louis directed as he guided Sabine to lie against the damask pillows on the bed. "That'll hold it secure. Now, let's see." Louis looked over the remaining fruits in the porcelain bowl. He'd already sampled the raspberries and persimmon. "Oh, this is too easy. I must be tricky." He snapped a green grape from its bunch and bit the rounded end off.

"Louis, are you eating? It's my turn."

He swallowed the evidence. "No, love. Here." He settled onto the bed beside her and touched the exposed meat of the grape to her lips. Slowly he rubbed the juice across her mouth. Candlelight sparkled in dancing licks over the sheen, creating a crystal sculpture of her parted lips.

"But I—"

"Ah-ah," he cautioned, pressing his forefinger to her upper lip so that she could not taste until it was time. " 'Twould be far too easy if I just let you bite into it."

The tip of her tongue lashed out, searching and finding his finger. "Now, flirting with the judge will not help you."

"Louis."

"Taste," he whispered in her ear.

The sight of her tongue working lazily over her bottom lip set Louis's heart to a rushing pace. A fine equipage of six trampled through his chest, increasing in speed as his desire threatened to exceed limitations. This teasing play had to end soon. But just a bit longer, he chided himself. Slow and sure will win her confidence.

"A grape," she said with a broad smile. "Not so very difficult."

"Ah, but is it white or black?"

"Oh, Louis. 'Tis not fair."

"I suppose not. It is white." He held the half-piece up so it caught the candlelight flickering behind it and he could see the fine veins meshed beneath the flesh. "A fine wine this little fellow would have made."

"Do another," she begged.

"Very well." With a snap of his fingers the grape sprang straight above Louis's head and landed with exact precision in his mouth. A trick any vintner's son learned while still in infant's skirts. There was only an apple and a sliced orange left. Both entirely too easy to guess. "Again, I must be tricky."

"I rather like your tricks." Sabine's tongue slid across her upper lip, only to end in a pout. "Are you eating again?"

"Change of tactics," he said as hundreds of tiny orange juice sacques burst between his teeth. Slightly tart at first taste, and then richly sweet. He winced as another bite dispersed the juice onto his lips and a stray droplet splat across his nose. "Ready?"

He took her silent nod the same way he understood his own body's incessant signals. Get on with it! Temptation can work for only so long before becoming a raging bull.

Louis pressed a juicy kiss to Sabine's mouth. Her delighted moan worked its way through his body like warm cherry wine teases the senses. The exploratory tracing of her tongue across his flavored lips enticed him to deepen the kiss. He plunged his tongue inside her mouth, spreading the juice across her teeth and on the underside of the soft, moist flesh of her lips.

"Any idea?" he whispered into her mouth.

"Mon Dieu, 'tis the finest orange I have ever tasted."

Sliding his arm behind her shoulders, Louis lifted Sabine into his arms. The movement allowed the slippery black silk to fall from her eyes and to her throat. He slowly trailed his other hand down the delicate hollows at the base of her neck. "I've another."

The mounded flesh that pulsed upward from her décolletage tensed at his sudden touch. Louis spread his palm wide and smoothed it over the side of Sabine's breast. "But it is a fruit *I* wish to taste."

The whisper of peach silk across satin sent a shiver through his body. Sabine lay still, a look of smiling curiosity on her face as Louis unhooked her dress. Once she was freed of the confining silk, Louis was able to feel the timorous beat of her heart beneath the gossamer linen of her chemise.

Louis pressed a kiss to the mound of her breast, lingering over her sweet-scented flesh.

"Louis?"

"Yes, my love?"

Sabine trailed a fingertip beneath his stubbled chin. "Are you afraid?"

As always, she could read his soul. "To be truthful? Yes, I am. A bit."

He slipped the blindfold from her neck and tossed it over his shoulder.

"Don't be." She smiled. "I am not afraid."

"No, of course you wouldn't be," he said with a relieved release of breath. "I've slain the dragon, there is nothing left to fear."

"Make me your wife, Louis," she whispered in her husky, knowing, woman's voice. Carefully she drew her fingers up over his shoulder, under his frock coat, and pushed it down over his arms. Lightning sparks traveled his arms, following the wake of her touch.

There was no going back. No controlling his desires. He had wanted this woman for too long. Tonight she would be his. Forever.

Her skirts were untied and shed in the blink of an eye.

Grabbing a fistful of cotton petticoats, Louis pulled them down over Sabine's hips and tossed them rustling to the floor. Candle-light played over the diaphanous chemise she wore, highlighting her breasts, her erect nipples, her thighs, and shadowing the curves beneath her breasts and the valley between her legs.

Sabine reached out. Delicate fingertips pleaded. Louis curled a loose fist beneath her fingers and kissed each one. Her wrist was narrow and smooth. Gardenia led his nose up her arm and to the cove of her neck. Kissing her through her hair, Louis found her life's pulse. She gasped. He reached up and pressed a quieting finger to her lips. Each exploratory kiss to her neck, behind her ear, across her shoulder, was matched by a loving kiss to his finger from Sabine's lips.

He felt her tense as he moved lazily down to her breast. Pleased, Louis kissed through the linen until her nipple hard-ened to a pebble between his lips. He felt her enclose his fingertip with her mouth as he enclosed her. She nipped, and he did in kind. "That shall teach you to be so feisty."

"Oh, Louis."

"Though I do rather like your feistiness."

Rising on his knees, Louis eyed his wingless fairy. He held her gaze as he untied her chemise and spread the lawn fabric wide. Her body arched toward heaven as he ran his fingers lightly across her breasts. Gorgeous mounds of flesh filled each of his palms and warmed to a wanting heat. Divine. Blissful. So very right. This was what it felt like to touch a woman again. And not just any woman. His wife.

"It feels so wonderful," Sabine whispered. "Your touch . . . your hands . . . oh, Louis."

"I could touch you forever," he replied huskily. "Your flesh is of the softest silk. Your breasts are fruits of a most exotic flavor. Ah, Sabine, you make me want you so badly."

"It is a want I've come to know myself, Louis. Remove your shirt. Quickly. I want to feel your body pressed against mine."

Never had a simple knot caused him so much vexation. Louis struggled with an end of his shirt tie, until finally, with a laugh, Sabine sat up and released it with a touch of her magic.

"There." She smoothed a hand down his hard chest, setting the fine dusting of dark hair to alertness. "So soft," she said, her attentions rapt on his body. "Louis, you are perfect." The sleeves of his shirt slunk down his arms at her direction, billowing in folds around his waist. "I've never touched a man like this before. I never imagined that flesh could be so hard and muscular, yet still feel so soft and warm."

"You haven't discovered it all yet, my lady. There are some places on me that are ... ohhh ..." He caught his breath as her fingers accidentally brushed over his groin before sweeping back up his stomach. "Very hard."

"Really?"

Innocent. Trusting. Fairy angel. God above, did he love this woman!

"Really. But that will come."

"When?"

"Oh, soon. Very soon."

She lifted her arms as he pulled the chemise over her head. Sabine lay back against the pillows, staring brazenly at Louis. She did not know to be embarrassed by her nakedness. Sweet heaven above, she lay there so confident and ready. One hand splayed across her smooth, flat stomach. A tender nest of dark blond curls bloomed between her legs.

Oh, it must surely be a crime to want someone so much!

Easing his palm over his breeches, Louis reminded himself to go slowly. He traced the softness of her thighs, lingering, memorizing the texture of the fine invisible hairs moving beneath his fingers. Following the dancing flashes of candle-light, Louis found her stomach was smooth, gently rising and falling to the beat of his heart.

"Your touch is like fire," she said urgently, and twisted a

fingertip through the ends of Louis's hair. "Are you sure that you are not a dragon in disguise?"

Straddling her, Louis bent forward to kiss her juice-sticky lips. "No, my lady, a knight I am."

"I think I like what lies beneath the armor."

Sabine grew more brazen in her responses, pulling his head down to coax his kiss a moment longer. Pressing the length of his body against hers, he ground his erection into her belly, relishing the sweet spark of teasing tension.

"What is that?" she gasped, and propped up on her elbows.

The heat had jeweled in liquid crystal in the hollow below her neck. Louis kissed her quickly, licking the moisture from her collarbone. "God made man and woman to fit together as one, Sabine." He pulled her hand down and placed it over his breeches. "I will fit inside you. That is the true consummation of our vows. You mustn't worry," he said quickly as he saw the wonder flee from her face. "I will be gentle. I would have it no other way."

She held his gaze for a few tense moments. Louis felt the curious tracing of her fingers down the length of his member. He didn't know how much longer he could bear such sweet torture.

"I want to see." Her hand found the metal buckle on the back of his breeches. *Click.* Louis touched the buttons at his waist, but Sabine was already loosening them from their slots. She gave a tiny gasp as he slid down his breeches and kicked them from his feet. "May I touch it?"

"Oh!" Louis rushed a staying hand to her curious touch.

"It hurts?"

"No, no. It just feels . . . so very . . ."

He forgot what he was going to say.

Sabine wriggled free from his grasp and stroked firmly yet curiously down his shaft, causing Louis to curl his fingertips tight into his palm and grit his jaw. Merciful heaven above!

"You like this," she concluded with a mischievous smile.

"Very much." Louis wilted into the bed pillows and allowed his inquisitive wife free rein over his aching body. Her slow and sensitive touch caused his entire being to pulse, to shake in anticipation of more.

"I understand now, Louis, how we will fit together. Can it happen now? Please?"

He hadn't the strength or willpower to delay any longer. "As you wish."

He rolled her to her back and gently coaxed her legs apart, slipping a single finger deep within the creamy depths of her. Her torso arched heavenward as his finger found her hidden pearl and began to stroke it tenderly, patiently, watching as he gauged her reactions. "Yes, you are ready, my love."

"I've been ready for hours, Louis," she gasped. "Oh, I feel as though I may begin to fly at any moment."

No longer able to delay their union, Louis slipped inside Sabine. A slight resistance, not enough to make her cry out, and then smoothly sliding in and out. To be enveloped inside her brought forth the most incredible sensations. She was his guide in his return to the place within himself, a place of innocence, a place of complete and total surrender. And he could feel her light radiate from within. Brilliant and warm and all-encompassing. It coated every portion of his body inside and out.

She gripped his upper arms. *"Mon Dieu,* this is heaven, Louis."

An indescribable wave of ecstasy overtook Louis the same time as Sabine. Her cry of joy was more thrilling than the finest opera. Shuddering over Sabine's body, Louis could not help smiling widely. The light she possessed twined them into a weave of love, hope, and peace.

"Mio Dio!"

Cristoforo blinked his eyes open. His entire body shuddered

with the remainders of what felt to him like sexual release. He couldn't have. Could he?

He glanced to the figure lying still beside him, the fine white bed sheets underlining her sagging breasts. Another old crone. Her name escaped him at the moment. Vicountess something or other. The wait at the de Lavarac estate had proved far longer than he'd expected. As darkness fell, Monsieur de Lavarac had decided that his brother hadn't plans to return this eve. Unable to bear the thought of spending a night in a *country* château, Cristoforo returned to Paris, tired, disappointed, but mildly enthused to find the missive from the vicountess waiting for him.

And now!

He shoved a hand beneath the sheets, feeling between his thighs the hard evidence of his arousal. It had really happened. And it had been beyond incredible. Unlike any sensation normal coupling had ever brought him.

The vicountess snorted in her sleep. She hadn't done this, Cristoforo knew. Why, the wrinkled old purse had barely flopped on her back before she'd been moaning and screaming. Hadn't been touched by a man for decades, he was sure.

Careful not to wake the snoring wench, Cristoforo slid from between the sheets and tiptoed to his clothes. Still stunned over what he'd just experienced, he punched his arms through his sleeves, vainly wishing Pietro were not asleep out in the carriage. But he could not bother with that right now. How could something like this have—

No! It could not be.

Cristoforo gulped down the shock at his own realization.

Had *she* been the cause of this?

But of course. If he could sense and experience the pain of her madness then why not also know her joys?

"It is not right," he hissed. "I cannot allow this to happen again. To allow her to feel such pleasure and I remain but a blind receiver? No, no, and no!"

Stuffing his long legs into his breeches, Cristoforo fumbled to button the sides, but was too vexed to continue. Draping his frock coat over his arm and hooking his shoes on his fingertips, he made for the door.

But . . .

Backtracking to the Chinese cloisonné vanity on which the Vicountess of Hagdom kept her perfumes and laces and jewels, Cristoforo perused the sparkling display for a moment. Plucking up a necklace of rubies and diamonds befitting his private performance tonight, he turned on his heel and left.

''Wake up.''

Vaguely aware of a soft voice fluttering near his ear, Louis growled in his sleep and turned to his left side, thinking it only his dreams that had become so vividly clear.

''Louis!''

But dreams do not shove you. ''Huh?''

Louis sprang upright in his bed and groped about in the darkness until his sleep-numbed fingers fell across a fall of soft and luxuriantly silken hair. ''What?''

'' 'Tis only me, Louis. Sabine,'' she whispered. ''Your lady wife? You remember?''

''Yes. Yes. I was just . . . sleeping.'' He rolled his tongue around his mouth and shook his head. He'd been sleeping like death itself. So well. For once.

''Get dressed.'' Moonlight flashed across her hair and twinkled in her eyes. She pressed a bulk of cloth into Louis's hands and leapt from bed, wearing her night robe and his periwinkle frock coat. What was going on? Louis squeezed the bulk in his hands and realized it was his breeches.

''You must come now. They're here!''

But it was the middle of the night. Wasn't it? Shaking off the last remnants of sleep, Louis's eyes slowly adjusted to the darkness. ''They're here? Who?''

"Hurry," Sabine whispered from the doorway. "Before they are gone."

Whatever she spoke of, it seemed urgent.

"No shoes," Sabine chided, and slipped her arm through Louis's. "They'll hear us coming."

CHAPTER FOURTEEN

Louis settled onto the clipped grass surrounding the pond in the hotel garden. Sabine's nightgown hissed across the grass as she cuddled close to him and pointed to the dazzling light show above the moonlit pond waters.

"Fireflies," Louis exclaimed as he took in the magnificent sight. There had to be hundreds of the dancing golden lights. He'd never seen so many at one time before.

"They've come for the fête," Sabine giggled. "They're always present when the fairies have reason to celebrate."

Louis smoothed his palm over Sabine's shoulder, pulling the ends of her hair out across the moist grass. Hers was a strange and magical mind. He knew not how it worked or what wheels had to be turned to induce the unusual images she saw. All he knew was that he wanted to touch it. He'd already had her body, now he needed to know her mind. To feel it breathe and to trace its inner workings until he knew her to the very soul.

He leaned close and kissed the spot just beneath her ear. She tasted of their union, sweet and salty at the same time. And still the faintest hint of orange juice mixed with grapes and persimmons lingered like a divine concoction offered up for the gods. Although she sighed happily at his attentions, her gaze remained concentrated on the fireflies, her eyes wide and glimmering with moonlight. "Tell me about it. The fête."

"Very well."

An orchestra of crickets arrived to serenade the festivities, and just above their heads a golden-eyed owl kept watch.

"The king and the queen of the fairies have come." Sabine began to narrate in a soft voice. "The king is the first to arrive. Six fine mouse steeds adorned in silver and crimson livery carry him upon a gleaming red maple leaf. The king's dew-kissed toes dangle over the edge of his throne, catching the light of the fireflies with every bouncing step of his fine equipage. He is dressed head to toe in finely spun gossamer robes dyed brilliant gold from the juice of saffron. His hair, long and fine as a spider's webbing, is twined in matching braids down either side of his head with gilded threads spun by silkworms."

Louis closed his eyes, and yes, it was so easy to see what his wife saw. "Go on," he whispered. He absently wove a finger through her bounteous hair. "What of the queen?"

"Ah, the queen follows the king. She arrives upon a silver-encrusted settee that straddles a sapphire dragonfly. Its wings flit crisply through the air, its flight steady so as not to upset his royal passenger. The queen's shimmering gown clings to her tiny body in worship. Her iridescent wings change colors with each graceful movement. She sings a most delicate and fanciful tune that brings all the royal fairy subjects to their feet.

"And they dance beneath a constellation of fireflies, the king bowing grandly to his beloved wife. Their subjects sing praise and applaud, with fairy wings of translucent crimson and tiny jewels of diamond and ruby to decorate their clothes."

"And what of the fairy princess?"

"The fairy princess?" she wondered. "But there is no—"

"I see her!" Louis pointed across the pond, where the fireflies had formed two almost perfect parallel lines, as if laying down the path for his imaginary princess to walk. "The fairy princess," he began, "is the daughter of the king and queen, and by far the loveliest, most desirable princess ever to take flight in the imagination of a young woman's mind. Can you not see her?"

Sabine shrugged, looking about in her perplexity.

"Her robes are of gossamer white, fashioned from the labor of royal silkworms, painstakingly stitched by hand and adorned with the tiniest and lightest of diamonds so as not to bend her fragile wings. She carries a pansy petal purse in her delicate hand. And there, do you see? She has stepped down from her dragonfly's back and her feet dance across the grass tops."

"She's so lovely," Sabine cooed. "Oh, Louis, I can see her. I really can!"

"And her hair . . ." Louis turned to Sabine and slipped splayed fingers up through her tresses. "The fairy princess possesses a great mane of golden hair, so soft and silken that the flowers weep and bow their heads in her presence." He tilted Sabine's face up to look at him. He could see in her eyes that she finally realized he spoke of her. "And her eyes—her eyes possess the secrets of the world. Brave men lose their hearts in the silvery, moonlit pools and can gaze into them only with adoration."

"Oh, Louis." Sabine nuzzled her cheek into his palm.

"But there is a knight!" Louis could not let his tale end just yet. "He is neither worthy nor brave. Ravaged by battle and lacking faith in mankind, all he possesses is a love of beauty and a gentle care. He kneels before the king and queen, not knowing what he shall say. Dare he ask for the fairy princess's hand? No, he mustn't be so bold. For surely all of Faerie would laugh and have mirth with him. Instead, he simply asks what he may do to make the princess happy. If she have one request, he will grant it. No matter how far or long it should take him. He would give his life to fulfill her wishes."

"And what does she request?" Sabine whispered, her eyes searching his.

Louis felt his heart rise to his throat. "I know not. What *does* she request? You are the fairy princess. Your wish is my command, Sabine. My heart shall not rest until you have what you wish."

"Very well." A veil of golden softness fell over her face as Sabine looked down thoughtfully, her fingers twirling in the thick carpet of grass. She was a prize for any knight's dreams. Lovely, sweet, unique in mind and spirit. And when she looked up, Louis had to restrain himself from pulling her face to his and kissing her, a simple gesture to prove she was truly his. "The fairy princess has only one request of the knight."

"By your leave, my lady."

"You must give to me your heart."

Fireflies danced in his breast, burning proud and bright as Louis enveloped Sabine in his arms and sank into the grass. Everything was so right. In fact, he was almost sure he heard the gay cheers and singing voices of the royal fairy fête. For he was loved by the most treasured inhabitant of fairyland, their royal princess. Sabine. Princess of all that was magical and enchanting. A misunderstood fairy child lost in the land of mortals.

"Granted," he whispered, and kissed her deeply.

And he kissed her, and kissed her, until his own reality meshed with her world of fairy dust and unicorns. Sensations took on tints and colors instead of tangible feeling. Her lips were sweet and ruby and hot at the same time. Her breath twined with his into a swirl of pink clouds. Love became so vivid and real that he could see it.

"Louis, your kisses make me burn."

"What?" He levered himself away from her, propping one elbow near her shoulder. "Are you in pain?"

"Oh, no, I mean, they make my insides so warm and tingly. I love it, Louis. If I could spend every minute of every day kissing you, I would do it."

He dotted brief, teasing kisses across her forehead and her eyelids, then whispered across her parted lips, "And what of making love?"

"Oh, that is heaven on earth, my love. Can we do it again? Please?"

"You'll receive no argument from me. Let's go to our room. After we've thoroughly sated each other—"

"Do you think that can happen?"

He waggled a brow. "I hope not. But later I should write to Henri to let him know we will be in Paris for a few more days."

Sabine raised a brow. "You think the Dragon Lord would approve?"

He smoothed his palm over her loose hair. "It does not matter, fairy angel. I love you. And I'll have no one tell me differently."

"She is with you?" L'Argent looked up from his stack of papers after Louis had explained his visit in Paris. "Where is she now?"

After a leisurely morning of lovemaking—just the memory of Sabine's kisses and the warmth of her body nestled against his, as if designed to fit only him—stirred up a lazy want in his loins. Louis felt he could make love to his wife for an eternity and never become sated. It had been near to impossible to leave her arms that afternoon, her nightgown opened to expose the creamy mounds of her breasts, her seductive smile curling behind a glistening wedge of orange as she stood in the doorway beckoning him to stay just a bit longer. Ah, those delicious citrus kisses!

If he hurried, he could finish all necessary business within the hour and be back in her arms before the juice on her lips lost its tangy flavor.

"It is of no matter to you."

"And what matter should it be to you? Why would you drag Mademoiselle Bassange along to Paris for a simple visit to my office? Seems rather presumptious myself. Have you designs on the girl?"

Designs? If L'Argent only knew. She was his wife! And he was damned proud of that fact. But for some reason he felt it best not to tell the lawyer about his new marital status. Not yet. He wasn't too sure of the man. Where his alliances fell. Perhaps it was a good thing Sabine offered to stay at the hotel while Louis spoke to l'Argent. As much as he wished to share everything with her, he had no idea what l'Argent would have to say. And he didn't wish to upset Sabine unnecessarily. Hell, he was afraid of his own reaction should the news be bad and l'Argent had located the other beneficiary. He would need time to put on a smile before breaking such news to his wife.

But, by some odd fortune, he had worried for naught.

"There is no news of the heir," L'Argent recited as he glanced over his papers, seeming miffed now that Louis had skirted the whereabouts of Sabine. "Nor of the woman, Evangeline."

"How hard can it be to locate the heir if his or her name is listed in the will?"

"Not difficult. But there are legalities, time constraints, *distances* to be crossed, Monsieur. Worry not, I feel sure contact will be made within the next few days."

Louis would not leave Paris without knowing the outcome of the Bassange estate.

"As for Evangeline, I've sent word to England in care of—"

"No!" Louis quickly stopped the spit-sucking notary before he had a chance to offer the name. To know the man's name would have only worked to further shape Louis's nightmares. It was hard enough that Evangeline screamed her vengeance in his dreams.. "It is not necessary Just . . . find her."

Sabine left a note with the hotel concierge, telling Louis he could find her out behind the grand building in the formal gardens.

The park had cleared quickly with the imminent setting of the sun. Though a good hour of muted daylight still remained, everyone was returning to their homes to eat and chat about the day's events and to prepare for the evening's program of theater and promenade.

Sabine sat inside a splendid cove hidden deep within the park, kicking her toes beneath the hem of her lavender skirts. Great boughs of thick greenery created a canopy that seeped a heady scent of pine into the humid air.

The rains would soon fall. Her clothes clung to her body, heavy with moisture. But she did not mind. The fragrance of the air, clean and clear, just waiting to spill forth a gusher of nature's liquid perfume.

Everything was so perfect. So right. It was too much to bear without releasing the emotion that welled in her breast.

As the sound of Louis's boots chuffing across the finely clipped grass brought him into view, Sabine set loose a fountain of tears.

Rushing to her side, Louis gripped her face between his palms. "No, my love, don't cry!"

Frantic, he pulled her to his breast and tried to smooth comfort across her back with his hand, but she struggled away.

Reluctantly, Louis released Sabine's shaking body and knelt beside her voluminous skirts on the grass, for the grotto bench was much too small for the two of them.

With eyes closed and head tilted back against the ivy-covered wire form that shaped the grotto wall, Sabine held out a staying hand. The force of her emotions would not allow her to speak at the moment, though she did not want Louis to take her tears in the wrong way.

"Sabine?"

A swallow and a sigh broke through the wall of silence her emotions had forced on her. "Fear not," she said in a strong voice. She was glad when a smile suddenly curled onto her lips. Louis would know she couldn't possibly be sad. Sabine opened her eyes to look straight into Louis's. "I'm sorry to have frightened you. It was just so nice"—she glanced up and around the tiny cove that surrounded them, her tears still sliding noiselessly down her face—"to find such peace."

"But, my love." Louis touched the warm tears that dribbled beneath her chin. They quickly spread down his forefinger and across his knuckle. "Why the tears? I thought you were happy. Is there something I should know? Sabine, please, it pains me to see you so upset."

Her smiling laughter pushed the worry from his face.

"It is not sadness that has brought my tears, Louis." She swiped a hand across one cheek, sniffing as she did. "I cry from my heart, and my heart sends up tears of joy. Oh, Louis, I was walking through the gardens and I was suddenly overwhelmed by pure happiness and delight. My life these past few weeks . . . you have given me great reason for celebration. Forgive me for pushing you away. I was caught up in my own world. But now . . ." She took his hand and pressed it to her cheek. "Feel my joy, husband. It is you who has given it to me with your vow of love and your unquestioning heart."

"Tears of joy?"

She nodded.

Standing, Louis pulled Sabine up and into his arms. "From your heart to mine," he whispered into her ear. "Your joy is infectious. Forgive me for thinking differently. You know I will always worry about you, Sabine."

"Yes, but not today." Gifted with a sudden whimsical desire, she pushed gently against his chest and he toppled to the bench, pulling her upon his lap to sit as he did. Their motion ruffed Sabine's skirts across the box hedging near the bench, which dispersed a heady fragrance into the air.

The sudden invasion of a nightingale to their little cove startled Sabine into a cry of surprise, followed by the most exquisite laughter. Louis joined Sabine in her glee as they watched the tiny bird flit about the opening to the grotto, in search of flower nectar, until finally it decided that nothing but silly human babbling could be found here and left in an invisible flash of wings.

" 'Tis a good thing the gardens are abandoned this hour of the day," Louis offered as his laughter died down. "We would have attracted quite the crowd with our silliness!"

"The crowds seemed to like our performance yesterday," Sabine said. "I'm sure 'tis not very often that one is witness to an actual dragon slaying."

"I'm sure not. Come here, my lady of the fairies." Louis helped Sabine to readjust her position on his lap, one leg to either side of his thighs, so that she could snuggle close against him. She pulled her skirts up and fluffed them out on so that his legs were entirely covered, and so that he could feel the heat of her body press against his. "Mmm, perfect."

"I love it when you hold me close," she said, and smothered Louis's reply with a kiss.

Louis smoothed a hand over Sabine's rising décolletage and found the first hook that closed her bodice. His touch, and the pleading look in his eyes, were irresistible.

"Can we make love?" she gasped in between kisses to his eyelids, his ears, and his chin. "I want to ride this feeling beyond the rainbow."

"Not only are you a fairy angel, but you possess powers to read a man's mind as well."

The last hook sprung, Louis folded back the lavender satin to expose her touch-starved nipples. "Mmm, such wicked sorcery." He closed his eyes, allowing her to continue her rain of kisses, while he lost himself in the task of feeding her needs. Each brush over her breasts elicited wanting moans from Sabine's lips. She could not help the sounds she made. It was as if passion had its own voice, and by forming it into a sound it only spurred her desires.

Her nose slid down to his ear and she nibbled gently on the lobe. "What if we are discovered?"

"We won't be." Holding her firm with one arm around her back, Louis taunted her nipple with alternating nips and long, languishing sucks. "I've a good view of the gardens from here. Besides, the sun is setting and everyone is home, eating."

"Are you hungry, Louis?"

"Ravenous."

She giggled because she understood his meaning. It wasn't a need for food that worked her lover to a frenzy, but a need for her body. A need she had come to know all too well.

"Do you trust me, Sabine?"

His hand journeyed down and under her skirts. She shivered just a little as Louis's hand found her narrow hip and coaxed the flimsy chemise up her thigh.

"With all my heart."

She reached beneath her skirts to find the buttons at the waist of his breeches. Paris was lost in a rush of desire and want. The garden smells twined into an aphrodisiac perfume that curled its invisible fingers through their hair and traced them across their bodies. Slowly Louis guided Sabine down upon his erection, his jaw tense to prevent his own cry of passion, lest they he discovered.

Pressing his cheek to her exposed breast, Louis moaned into her heart, speaking in the lover's tongue of all that had become sacred between the two of them. Sabine moved gently, barely drawing herself up his length. She liked this feeling of being on top of him. She was in control.

He nipped her breast, and Sabine giggled and squeezed her thighs.

"Oh!"

Sabine clapped her hand over Louis's mouth. "Careful, lover," she admonished him at his sudden cry.

"It was your laughter," he gasped. "And your actions. You . . . moved. Inside. It was as though you were . . . hugging me."

"You mean . . ." She looked down to where their bodies joined, concealed from all. Her muscles had flexed when she'd laughed, squeezing her thighs closer around his waist and squeezing . . . deep within. Had she somehow . . . There was only one way to know for sure. Another giggle produced the same result.

Louis clung hard to her body. "Do that again. If you can."

And this time, without so much as a single peep of laughter, Sabine felt the strong muscles of her stomach contract against Louis's, and in turn her feminine muscles closed tight about his member, drinking from him the passionate elixir of love.

"Strike me down with the horn of a unicorn, it is more fairy glamour." He bowed his head into the cradle of her breasts.

"Oh." Sabine's fingers curled and pressed tight to his back, twisting the ends of his hair beneath her palms. "It brings me to the edge when I do this. I need to let go, Louis. I want to fly like the nightingale. Catch me!"

Twined tightly together, the two surrendered to the waves of orgasm and rode the fluttering climax on dragonfly wings until they were both loose and relaxed in each other's arms.

Just then, soft sprinkles of cool crystal water peppered

Sabine's skirts. She tilted her head back and opened her mouth to release a silent cry of triumph.

"My fairy angel," Louis whispered as he laid his head on her breast.

CHAPTER FIFTEEN

Sabine's skirts rustled softly between Louis's legs. He tried desperately to steer her closer to the side of the buildings, for after the light rain the streets were muddier than usual. But she was blind to the ugliness and stench of the city. Her eyes saw only wonders and beauty.

And after their lovemaking in the garden, Louis found it impossible to really mind the odor and mess himself.

"Louis!"

Suddenly Sabine was tugging him up to a set of carved oak doors. "The Opéra."

"Yes, I can hear they've started already." He examined the billet pasted to the smooth wood door of the new oval hall. "Cristoforo. Hmm. Another capon imported from Italy. Ah, but they do have incredible voices. Would you like to go in? Sabine?"

She had fallen into her wide-eyed stare so suddenly that it frightened Louis. No! Not after they had come so far. He gripped her upper arm. "What troubles you?"

"Hmm? I—yes, let's go inside," she said slowly.

Still not normal, he thought with a sigh. But getting closer every day. And for the moments he held her in his arms and made her his wife, she was totally whole. He praised the Lord for that.

After purchasing the seats of an absentee box holder, Louis led Sabine up the winding red-carpeted stairs and into the opulent theater.

" 'Tis beautiful," she whispered.

Her gaze was bright as it fell over the great velvet stage curtains and across the mahogany stage. Lumieres set at the front of the stage were polished to a sparkling copper glow and cast crooked shadows across the faces of the musicians sitting in the orchestral pit. Violin bows moved in graceful unison, and occasionally the thin hand of the conductor would rise to redirect the rhythm.

Sabine's lips parted in silent awe as she leaned over the balcony and seemed to count each and every velvet padded seat. Marveling, she pointed out to Louis a lady's wig done in the shape of a ship, replete with pink silk sails and sparkling sapphire waves.

The audience sat enthralled. Odd, thought Louis, for the only other time he'd been in a theater, it had been chaos. No one attended the opera to watch the performance. It was to see and be seen. To tend business and liaisons, and gossip, gossip, gossip.

But the reason for the rapt attention was clear.

There, on the stage, was the most astounding sight. Louis found himself sighing along with Sabine. A lone singer stood tall and erect, commanding the entire room with his imposing carriage. The grand headpiece he wore, feathered and gilded into the shape of a swan, added another foot and a half for sure. He was robed in a costume of heavy ivory damask and remained perfectly still in very center stage. His only movement was to direct his voice with his long fingers and turn above the waist as his eyes scanned over the intent audience.

Long wisps of honeyed hair slipped from beneath the headpiece and flowed across his crimson-velvet-caped shoulders. His lips were painted the same deep, enticing bloodred as the ribbon in Sabine's hair.

And the sound coming from the man's mouth . . . It was amazing. So heartwrenching that Louis settled into his chair, transfixed. Such beauty the man possessed, along with the voice of a cherub. Not even a woman could reach such high notes, nor could any singer Louis had heard fashion plain notes into such utter poignancy.

Librettos had been sold out and so Louis hadn't the slightest idea what the man sang. He'd never learned Italian, just a bit of Dutch during the war. But he was sure just from the lilting and longing melody it was a love song. A yearning plea to join with the beloved. A lost soul searching for its mate.

It was as if the man sang of their passions only moments before in the gardens. Had been a witness to their stolen embrace.

As his voice grew louder and louder, extending each note to an impossible length, the singer's eyes locked into a stare. They were colorless from such a distance, lost beyond the white face paint and the billowing crown of ostrich feathers.

Is he looking at me? Louis wondered uncomfortably.

He glanced to Sabine. Her features appeared frozen in dread, eyes wide, lips slightly parted, while her fingers fell loosely across her skirts. Louis jerked his gaze back to the stage. Cristoforo looked at her! At his wife. The rogue!

Louis clutched Sabine's hand, finding it oddly cold.

"Sabine?"

Glass shattered beyond the stage curtain. The audience rustled. Cristoforo faltered. Sabine spun around to face Louis, her eyes wide with terror. "We must go!"

* * *

Bringing his performance to a shaky conclusion, Cristoforo
dashed for the stage curtain, parting the heavy velvet with a
kick of his toe. He nearly knocked the waiting contralto over
as he elbowed past her and had to juggle his steps to avoid the
shattered water goblet.

"That was you, Pietro?"

The boy looked up from the scatter of thin crystal. "Forgive
me, master. It is just sometimes I become so . . . caught up!
Enthralled!"

"Yes, yes, whatever. Pietro, she's here!" He dodged the
black mare upon whose back he was to sing his third act solo.
"We must hurry."

"But your duet?"

"Follow me!"

The concierge bowed grandly as Cristoforo appeared in the
lobby.

"Did you see a girl?"

"Yes, Signore, with a man." Fingering the hem of his blue
livery, the concierge nervously eyed the singer. "Signore, are
you not supposed to be—"

"Silence!" Cristoforo yanked the heavy headpiece off and
stuffed it into the concierge's arms, stirring the whiff of white
feathers to a fluffy cloud. "Come, Pietro."

Pietro was already at the door. Cristoforo raced behind him,
out into the street, his soft satin slippers soaking up the mud.
He slipped, but caught himself against the stone facade of the
building before losing his balance. A maid tiptoeing along in
high wood pattens gasped and dropped her basket of flowers
at the sight of Cristoforo.

"Is that her?" Pietro asked of the tall, slim woman in violet
skirts who was hurrying away from the Opéra, her arm threaded
through a man's.

"Yes." Sudden dread coated Cristoforo's throat, threatening

to seal off forever the beautiful sound that he mined there. But there was a strange pleasure in having finally *seen* her. "Follow them."

"Yes." Pietro dashed across the mud, then halted abruptly and turned back. "Er, shall I . . . dispose of her?"

The singer pulled himself erect and released a great sigh, noticing with distaste that the maid ignored her spilled basket and stared at him with that ever-sickening adoring gaze. "No." Sabine Bassange was *his*. Not another soul would take that from him. "Follow them. Listen to their every word. Return with a full report."

With a confirming nod, Pietro dashed down the street and Cristoforo slunk against the wall of the Opéra. Ignoring the swooning wench who'd yet to jerk out of her frozen state, he pressed his fingers to his forehead. But the wretched pain was not there. And if truth be confronted, Cristoforo had to admit that this night had been a rather good one. Why, just before taking the stage he'd clung to a white prop column as a now-familiar pleasure had coursed through his body.

"What has become of you, my mindless, mad Sabine? You walk the streets of Paris dressed in fine silks and on the arm of a rogue. And suddenly my nights are filled with pleasures beyond my belief. This is not you."

You must never tell. It is what I've dreamed of for years, Sabine. Please, keep it a secret.

You'll not take my son!

Fairy light, fairy bright, who shall be my love tonight . . .

The hum of her inner voices taunted and tore at her rational thoughts so that Sabine found it impossible to do little other than follow Louis. Thank God he held her hand, or she might have begun to wander.

Shall we dance? The sun is high and so are my spirits. One last dance before I must leave.

Yes, to dance . . .

The compulsion struck without warning.

Sabine yanked her hand away from Louis's and twirled away in a graceful spin. The cobbles were slick and rank beneath her soft slippers, but she did not care. The motion, the freeness, obliterated the confusion in her mind, dimming the voices so that they were bearable.

"Sabine!"

"I'll never tell, Christophe, I promise," she singsonged.

"Sabine." Louis caught his wife before she spun right into the paned glass window of a pastry shop that boasted glazed fruit swimming in a delicate cream sea. He huddled her tight in his embrace, feeling at first the tension stiffen her body. "It's Louis," he whispered, sensing he'd lost her once again. "I am with you, Sabine. Sabine?"

Finally he felt her body relax and melt into his. A dreamy smile brought the brightness back to her eyes. "Kiss me, Louis."

He wasn't sure where her mind resided at the moment. But a kiss always brought Sabine over to his side.

They kissed beneath the creaking tin sign of an apothecary shop, completely deaf and blind to the evening crowd that infested every inch of street. The street was barely wide enough for two carriages to pass side by side, and not a few were haggling and yelling to make way. The bustle of carriages lightened the darkness, for on each one dangled a glass-enclosed light or two, one to either side of the driver. The intermittent light show captured diamonds laced around sausage necks and made them sparkle in fleeting glimpses. A cloud of powdered wigs bounced and floated past.

He'd rescued her. She was his again, clutching his body tight to hers as their passions teased one another to quick arousal.

But Louis's mind was not totally at ease. Deep in the throes of his wife's kiss, Louis could not understand why Sabine had insisted they leave so quickly. Had the capon's seductive stare frightened her? Or was it something more? Something that only her tortured mind could ever understand.

Something had pushed her into the darkness again.

Louis wanted only to whisk Sabine back to their room, strip her naked, and make love to her for the rest of the night until the dawn shone its pink fingers of light across their sated bodies. For when it was only the two of them, he knew that she was safe from the madness that tormented her. But that could not happen until his worries were calmed.

"What was it that frightened you, fairy angel?"

"It's ... nothing," she whispered against his lips. "My mind was wandering. You know how it does wander."

Her hesitation caused Louis to wonder. Had she just told an untruth? But that was unlike her. She'd been so honest about her tears earlier. "Look at me, Sabine." When she was unable to meet his gaze for more than a brief second, Louis grew even more uneasy. "You must tell me everything. You know you can trust me."

"I do, Louis."

"Then why do I feel as though you are not telling me the entire truth?"

She looked away, over his shoulder. "You must never tell," she whispered in a faraway voice.

"What did you say? Tell what? What secret is it that haunts your mind, Sabine? Tell me," Louis pleaded. He felt so close. So close to reaching that inner part of Sabine that refused to show itself, that cowered in the darkness in a vain attempt to protect her. "Trust me enough to share whatever it is that troubles you. We can work this out. Together."

"No." She shook her head and crossed her arms over her stomach. "I promised."

"Promised? But who?"

At her silence, Louis released a frustrated breath. The key to erasing his wife's torment dangled so close. Yet still so unreachable. "Very well. But answer me this. Does it have something to do with the singer? The way he looked at you, Sabine. I—''

Sabine suddenly spun into a dancing circle, her path weaving her through the crowd of people and into a clearing in the center of the street.

"Not now," he barely whispered. "What has happened to reverse your recovery, my love?" As he pushed his way past a red-frocked dandy and his overstuffed paramour, Louis spied the carriage rumbling at a pace too fast for the thick traffic, its urgency forcing the finely dressed crowd to part. It was headed right for Sabine, who was quite oblivious, lost in her dance.

"Make way!" a mud-spattered footman who preceded the carriage yelled as his lantern dangled precariously from the end of a long wooden pole. "Make way!"

Louis dashed into the street. Instead of grabbing, he had time enough only to push his wife. His hands slipped over her satin dress like water over stones. He heard the horse's frightened whinny. Felt the sharp, jabbing hooves against his side and shoulders. The force of impact sent him flying, parting the crowd. Blackness took his sight as his head smashed into the stone facade of the apothecary shop.

"Louis!" Sabine cried, and raced for her motionless husband.

CHAPTER SIXTEEN

"We have sacrificed much, have we not, Sabine?"

The nine-year-old child that Cristoforo had kept secreted away so safely deep within now clawed to the surface with screaming vengeance.

"No, Papa, run!"

"Silence, you miserable little rat," barked the whiskey-laced voice. A voice possessed by the biggest, ugliest man Christophe Bassange had ever seen. "Get inside the carriage."

Christophe lost his scream as it was smothered beneath a thick wool blanket pressed to his face. He struggled against his captor's manacling grasp, but his weak child limbs soon gave up and he began to sob into the scratchy wool.

What he had seen!

Grand-père had promised that Papa and Mama were pleased he was going to Naples. There he would perfect his vocal skills at the Sant'Onofre *conservatorio,* studying under one of Italy's greatest teachers, Antonio Bernacchi. He would be happy and never want for another thing. *Grand-père* had said so! "Do not worry about your papa and mama. You go, Christophe, make me very proud of you. I will follow soon.''

But Papa . . .

Images of Papa, begging on his knees. ''You cannot take my only son away from me!'' And then the blinding flash of steel and sprays of red, gushing blood.

''Master?''

Cristoforo released the crumpled velvet drapes with a sigh. A fringe of scarlet brushed across his cheek. He pressed tension-wrought fingers to his forehead. But the images were already gone. Fighting his way back from the vicious memories had become easier over the years. As simple as a sigh or a refused cup of chocolate. ''You let them go?''

''I was not told to detain them.''

''That is correct, Pietro. What did you learn?''

''Nothing. Though she did kiss him more than a few times.''

''Really.'' Cristoforo wondered what de Lavarac was up to. Kissing a lunatic? He knew she was mad. Both brothers knew. L'Argent had said as much. Monsieur de Lavarac's intentions—sick as they may be—were lost on the idiot. She did not understand. She *couldn't.*

A shock of red fire coursed over his forehead, streaking from temple to temple. Cristoforo clutched at the pain, but by the time his hand touched his face, the torment had left. So sudden. So vexing. But he sensed it an odd prelude to . . . something.

''The man was struck by a carriage.''

''You don't say.'' So that was it. But why was *he* feeling the pain?

''I'm not sure how badly he was injured. The girl remains unharmed.''

''Of course.''

Sinking into an overstuffed day chaise, Cristoforo closed his eyes and let his head fall into the cushioning feather pillow Pietro had fluffed for him. He hadn't had a bad headache for days. Though he could still sense her presence. Dark and cool, yet at the same time enticingly tempting in its elusiveness, almost seductive.

And now these sharp jabs in his head. She was suffering. Somehow.

He squeezed his fingernails into his fleshy palm, forcing himself to feel a tangible pain. "You'll not seduce me into your tainted clutches, madwoman. I am damned while you walk the earth free. I never know when your hideous mind will connect with mine and bring me to my knees. And yet . . ."

There was always the lingering question of whether she felt his pains and joys too. He had no way of knowing. But why should she not? They had always had the ability to sense each other's thoughts. Sometimes they would finish the other's sentence. Or when one was sad or lost, the other would come, as if called. Sabine had even once cried out while playing in the meadows, only to find Christophe had cut his ankle on a sharp stone while carrying in firewood.

They had relished their magical connection. They'd never once told Mama or Papa, keeping it as a wonderful secret that would bind them forever.

But the childlike wonder was long gone. Hardened and honed to be the perfect vocal instrument by severe teachers and endless days and nights of practice, practice, and yet still more practice, Cristoforo had lost all feeling for the crazy wretch who tormented his life even when he was as far away as Naples. She was nothing to him but a threat to his art; he could not perform without the fear of failure as he stepped on the stage each night. For her wicked sorcery struck without warning.

And now de Lavarac had been injured. When it should have been her.

"Forgive me, Sabine," Cristoforo whispered. "But you must die—aaah!"

"Master?" Pietro rushed to catch him before the pain wrenched him out of his chair to the floor.

"It is like fiery blades. . . ." Cristoforo gasped as he fell into the boy's arms. His body convulsed, fighting against the unseen army of devils that marched up and down his temples, thrusting and poking with their angry spears. "Help me . . . ice, Pietro! Run quickly. Take my purse. Must . . . put . . . out this fire!"

"He has not moved since last night," the surgeon explained to Henri. "I've finally been able to force a few restoratives down his throat. They should reestablish the equilibrium between the humors. I hope. If not, I'll bleed him again."

After receiving Louis's letter describing his marriage to Sabine, Henri had hastened to Paris. What madness! For his brother to actually vow before God that he would serve and love such a damaged human being? While for one brief moment Henri had considered the benefits of his brother marrying such vast amounts of money—an heiress, she was—that had been only a foolish fancy. The de Lavaracs were well off enough without polluting the bloodline for a few tarnished coins.

Besides, was it even legal for a man to marry one such as she?

What a further shock to learn that his brother lay in the infested halls of the Hôtel-Dieu, motionless, struggling for life.

"He took a blow to the head. The swelling has gone down some. I've been bleeding him. Only time will tell." The physician gave a helpless shrug.

From his black clothes Henri presumed he was a doctor. One could not be sure in this hospital. Not too many in the medical profession graced these filthy halls.

"What of the girl?" Henri hadn't seen Sabine. Was it too much to hope that she'd been lost in the confusion?

The doctor's brows drew to his nose. "She's in there with him. A curious one, she is. Hasn't spoken a word since arriving. I got no more than your brother's name from her. Just sits there, holding his hand, staring into space. I suppose it must be a shock. Especially for one newly wed. Oh, she did tell me that too.''

Newlyweds. Henri's rage curled his fingers into tight fists. She was to blame for this. Should have never happened. If the girl had not accompanied Louis to Paris, perhaps he might not be lying near death right now. Her presence had blinded Louis since the first day she arrived. And his blindness had brought upon his injury. ''Might I see him?''

''Of course.''

Down the dirty halls Henri followed the black-robed doctor. If only Louis had been brought to the Hôtel des Invalides. The military hospital was so much cleaner and more modern.

As they entered a great room filled from wall to wall with roped beds separated by draped sheets, a pungent, acid odor blasted Henri's senses. He fumbled for his handkerchief and pressed it to his nose. Sunken eyes stared up at him as he walked by. Some beds held two figures, some three if they were children. Thin windows, set high into the walls, were all sealed tightly, the glass stained a foggy yellow.

At the very far corner they came to a stop. The late afternoon sun barely whispered across the foot of the bed, allowing cold darkness to seep across the walls and floor and the fetid air. At least only one figure lay on the narrow bed.

''I'll leave you.'' The doctor turned and went, his shoes pounding echoes across the floorboards.

Henri swallowed. He was thankful for the poor light, for he could not bear to see his brother in pain. The night he'd found Louis beneath the gnarled elm at the edge of the vineyards, the blood flowing from his wrists, had brought him to his knees. His own flesh and blood. It was not right. He had never been one to be overly emotional. Janette had seen him cry only once, the moment their child had died. And he had not cried since, even standing at her graveside; it seemed he had no more tears. But Louis's attempted suicide was a terrible blow. He had not realized Louis was in such despair after his return from duty. Perhaps he should have been more understanding.

A hot burn simmered beneath Henri's heart. Was this all his fault?

Thinning linens, stained with blood, draped Louis's motionless figure. His fancy dress shirt lay across the end of the bed, one sleeve stained with blackened blood, the hem tattered and crusted with mud.

No, it was *her* fault.

"Pitiful." Henri's comment was not directed toward the silent invalid lying in the bed, his eyelids blackened and his head bandaged. No, it was the soulless creature who sat next to him, her pale fingers holding a death grip on Louis's immobile hand. She sat at his side, her body erect, her violet skirts splashed with dried Paris mud and the visible tips of her satin shoes covered with more of the abundant slop.

Made uneasy by her wide-eyed, vacant stare, Henri approached his brother with the utmost care. Sabine did not even acknowledge his presence. Though he couldn't be sure that she wouldn't jump into some insane fit if prompted.

Squinting, Henri observed his brother's rising chest, then he pressed his flat palm over Louis's heart. "His breathing is good," Henri whispered, trying to assure himself.

When he pulled the flimsy separating curtain back and away, hazy light crept across Louis's face and dust motes became visible everywhere. Henri was able to see that Louis's lips were cracked and colored a deep purple, a dried trail of spittle twisting down his neck. "Damn, I'd like to know who the hell owned that carriage. Why did he not see?"

Of course Henri knew that it had to have been a rich man's carriage. Nor would the owner have given a backward glance to the destruction left in his path. The beau monde simply hadn't a care for the common man.

His attention veered toward the mute wraith sitting not two

feet from him. He knew exactly why Louis had not seen his impending doom. *"Madame* de Lavarac, eh?"

Surely the lunatic had witnessed the accident. Determined not to let her get by without an explanation, Henri knelt before Sabine and placed his palms on her lap. The faint whiff of expensive perfume told him Louis had been generous to a fault with the wench. It disgusted him to know that his brother could be so foolish. Did he think to cure the madness that held her eyes wide? What a fool to marry her!

If he could do nothing else, something would have to be done to right this terrible mistake. For Louis's sake.

"Sabine?" Having watched Louis many times, Henri knew that he had to make eye contact to get anywhere with the mindless simpleton. "Look at me, lunatic."

A touch to her cheek startled her from her frozen state. Eyes that were on occasion brilliant jewels were now clouded with a haze as foggy as the stifling air. Her mouth fell open and a miserable groan sifted over her parched lips.

"Sabine, do you know who I am?"

"Drag—Henri," came her meek answer.

"Good." He flashed a genial smile, knowing that he must be cordial to her. He must establish a rapport.

Her hair was tangled over her left ear, a scarlet ribbon hanging by a few strands of her golden locks. The circles beneath her eyes cut deep and black. Henri placed an experimental hand to her hair. So soft. It reminded him of Janette.

No, do not even begin to compare the two!

"Why did he not see?"

Sabine turned her blank gaze on him. Utter emptiness. Not even a flicker of compassion or sadness in her wide eyes. But still, she had recognized him. She was playing. Yes, hiding behind her affliction.

Henri quirked a dark brow, his inner anger roiling into a fierce storm. But he would not unleash the rains. This situation required a much lighter hand.

"Sabine." Her hand was cold, so icy. Like her stare. "You've been through so much. You'll be lying in a hospital bed yourself if you do not rest."

"No," she whispered. "Louis—"

"Will recover." He hoped. Henri glanced to his brother. He wanted desperately to lift Louis into his arms and carry him outside. Into the light and fresh air. To hold him close and provide the healing touch he so needed. But alas, he knew not how to begin to connect with his brother, to renew the close bonds of brotherhood they'd once had.

He would help Louis. In his own way.

"Louis needs time to rest. And so do you, Sabine. Have you slept? You look a fright. Poor girl." He drew out the words in false sympathy.

"I mustn't leave him," she whispered, clutching a wedge of material from Henri's brocade frock coat between her pale fingers. "We promised to always be together. I cannot leave, Henri. Louis needs me."

"Oh, but just for a little while, Sabine. A rest and perhaps a nice bath to refresh yourself. And then you may return. I . . . hmm . . . I have already secured a room for you at a nearby . . . er, inn. Yes. And you need to eat."

"No."

"Now, you mustn't argue, Sabine. You can be of no good to your *husband* in your state." Henri sucked on the inside of his cheek. How he hated condescending to this creature. Her inheritance would be tainted with Louis's blood. She was the cause of Louis's condition. "Just a few hours' rest. I promise I will return to bring you back to my brother's side." He smoothed the back of his palm across her cheek as he'd witnessed Louis do many times before. "Be a good girl now, Sabine."

"You promise?"

All he could manage was a mute nod.

"I am rather tired."

"And hungry, I'm sure," Henri offered.

"Yes, but—"

She resisted his direction. Henri lifted her hand from her mud-spattered lap. The fingers were long and narrow. *Just like Janette's.* His heart stuttered inside his ribs. "Louis would understand, Sabine. I promise you, it will be no more than a few hours. All right?"

"Very well." She stood and gazed over Louis's helpless body.

Henri stood, waiting, resisting the urge to yank her by the arm and pull her outside. But he could not have her suspect.

He watched with restrained impatience as Sabine opened her fist over Louis's chest. A short, thin twig fell to the stained linen. "Never farther than a heartbeat away," she whispered, then turned and accepted Henri's outstretched hand.

The ride to the Jardin des Plantes quarter took less than ten minutes. Henri directed the carriage driver to stop just ahead. As they wobbled past the public herb gardens, Henri drew in the delicious scent of crimson-berried yews and the arresting shock of the acrid odor of monkey. The beasts had been imported from India, he had heard. For purposes of studying them in relation to man. Monkeys and men? What nonsense!

But no more foolish than the mess Louis had involved himself in.

Surprised at the lunatic's normalcy during the short ride, Henri had a moment of soul-searching. Was he doing the right thing? This was now his brother's wife. If he were like any other married man, Louis had consummated his vows already. The thought of his brother making love to this woman—who was by no means ugly or disfigured . . .

Ah, but her mind was far more disfigured than even the most hideous of cripples.

Pray God Louis had not had relations with her. For what would become of a child that resulted from their union? Surely it would be as tainted as the mother?

A glance at the frail specimen sitting across from him found Sabine silent, her mud- and bloodstained skirts spread carelessly across Henri's knees. A surge of anger scratched inside his throat. *Louis's blood. His* flesh and blood. Not hers. Never would she have a place in the de Lavarac family. Never!

Could Louis forgive him for what he must do?

He must. Louis was too blinded by a pretty virgin to see things clearly.

If Louis questioned his wife's absence, Henri would simply tell him he had never seen her. She must have become lost in the confusion after the accident. The surgeon would agree if he paid him well enough. And should Louis press for a search to be mounted, Henri would, well, he would worry about that later.

Though he'd never lied to his brother in all his years, *this* lie was necessary.

Sabine patted a palm over her messy hair and gave Henri a sheepish smile.

"A little rest will take care of those horrendous circles beneath your eyes."

She touched the flesh beneath her eyes, obviously unaware of how bedraggled she looked. Rather like a child come in from a day's hard play, Henri mused. Rosy-cheeked and tousled hair, save the haunted look in her eyes.

The carriage stopped and Henri open the half-door, which emitted a whining creak. He stepped down, his boots crushing the pebbles on the ground. "Come now."

Her hand was like a child's, so fragile, Henri felt sure he could crush her bones with one sure squeeze. She stepped down from the carriage and, brushing her hair from her face, looked over the building before them. Hôpital de la Salpêtrière. Once an old powder factory used in making explosives, Louis XIV founded the hospital to help sick and socially disadvantaged women. The institution also took in the insane.

The great domed chapel sat like a sharp-edged cap upon the

sterile and ugly building. Evening shadows fell across the narrow flower gardens that led parallel lines up to the entrance steps. The faint odor of ripe alcohol, like wine gone bad, touched Henri's nose. Filth disguised by a few sprays of colorful flowers and a well-manicured lawn, that's all it was.

And—if he turned a blind eye—Henri could allow himself to see only the surface.

Running the knuckles of his loose fist down her back, Henri gently coaxed Sabine forward.

She balked, freezing at the edge of the lawn. "This is not an inn."

Henri pressed his flat palms to her shoulders, readying for any sort of insane reaction. Already she was so resistant to moving forward that he found himself pushing just to hold her upright.

"What is this place?" She turned to him, her eyes flashing wide. "There are bars on the windows, Henri. No! You cannot do this. Louis! He is my husband."

An attendant from the institution appeared on the steps. Henri saw that he was eager to assist. "Grab hold of her!"

She would receive the care she so desperately needed here, he reassured himself silently. This was best for all. Henri released Sabine into the capable hands of the attendant.

A bitter streak of guilt weakened Henri's resolve for a moment as he watched the attendant secure Sabine's arms from behind. The violet silk of her dress tore at the shoulder as she jerked and twitched, the sound like a sword ripping the muscles of Henri's heart.

Her horrid lunatic gaze fixed on him as her struggles and screams brought out two more attendants. "We'll take care of things," one assured. "The wench will be restrained. Jean-Luc will go over admissions with you."

Henri swallowed. "Good."

Sabine's screams were abruptly muffled by a hand to her mouth. One man held her legs while another helped lift her by the shoulders. The last thing Henri saw of his brother's wife before they carried her into the hospital were her raging violet eyes. No longer hazed by madness. Wild. Violent.

Knowing.

" 'Tis for the best," he muttered, choking down a breath-stopping gulp. He pressed a hand to his thudding heart. "I must believe that."

CHAPTER SEVENTEEN

L'Argent had reported that Monsieur de Lavarac stopped by his office just yesterday afternoon. More toward evening, he'd quickly corrected himself. And no, the *notaire* had given him no information other than to assure the man that he still searched for the beneficiary.

As for seeing him later that evening, l'Argent could not recall. He'd attended the opera, had adored Cristoforo's performance—of course—but he couldn't remember if he had seen the man accompanied by a woman in lavender skirts.

Cristoforo knew Paris was a big city, and the pockmarked *notaire* was so ill sighted, he could not see his own thumb held before his nose. Pietro's search for Sabine and Louis also turned up nothing. It was as if they were right beneath his thumb but cloaked in an elusive glamour.

Cristoforo instructed both men to check the local hospitals. If de Lavarac really had been injured, then surely he could be found. As for Sabine, well, it seemed wherever de Lavarac went, she was not far behind.

Resigned to wait until he heard some news, Cristoforo dug out the satchel of legal papers he'd held since his thirteenth birthday. A gift from *Grand-père*. But after settling onto the crimson damask day chaise, Cristoforo did not even bother to untie the scrolled papers. He knew every exact word.

A boy so young could have never imagined the magnitude of the deal he had agreed to. To never want for another thing. To travel to Italy. To be granted the fine schooling Sant'Onofre offered so that he may become a master at his craft and live off the music he so loved.

Yet the allowance of five percent of all earnings had proved to be far less than his child's mind could have imagined. *La dolce vita* it was not.

It was not long after that he grew to hate his flaxen-haired sister. For the connection between their minds had never been the same since that humid day in August when the Italian bravos had come to take Christophe Bassange away from his family forever.

His mind shifted to the odd evening he had spent in a dark wine cellar in Italy with his kidnappers. They'd poured him pale wine and treated him quite gently. Frightened, Christophe had gratefully accepted the wine and drank heartily, finding its heavy bite washed over the ugly horrors that taunted his mind. When he'd reached the point of inebriation, the proffered milk bath had seemed too luxurious to pass up.

To his dying day, Cristoforo would never forget the gushing fountain of red that spilled up to the surface of white water. He'd felt no pain, so soused he was. But the realization of his fate had hit hard days later.

Castrato. The whispers filled the halls of the *conservatorio,* chilling the blood in his veins. One of *those* boys. One to be ridiculed and gossiped about and shunned by child and adult alike. One of the *evirati,* possessed and kept in a gilded cage like a wingless songbird. Prized only by the music teachers.

The Church would not even acknowledge publicly that the knife had ever been used to create one of their angels.

"It should all be mine," Cristoforo muttered as he tapped the coiled will against his forehead. "You were very clever, *Grand-père,* having all my earnings transferred to an account in your name. Keeps it out of the hands of the lecherous accountants and Italian lawyers and teachers, you said. Sounded good and well at the time. Yet now you give half to that miserable bitch whose madness will be my end. Well, I shall not allow that to happen."

Cristoforo's long fingers curled around the will. "The missing heir will appear."

He'd thought that forcing l'Argent to keep his name a secret for a week would give him enough time to remedy his distress. But she'd slipped from his grasp. Now no one knew of her whereabouts.

But Cristoforo knew she was here. Still alive. In Paris. So close.

"Pietro! Ready my cabriolet, we must go see l'Argent. He must have found the girl by now."

The liquid that spilled over his lips was barely tepid. It tasted horrible. Like water-drenched lamb that had been boiled in a dirty pot for days. Disgusting. But it was sustenance. And though his mind wasn't clear enough to do anything beyond swallow, Louis's body sensed what it needed and acted of its own volition.

He struggled to open his eyes. Just one eyelid. But it seemed there were great weights holding them tightly shut.

Another spoonful of liquid. Well, at least it wet his dry throat.

Louis tried to determine what exactly was going on beside the fact that he was being fed by someone he could not see or hear. Every portion of his body ached in ways he'd never imagined possible. While battle wounds flared mad red for a brief time only to settle to a dull ache, this pain was entirely different. His body felt numb, like sleep tingled just beneath the surface, holding him frozen to some hard, flat object he could not discern. And to make matters a thousandfold worse, a gripping ache cut into his side. Louis felt as if someone had tried to weave a basket with his ribs.

And then there was the pulsing mass atop his neck. It felt ten times too large for his eyes. As if, should he try to stand, the mere weight of his oversized head would topple him to the ground. Sounds were muffled in his left ear. Every time he moved his head, a muted rustling, as though wads of linen had been stuffed in his ear, frightened him.

Another spoonful of liquid passed over his lips. He could not judge the contents of the broth by its faint smell. But there was a distinct odor somewhere. More like urine and rot, he thought. Must be his surroundings. Pray God, let it be his surroundings.

His hearing wasn't clear, nor did he feel he could speak, but he gradually began to recall what had happened.

Sabine . . . ah, Sabine. Spinning in her mindless dance in the middle of a busy Paris street. Why she'd suddenly slipped into the grasp of madness when he'd felt that they had finally come to the brink of her recovery he would never know. The streets were ill lit, but all had seen and heard the oncoming squeals of destiny. He'd dashed into the carriage's path and pushed her out of the way.

He had, hadn't he? Hopefully. Of course he had. That could be the only reason he lay in such a state. The sting of the horse's hooves as they had kicked and stomped his body returned to bite his aching side.

Louis winced and spit up broth.

"Monsieur! Pardon me, is that too much?"

Ah, a soft, tender voice. Sabine. So she was not hurt. Thank God.

The memory of their marriage vows spoken beneath the

showering rose petals seemed unreal. As untouchable as fairy wings. As if he stood in the clutches of the topiary dragon and could only watch his nuptials from a distance.

But now memories of losing himself inside her, nuzzled tight by her womanhood, were so vivid. The sweet perfume of her body was like wax to his flame, melting into his senses. They'd stolen a moment of pure bliss in the gardens. Ah . . . So safe, so loved, she made him feel. Persimmons, candle flames, and Sabine's sweet kisses . . .

She was here. By his side. His fairy angel.

"Sa—"

"You mustn't speak, Monsieur. You need to rest. Would you like more broth? Or have you had enough?"

No, she did not speak like Sabine. Too harsh her voice. Where is Sabine?

Louis jogged his tongue back and forth inside his mouth. Everything felt swollen, unusable, damaged.

Something was missing. A presence.

"Sabine," he was finally able to whisper in the weakest breath.

"No, no, Monsieur. I am Béatrice.

"Where—"

"I'll leave you to rest. I'll return to change your dressings in a short while. Oh, what is this? So you've had a visitor, eh?"

Louis saw through the thin slit of his eyelids the fuzzy image of something red, maybe orange—it was just too hard to focus—dangling before him. It took all his effort to squeeze his eyes tight and pop one eyelid open. A flash of scarlet ribbon. *Will you thread this through my hair?*

She *had* been here. Left behind a trace of her essence in the vivid memories that caressed his aching mind.

But where is she now? And where exactly was *here?*

"I could use this—"

"No!" He was able to force out in an exhausted breath.

Béatrice jumped. "Forgive me, monsieur. Here. I shall leave it with you."

He felt the soft tickle of the ribbon dance across the base of his palm as she placed it in his hand and curled his fingers closed over it. And then he noticed the sharp scrap of something else across his fingers. Something lay in his lap. He wobbled his forefinger over the hard cylindrical surface.

"Oh, that," the woman said. "I shall remove that for you, Monsieur." Louis felt something rough scrape across his knuckles and then saw the stick in the woman's fingers. "I don't know why it wasn't removed immediately. Looks like you've brought part of the forest in with you!"

"No!" The muscles in his left arm stretched and screamed as he shot his hand up to reach for the precious item. "M-mine."

Béatrice's eyes narrowed and her mouth twisted up on one side. "If you insist." The woman placed the stick in his hand and curled his fingers tight around it, enveloping ribbon and branch together. "Must have taken a blow to the head, poor fellow."

Louis squeezed his fist, sensing that his lack of strength threatened no damage to the fragile stick. Visions of watching his fairy angel work fastidiously at sizing her twigs just so danced across his vision with the swiftness of a fall breeze.

That was what was missing. The magic of her presence.

"Need . . . you . . ."

On his return visit, Louis was sleeping. Henri hadn't wished him woken, for he knew his brother needed rest to recover.

They would keep watch over Louis and notify him as soon as any changes occurred. They had better. Henri paid Béatrice and the attending physician well enough. A necessity unless he wished his brother virtually ignored. The hospitals in Paris were notorious for allowing patients to die without so much as a care. Three silver écus, nearly an entire week's wages, had seemed to capture the attendants' attention. Henri made sure Béatrice knew which inn he stayed at. She would contact him should Louis show sudden signs of improvement, or should a priest need be brought.

With nothing more he could do for his brother, Henri reluctantly left the stifling halls of the Hôtel-Dieu. Hell, he wasn't reluctant. He was damn glad to be on the opposite side of the hospital walls. Sickness and death did nothing but stir up memories best left buried.

The afternoon was full and humid, coaxing the sweat down Henri's face in dirty streams. The sun was high and bright, a perfect day for the vines. The dark grapes would drink in the sun's heat and become sweet and full.

Henri swiped his arm across his forehead and blew a strand of sweat-drenched hair from his nose, his mind filled with more than mere concern over the vines.

Only a coldhearted man could have done such a thing. You took his own wife away from him. Should he recover, he'll never find her, thanks to you.

Regret's voice spoke louder and louder as the day progressed. Henri tossed four sous onto the tavern bar located below his room and swigged down the last of his summer-hot ale.

What was it about the lunatic and her strange attraction?

Louis had never known a true love, had always gone cow-eyed over any lovely girl who would give him the time of day. It wasn't a surprise that he'd become so attached to a girl as pretty as Sabine.

Pretty? Henri smirked, and swiped the back of his shirt-sleeve across his lips. Yes, pretty. But could his brother not see through the beautiful facade to the inner ugliness?

She would never take a turn for the better. No matter how much Louis felt his presence worked to change her. Madness was an incurable malady that demanded constant medical care.

The kind of care Sabine would now get at Salpêtrière, Henri reassured himself.

But his conscience was not so sure.

The place is a festering hellhole. Far worse than the miserable conditions at the Hôtel-Dieu. You heard the disembodied screams echoing from behind the stone walls as you signed your name to her admissions form. You almost gagged at the wretched smell. Her mind will grow worse. 'Tis no place for such a gentle soul. You know it!

"Forgive me, brother," Henri muttered to himself, and then ordered his sixth tankard of ale.

CHAPTER EIGHTEEN

"I don't believe you."

"What do you think, I've hidden the girl away somewhere? And to what advantage would that be?"

"I don't know." Cristoforo clenched his fingers around his purse strings, checking to be sure they were attached tight to his shirt ties. He'd be damned if he would allow this jellyfish of a man to tell him what to do anymore. "You lawyers are all alike. You wrote this contract! It was you who saw to it my life's wages would not be mine."

"At the vicomte's request."

"Yes, well—" Stating the obvious did not help. Cristoforo shrugged both hands back through his hair, pressing hard against his skull. He had no idea what he could do to gain control of his own finances. For l'Argent insisted that until the girl received a complete medical examination—if and when she was found—and was proved to be incapable of handling her own finances, he would not allow Cristoforo to garner control of his money. Why, oh, why, had the old man done such a horrid thing?

"You did sign the papers."

"I was but a child!" Cristoforo pressed his fingers to his aching temple. The pain was dull, but it had been incessant for days now. The girl was in a state of constant torment. Why, he knew not. "I don't know what to believe anymore. You lie!"

"Do not falsely accuse me! I told you the truth when I said de Lavarac came to me two days ago, but I've not seen him or the girl since. I wish I did know where she is. You are aware that I do not receive my fee until she is found and all the papers are signed?"

Cristoforo shrugged. Fee? *Diavolo!* He could hardly believe by the expensive Dresden figurines that graced his office and the fine Italian leather of his boots that l'Argent had not been dipping into his funds for all these years.

"It would be best if we worked together," l'Argent said. "Perhaps I should alert the guard."

"No! I don't want to involve the law. In case she were to be found dead—"

"Dead?"

Realizing his slip, Cristoforo drew his arms tight across his chest, more as a comfort than defense against the sloe-eyed *notaire*. "We don't know this man. He may . . . harm her."

"He seemed to me to be genuinely concerned about her. And if he's injured—"

"Perhaps concerned about her money!" Cristoforo raged. "Which is really *my* money. Is there no one who does not want a piece of me? Must I feed the masses in return for my fame? Is that it?"

"*Sst, sst.*"

"So you say! " Cristoforo dove at l'Argent and stabbed a finger into the man's chest. "I want the papers prepared this day, do you understand? I'll not give you or anyone else one single day longer to spend my money.''

"But we need the girl's signat—''

"Forge it!''

L'Argent squeaked out a breath as Cristoforo grabbed and twisted the tied knot of lace at his neck. How he'd love to keep twisting until the man's face turned blue. ''Do you understand me, little rat?''

L'Argent shook his head rapidly. He gasped for air, his skin flushing to a deep maroon. Just a minute more and he felt sure blue would come. But until he found the girl and got his hands on his money, he needed this man.

The *notaire* crumpled to the floor at Cristoforo's red-heeled shoes, wheezing in the stale office air. ''I'll send Pietro for my first withdrawal in the morning.''

Long, hair-thin legs skittered down the wall, a wall stained and smudged with substances too foul to imagine. The constant odor seemed only to increase in intensity as the heat of the day warmed the stone walls. But the spider did not seem to mind.

Curling her legs tight to her body, Sabine began to rock back and forth. Her only companion in this chamber of horrors made a zigzagging escape toward the barred window at the top of the cell wall. A window she was unable to reach. And even if she could, it was barely the size of her head. Not large enough to look out and see the sky. Not even large enough to let in fresh air, it would seem.

A loud, groaning male voice echoed down the hallway outside Sabine's cell. Close behind that came the hair-raising shriek of another. Always the noise. Chains clanking against the floor. Iron doors creaking and slamming. Idiotic laughter. Frightening her. Crushing her sanity.

This was not the kind sanctuary the gruff attendants had described as they'd carried her inside the walls, kicking and screaming. *You shall receive the help you need. Relax, we mean you no harm.*

Harm? Of course they meant her no harm, they also meant her no attention, no care or compassion. They'd thrown her to the cold stone floor and clanged the iron bars of her cell door shut. Sabine had lain there listening to the hideous echoes of their laughter until finally the deep-throated glee had blended into the cries for mercy surrounding her on all sides.

This isolation would prove far worse than the years she'd spent alone with only her *grand-pére* growing gradually blind and deaf. At least at the castle she'd had her freedom. At any given moment she could dash out into the meadow and spin until she lost herself in the joy of the day.

But not here. Here the rotting straw beneath her bare feet squished with every step and worked its way between her toes. Here her view of the sky was only a tiny square of azure. Here her senses were assaulted by sounds of pain and calamity and violence. Here she would not survive.

Unless . . .

Help me . . .

Closing her eyes, Sabine reached deep within. She curled a mental grasp about the darkness—so familiar and always there—knocking, pleading for entrance. Rescue me, she screamed to the shadows. Cover me with your numbing pain. Anything to escape this nightmare.

"You are looking a trifle better, despite lying in this hell-hole."

Louis smirked at his brother. One of the few places on his body that did not hurt was his mouth. "You speak the truth of this place. Why was I not taken to the Hôtel des Invalides? It is much cleaner there. By God's green earth, I crave fresh air."

"I was not here at the time of the accident, or I would have arranged more suitable accommodations. The doctor said you must rest a few more days before attempting to go home,'' Henri said. "You've broken bones. Healing takes time.''

Yes, didn't it? Healing of many different wounds. The wounds on his wrists were closed over, almost smooth, but the mental healing had only recently begun. Thanks to Sabine.

Ah, precious Sabine. Her name traveled through Louis's mind on fairy wings, touching his senses with fleeting memories that grew paler by the day. Like the tears of joy she had cried in his arms, slowly they had evaporated, finally leaving nothing. He had to get Sabine back before the memories were lost forever.

"I know she was here,'' Louis snapped.

Jerked out of his study of the dried mud on his boot, Henri looked up. "Who?''

"My wife,'' Louis spat out. He held up the slip of dirtied red ribbon and the stick. "She was here. And now she is not. Where is she, Henri? She could be lost.''

"I . . . had no idea she was here.''

"You know that she was with me when I came to Paris!''

"Yes, yes, but I have not seen the luna—er, Mademoiselle—''

"My wife,'' Louis supplied. "You must have received my letter. Why else would you be in Paris?''

"Of course,'' Henri said, lowering his voice. "Your . . . wife. I do not know what to tell you, Louis. If our paths had crossed, I would have escorted her along with me. Have you questioned Béatrice? The physician?''

"He merely shrugs his shoulders. I do not trust the man. He is a charlatan. I've had this damned mustard plaster on my ribs for two days, which does nothing for the pain but distract me with its stench. She could be anywhere, Henri.''

"Yes, and in her state—''

"Her state was fine until—mon Dieu—'' The realization hit Louis with the force of a horse's kicking hoof. The last time he saw his wife she was in a state of madness, lost in her own little world. He hadn't seen her since. She could not return to lucidity without him. Even if she were found, no one would be able to understand her. "She must be so lost without me. Oh, Henri, she cannot survive by herself."

"You see, even you know the truth."

"Don't do this to me now, Henri." Louis's voice cracked, as did his heart. "I need your help."

Long seconds passed as Henri stood at the end of Louis's bed, tapping the rusted iron railing with his knuckles. Nervous, he seemed. But what could Henri possibly have to be nervous about? When he spoke, his voice was a husky whisper. "Perhaps . . . it was the capon."

"Capon?" Louis jerked his head in question. What the hell was he talking about?

"Signore Cristoforo. A castrato," Henri ground out through a tight jaw.

"A singer?" Louis drew up the corner of his lip. He tapped the end of the worn stick against his stubbled chin. The name was so familiar. "Cristoforo—yes, of course, we just saw him, at the Opéra—the evening of my accident. Yes, I remember. He looked at Sabine. So oddly. He frightened her." Damned castrato, if he had laid a hand on his Sabine! "But what does a singer have to do with my wife?"

"You do not know?"

"Know what? I have been a refugee from the world for days. Tell me, Henri. My wife is missing. If you have any clue as to where she is you tell me now!"

"Settle down. The more you move about, the longer you'll be consigned to rot in this place. I will explain everything. Though I'm not sure you'll want to hear. This Cristoforo, he came to the château days ago in search of Sabine."

Louis pushed himself forward in bed to rest his elbows on his thighs. A painful maneuver, but the stretching of his back muscles felt good. "He came to our home?"

"Yes, he arrived the eve you had left for Paris."

"But why?"

Louis searched Henri's eyes, shot through with red veins, waiting, wondering why he was so reluctant to explain. But finally—

"He is the missing heir. He had just been informed by l'Argent regarding the vicomte's death. He is . . ."

"What?"

"A relative. Or so he tells me."

A great suction worked below Louis's heart, draining him completely of his life's blood within a flash of a moment. He clenched his fist. This had been the one thing he'd prayed would never happen. That a relative would appear to wrest Sabine away from him forever.

The twig snapped. As did his heart.

"She has never told me of a relative."

"Perhaps she has kept him a secret for a purpose."

"Secret? Sabine would never keep a secret. She is far too good-hearted. She does not even know the meaning of a secret." Maybe . . .

"Or so you believe."

Louis recalled the words his wife had whispered outside the apothecary shop just before she'd spun into the streets. *You must never tell. I promised.*

Who? Who must she not tell? And what was it she held secreted away?

"Perhaps," Henri was continuing, "she thought to hide this relative from you so that she might stay with a man she feels will care for her."

"And how do you know he is her flesh and blood? Have you seen proof?"

"Only in his eyes," Henri reflected. "They are Sabine's."

Louis swallowed the sickening rise of bile that spiked up his throat. "Did you tell him that she is wed?" he managed to ask. "That I am her husband? I'm surprised he has not searched me out?"

"He is a very busy man. Singing for a king and all."

"Yet he has time enough to secret Sabine away! Does he not think that stealing my wife from under my very eyes would not cause me undue amounts of dread? Where is this singer?"

Henri shrugged. "He is to give a performance tonight at the palace for King Louis. You'll not have a chance to see him, Louis. You are far too weak to be paying social visits to anyone."

Louis swung his legs over the edge of the bed. His ribs squeezed like hot pincers. He gasped. "This will not be a social visit." He scanned the floor for his shirt, but saw only the discarded bed linens from last night and a black beetle crawling across the stained and wilted folds.

"I cannot allow this." Henri rushed over and placed his hand on Louis's shoulders. "You need rest, brother. The color is already draining from your face. You mustn't bother with this. I don't think it's anything to worry—"

"Worry?" Louis slapped his palm down over Henri's. He felt the muscles tense in his brother's hand. "You would keep me from my wife? When you know she needs constant attention, someone who understands her?"

"Of course not, I—"

Louis pulled the thin coverlet back and made to get up. "I must find her."

"No!" Henri ripped the shirt from Louis's hand and flung it back to the floor. "Cristoforo will take good care of her."

"But she is my wife! Sabine needs me. This man cannot just spirit her away and remove her from my life without so much as a by-your-leave!" Louis drew in a deep hissing breath, malice heating the embers of his growing vengeance. Pain was blissfully disguised by anger. "You do not care for Sabine's welfare, Henri. You have disavowed her presence in our home from the very day I brought her to live with us. You could not be more pleased."

"Nonsense!"

The curious stirrings of the patients around Louis's bed alerted both men to lower their voices. Henri leaned close to Louis's chest, laying his hands across him gently, but all the same staying. "I would never wish Sabine harm. I want only what is best for her. To see that she receives the proper care."

"Then help me." Louis gripped Henri's upper arm in a desperate lock. Conviction colored his words a bruising deep maroon. "I must leave. I need to find her. To find this Cristoforo."

"Let me look into it," Henri reassured his brother. "You lie still. Rest. I'll report back to you in the morn. I mean it, Louis. You'll do your wife no good if you're lying facedown in some sewer because you were too weak to hold yourself up."

Silence froze the air in an icy chill. The beetle touched the tip of Henri's boot with its hairlike feelers. A wave of dizziness curled through Louis's head. So easy it would be to close his eyes and sleep.

It seemed forever before Louis could mutter a few lackluster words. "Of course, you are right." Louis settled back into bed, the ropes groaning at his shift in weight. He pushed both palms roughly over his forehead and across his dirty hair. "But you'll speak to this Cristoforo tonight?"

"I shall do my best. Perhaps I can locate him before he arrives at the palace. You know I won't gain entrance there."

"Yes, yes."

"Monsieur, it is time for your brother to leave." Béatrice appeared at Louis's bedside, her flowing white novice robes stained with a slash of crimson at the hip. "You need your rest."

"So I've been told." Louis sunk into the bed, crossing his arms over his chest. "Very well. I trust you, Henri. You will not forget your promise?"

"Of course not."

Henri touched Béatrice's elbow and guided her around the curtain and down the hallway. "Perhaps he should be restrained,'' Henri suggested quietly. ''He's developed this insane notion that he wishes to leave. I shouldn't wish him to wander about foolishly. He does not know how weak he still is.''

''I understand, monsieur. Weakness tends to blind a man. He hasn't the strength he believes. I'll watch over him, I assure you. He'll not leave the Hôtel-Dieu tonight.''

''*Merci.*''

Henri reluctantly bade Louis adieu and left, his heels clicking in dull thuds down the hallway.

Weakness tends to blind a man. Henri flexed the muscles in his fisted hand. *I am not the weak one. It is Louis.*

He hoped.

CHAPTER NINETEEN

You like it here, do you not?

"Oh, yes, it is splendid. A heart could dance for eternity. Might I stay forever?"

Of course you may. Once one steps beyond reality, there is no turning back. You will be our guest forever, precious child. Enjoy yourself! Over there! You must dance with the fairies. And there! Don't forget to ride the unicorn, 'tis a dream come true.

"Oh, I won't. Everything is just so perfect."

She stopped at the edge of the meadow, a meadow brilliant in color and smell. Every flavor of the rainbow danced before her in enticing waves that caught the sunlight in brilliant gemstone flashes. Clean, fresh air draped her body in seductive perfume. The wings of a sapphire butterfly kissed her shoulder. Too good to be true.

A wistful frown turned her lips down. "But what of the darkness?"

What of it?

"I do so dread the visions." She pressed crossed hands to her breast. "It hurts me deep inside. It makes me scream and tear at my hair. Can you not stop it?"

There is simply no way. 'Tis your soul that is shadowed, child. You must accept the darkness. For without darkness there can never be the magical realm within which you have chosen to dwell.

She thought for a moment. "I cannot have this place without the horrors?"

Exactly. 'Tis far better than what the real world has to offer.

Sabine sighed and watched as her breath floated in shimmery pink waves across the sky, painting a delightful swirl above her head. "I suppose. But what of Louis?"

Louis?

"My husband? May I have Louis too?"

No. It is impossible. Stay here, child, forget about that man. He can only hurt you like—

"No! Not Louis. He loves me. His heart is kind and gentle. There is no other like him, no one who really knows me as he does. I want to be with him always."

Impossible.

"Impossible? But without Louis . . ."

The pain will subside. Seek protection in our arms, child. It is we who love you. We will never abandon you. Never . . .

"It was not he who left . . . oh dear God, I left him!"

Abandoned . . .

"No! It was I! I've betrayed my husband. We promised never to leave each other's side."

Then why are you here?

"I was frightened. Of the sounds, the screams . . . It was that man. The Dragon Lord, he led me away. Oh . . . I don't belong in this place."

As Sabine glanced around, the pink-painted sky suddenly shimmered and melted away, revealing the stained, cold walls of her cell. Iron bars barricaded her flight to freedom.

"Please," she whispered to the stone ceiling.

But there was no answer. No one else could hear her cries.

She closed her eyes tight, mining deep for the sanctuary, reaching with her arms to grasp it before it faded completely away. A flash of blue sky blinded her. The smell of summer grass, the kiss of spring rain . . .

She was back.

"Very well. I shall stay here. 'Tis where I belong."

"Good afternoon, Monsieur de Lavarac. No, no, do not try to rise. I'll just sit here by your bedside."

Louis recognized this man from somewhere. Fancy frock coat and breeches. Double-stitched embroidery in silver threading. A shiny gold chain stretching across his stomach. If he'd pull his tricorn up a bit to reveal his eyes, he'd remember. *Always look the enemy in the eye.*

"I've a few questions for you. *Sst, sst.*"

Of course. Ambroise l'Argent. How could he have forgotten so quickly?

"It took some sleuthing to find you," he said on an abbreviated chuckle.

"I've been right here for a week," Louis muttered, unable to see the humor in his situation.

"Yes, but I was not aware of the abundance of hospitals in Paris until I began searching through them."

"How did you know to look for me in a hospital?"

The man bristled and jerked his head away toward the high window in the wall. Dirty sunlight painted odd shadows across his face.

"Have you spoken to Henri?"

"Ah, yes!" the man quickly picked up the conversation. "It

was your brother I ran into, Monsieur de Lavarac. He told me you had been injured. Unfortunately at the time I didn't ask for the name of the hospital, which ... explains my search. Yes, very good. So! You see, I've need to discuss something with you.''

''You've been able to locate the woman? Evangeline?''

Louis wasn't sure why that particular question had just flown out. He hadn't thought of Evangeline for days. His only concern now was truly that of locating his wife.

''I feel my connections are bringing me closer. Much closer, Monsieur. The English roll officer plans to send word of anything he uncovers regarding the woman.''

''Very good.'' Louis's voice had returned over the days he'd lain in this stinking hospital. His head ached less and his ribs hurt only when he moved. But he knew he would not fully recover until he set foot outside the Hôtel-Dieu and breathed fresh air. And not the stifling air of Paris. It had to be the good, clean country air of his home. ''I understand the heir has been located?''

''Er, yes.'' L'Argent appeared to weigh his words carefully. ''So you have been told the beneficiary's identity? *Sst sst.*''

''Henri informed me earlier. He's gone to see him. Cristoforo. Sabine's ... relative?''

''Your brother has gone to see him? But that is hardly necessary.'' The lawyer shifted uneasily.

''Is there a problem, Monsieur l'Argent?''

The damned little squirrel most certainly did not like to look Louis in the eye. Always darting his bulging eyes. Made Louis nervous. If only he had the strength to just reach out and wrench the man closer.

''You see,'' l'Argent started cautiously, ''we would like to execute the will immediately, but it seems we cannot now locate Mademoiselle Bassange.''

''But I thought Cristoforo—'' Dread suddenly clenched Louis's heart, digging its long claws deep into the throbbing muscle. "Doesn't the singer have her?"

Henri had seemed most positive that Cristoforo would have Sabine.

"The devil, where is she? My wife . . ." Louis whispered.

His fairy had fled. And he had only a tattered ribbon and broken twig to remind him of her presence.

"Your . . . wife?" L'Argent snapped his portfolio shut and leaned over Louis's chest, his scrawny elbow digging into the thin mattress. Fish eyes, Louis thought of the man's bulbous gaze. "Monsieur, this is highly irregular. You are aware that permission was never granted to wed Mademoiselle Bassange? And the girl is not exactly—"

"She is of her right mind, if that is what you mean, l'Argent," Louis said, suddenly on the defense. He wouldn't allow this namby fishhead to order him around.

"Well . . ." The wooden chair creaked with l'Argent's weight as he straightend. "That is to be debated."

"And have you seen her lately? Have you held a conversation with her?" Louis felt the rage build in the muscles on his arm, tensing his fingers into a fist. But his weakness quickly released the tensed muscles like a broken spring. "She is sane, Monsieur l'Argent. She knew exactly what she was saying when she took our marriage vows, as did I, and I'll let no man question them."

"*Sst. sst.* So you say. But this must be discussed with Signore Cristoforo—"

"Signore?" He hadn't even met the man, yet Louis harbored instant hatred for him. "Is he not a Bassange? A Frenchman? What, has he abandoned our country for another that suits him better?"

Stop it, Louis's inner voice screamed. That is the soldier talking. The part that blindly took sides for no reason other than that he had been told to do so. *You've sacrificed that part of you for a kinder Louis, remember?*

"Signore Cristoforo has lived in Italy since he was just a

child. He did not abandon France. If anything, she abandoned him. Yet he has the greatness in his heart to return to France and gift us with the divinity of his voice." L'Argent was speaking ever more passionately. "To hear the man's voice is to fall madly in love."

"Really." Louis would never understand the veneration the masses heaped upon the castratos. Henri was right. A capon he was, a mere facsimile of a man.

"Yes, but returning to business." L'Argent leaned back in the chair, his coat parting to reveal the gold chain of his pocket watch. "You know where Mademoiselle Bassange is, Monsieur de Lavarac?"

Louis shook his head. "She was here." He lifted his right hand to reveal the scarlet ribbon, but it quickly fell back to the bed. The stick, now in two pieces, was sweaty and tight in his other palm. "But now she is not. I assumed your Cristoforo had her."

"Hmm. I don't . . . believe so."

Louis caught the searching wonder in l'Argent's voice. As though he weren't sure himself whether the singer had her. What was going on? He understood that l'Argent was working for Cristoforo. Was it possible that Cristoforo could have Sabine without l'Argent knowing?

Yes, that had to be the case. For Louis could not bear to imagine his wife wandering the streets of Paris alone and lost and in an irrational state. "Where does this Cristoforo reside when he's not performing?"

"Hmm? Oh, he's an apartment on the Rue St. Honoré. Very convenient when getting to the Opéra. Now, you say she was here?"

Louis nodded, silently gauging the darting eyes of the *notaire*. No. The man truly had no idea what was going on. Which meant only that the answers lay in the hands of the castrato.

"Very well. I am sorry to trouble you, Monsieur de Lavarac. I should return to my office. I've much work to do for you, to search for these two women." L'Argent stood and checked his watch. Satisfied with that, he began to walk away, but paused. "Oh, and you can be at ease, monsieur. We will find your wife. I promise you that."

Louis waited until l'Argent's smirk was out of view before gripping the flimsy bedsheets in both hands and tearing. The splitting sheets disguised his own inner scream. Never mind Evangeline. They would find Sabine before him. And when they did he would never see her again. From the little he had learned of Cristoforo thus far, he could not believe he had any intention of caring for Sabine. She would be locked behind the walls of an institution and the capon would leave for Italy.

"I must find you first, Sabine."

"What the hell is that scrawny excuse for a man up to?" L'Argent stepped down the stairs before the Hôtel-Dieu and drew in a cleansing breath of air. He tapped his silver damask shoes against the bottom step, shaking off the rotting straw that adhered to the heel. Bothersome that he'd had to enter such a hideous place.

Forge it! The evil command from his employer resounded in his mind.

The temptation to follow the singer's demands was great. Only one signed copy of the document was needed, and l'Argent would receive his sizable fee. Not that he hadn't been trimming a little off the booty here and there through the years. What had the Vicomte Bassange expected?

Which reminded l'Argent; he needed to stop by the milliner's and see that the buttons on his silver frock coat were recovered. Wouldn't do to be wearing ill-cared-for clothes.

But back to Cristoforo. Just what was the man up to? Could

he possibly have the girl? *Do not inform the police. I shouldn't wish for them to be involved if she were found dead.*

Was it possible? L'Argent hailed a cabriolet and tossed a shiny sou to the young boy who scrambled to help him into the two-person cart.

Possibilities were endless when associated with Cristoforo. But to kill? No. Not a man capable of such tender, sweet music. Could he?

L'Argent was determined to find out.

"He's hiding something."

Cristoforo tilted his head to the left to allow Pietro access to his aching neck muscles. Ah, the boy's hands were heaven, greased and slick with angel's mead. "Lower, Pietro. Right at the base of my skull. Oh . . . there . . . yesss."

"Who's hiding something?" Pietro questioned as he dutifully kneaded his master's flesh with the warm spice-scented oil.

"That insipid *notaire*. The snot-sucking rat. Why he would want to keep her whereabouts a secret is beyond me." Cristoforo propped his elbows up on the bed and flipped his hair from his eyes. "The man will benefit only when the papers are signed. What advantage is it to him to prolong this whole miserable mess?"

"Perhaps he likes to vex you, master. He's got that look in his eyes."

"Yes, yes." Cristoforo pressed his cheek into the pillow and closed his eyes. "That look of disgust. The same look every man gives me."

"You mustn't let it trouble you," Pietro cooed. "You do not disgust me, master. And even if those men do look down on you, there is no denying that you capture their attention and their desire each time you sing. They love you, Cristoforo. All the world loves you."

Allowing a smile to twist his lips, Cristoforo hugged the pillow with one arm. "They do, don't they, Pietro?"

The touch of Pietro's warm kiss on the back of his neck appeased Cristoforo's vexatious mood.

"Always and forever, master."

CHAPTER TWENTY

He felt as though one of his ribs were poking through his flesh. Each movement changed the rib's target. Sometimes his upper left side, sometimes his gut, other times his heart. But Louis knew that the pain in his heart was not a physical consequence of his injuries. Every minute, every hour, every endless day spent without Sabine, tore another long gash down the fragile muscles of his heart. And though he felt with each step he took that death stood just around the corner, Louis vowed that he would not die until Sabine had returned to his arms.

Louis pulled up his breeches and fastened the cloth-covered buttons at his waist and below his knees. His chest felt hollow and deflated, and his lungs gasped with each movement. It was no wonder countless numbers died in the Hôtel-Dieu. The stench alone was enough to suffocate even the strongest man, and what with the rodents and the filthy linens, he was surprised he'd not worsened instead of gaining his strength.

Pulling his shirt over his head, Louis eyed the door at the end of the corridor. No attendants. They rarely walked the aisles or tended patients unless someone called out. Loudly. Small wonder, Louis thought as a vile spike of urine curled its way up his nostrils. He unwound the filthy bandage from his scalp, wincing as the linen pulled at the serrated wound just over his left temple. A touch to the sore injury proved it seeped but did not bleed.

He stood still for a moment, judging his inner strength and his outer as well. He was strong enough to stand. His resolve could smash a thousand dragons to bits if only his body would allow. But it was enough. Strong enough to rescue his damsel.

"It's not that I don't trust you, Henri." He tied his collar and sleeves and pulled on his dirty frock coat. "But I fear a true dragon has come for my princess."

She danced across the meadow grasses, her feet at first slipping in what might seem to be rotting straw, but as her mind drew deeper into her soul, the coolness of the grass was a tangible feeling beneath her bare toes.

And the stone walls became bright and clear skies. No ceiling blocked her view of the fluffy white clouds. A bird flew overhead, its breast a brilliant red. The scent of fresh running water in a clear brook and soft bordering mud was a delight.

With her eyes closed, Sabine spun across the soft summer grass, no worry should she fall, no care for boundaries that might be there in the guise of cold stone. She hummed and took great delight in the lilting rise and fall of her voice.

A grand spin lifted her pristine white skirts above the crimson poppy heads in a swirl of fine watered silk.

And all about her head, dancing in unison to her song, were the fairies. Every color of the rainbow glistened in their fine wings. A sparkling shower of fairy dust sifted down over Sabine's hair and kissed her lashes and settled into the pores of her skin until she flashed beneath the hot sun.

"Oh, you were right," she said with a satisfied sigh. "The real world is no place for me. I like it too much here."

Curse the invention of the carriage! Paris's streets were clogged with a sort of mechanical jam of carriages and horses and vendors' carts all intent on holding their ground until someone else backed down and moved aside.

Vendors hiked up their unsold goods and buyers bustled home to eat and then dress for the theater. Thieves and pickpockets sorted through the day's meager take in hope of a much grander prize as soon as the sun set.

Pinned against a wall of the Blushing Maiden tavern, Louis pressed a hand to his chest. The pain screamed and bit with each step he took, but he hadn't the patience to stand around and wait for the devil to rise up from the ground and start pitching carriages this way and that.

He felt along his upper thigh. No sword. He'd not drawn steel since battle. No. That wasn't true. He'd killed the bravo at the Bassange estate. No regret, no guilt.

I love you, Louis.

Her voice felt sweet inside his head. Soft and tender. His fairy angel needed a soldier, a man who spit upon pain and forged ahead until the battlements had been breached and the damsel could be rescued.

"I'm coming for you, Sabine."

Grabbing hold of the leather tack on the back of an equipage, Louis drew himself astride a horse mounted before a fine gilded carriage. He slid atop its back and carefully levered himself to its mate's back. Almost jerked off balance, Louis caught himself with a hand to the second horse's neck. There was nowhere for the beasts to go, so his daring maneuver worked well enough.

"Demon!"

"The devil yourself!" Louis waved a fist at the carriage driver as he jumped to the belly of a vendor's cart. There were only two sun-ripened fish lying in the bottom of the wooden cart. Just enough to make the footing hazardous. Slipping on fish scales, Louis toppled forward, but caught himself. He clambered over the side of the cart and landed on the other side of the jammed street.

"A thousand devils," he gasped, and gripped at his pulsing chest. His breath had been sucked away by his acrobatics, the pain increased tenfold. He gagged up blood and spit it on the muddied cobblestones.

Two young boys pushed past him, oblivious of anything but their play.

Pulling himself up by the side of a building, Louis staggered onward, his boots ruffing across the cobblestones, for he could not step as lightly and quickly as usual. He stopped, squeezing his eyes tight to shut out the pain.

Endure. For Sabine.

The Rue St. Honoré, where l'Argent had said Cristoforo resided, was on the right bank. Not far from the Hôtel-Dieu, but a good enough walk considering his injuries.

Louis, my love.

Louis reached out and grasped the vision that wavered before him. A fairy princess of sun-kissed hair and an enchanted smile. "I'm coming Sabine. Hold on."

The street was in a constant state of construction, though the stretch paralleling the Tuileries was nearly finished. It was not too hard to locate the great Cristoforo's dwelling. A wreath of fresh bloodred roses had been fastened to a window of the third-floor apartment. Rose petals, trampled to a mucky pulp, had been scattered over the mud- and refuse-ridden street in front.

A spindly young man who appeared no older than a teenager and who gave his name as Pietro reluctantly allowed Louis entrance. The young boy raised a handkerchief to his nose and gave Louis a wide-eyed once-over. Louis sniffed. Fish. A hell of a lot better than death and sickness though.

When Pietro saw that Louis was in pain and noticed the wound on Louis's temple, he hastened him to a sofa and said he'd procure him some refreshments.

"I just want the capon," Louis ordered in a huffing breath.

Pietro left, leaving Louis alone in an ornate drawing room. No expense had been spared in the furnishing of this plush, gilded spectacle. Boiseries that lined the walls were in gold, not simple carved wood. Even the English paper was overlaid with gold. Candelabra held black guttered candles twisted with cherubs and vines. Everything was either fringed or gilded or plated with some extravagant substance.

Louis pulled tufts of his hair down over his temple in an attempt to hide the wound. His head had collided with a wall. A hardheaded man, Béatrice had laughingly exclaimed. Yes, Louis thought. And not about to soften now.

He smashed his fist into his opposite palm. "Where is she?"

Moving his tongue around inside his mouth, Louis tasted the blood that had risen from his throat. He knew not why he bled, but assumed that he had internal injuries as well. Most likely upset by his jaunt over the traffic jam. He felt dizzy, but since sitting down, his equilibrium slowly returned. He propped his head against the plush chair cushion and lifted his feet to rest them on a silly fringed footrest. Wrapping his left hand about his right side, he settled into a reasonably comfortable position, and waited.

The stick he'd found lying on his lap felt like fire in his hand, the living, breathing, enigma of Sabine Bassange possessing its deadened bark.

Kiss me, Louis.

Untouchable images of her summer smiles, echoes of her breezy voice, filled the room. Louis reached out for the fading vision of his fairy angel.

Make me your wife . . . body and soul. I love you, Louis.

Ah, to feel the warmth of her flesh upon his. To twine his fingers deep within her honeyed hair. They had been so close to starting forever!

Her image faded with a snap just as Louis tried to touch the side of her face. Clasping his empty fist to his chest, Louis swallowed back bittersweet tears. Was this what it must be like for Evangeline? To possess the memory, yet to never again know the true flesh and blood? To never taste her husband's kisses again?

Regret threatened to cloud over all Louis had accomplished since meeting Sabine. Be strong, he coached silently. Do not revert to that hideous excuse of a man you were just weeks ago. Be strong for Sabine . . . and Evangeline.

It seemed forever before the capon emerged from a side door. Vicious red damask enrobed his slim figure. His blond hair gleamed under the candlelight, a perfect match to Sabine's butter-cream tresses. He was . . . pretty—the devil take his soul for even thinking such a thing of another man—far prettier than a male had a right to be.

Forgetting his troubled thoughts, Louis drew in a fascinated breath. This man's presence truly bespoke greatness. His carriage was so straight and tall. He moved with such grace. He seemed almost to freshen the air with each step he took. Royalty, Louis would have thought if he had not known otherwise.

The singer pulled up a chair opposite where Louis sat and positioned himself regally in it, then raised his eyes and matched Louis's gaze.

Louis gasped in a breath. It was as if *she* were here. In this very room. Cristoforo had stolen her fairy eyes, stained violet from the juice of the nightshade. Had pilfered her soft, smooth peaches-and-cream skin. Had borrowed her lovely rose-petal smile. There was no doubt, Cristoforo and Sabine were related.

"Quite remarkable, is it not?" the singer said in a soft yet commanding voice.

Louis snapped out of his dumb stare and settled back in his chair, not sure what to say.

"I was equally amazed upon first sight of her in the box the other night." Cristoforo, too, settled back into his chair. He pressed his abnormally long fingers to the soft waves of white silk draped about his neck. A singer's precaution, Louis figured. Though most likely vanity also, judging from the diamonds that graced his satin slippers.

"You are Louis de Lavarac, the man who has been watching over my sister?"

"Sister?"

Battle mortars exploded in Louis's heart—

"You didn't know?

—smashing his soul to bits—

"Of course, how could you?"

—sister.

"Yes, Sabine Bassange is my sister."

"Mon Dieu, I never . . ."

Cristoforo raised a graceful brow. So much like Sabine's expression.

Brother? No, this cannot be!

She'd never once mentioned . . . Although there had been that one time when Louis had suspected she was not saying everything she knew. No, this was a thousand times worse. A brother. Surely he will take his fairy angel away from him. Reclaim his own flesh and blood.

Oh, Sabine, my precious Sabine. Where are you?

"Is she here?"

"You do not know where she is?"

"As you can see, Signore, I've been hurt."

"Yes, I see. And been for a swim with the fishes too. You are comfortable?"

"No, but I don't think it possible. I was hit by a carriage over a week ago. I know that Sabine was with me at the Hôtel-

Dieu, but now she is nowhere to be found. I thought surely her own her—brother—might know her whereabouts.''

''You mean twin,'' Cristoforo said in a slow drawl.

''Twin?'' Louis swallowed.

Another battle cry. His final defeat.

Mon Dieu, twin?

But of course. They were so very similar. Which proved that their bond was far deeper than Louis could have ever imagined. Would it be right to separate them further, when Sabine now had the chance to be with her flesh and blood again? Would Sabine choose to go with her own twin or her new husband?

Deep in his gut, Louis knew the answer to that question. Sabine loved him as he loved her.

But would the castrato let her go?

''I—I am her husband.'' He eyed Cristoforo for response, but the man remained strangely calm. Unmoving. ''We were wed eight days ago in the Tuileries. I love your sister, Signore Cristoforo. I need to find her.''

Suddenly Cristoforo's laugh burst out as a snort. ''You actually married the madwoman? Ha! Although''—he pressed a thoughtful finger to his lips—''it has been said that marriage is a cure for insanity—''

''She is not mad!'' Louis sucked in a breath as the pain pinched his gut.

''I know that she is!'' Cristoforo rose like a marionette on a taut string, instantly straight. He leaned into Louis and focused Sabine's gaze upon him. ''I feel her lunacy every day of my life. Do not tell me Sabine Bassange is of her right mind, Monsieur de Lavarac. For I know better.''

Slightly daunted by Cristoforo's overwhelming presence, Louis did not say anything. Could not. The man was a stage performer; of course he would know how to put things, how to act in order to command a man's attention. And he certainly had his.

Now Cristoforo stepped back and began to pace the floor,

his fingers propped over each narrow hip, his red robe flying out like massive wings.

"I'll admit she has her moments," Louis finally said slowly, for the pain had started to pulse in reminding bites. "But you have not seen her lately."

"You mean since you have taken her into your care?" Cristoforo said with a laugh.

"Yes! She has changed. The madness no longer controls her life. She controls it."

Cristoforo stabbed the air with his finger, turning on Louis with a challenge in his simmering eyes. "If that be so, then why is it my performances continue to suffer?"

"I do not understand."

"You do not know the way of twins, monsieur. We are connected. Have been since we were very young." He gripped the arm of Louis's chair and grasped the air with his other hand as if clutching a man's throat. "I can feel her madness. I know when she is happy. I know when she is sad." He leaned closer to Louis's face until Louis could feel the man's heated breath on his neck, taste garlic and wine on his flavor-starved tongue. "And when she is mad, then I, too, suffer. It grips me like a devil riding my skull. Her torment becomes mine."

"And what of her?"

"What?"

"You care not for her feelings. You say you can sense each other's feelings. Perhaps it is *your* ill moods that brings on *her* insanity!"

"Nonsense!" Cristoforo paced away from Louis, his robe flying up in a whooshing arc as he did. "You know nothing about suffering, Monsieur de Lavarac. You know nothing of what I have endured because of that wretched facsimile of myself!"

Louis nodded. He wanted to hear everything. Perhaps this would-be man held the key to Sabine's struggles. Secrets that would shine light upon her darkness once and forever.

"Tell me," he coaxed. "I want to hear. Tell me why you hate your sister so. Tell me . . . of your parents."

Cristoforo's jewel eyes widened, then narrowed to slits.

"Very well. You should know this. Someone"—Cristoforo plopped down on the chair with a pouf—"needs to know of *my* pain."

CHAPTER
TWENTY-ONE

"You speak the truth, *Grand-père?*"

"Christophe, your voice is of the angels." The old man unlocked a carved alder chest and drew out a paper. His twisted hands, which reminded Christophe of pond-wrinkled tree roots, shook. "The world should not be denied the magic you possess."

"Then I can go to Naples?" Christophe could barely contain his excitement. He felt like running, screaming at the top of his lungs. Announcing to the world his great fortune. But no, that would damage his vocal cords.

Ah! Many times he'd tried to beg Papa to allow him to study music. I want only to sing, he'd plead. But Papa would always say he should not be so vain. Vanity is the devil's work. To sing for the masses would only bring sinfulness. Besides, Mama would be heartbroken if either one of her precious angels were to leave her side.

"Papa has agreed?"

Christophe did not notice the twitching muscle in *Grand-*

père's jaw, for the right side of his face was illuminated by the brilliant afternoon sun. "In so many ways. But see here."

Christophe scanned the fancily scrawled paper that *Grand-père* pushed beneath his trembling fingers. He was quite good with his letters, but this script had too much of a flourish for him to really read. "My acceptance to Sant'Onofre?"

Grand-père nodded, his time-faded eyes sparkling periwinkle instead of the vivid violet the Bassange family had been gifted with.

"Oh, *Grand-père*, I'm so pleased!" Christophe dove across the trestle table and wrapped his arms about his grandfather's neck. Cherrywood tobacco scented the old man's flesh and his hair. A sweet fragrance that Christophe could sense before the old man entered a room. "I must tell Sabine. She will be so happy for me."

"No!"

Christophe winced at the pain in his upper arm, where *Grand-père* held too tight. "We must keep this our own little secret, Christophe. I know of a way to announce your great fortune. But allow me to do it?"

Christophe studied the dark pupils in his grandfather's eyes; they shimmered with liquid, but held steady, pleading. "Of course, *Grand-père*. Oh, I love you. And you'll come to Naples as soon as I've settled?"

"I will, my child. Nothing can keep me away."

"When am I to leave?"

"Tomorrow eve your transport to Italy will arrive. You'll have no need to bring anything. Just your golden voice, my child. Just your voice."

Christophe caught his sister around the waist as she came dancing around the west side of the Castle Bassange. Her shiny, long hair fell over her bright smile, and her sun-splashed laughter seduced his own to rise in his throat. "What is it, Christophe?"

"What do you mean, my fairy princess?"

"You are so happy! I was in the meadow chasing butterflies, when I felt it deep inside my breast. Your joy! I ran as quickly as I could. Oh, Christophe, tell me, tell me, please!"

He cracked a sly smile and leaned against the castle wall, the old stones warmed to a pleasant temperature by the sun. A green katydid fell from the climbing rose vines overhead to Christophe's shoulder, but he flicked it away.

"Oh, you're not going to tease me, are you, Christophe?" Her impatient bounces set her hair to a glittering shiver across her shoulders and made the hem of her gray muslin skirts move in delightful waves over the tops of the grass.

"And why shouldn't I, Mademoiselle Tease?"

"Me?" She mocked a horrified expression and lay her arm dramatically across her forehead. "Why, whatever do you mean?"

"I've been allowed to help Mama bake the gooseberry pies," Christophe singsonged in a mocking voice. "I've been asked to tend the garden this afternoon. You cannot help. Mama picked me."

"Oh, brother—"

"That's me. And still you tease me so, you little hen!"

The air echoed with laughter as Christophe spun Sabine about by her waist. As tall as she, he was still a might stronger and was able to lift her feet from the ground.

"Enough, Christophe. I relinquish! I was just feeling a little feisty this morning. You did get to ride with Papa to Paris last month. And I so wanted to go."

"Very well, then, we are even. And now I shall tell you." Christophe slunk down against the castle, his breath winded from spinning. He held out his hand to pull his sister to the ground next to him. "I owe you that much for the Paris you missed. But you must swear upon your soul that you'll not tell Papa and Mama.''

"I swear it." She pressed a hand to her heart. "But why can't I?"

"I'm not sure." Deep inside, Christophe sensed that his grandfather had not gained permission from Baptiste Bassange to send him away. But to look at the other side of the coin, who was he to argue? He was going to Naples! To study with the greatest musical teachers. His only dream was to finally come true. "Just keep it a secret like we keep our special bond a secret, will you?"

Sabine lay her head on Christophe's shoulder and toyed with the fabric button sewed at the knee of his tan chamois breeches. Her touch briefly ignited the pain in the scrape on his knee. He'd injured it on a tree limb days ago, but Sabine had been the one to scream. He'd grown too old to cry out. Well, most of the time anyway.

"I will keep this secret forever and always," she said in her doll-soft voice. "Now, tell me before I expire from curiosity."

"I am going to Naples."

"To sing?" She knew of his desire to sing professionally. Sabine shared his same excitement for music and the elegant arts.

"Yes, to study and to sing. *Grand-père* has arranged for everything. I leave tomorrow evening for Sant'Onofre."

"Oh, Christophe, I am so thrilled for you! You shall be the greatest singer in the world. Your voice will capture the hearts of all and seduce each and every soul to be your slave."

"I rather like the sound of that." He spread out his fingers, and Sabine locked hers within them. They always held hands. It made the bond so much stronger.

"And I shall come see you every night."

"Dressed in diamonds and the finest gowns, of course."

"Oh, of course. With my hair done up in a towering design

and bright rouge upon my lips and cheeks. And Mama and Papa—''

Christophe jerked their clasped hands up to cover Sabine's mouth. ''You promised, Sabine.''

Her eyes studied his, carefully reading the warning. ''So I did. But they will know sooner or later, will they not?''

''I imagine so. Hmm . . .''

Well, that would be for the best. He shouldn't wish to keep this a secret from his parents forever. *Grand-père* would explain everything to them. Christophe counted on his grandfather.

A soft breeze swirled over Christophe's cheek. He pulled his sister's hand to his chest and held tight, closing his eyes to his fantasies of life as a famous singer. No longer would the towering elm trees and the birds be his only audience. He would finally have the chance to live out his passion. To make the music his own and to share it with the people. To step onto a stage dressed in fabulous costumes and sing the audience into another realm, a world where music set the course and painted the scenery and ruled supreme. A place where he felt a king, master of his destiny.

''Come, let's dance!'' Christophe jumped up and bowed grandly before his sister. ''The sun is high and so are my spirits. One last dance before I must leave.''

Sabine's skirts swished across the meadow grass, creating a hushing rhythm to their spinning footsteps. Laughter bubbled unbidden until, dizzy, the two fell into a giggling tumble amid the poppies.

Spreading his arms wide above his head, Christophe closed his eyes and grasped the warm air. His future, clean and ready for his own design. So perfect. A desire he put above all others.

The breeze began to tickle. Christophe realized Sabine ran her fingertip over his cheek. He could feel her loving gaze upon him. Sense her sudden sadness as easily as he felt the sun warm his flesh. ''What is it?''

''I shall miss you.''

He kissed the back of her hand and turned to press a kiss to her forehead. "We will always have the bond. I shall never be far from your side, Sabine. I will know your happiness and your sadness. As you shall mine."

"I know I shall never feel your sadness, Christophe. You are to venture on a great and exciting journey. Life is opening its doors to you. You must grasp this opportunity and follow its course. For then you will always be happy. But you will promise to visit? I fear your distance will weaken our bond."

"I shall never be more than . . ." Christophe pushed up to rest on one elbow and glanced about until he found a device to explain his emotions. He snapped the foot-long alder branch in two and then wrapped his fingers about it and snapped the exposed ends off near his palms. "Here." He held the stick up before the two of them. "They say that a man's heart is the size of his fist. Approximately this wide." He turned the stick from end to end and then pressed the simple twig into his sister's palm. "This is a measure of my heartbeat, Sabine. And I promise you, I shall never be farther than a heartbeat away."

She folded her fingers over the stick and pressed it to her lips, kissing it softly. "I will hold you to your promise, Christophe. Never farther than a heartbeat away."

Louis fingered the stick in the pocket of his frock coat. *Never farther than a heartbeat away.* She'd left it for him as a sign, a message of sorts. *Where are you, Sabine?*

He looked to Cristoforo and found his wife's innocent gaze studying him.

"You and Sabine were very close."

"We believed ourselves to be one soul divided at birth."

"And that is why you can *sense* each other?"

"Feel each other's pain, happiness, and joys," Cristoforo explained with a bored flip of his hand.

This was all very fascinating to Louis. He'd never imagined

such a thing. Of course, it did make sense to him now. To sense and feel another's pain from such a distance . . . why, surely it would bring about the madness. And the Italian opera verse that Sabine sang without so much as a clue to its origin . . .

It was all beginning to make perfect sense.

But he could not allow himself to be taken in by Christophe Bassange's story. The man was not an imbecile. "But you must have suspected the vicomte's intentions?"

"I was but nine."

"The age of reason," Louis argued, refusing to allow this man to bring more sympathy upon himself than necessary.

"Correct. Of course I did not feel as though *Grand-père's* intentions were pure and honest. I sensed—no, *knew*—he had not spoken with my father about my journey to Italy. Papa was very set against my leaving home. Singing was a vanity. Even for the church. And to sing for money appalled him.

"And so it was not so difficult to overlook *Grand-père's* indiscretion. You see, as a nine-year-old child, it is much easier to see your own wants before you can see rights and wrongs. And I wanted so desperately a life of music. To travel to Italy and study with Bernacchi, to hone my voice to an instrument of perfection. I was promised this," he said in a harsh voice that settled to a hint of a whisper. "But I was not prepared for the horrors I would have to endure thanks to *Grand-père's* scheme. He'd sold me, you see." Violet eyes gauged Louis for a reaction. "At least, that was what I was to discover much, much later, when I had begun to travel and tour."

"Sold you?"

Cristoforo cocked his head. "Greed tempts men to do evil things."

Christophe stood just inside the twisting castle stairwell, listening intently to the hushed conversation outside. He'd changed into his best pair of breeches—only the knees patched, while his shirt was white and clean, the lace around the wrists recently repaired by Mama so that it looked almost new.

His insides were as fluttery as a hummingbird's wings. But he practiced appearing calm on the outside. He must start now, so that it would come naturally when he performed onstage.

The carriage had arrived just as *Grand-père* had said. But it hadn't taken more than a few moments for Baptiste Bassange to arrive in its wake. He'd left in the morning, intending to spend the night in Paris—supplies such as flour and a new field scythe were needed; but being able to haggle a good price immediately, Papa decided to return home.

Even from the distance of nearly three hundreds meters, Christophe could see the color of his father's face. Red. Papa was outraged. It took only minutes for Baptiste to discover what the strange Italian visitors had in mind.

"Leave us!" Papa cried.

"We've a contract." A faceless voice reached Christophe, and the funny Italian accent caused him both excitement over his future and worry. "I'll not leave until the boy is in hand."

"This is madness." Papa must have turned to *Grand-père* for Christophe could barely hear his whispered tones. "How could you? My own son?"

"Christophe!"

At *Grand-père*'s voice, Christophe stiffened. Dare he go against his own father? This was a dream too good to pass up. A chance he'd never again be offered. But Papa's anger . . .

You want this. You must be brave. Show your father that you control your own destiny.

Drawing his shoulders square, Christophe smoothed his palms over his best Sunday frock coat, cream satin and black embroidery, and marched out into the twilight. Overhead, the moon, already visible as a white disk in the heavy amber sky, waited the darkness.

"Get yourself back inside!" Papa shouted at him. "You don't know what you're dealing with, son. No!"

One of the large Italians had appeared from behind him and gripped Christophe around his upper arm, his fingers meshing together beneath his arm, they were so huge. He started to direct Christophe toward the carriage, swerving to avoid the anticipated anger of his father.

Don't look back. Christophe steeled his conscience as he coached his feet to move and not slide along in the dusty ground. *You want this. This is for the best.*

"I'll kill you, goddamn Italian bastards!"

Christophe winced at his father's blasphemy. Never had such vicious words crossed his God-fearing lips. He could not bear to leave this way. Not without appeasing his father, making things right. Christophe wrenched himself around and yelled, "No, Papa, do not say things like that. This is what I want!"

Baptiste Bassange raised his fist to the Italian. "Release my son."

Christophe noticed *Grand-père* had faded away, his hunched figure slipping into the shadows by the castle wall.

Where was Sabine? Christophe strained against the Italian's hold. *Mon Dieu,* he'd forgotten to bid his sister farewell!

He twisted his arm, trying to release himself from the tight grip that pulled him away from his father. "I need to say good-bye," Christophe argued.

"No time," the man grunted, and jerked Christophe around toward the waiting carriage.

But it was too late.

Something went terribly wrong.

Papa's last words, another plea for the release of his son, were garbled and split wide by the flashing steel of the Italian's blade.

Christophe froze. Everything seemed to slow as Papa fell to his knees, his fingers clutching and slipping in the flow of crimson blood that spurted from his throat.

"Fool!" The bravo's voice sounded oddly deep and distorted by the strange process that was taking place in Christophe's head. He raised his bloodied knife to the old man cowering in the shadows. "We had a deal!"

"Baptiste!"

"No, Mama!" Christophe wanted to run, to scrape through this horrific scene and protect his mother as she came running toward his father. But his knees were locked. He could not move.

Mama's striped skirts whipped between her legs as she dashed for her husband, her face screwed into a mask. Oddly, she bypassed Papa and went straight for the Italian, her fists mashing into his face. Steel caught the last hint of sunlight, flashing in Christophe's memory. Imprinting the hideous flash of death forever.

"Mama!"

Sabine's tiny cry pulled Christophe from his slow-motion nightmare. He jerked his head up to see his sister struggling within *Grand-père's* encircling arms. Sounds ceased. Sabine's mouth stretched wide, but Christophe could not hear the pain of her scream or feel the terror in her eyes. He fell deaf to their bond at that moment.

He could feel *nothing.*

Clutched around the waist by two impossibly strong hands, Christophe could not struggle, could not argue as the Italian tossed him into the carriage and he heard the exact click of the lock. Odd how he could hear something like that. A tiny, precise metallic click. And still the screams of his twin were silent in his head. But as the carriage wheels rocked and began to turn, the silent screams took on a pulsing rhythm in his temples. Pounding and ripping from the inside. A new and unique pain that stayed with him all the way to Italy.

"It was the vicomte's fault," Louis said in amazement. "The death of your mother and father."

Exhausted from his tale, Cristoforo merely nodded and laid a long finger aside his cheek, resting his head there.

"Sabine's madness . . ." Louis sat straight in his chair, no longer aware of the pain in his chest. "That is his fault as well. And she was left to rot with him. By all that is sacred, I thought I understood, but this . . . my poor Sabine."

"And what of me?" Cristoforo asked matter-of-factly.

"But you were safe. You were pampered and fed and had the world at your feet. Sabine suffered!"

Cristoforo's face was in Louis's space before he knew the man had moved. "I suffered! Do you think a nine-year-old child should be left all alone in another country? He was supposed to join me! We had agreed that as soon as he could, *Grand-père* would travel to Naples to stay with me. To care for *me!* Not that insufferable bitch!"

Louis felt the blow of Cristoforo's words as if the man had physically struck him. The sudden silence of the room was jogged by the whipping flutter of the candle flames all around him. "Why do you hate her so? She cannot help this bond between the two of you. She could not help that her mind chose to retreat after witnessing such horrors—"

"She took *Grand-père*—the only protector I had—away from me." Cristoforo reiterated by beating a fist against his damask-covered chest. "Don't you see? She robbed me of my childhood *and* my peace of mind. I received a letter weeks after I had arrived in Naples. From *Grand-père*. Forgive me, Christophe, I know you expected my arrival very soon. But you must understand the tremendous guilt that pins me to the ground daily. I never intended for things to go so wrong. And now poor Sabine—*poor Sabine!*—she is not right in the head. *Dérangé*. I must stay with her. She needs me."

Cristoforo pounded the table of inlaid marble near his thigh. "*She* needed him? *I* needed him! But because he was overwhelmed by regret, he chose to stay with her. Regret! Regret does not bring back the dead, Monsieur de Lavarac!"

Louis drew in his breath. *Regret does not bring back the dead.* Sabine had said exactly the same after he'd pressed the tip of his knife to her throat.

"I never asked for this fate." Cristoforo continued to rave, proving without a doubt to Louis that the madness had not spared him. "Do you think that when I arrived in Naples I asked to be castrated?"

Louis could not move, nor answer.

"I never imagined, Monsieur de Lavarac, never in all my dreams, that this"—he gripped his groin with long fingers—"this was what awaited me!"

Louis swallowed.

Seemingly pleased with his silence, Cristoforo's raging features smoothed into a smile. "They get you soused, you know. I do not even recall how many bottles of wine I shared with the bravos upon arrival in Naples. To celebrate my future, they declared. And you know, I didn't even mind when they offered up a delicious milk-bath scented and speckled with pink rose petals. I had to be lowered into the tub, I was so weak on my legs. I think I passed out. Yes, I know I did."

"I didn't even feel the pain," Cristoforo said with a matter-of-fact air. "Not then anyway."

Cristoforo settled back into his chair. Louis wanted to press his hand over his own breeches. Just to be sure. But he still could not move.

"And do you know what it is like to fend for yourself at such a young age?"

Not easy, Louis knew. But also not so hard as one might think. His own father had raised a brood of six brothers and sisters after his parents' death, and he was only twelve at the time.

"You cannot imagine the world of perversion I was plunged into, Monsieur de Lavarac. Never"—Cristoforo squeezed his fist before his eyes—"in your most bizarre dreams."

"I don't need to hear this." Louis tried to rise but found his chest ached with each movement. He'd become too comfortable to notice his broken bones had settled into an unnatural position.

"You don't need to or you don't *want* to? You have fallen in love with a madwoman, monsieur. How is it that you can have no sympathy for me, then? I am of her blood! And I certainly deserve the same respect as some lunatic."

"You are the lunatic! And if you do not know where Sabine is, then I must go. She could be anywhere. She needs me."

Louis pulled himself to a standing position, only to find that Cristoforo snapped his tall figure right before him. The edges of the man's robes brushed across the fine lawn sleeves that over the days spent at the Hôtel-Dieu, had become soaked with Louis's own sweat and blood.

"Out of my way."

"I need her too," the capon said with a sly curl to his lips. "You've not heard the end of my tale."

"What? That you lived happily ever, getting rich, getting drunk, and leaving your own flesh and blood to rot?"

"No!"

Louis paused at the touch of Cristoforo's hand to his own. He wanted to jerk away, but the thought that this man was of Sabine's flesh and blood—his only link at the moment to his wife—stayed him. "Tell me, then."

"I shall make this quick." Cristoforo's eyes flashed with a wicked glee as he drew them over Louis's swaying figure. "It doesn't appear as if you've much time to spare."

"On with it!"

"The papers I signed after leaving my family, the papers that remain in a lawyer's hands—Ambroise l'Argent—doled out an allowance to me. Five percent of my earnings. Which, as a child, I thought quite reasonable. All I wanted was to sing. My aspirations far outweighed my financial knowledge. The remaining funds were to be transferred to *Grand-père's* account, which he would then hold for me until I was older and wise enough to handle my own money.

"Of course I eventually discovered that it is not easy to live on five percent. I quickly learned that when it came to women, the young ones were sweet, but it was the old and wrinkled widows who held the largest and most generous purses."

"I've no interest in how you pursue your carnal pleasures."

"Really?"

This time Cristoforo's gaze did nothing but sicken Louis. The man did not disguise his lingering summation of him as he drew his eyes slowly across Louis's face, seeming to pause forever on his lips. Why, he looked him over as a man would a woman! These castratos truly were a foul bunch.

"I am leaving." Louis pushed past Cristoforo and hobbled awkwardly toward the door.

"You can well imagine my anger when *Grand-père* sent me a copy of his will years ago," Cristoforo spoke loudly, as Louis's steps did not cease. "The gall of the man to give Sabine half of all my earnings—after all the pain she has put me through! Do you see? She is not deserving of my money. Money hard-earned. Money that is mine. All mine!"

"It is the least you can give to your sister for the misery you have caused her!"

"I? Oh, no." Cristoforo broached Louis's side in a moment. He waved a chiding finger back and forth between the two of them. "I did not cause the misery. The Italian bravos that came for me that summer's eve. *Grand-père* and his vicious scheme. But not I."

The man had no idea that others might also possess feelings.

"You are a sorry excuse for a human being."

"No sorrier than the man who stands swaying before me, his feeble heart captured by an unholy lunatic. Never will she be sane! And always I shall be cursed with her madness."

Louis swung the door wide and staggered across the threshold, his anger and disgust for Cristoforo carrying him quickly down the hallway of gilded boiserie.

"She must die, Monsieur de Lavarac!"

Louis winced and hobbled faster. He had been in the dragon's lair. And the beast had his fairy angel in its sights. He must get to Sabine before she fell victim to the dragon's fiery scream of death.

CHAPTER
TWENTY-TWO

The aging facade of Salpêtrière took on a dull gray sheen in the feeble light of the early morning. Henri trudged down the steps and wandered the Rue Buffon to the box hedges of the Jardins des Plantes. Masculine calls from the Pont d'Austerlitz reminded him of Paris's unending cycle of life; the city never truly rested. While the hawkers and bakers had already sold out their morning wares, boats and barges just beginning their day carried cargo down the murky waters of the Seine.

Once out of the clinging shadows of the asylum, he allowed himself a breath. But the simple breath seemed to unlock all the past days' worries, and Henri fell to his knees.

"What have I done?"

As each hour passed, the guilt over his actions haunted him twofold. He hadn't been able to think alone in his room at the inn. The night had been sleepless—tossing and turning. Sitting by Louis's bedside had only further twisted the choking rope about his neck. Regret flamed bright and cracked loudly everywhere he stepped. As if each footstep crushed the fragile shell of a black beetle. An innocent victim of his own stupidity.

Had he cracked her shell? Delivered the final crushing blow to Sabine?

If truth be confronted, Henri had to admit that she *had* been closer to normal, as Louis had said. So like all others. *She will triumph. She has not lost yet.*

So like Janette.

"Forgive me," Henri whispered to the heavens, his plea aimed at the memory of his wife. For he felt sure her spirit roamed the glistening white clouds, her arm clasped around their newborn, her long, straw-colored hair dusting their child's pale flesh. And sometimes—sometimes—Henri felt as though he could feel his beloved wife's gaze shining upon his shoulders. "I thought it for the best, Janette. But I am not so sure anymore. I just don't know—"

The few days he'd been away from the château had begun to clear his senses. Exhaustion was common in his life, more so with the imminent harvest. For weeks Henri had been up around the clock. He'd raced to Paris half asleep, half walking in a waking dream. Would he have done the same—committed Sabine to Salpêtrière—if he'd been well rested? Thinking straight and sure?

Henri would never know.

Sabine would get the help she needed. She would! He must keep repeating that to himself, for eventually he would begin to believe.

The rumble of carriage wheels prompted Henri to his feet. He did not want anyone to see him huddling in the shadows of the garden, feeling so odd.

He recognized the face that peeked out between the carriage draperies, and his heart sank when the passenger called the carriage to a halt. He looked about. Nowhere to dash. No place to hide and cower from his mistakes.

Ambroise l'Argent greeted Henri with a curt *monsieur*.

"Strange to find you in the shadows of the Salpêtrière. Visiting relatives?"

Henri swallowed. What to say, what to say?

"Monsieur?"

"No," Henri finally said. "Just out for a walk. Lovely morning. Nice breeze. Needed a change of air from the hospital."

"Quite a ways from the Hôtel-Dieu," l'Argent said with a gesture down the Quai St. Bernard, which led to the wretched place. "*Sst, sst.* How is your brother? I spoke to him just yesterday. Seemed he was holding his own."

"He is stable. The surgeon says that he will be able to travel home in a few days. Recovery will come much easier in a familiar place."

"Good. And Mademoiselle Bassange? Er, that is, *Madame* de Lavarac. You've not yet located her, I assume?" L'Argent's glance traveled over Henri's shoulder to the institution walls.

Henri tried to remain nonchalant. Just a stroll in the garden, he reminded himself.

Perhaps he should tell the lawyer of Sabine's whereabouts? Release this tremendous worry from his shoulders. It couldn't hurt. L'Argent of all people could see to Sabine's proper care, perhaps inform the capon. For wouldn't the great Cristoforo provide her with the best possible care? With their combined inheritance, Sabine would most certainly be promised a good life. Far better than Louis could ever grant her. Why, the vineyards supplied just enough each year for the two of them to live comfortably. To even think of supporting another family—

"I've brought her to Salpêtrière," Henri blurted out. A welcome wave of relief suddenly overcame him.

L'Argent's eyes twinkled like two fallen stars. "Very good, monsieur."

"You'll inform the capon?"

"Um . . . if that is what you wish?"

"Yes."

* * *

L'Argent wasn't terribly surprised to find Cristoforo, accompanied by a delicate-looking boy, waiting in the chair behind his desk. Steeling himself to remain casual, l'Argent slowly slipped his frock coat from his arms, smoothed the satin sleeves into a nice fold, and hung it on the iron rack nailed to the back of his door.

As he crossed the room, and the mocking grin on the singer's face grew wider, l'Argent's resolve strengthened.

"You are sitting in my chair, Signore."

Cristoforo jumped immediately to his feet. "By all means, we mustn't allow improprieties."

The singer walked around one side of the desk, while l'Argent paralleled him on the other side, until finally Cristoforo stood where l'Argent had once been and l'Argent could sit himself in his chair. The singer's strange shadow peered from behind his master's right shoulder. A shadow of what might have been, had Cristoforo's voice not allowed him to achieve such success.

"*Sst, sst.* And to what do I owe the pleasure of your visit?" l'Argent offered while his right hand clenched the wooden arm of his chair. For the first time, he'd rather not share words with this man.

"It truly is a pleasure, isn't it? To be gifted with my presence?"

Cocky bastard. As much as l'Argent had revered this man's singing, the events of the past days had put him on guard. "You know I adore your singing, Signore Cristoforo—"

"Pietro!"

With military precision, the boy took a step to the right and snapped a hand-sized flintlock in position toward l'Argent's head. Quite unexpected, to say the least.

"Where is the girl?" Cristoforo growled.

"I don't—"

"You do!"

The slam of Cristoforo's palm on the desk before l'Argent made him jump. His grip on the chair arms loosened; he also felt his bowels loosen.

"Sst."

He daren't take his eyes off the pistol held remarkably still by the boy. But the flames in the singer's eyes coaxed l'Argent into their trap. Gulping down a swallow the size of a large boulder, l'Argent reminded himself that the girl could very well be in danger from this man. Her own brother!

"I'll not reveal her whereabouts when you stand threatening my very life. And possibly hers!"

"Ha!" Pushing away from the desk, Cristoforo paced around and behind Pietro as calmly as if he hadn't a care. He even paused to look out the window. The great damask robe he wore over his silk finery made him look like a king overseeing his castle. Sunlight sparkled in his smooth golden hair. But when he turned, all it took was one great stride to pull up behind his lackey's back.

L'Argent felt the bile rise in his throat as he watched the castrato curl his snaking fingers over the boy's shoulders and begin to gently massage. The pistol remained as steady as a miniature cannon.

"What do you think, Pietro?" His voice was seductive. "It's obvious the man knows the girl's whereabouts, because he has just said he would not reveal it."

"I—" L'Argent choked. *Mon Dieu,* he had! Fool to have let such a thing slip!

"Shoot him," was Cristoforo's casual command. And then, as an afterthought, "But not in the head. Not yet. Dead men don't speak."

As the boy's finger cocked the trigger and made ready for release, l'Argent's kidneys surpassed his bowels and the hot liquid spread across his lap.

What was he doing? His silence would serve no one! Not even himself!

''She's at Salpêtrière!''

The singer slapped the pistol barrel down just as sparks flashed. Splinters sprayed up from the floor as the ball lodged itself near the front left leg of the mahogany desk.

So close to further soiling himself, l'Argent squeezed his thighs tight. A bead of sweat used his nose as a springboard to descent.

''You've had her committed?''

''Not I!'' l'Argent was quick to offer. ''It was Henri de Lavarac.'' The man *had* said that Cristoforo should be notified. So it wasn't as if he had revealed a secret. Damn the girl's safety! It was time l'Argent looked after his own neck. ''He doesn't want his brother to have anything to do with the girl.''

''Not surprising. Good, good. That is one of the things I wanted from you; now for the other.'' Cristoforo gave a regal, stageworthy gesture with widespread arms. ''The will. You have it?''

''O-of course.''

Eager to be rid of the devil himself, l'Argent reached down and grasped the drawer pull.

''Ah!'' At Cristoforo's command, Pietro again snapped the pistol up toward l'Argent's head.

''I am merely retrieving the requested document! It is in my drawer.''

The singer seemed to accept that and nodded that he continue. ''Call off your hound!''

Another nod released the boy's tension-wrought aim, and with that l'Argent was able to release his own tension. The scent of urine had begun to overwhelm. He prayed the others wouldn't notice.

Before he even had time to lay the document flat on the desk, Cristoforo was there, spinning it around and reaching for the quill and ink. He hastily scrawled his own name, Christophe Alain Bassange, on the first line, and then gestured to Pietro. The boy exchanged the pistol for quill.

"Careful now," Cristoforo coached. "Sign it Sabine Margot Bassange. Oh, such lovely handwriting, Pietro. I never imagined. There! Good indeed."

The exchange of weapons was again made. Slowly and with a wide, evil grin affixed to his face, Cristoforo handed the quill to l'Argent. "Your turn."

Squeezing his eyes tight, l'Argent bit his lip. Damn the castrato and his sickening ability to seduce. He would swing in the gallows for sure for being accomplice to forgery. This wretched excuse for a man had no right demanding such submission!

But on the other hand, one could not swing from a rope if one was nowhere to be found.

L'Argent accepted the quill, being careful not to touch the flesh of his former idol. As soon as this man and his monkey crossed the threshold, l'Argent had plans to be on a coach for . . . Spain. Yes, that's it!

His nervous scrawls danced quickly beneath the feminine signature. Ha! The boy had a talent indeed, besides obeying his master like a trained circus animal.

The document was quickly retrieved by Cristoforo's greedy fingers.

Slamming the feather writing instrument on the desk, l'Argent spat out, "Done. The majority of your finances are in banknotes redeemable only by an Italian bank. I've invested a small portion, which I'll have my clerks draw out for you."

"This will be done by your command?" Cristoforo interrupted.

"By the command of the will." L'Argent's voice was nearing a shriek. "My clerks need only that paper to dole out your inheritance. The notes and the investments will be delivered within the week. Now, be gone with the two of you. I wish never to hear your wretched voice again."

Cristoforo paused at the door, his hand on the door pull.

"Wretched?" He glanced to Pietro, who still held ground in the center of l'Argent's office. "Did you hear that, Pietro?"

"I cannot believe my own ears," the boy said. "The man must be mad."

"Oh, hell." L'Argent stood, forgetting his soiled breeches, and pounded the desk with his fist. "Be gone, you devils!"

"Yes," Cristoforo said thoughtfully. "I suppose 'tis high time we did take our *wretched* selves and vacate the premises. But you first."

L'Argent felt the burn of metal lodge in his throat before he heard the charge hiss and snap. He gagged, swallowing molten steel. His eyes fixed. The sudden spray of golden sparks from the boy's hand seemed almost too beautiful to imagine.

And then the bite of death opened wide over his heart and brought him to his knees. The stench of excrement was the last thing l'Argent registered before closing his eyes forever.

"You've but two hours before tonight's performance, master," Pietro warned as Cristoforo exited the carriage. The evening air was heavy with perfume from the nearby gardens.

"Are you going to carry my valise for me? We mustn't lose track of the will." Cristoforo had little time for Pietro's insolence tonight. Thanks to l'Argent, he had plans. Things needed to be done. He knew as well as Pietro what little time he had. But he wanted to do things right. Dramatically. Usually he was content to sing, and leave the acting to others.

But not tonight. The pre-show, with its audience of one, would knock them off their feet. Or, rather, . . . *her* feet.

CHAPTER
TWENTY-THREE

Louis followed his body's own demands for rest and slumped down against a brick wall within the shadows of a four-story apartment building. He had wandered mindlessly after leaving Cristoforo's apartment. And though he'd tried to fight his weakness, it must have been a faint that pulled him down against a wall to sleep. He'd slept well past noon, and only later, upon finding a rogue apple lying in the street did he finally lose some of the dizziness. He thought perhaps he might now be somewhere near a city garden, for the enticing scent of flowers permeated the street stench with the faintest whisper.

His boots skidded across the moist cobblestones, his leg muscles releasing themselves like a wound child's toy. He groaned quietly when his ribs jabbed at his insides. Though Béatrice had carefully felt across his chest and assured him that none of the bones protruded in any odd fashion, she did suggest they were surely cracked and would cause him great pain for weeks.

The streets of Paris were surprisingly quiet. After nightfall one could expect to hear the rowdy hoots of rabble-rousers and criminals as they scoured the streets in search of victims and excitement. Or a prostitute's shrill giggles echoing down from an open window. Cats meowing and muted horse hooves clopping through the muck. But it was quiet here where Louis sat.

At least some semblance of peace.

He had wasted an entire day already. He needed food, strength to endure.

Tears overcame him before he could stop them. The pain of loss, of unknowing, clenched at Louis's gut and folded his legs up to his chest. He sobbed into his cupped palms.

Where was she? Where in this godforsaken hellhole of a town was his precious fairy angel?

He felt so helpless. He knew not where to go, where to look. He'd questioned everyone who might have an idea of Sabine's whereabouts. No one knew a thing. And Louis believed that Cristoforo did not have her.

Incredible to think that monster could be his wife's flesh and blood. *Twins.* Much as he had hated hearing the singer's tale of his childhood—and Sabine's—Louis had had to hear it.

It was the vicomte's fault that she was encircled in this darkness!

He swiped a hot tear from his face, and as he rubbed the liquid between his dirty fingertips he remembered their stolen tryst in the gardens. How she'd cried from joy. Such innocent happiness.

"I cry from the heart too, my fairy angel. But it is a great sadness that taints my tears."

Closing his eyes and bowing his head to his knees, Louis was able to conjure the vivid scents and sounds and textures as his wife had mounted him in the gardens and together they rode to ecstatic oblivion. The smell of clean, new grass, the soft flutter of nightingale wings, and the hot smoothness of Sabine's flesh gliding beneath his fingers, his tongue, his lips.

"Monsieur?"

Louis jerked his head up and scanned the darkness. His gaze fell upon a shadowed figure standing five meters away, framed on either side by the straight lines of the buildings Louis sat between. Twin orbs stared back at him. Silent and wide, set into a child's dirty face. So frightened. So alone . . .

"Sabine." Louis reached out, his fingertips vying to touch the child, but he was too far away. Wide and dark, the eyes. Not so much as a blink. "Come to me?"

The child turned and scampered away, its bare footsteps squishing softly in the street muck. But the image of her vacant stare remained imprinted in the air before Louis.

That is how her eyes are right now. Wide and lonely.

"Leave us." Cristoforo gestured with his handkerchief to the attendant. "I promise a reward for your assistance. But not until I am ready to go."

"Monsieur." The guard hawked and spit a generous wodge, barely missing the toes of Cristoforo's silver damask shoes. He trudged away down the filth-ridden hallways of Salpêtrière.

"Would you like me to stay?" Pietro asked, holding the flamboyant white-feathered headdress out for his master while his pale brown eyes worriedly trailed up and down the unclean walls. Shrieks and desolate cries reached them from all angles. Invisible ghosts of an unholy and hideous realm.

His concentration focused on the task at hand, Cristoforo fluffed the tips of the frothy ostrich plumes. "No, Pietro, I must be alone. You wait below for me. Don't stray too far. Who knows what becomes of those visitors who never find their way back out of this labyrinth of madness. If I don't return within the hour, come for me."

Cristoforo bent over, and Pietro placed the headdress carefully upon his master's head, pulling the gilded collar down around the white robe Cristoforo wore. From his pocket Pietro produced two small pots of theater paint. Within minutes Cristoforo was transformed into Michael, angel warrior of God.

"How do I look?"

Pietro could not disguise his glossy-eyed adoration, which pleased Cristoforo immensely. "Come, Pietro, you can swoon later. Just tell me, do I look angelic to you? Would you believe me to be an angel from the heavens come down to save your godforsaken soul?"

"Yes, Cristoforo. If an angel should ever come to me, I can only wish it would be as beautiful as you."

Satisfaction curling his gold-flecked lips, Cristoforo gifted Pietro with a careful kiss to his forehead, leaving behind a faint smear of paint. He wiped the smudge away with his handkerchief. "You serve me well, my sweet one."

The boy blushed so exquisitely.

"Now, go." Spreading his arms artfully out and affecting a somber, angelic poise, Cristoforo turned to the barred door which the guard had unlocked. "I've a performance to give."

His fingers curled involuntarily near his hip. Searching for a battle saber. Pining for the extension of power that would heap destruction and violence upon any who should cross his path.

"No!" Louis yelled against his own inner torture. "That is not the way," he whispered. "I will not harm another soul. Never. I cannot."

But what if it is necessary to get her back?

"Only then," he huffed, straining against the constant pain.

Stumbling onward, his steps echoing against the brick walls that paralleled him, Louis could see ahead the Hôtel-Dieu. Damn if he would ever tread those filth-ridden floors again. He staggered and stepped backward when the footsteps of another man caught his attention. Quickly they increased their pace, until the man was right at Louis's side.

"What are you doing? This is madness."

He instantly recognized the voice. Blindly reaching for his

brother's body, Louis felt his hand slide across Henri's arm. "And you do know your madness, brother, do you not?"

Laughter tickled his throat, but Louis was too exhausted to release it. Instead, he reached again for Henri and pulled him close, hugging him. He needed this. This reminder of his own sanity, the warmth of his own flesh and blood, the unexplainable relief of being sheltered in a comforting embrace.

"I will help you back to the hospital," Henri said in Louis's ear, still holding him close.

"I will not go back there to die."

"You'll die like a beggar in the streets if you are fool enough not to return. You are weak, brother."

"No." Louis pushed Henri away. In the dim glow of a nearby streetlight, Louis could not read Henri's expression. He suspected the man was just as weak and tired as he. "You need rest too, Henri. You go. I—I will not rest until she is found."

Ready to step forward, Louis was stopped by Henri's hand. The two brothers held each other's gazes. Louis waited. It seemed Henri wanted to speak, but he remained silent. The sudden creak of wood snapped close by. Floorboards inside a warm and comfortable home.

Finally, Henri drew in a deep breath. "I know where she is."

Louis gripped Henri's arm, steadying himself. He could not speak. Henri's admission was too incredible to believe.

"I took her to Salpêtrière."

Louis's lower jaw fell slack. Words would not form on his tongue. Salpêtrière was an institution for the insane! The very walls of which he had vowed Sabine would never see. He felt the familiar battle fire spark in his soul and threaten his resolution to avoid violence. He'd like to wring his brother's neck for what he had done to Sabine.

But the thought was only fleeting thanks to the realization that he now knew the whereabouts of his wife. He could be at Salpêtrière within the hour if he found a sedan. And now more than ever, time was of the essence.

"I thought it best at the time," Henri continued. "But not so anymore. I will do everything I can to help you. Please, you must forgive me, brother."

"Forgive?" Louis caught Henri by the shoulders and turned him to study his nervous gaze. "You have consigned my wife to a living hell, and you ask forgiveness?"

Henri drew in his upper lip.

"I shall deal with you later," Louis hissed, and marched down the street.

Sabine jerked her head. What was this?

An angel amid the dour walls of this hell?

But why? How?

So beautiful this creature that stands before me. Robed in white satin and crowned in regal clouds of frothy white. Thick circlets of gold wrapped about its arms and belting the flowing robes. Ah, heaven.

Sabine lowered her gaze. *Yes, humble yourself.*

But . . .

At least she knew subservience. 'Twas high time the vexing little wench bowed before him. Showed her humility. After all the pain she had caused him. Cristoforo's long fingers wrapped tight about the cool column of leather-wrapped steel hidden beneath the folds of his robe. He hadn't thought much on what method to employ other than to keep it quick and simple. And final.

Drawing his right hand up within the billowing volume of his sleeve to conceal the dagger, Cristoforo approached the frail girl who cowered before him. His steps were light, floating, an angel's gait. His face remained a gentle mask to hide the evil that boiled within.

So this was Sabine. His blood sister. His twin. The fragile

limbs that had hugged his within their mother's womb were
still so fragile. The sweet little imp who had romped through
the meadows with him in his childhood remained, yet in the
guise of a grown woman. The wide-eyed maniac who transferred her pain to him at the most inopportune moments. There
. . . somewhere.

For all Cristoforo knew, she received his triumphs and pains
as well. Would that not make sense? She had felt them as a
child, as had he. There was no reason she could not now.

But I am not mad.

She could never suffer such debilitating headaches because
of him. Never would his dark moods send her screeching and
stumbling in pain. His mind was not a tangle like hers.

But a beautiful tangle it was.

It was all Cristoforo could do to restrain himself from bending
forward and touching the silken hair on her head, dirtied and
tangled from her imprisonment, yet still oddly enticing.

Allow yourself to enjoy this. It is owed you.

"Yes." Stretching his left hand out, Cristoforo bent and
smoothed his forefinger along her hair. Sabine jumped as if
she'd been jolted by an eel and slid back across the filthy floor
until her back pressed to the wall.

"Do you fear me?" Cristoforo whispered a *mezza voce*.
Kindness seeped from his lips, gentleness radiated from his
outstretched hands. The feathered headdress was damn heavy
and beginning to slip for the sweat beading in his hair, but he
persevered.

"You are a-an angel?" she stuttered.

"How could you think me anything else?"

"I—I don't. Forgive me. Yes, forgive me, please. I've
never—but why? Why me? Am I to—to die?"

A sardonic grin curled Cristoforo's lips. "To die? I am an
angel of God, little one." He stretched his hand out, feeling
her strangely calm breaths wisp across his fingers. *Capture her*

life. Suck away her strength. "Take my hand. I'll not lead you astray."

"But—" She looked up.

A cry of strange desire welled at the back of Cristoforo's throat at the sight of the lucid violet jewels dancing curiously beneath her dirt-smeared brows. Twin mirrors to his own. And those lips. So pale and still quite soft even after her imprisonment. Would they taste of wine, sweet and rich? He could only imagine. And her hair, so buttery in its color, was exactly as his, though even thicker. It was almost as if he gazed into a mirror. His feminine image matched his curious gaze. An image he had portrayed many a time before the footlights.

And deep within her eyes Cristoforo thought perhaps there lay a sliver of knowledge. Of intelligence and understanding. No demons danced within. Only a haunting of memories. Fear that was present when he'd first approached her was now only curiosity. What did she think? *Could* she have rational thought?

Cristoforo knelt before Sabine. He needed a closer look. Contact with this enigma kneeling before him. A whiff of her essence, a feeling for the rush of her blood.

Bleed her of her soul.

A shrill *clink* startled Cristoforo. He pulled back abruptly. He'd forgotten the knife curled in his grip. Quickly he covered the abandoned instrument with his robe, noting when he looked back that Sabine had not seen the weapon. She remained fixed to his gaze. Was that a smile? Or a fearsome quiver twisting her lips?

"Come closer, Sabine," Cristoforo whispered. "Let me touch you. Yes, take my hand." Her fingers were like breeze-cooled willow limbs in his long hand. "Draw my divine power into your soul. Feel the warmth. Yes? I am like you."

Like a gentle fawn held transfixed as it listened for danger, Sabine's gaze was innocently fierce and deep. Cristoforo slid his palm along her cheek. So smooth. The cheekbones were set high beneath soft flesh. Just like his. Her lips were a little parched beneath his roaming thumb, but plump and promising. Cristoforo leaned forward, inhaling the dusty odor that surrounded his mad double. He lingered, feeling her soft breaths upon his parted lips.

Perhaps . . . a kiss . . . to taste the life that was once his.

Drawn by an inexplicable magnetism, Cristoforo leaned in, catching her shallow breath across his lips. She closed her eyes as he neared her. He smelled her sweat, sweet and acid, yet beyond the dirt and oily sheen lingered the faintest blush of perfume. Exquisite, expensive, seductive.

He brushed his lips across hers. She did not move. Blessed heaven, such divine temptation! Pressing firmly, Cristoforo closed his eyes and began to drink in the essence of madness that had taunted him so. Enveloped by memories long gone, he lost all conscious regard for his plans.

And then she whispered incredulously, "What are you doing, Christophe?"

The spell had been broken. Slashed to a gaping, gushing red fountain by the bravo's blade.

Suddenly gifted with wings of rage, Cristoforo rose and stepped backward, away from the vixen who shrouded herself in false innocence. He tore the clumsy headdress off and tossed it to the floor, where it landed with a dull thud on a rotting scatter of straw.

Before he could speak, Cristoforo noticed Sabine's gaze grow wide at the sight of the naked blade lying less than a stride from her knees. He dashed for it and wielded it brazenly against her fragile neck. "What is this madness that possesses you, yet still allows for such a clever facade? Hmm? Tell me, my little whore, why is it you play such games with me?"

"Christophe," she squeaked. She struggled weakly within

his grasp, not at all aware that each movement opened the soft flesh on her neck across his blade. "Why are you doing this?"

Noticing a thin spurt of blood color his pristine white sleeve, Cristoforo quickly jerked away. He did not want her dead. Not yet. Not until he'd made her completely aware of his suffering.

Dropping her, Cristoforo stood, stretching his grand height to its full length. With a pull to either side of his robe, the fragile silken eyelets opened up from neck to hem. Cristoforo tucked the blade inside the waist of his gray velvet breeches, placed his hands on his hips, and paced before the wild-eyed girl.

He hadn't expected her to recognize him. To be so utterly lucid. Was she not a raving lunatic? Screaming and pawing at the walls? How was it that these headaches tortured him, and yet she was so seemingly normal?

Cristoforo stopped his pacing. He turned to examine Sabine. *Seemingly normal.*

But not. He knew better.

"Do you know the suffering I have endured because of you?" he hissed. "Or is it that you are not really mad? Perhaps you are a witch?" His white robes billowed grandly behind him as Cristoforo dove to the floor and knelt on one knee. "That is it, isn't it?" He jerked her gaze toward his with a stiffened finger to her dirt-smudged chin. "You practice witchcraft. Oh, what a fool I've been. And that man."

"What man?" she pleaded. "Louis? You know of him? Where is—"

Cristoforo pushed her groping hands away. He would be a filthy mess if he allowed her to touch him. "Yes, Louis, you filthy whore."

"No!" she screamed.

"Yes, a whore. You've given your body to him, have you not?"

"H-he is my husband."

"And did you cast a spell upon him also? Did you chant

over your cauldron and weave odoriferous herbs into his clothing? Damn you, vile creature. You shall suffer!'' He gripped
the knife handle but did not pull it from his waistband.

He observed as Sabine studied his fingers as they worked
curiously about the leather grip.

"I love you, Christophe," she said in a faint voice.

"Love," he ground like butcher's sausage through his teeth.
"Like you loved Papa and Mama? And now you wish to do
away with me as you had done to your own parents?"

"No! I did not—"

"I saw it!" Cristoforo went nose to nose with her defiant
glare. "Ruby blood spurting from Papa's neck, gushing and
gushing, splattering across the ground, painting the yellow dai-
sies a hideous death."

"No! Do not say this!" Sabine covered her ears and hobbled
away on her knees.

Cristoforo rushed to her and pushed her up against the wall.
He pulled her rigid arms down and pressed his nose into the
musty-smelling hair above her ear. "And Mama's screams
opened wide into a gurgling cough of bloody bubbles. You
remember, don't you? Tell me, Sabine, did you laugh? Did
you do a mad dance across their graves afterward? So satisfied
were you that you had gotten rid of all three of us in one fell
swoop?"

"No," she gasped. No tears fell from her eyes; in fact, it
seemed to Cristoforo that the lavender jewels were becoming
glazed. Uncomprehending.

"That's right, wench. Retreat inside. Close your mind to
life's monstrosities. It has been so easy for you, hasn't it?
Living in a world all your own making. Not having to live by
society's rules. Not having to rise every morn at four and sing
to the sound of a whipping cane keeping time. To work and
study until your legs give way beneath you. To endure the
taunts and curses of those *normal* boys. The uncut ones. Their
laughter . . . the torment . . . oh! To return to bed well after

midnight, only to be pulled to the cold floor by some brute who turns you around and satisfies his lusts with your body.''

Cristoforo squeezed her upper arms, relishing the feel of her flesh bulging and growing hot between his fingers. She deserved this pain. It was long overdue.

''Do you know what it is like to perform for thousands? To have even kings and queens at your command, lingering on every note, savoring every last sound? And then to suddenly fall deaf to all but the screaming inside? These headaches you've cursed me with, Sabine, I live the madness too. Look at me!''

It did no good to shake her. Even as her head cracked against the stone wall, Cristoforo could not get Sabine to look up. To heed his words. To understand his sacrifices. He had suffered so much more than she!

''Be done with it, then.''

He pushed her away. Sabine fell like a doll to the floor, her eyes remaining wide, fixed on the hem of his open robe.

Cristoforo pulled the dagger from his breeches and tested the edge with his fingernail. *Damn.* He had sliced a thin sliver. Pietro would have to manicure it quickly before his performance. The performance! He'd almost forgotten.

Tilting her chin up with the tip of his blade, Cristoforo studied the frail line of blood that had started to clot on her neck. So clean. Perfectly drawn. Like a glissando sliding from one note to another, cleanly, easily, no tearing or faltering. He then moved to his twin's frozen gaze. It was as if she were dead, her eyelids yet unclosed by the priest. But her pulse beat in her temple, frantically pushing the milky flesh up with each throb of her blood.

Her death would come so easily. Yet . . . without the satisfaction that she had suffered.

A hideous thought came to Cristoforo. So evil and despicable, in fact, that he smiled.

Cristoforo stood and hid his blade once again. Retrieving

his plumed headdress and tucking it beneath one arm, he said, "I shall return, Sabine. But you will not be lonely, I promise. I think I can arrange a little entertainment for you until after tonight's performance. *Arrivederci.*"

CHAPTER
TWENTY-FOUR

The pain in his broken bones hurt less and less. But Louis knew that it was only because the greater pain in his heart masked his physical wounds.

Salpêtrière was still a good distance away. The entire city had suddenly gulped in a breath of darkness and spewed out the evening. All about him the bakers, the hawkers, the farmers carting wilted vegetables and flowers, skittered like bees in a hive searching their queen bee. Not a single person gave any bother for another. Theirs was the only path to follow, heaven be damned if you stumbled across their ribbon of territory. Dodging to avoid the path of a barber's cart, Louis pressed his back to the wall of an apothecary shop. If he took the narrow back streets, he could avoid the tight crowd.

Paris be damned, this bustling city life was not for him. Nor for Sabine and her gentle nature. She belonged with him, safe in his arms.

"I will find you, Sabine." Louis wound his fist around the hilt of the gentleman's rapier he'd borrowed from Henri. "And I'll let no one stand in my way."

* * *

Cristoforo watched dully as Pietro stepped up inside the waiting carriage. Only a half hour before curtain, his faithful valet had reminded him as they had walked quickly from the building to the accompaniment of haunted moans and screams for release.

But amid all the cries of pain and pleading screams for mercy, it had been the silence that bothered Cristoforo the most.

The silence of his twin. The wonder that had glistened in her eyes when he'd first entered her stinking cell. It had been far too long since he had beheld such innocent trust.

He could have done it. Easily. Drawn his dagger across her throat in a mimic of their parents' deaths.

But she had spoken.

What are you doing, Christophe?

And for one moment of defeat Cristoforo had given way to Christophe Bassange.

Now, as the singer rested his forehead against the cool exterior of the carriage, he wasn't sure who he really was. Cristoforo, the famous Italian singer? Or Christophe Bassange, poor, unknown Frenchman whose dreams of fame caused his own death.

"Master?" Pietro peeked his head out of the carriage.

Yes, of course. He remembered now. Cristoforo.

Flipping a graceful hand up, Cristoforo was pleased when Pietro dutifully placed a lace-rimmed handkerchief on his palm. It smelled faintly of lemon as he wiped it across his painted face.

"You mustn't!" Pietro cautioned. "Your performance begins soon. Unless you wish me to redo your makeup?"

No, he didn't. He didn't really wish anything at the moment. Except relief. Cristoforo tossed the thin linen to the floor of the carriage and nudged the edge of Pietro's frock coat aside. "Have you the whiskey still?"

The boy blushed at his master's knowledge of what he must have thought his secret vice.

"Give," Cristoforo said dully.

He'd noticed Pietro sneak sips from the brown glass flask on only two occasions, though Cristoforo had always suspected it a habit. He took a generous slug of the warm liquid, his eyes instantly tearing at the sting of alcohol to the back of his throat. It burned like fire and tasted horrible. It did not slide down his throat so much as caterwaul in fits of rage.

Releasing a gasping breath was near impossible through what felt like a shrunken windpipe. "Pietro!"

The boy knelt on the carriage floor and caught his arms around Cristoforo's body, hugging him tight, perhaps as a means of comfort. But he didn't want to be touched or appeased or even venerated at the moment. Pushing backward, Cristoforo stumbled against the dizziness spinning in his head and the sudden looseness of the gravel beneath his heels.

"Master, your voice, you won't be able to sing. Come, give me the flask and I'll see to it you are given a pitcher overflowing with icy water when we arrive at the Opéra."

The burn had passed. And the urge for another swallow of the vile liquid made Cristoforo clutch the flask tight to his breast. He shook his head violently and turned to sit on the floor of the carriage, his heels digging into the soft grass that edged the circumference of Salpêtrière.

"Do me a favor, Pietro."

"Anything."

The boy's soft breaths whispered across Cristoforo's back. All he could do was bristle and shake his shoulders. Pietro's breath felt like the death chill of Christophe Bassange's ghost brushing against his body.

"Ride to the Opéra and tell them I cannot perform tonight. Speak to Monsieur Avenette, the master of ceremonies. Tell them . . . I've a terrible pain . . ."

"Another head pain, master?"

Shaking Pietro's searching fingers away from his face, Cristoforo then pressed his palm over his heart. "No. It is somewhere else." He pounded once against the violent rhythms that beat beneath his hand. "She has injured me deeply, Pietro."

"She?"

"I wish to be alone for a time." He stood and stepped back from the carriage. *She had succeeded in mastering his fate.* He signaled the coachman to drive on. "Do this for me, Pietro!"

"But I cannot leave you alone in the dark of night!" the boy called as the wheels beneath him slowly began to turn.

"There is no one about!" Spinning in a circle, Cristoforo did not even scan the surrounding grounds. He knew the gardens flanked the institute. Hadn't heard another human voice in the time he'd been outside. There he would be safe.

Not that it really mattered anymore.

"I shall return as quickly as possible!"

Cristoforo waved off the devoted cherub and staggered through the loose pebbles to the cushioning softness of the garden's grounds.

A half moon barely illuminated his snaking footsteps. As he'd guessed, the grounds were silent, save the funny screech of an occasional monkey or the rustle of overhead tree boughs. Cristoforo lay across a marble bench on the edge of the Jardin des Plantes, one leg bent at the knee, the other flailing out across the grass. The flask of spirits dangled between two of his fingers.

The garden bordered the hospital, but the yew hedges were high enough that Cristoforo could not be seen. He had the sudden urge to rise and race for the sound of the spinning carriage wheels and Pietro's cries of worry as they passed by, but he could not.

He knew that he'd just given his final performance.

Cristoforo lifted the back of his head from the bench and sloshed another burning gulp of whiskey down, the dark liquid spilling across his paint-smeared cheeks and into his hair. When he raised it above his head, a fine slash of moonlight shone through the dark liquor bottle. Nothing remained inside the blown glass. Nothing left to wash away his torment.

And now he lay, reflecting.

It had all been wrong. It was not he playing one of God's angels. She had been the true embodiment of the winged deities. Innocence and gentleness pooled in her eyes. Her soft voice had been nothing less than ethereal.

How? How, had she—that seemingly innocent creature—been the cause of his devilish torment?

"I have seen my own death," Cristoforo muttered. "Her eyes reflect the truth. Mirror my future."

He felt numb. Not even after days of endless warm-up voice exercises, diction, and enunciation, the tense study of letters spent beneath the watchful eye of Bernacchi as he wielded his mahogany cane, and then still more hours and hours of voice control before a mirror, theory, and finally counterpoint on the slate board . . . ah, not even then had he experienced such dull numbness as now.

Exactly as it had been that night the bravos had kidnapped him away from his twin. Forever altered their miraculous bond of souls. Tainted and twisted their perfect union.

Click. Still the memory of the carriage latch locking into place haunted him like bones rattling in the dark.

The leather-wrapped handle of his dagger felt sweaty and hot in Cristoforo's palm. After she had spoken, he hadn't been capable of pulling the knife across her throat. Instead, he'd wanted to kiss her hard, to pull her body close to his so that he could taste their bond, to feel the woman she had become. Chart the origins of the madness that haunted him, that always found him with wretched accuracy. He'd actually felt the warm sun on his cheek, her girlish laughter kissing his ears. But too suddenly the red gusher of death clouded his memories.

Not her fault. Cristoforo knew it. Not his fault either. Maybe a little? He should never have gone to Naples. Never, ever allowed himself to believe *Grand-père*. Never . . .

If he had never wished for such a thing as the life of a singer. Thought only of himself . . .

And now it was too late. Their bond had been twisted and screwed into a fragile skein of torment and unknowing.

Christophe was dead.

Yet she still loved him. That had been clear. He'd seen it in her eyes, felt it in her voice, tasted it on her lips.

"Such an innocent," he moaned.

Through the numbness of his liquor-induced haze, Cristoforo finally saw things very clearly. Yes, *he* had been to blame for everything. Not only the death of his parents but the death of his twin. Guilt was the sharp instrument that cleaved his skull and burst the pain with exploding accuracy over the years.

His grand designs for making things right, for destroying what he thought had been the cause of his torment, had all been shattered with the simple words of an angel.

I love you, Christophe.

"Forgive me, Sabine." For at this very moment he knew the two lackeys he had paid were entering her cell. "Perhaps I have known all along . . ." This time the liquor did not even enter his mouth; instead, the last few drops spilled across his chin and curled in itching trails down his neck.

He imagined the high soprano scream Sabine was making right now as she struggled against the lackeys. And . . . he regretted his actions. There was only one way to appease his twin. Only one way to end his torture.

"I will make things right. It is the least . . . that I can do for you."

Drawn by the growl of a dragon, Louis raced across the trimmed grass of the garden to the white-robed man sitting on a bench. Hôpital de la Salpêtrière loomed in the background, the moon glinting just behind it, a shadow-cloaked castle rising out of hellish mist. All about him sharp yew hedging scratched across his shoulders and steered him into the grassy clearing.

As his battle-stealthy footsteps took him upon the man, Louis realized that Cristoforo did not even notice his approach. *Good. Always see the enemy first.*

Instead, the man sang to the gray clouds overhead, one long arm extended high into the sky while his voice soared even higher. Dragon sorcery, used to disguise his voice as that of an angel.

For a moment Louis allowed the rich notes of heaven to twine within his mind, playing their magic upon his heart. He did not recognize the Italian words, but their haunting tone signified something strange. Like a fallen angel pleading for return to the pearly gates after a rampage through hell.

No! He would not fall prey to the devil's magic!

Louis pushed Cristoforo back against the iron bench by his shoulders, choking a perfect high note to a warbled chirp. He positioned a knee between his legs to keep him at bay. Though it appeared the man was in no condition to fight or struggle. "What have you done with her?"

"Ahggh!"

At the man's cry, Louis looked down. His knee had wedged the dagger Cristoforo had been holding into the man's gut. Louis jerked his leg down and grabbed the knife. Only the very tip glistened with blood. He'd barely punctured the man.

Should have killed him.

No!

Louis dropped the blade on the bloodstained robe wrinkled across Cristoforo's lap. "You had plans to use that on my Sabine?"

"Yes," he said weakly.

Surprised at the man's brutal honesty, Louis pulled his leg away and stepped back. Whiskey caught his nose with a sharp pinch. The man's face was drawn, smears of apricot flesh showing through the white theater paint. He must have just given a performance. But the opera house was far from here.

"Have you been to see her?"

"Yes." A drunken smile snaked its way across the castrato's face as he drew a thin finger beneath his chin. "I went with the intention of slashing her milky throat from ear to ear."

Louis's fingers snapped into tight fists. Already trapped in a battle rage, he had no intention of controlling it this time.

"But I could not," Cristoforo said, stopping Louis's fingers inches from his throat.

"Not man enough—"

"I kissed her," Cristoforo continued in a slow and reflective drawl. "She tasted like sweet Italian ice flavored with the barest hint of lemon. She knew me from the moment I entered her cell, I am sure. Oh . . ."

Louis went on guard as Cristoforo raised his hand, the dagger clasped within his fingers. But he only rubbed the back of his thumb across his temple. Blood from the blade suffused a ruby trail across his hair. *Sabine's hair.* The singer winced and pressed at his forehead, which told Louis the man was in pain.

And after everything he had learned, that could mean only that Sabine was also in pain.

"Tell me how to find her. Where in that huge institution is my wife?"

"Not so quickly, brave one." Cristoforo admonishingly tapped the air with the knifepoint.

"Damn you, man! I've already listened to your pitying tales of suffering and woe. Where is she?"

Cristoforo slowly stood. The acrid smell of animal waste from the garden's monkeys mixed with the spilled liquor dripping down his neck to emit the foulest scent to the air.

"If you will not tell me, I shall find her myself." Louis sidestepped the decrepit angel from hell but stopped when he felt the brush of Cristoforo's fingers over his leg.

"She is inside . . . but . . ."

"But what?" Louis shouted.

"It is too late," Cristoforo panted. His eyes drew across the lawn, sullenly seeking. "All I have worked for means nothing to me. To look into an angel's eyes . . . and see your death . . ."

He held the blade out before him, the point directed toward his chest, the handle waiting Louis's hand. "Go on. I know you wish to do it."

Louis was startled at how much this man now reminded him of himself, of how he had felt when he'd tried to take his own life. How easy it would be to push the steel through the dragon's heart. But an invisible fist gripped at Louis's soul, holding him back. And for once he was able to see things from Henri's point of view. From any sane man's point of view. What a fool he had been!

Death was not the answer. It can never be. Not for any man. It was only the coward's means of escape from the struggles all must face.

Eyeing the dagger, Louis said firmly, "That is no way to stop the pain."

"You deem to know my mind, monsieur?" Cristoforo said in a slurred drawl. "But you can never know. You say you love my sister. But can you say you know her mind? Can you know any man's mind? We are all lost, Louis de Lavarac." His long fingers danced in macabre twists before him as he continued. "Life forces us to choose our own madness, our own sadistic pleasures. She is as much her own making as I am. We are simply too fearful to escape the shadows.

"And so . . . I beg you . . ." He tilted the dagger so that the moon reflected in a flash of silver. "Release me."

Madness once again tempted him. But so very different from the first time he'd encountered it in the dandelion-swept meadow outside the Castle Bassange. Louis felt his hand flinch and rise to reach for the blood-tipped dagger. His mind fought against the involuntary movement. How he wanted to wield the death sword to this evil man's throat!

She is your salvation. Do not mar your wife's love for you by washing it over with another man's blood. Her own flesh and blood.

Yes, thanks to Cristoforo's own flesh and blood, his twin, Louis could now step back and away from the wicked challenge offered.

"No."

An abbreviated chuckle popped from Cristoforo's mouth. "Very well . . . then I shall do for you what you cannot."

The murmur of steel piercing first through velvet and then through flesh and blood slid down Louis's neck and spine like fire. He remained frozen in place. Unable to lunge forward and pull the dagger free of the man's chest, nor able to turn and run away.

Still standing, Cristoforo groped at the dagger handle, but his fingers hadn't the strength to work the blade from the cement of his heart. Falling to the grass, he jerked his knees up to his chest, pushing the knife deeper into his body, through the golden lungs that served his fame.

By rights, Louis should have removed the knife, leaving the sorry capon to rot, but he couldn't bring himself to approach the thing that now writhed upon the grass. The man who had wanted his own Sabine dead.

Louis stumbled backward, his own pain tearing at his insides. But no regret. No, not this time.

It is too late . . .

What had the capon meant by that? A sharp spur struck at Louis's spine, tingling its prickling path up to his neck. "Sabine!"

Louis turned and ran for the steps of Salpêtrière.

CHAPTER
TWENTY-FIVE

His heart pounding frantically and his breath vying for release with each vicious heartbeat, Louis raced the empty hallways, weaving to the right as the guard had informed him. The walls were surprisingly freshly scrubbed. No bars on the doors. Not even an odor other than that of his own sweat and blood.

Had he been wrong about this place? Why, it was nothing as he had imagined.

Louis rounded another corner and raced up two half-flights of stairs. The shrill cry of a rat startled him. Fat and plush, the little beast gave Louis no mind as it scrambled across the straw-scattered hallway. The pungent scent of urine blasted Louis's senses. He raced onward, discovering with each turn, each flight of steps he took, the conditions worsened. Slowly the truth of Salpêtrière were revealed like a hideous scar hidden behind a veil of silk.

When he neared the end of the west wing, he stopped abruptly, his boots skidding on the shards of rotting straw that coated the hallway like a slimy carpet.

His bootsteps had awoken a clatter of chains and moans. Everywhere the sick echoes of pain and suffering deluged his senses. Rot and human waste clawed his nostrils wide. Louis coughed out a choking breath. He listened carefully. Each tormented scream burned like a fire poker into his heart. In his worst nightmares, this was what he had imagined.

And then . . .

Sabine's voice echoed from behind the wall to his right. But it wasn't soft and floaty like a summer breeze, rather . . . a scream.

Two men staggered out of the last cell, their waistcoats and shirts stained with liquor and brown trails of tobacco juice, their eyes wide.

"Call for the chains! She is mad!"

"You'll not have your pleasures today," the other said to Louis as they hurried past him.

Louis raced to the open door. At the sight of an enormous man bent over on the floor, Louis felt the bile rise in his throat. *Pray God, this is not her cell.*

He saw the frail leg of a woman sticking out from under the man's sagging belly. A wisp of lavender silk. "Sabine!"

Louis struggled to pull the huge man off his wife. But struggle with an elephant might be far easier. The man did not move, nor did he fight. It was almost as if . . .

One brute, rib-cracking heave sent the man rolling to his back. Louis gasped in a pinching breath. Fire blazed in his chest. He'd broken something not already damaged, or rebroken something. But he hadn't time to worry of his own ills.

On the floor where the man had been, Sabine lay still, her eyes closed, her lavender dress—the same dress she'd worn the last time Louis had seen her—torn down the middle to reveal her dirt- and sweat-smeared breasts and stomach. In her hands she held a rusted street dagger. Blood spilled from the blade onto her stomach.

"No!" Louis dove to his knees and ripped the knife from her motionless hands. He pressed his palm to her naked stomach but found no wound. He glanced over at the man. His gut had been ripped wide, the flesh lacerated and red. Dead.

But what of his wife?

Louis pressed a shaking hand to Sabine's pale cheek. So cold. Her eyelids did not even flutter at his touch. "Sabine!" He shook her. It was possible she'd been crushed lifeless by the monstrosity that had lain upon her. A flashing thought that she'd been debauched came to Louis. He pressed a hand to her upper thigh, cautiously sliding it down against the other. No. A glance aside found the dead man's breeches were still fastened.

"Dear God above, I send you my thanks."

But his prayer would mean nothing if his wife did not breathe.

He touched her throat. A tiny pulse. A line of dried blood cut below her chin. What?

Her soft whimper flooded like redeeming holy water over Louis's heart. "Alive." He brought Sabine's body up to cradle against his. Her hair slipped across his lips, her hands falling limply over his knees. "Sabine, it is Louis. Oh, my love, you are safe now. I will take you away from here."

Her eyes fluttered open and slowly scanned the room. They fell across the dead man's belly without so much as a blink. The bloody knife lay at Louis's feet. Flashes of her macabre fascination with the dead bravo's blood hit Louis like a slap to his face.

Please let her survive this. Please, God.

Louis watched as Sabine's eyes followed the length of his leg up across his breeches, the thinning brown cotton filthy from a week spent in the Hôtel-Dieu. Her hands lay lifeless near his waist as her journey drew her tearstained gaze up to his shoulders, to his chin, where the stubble had darkened to a burgeoning beard, and finally to his own eyes.

Louis's heart lurched. Her expression held an awful familiarity. Violet jewels, glazed and empty. The madness had returned. No. *No!* He squeezed her tight. But what could he expect after the hideous week she had spent alone in this hell-rotten hole? And after this man had tried to kill her?

Damn Henri!

Louis squeezed his eyelids tight. His body swayed gently, his wife a tangible salvation in his arms. He had almost cured her. His love, that is. Together they had been *so* close. Her mind had been cleared of the darkness. Had it all been for naught?

"Sabine." He touched her cheek. Still soft as a rose petal. A rose shadowed by the darkness, so desperately in need of redeeming light. "Speak to me, Sabine." He felt the tears well in his eyes, urgent and stinging. "Say my name. Please . . . something . . ."

She touched the sharp, bristly hair on his chin with a crimson-stained finger. Perhaps she did not recognize him? A week's growth of beard and barely a splash of water on his face . . .

Her eyes took on the beam of moonlight from the tiny arrow-hole window. Her tongue crept out across her lips to moisten them. Louis watched, his breath held, as a subtle change washed over her features. Sun spreading across a shadowed rose.

"I am Louis," he whispered against the trembling press of her finger. "Your husband."

The rose smiled. "And I am Sabine, your wife."

Henri arrived moments later, and it was with his signature on the release form that the warden of Salpêtrière released Sabine into Louis's care. Slipping off his frock coat, Louis quickly helped Sabine into it, for she clutched her slashed bodice with fretful fingers. He carefully closed each button right up to her neck, where he pressed a kiss to the red line in her flesh.

The sight of her abundant smile beaming up at him, silently rejoicing, worked magic in Louis's heart. Covered in filth and looking like she'd been through a hell of her own, his wife still shone with a brightness to shame even the sun.

They trudged slowly, silently, down the crushed-stone aisle from the doors of the institution to the Rue Buffon. As happy as he was to feel his wife's hand pressed into his, Louis could not speak. How would he ever begin to take away the pain Sabine had endured—all through her *life*—with a few simple words? The feel of his wife's narrow fingers clutched tightly to his body was all he could concentrate on. He would never let her go.

He must not.

It was with sudden urgency that Henri dashed a few steps in front of them and fell to his knees before Louis and Sabine. Fending off the anger that strove for birth, Louis pulled Sabine close and pressed his lips tightly together as he glared at his brother's upraised face.

"I bring myself to my knees before you," Henri said, his voice serrated and tired. " 'Tis where I belong. I have been the worst of all enemies to you, my brother. I beg your forgiveness. Please."

Louis felt Sabine gently pull out of his embrace. Stepping away to allow him wide open space to fight it out with his brother? It would please him immensely to burn his fist across Henri's face. To shake his body until his bones clicked against one another. To drag him through the doors of the hideous asylum that loomed behind them and lock him away in darkness and chains.

Moonlight pearled upon Henri's brow and glinted deep within the dark circles of his eyes. Just as troubled as himself, Louis knew. Henri had endured equal torment and loss, and yet somehow he had not shown his misery. He'd kept it all inside. Perhaps far more dangerous than acting on your grief,

Louis thought as he pictured the scar across one wrist. For no one could ever know another man's pain. Until it was too late.

Louis glanced to Sabine. She stood apart from them, her gaze locked on the golden disk above. He sensed that she had not retreated to her world. Or maybe she lingered just at the edge, not sure whether to step across, waiting perhaps for a pull from his side.

"It is not I who can grant you the absolution you seek." He looked to Sabine and felt Henri's gaze follow his own.

"Sabine?" Henri's voice whispered nervously. Not a bird cawed, nor a carriage wheel creaked. All was silent.

Pressing his fist to his lips, Louis watched as his fairy angel padded across the grass to Henri. Hiking up the filthy hem of her lavender skirts, she knelt before him, dirty strands of her hair sliding across her face. Captured by her questioning gaze, Henri remained motionless, allowing her to touch his cheek. She was looking deep within, Louis knew. Mining Henri's soul as she had mined his so many times. Working her fairy magic with the gentlest of care.

Sabine spoke. "You loved her with such desperation."

Tears shivered in the corners of Henri's eyes. Louis bit down on his knuckles.

"Love is forever, Henri. You mustn't besmirch the memory of Janette. Cherish it always. Release the pain that darkens your soul, for if you do not, you will continue to harm others."

Henri bowed his head and began to sob into his cupped palms. "I was only worried about my brother. I did not know . . . about you. I—I was frightened by you."

Sabine's soft laughter touched Louis's heart, reminding him of the arrow that Cupid had firmly lodged there. He pressed a hand over his breast. Forever it would remain.

"Come to me, Henri." Sabine spread her arms around Henri and cradled him into a rocking embrace. "I love you, Dragon Lord. And I promise I shall try not to frighten you so." She glanced up to Louis. "If you will promise to accept my love for your brother."

"I do, I do," Henri cried out from within her grasp.

If she had the strength to forgive Henri for imprisoning her in such a hell, then by God's grace Louis must too. It was the right thing. For all of them. He put his hand on Henri's shoulder. "All is forgiven, brother."

The trio jerked their heads up at the sudden intrusion of clattering carriage wheels and clopping horse hooves.

"There!" a man who stood upon the sideboards cried out. "Louis de Lavarac!"

"The guard," Louis said in curious wonderment. He exchanged glances with Henri, and his curiosity melted to dread.

Sniffing away final tears, Henri jumped to his feet, bringing Sabine up with him. Before the carriage rolled to a halt, the man who had called out Louis's name jumped to the ground and advanced on the trio, his sword clicking by his side. "You are Louis de Lavarac?"

Louis received Sabine in his arms. She clung fiercely, her sweet gaze nervous as it traced his own. He hadn't the chance to hold her, and now he stole a quick kiss to her forehead. A brush of her hair stirred up memories. The faintest fragrance of soft flowers broached his senses. There would be time later for making love and for starting their forever.

But now he wasn't quite sure what was going on. He nodded reassuringly to her, and then answered, "What is the problem?"

"By orders of King Louis himself, you are under arrest for the attempted murder of one Christophe Bassange, also known as Cristoforo."

CHAPTER
TWENTY-SIX

Sabine stiffened within Henri's embrace. Henri loosened his arms. She did not move, did not speak or even cry out as they watched Louis step aboard the carriage. It was not the iron-barred wooden box the guard usually used to transport criminals, rather a flat-topped carriage. Thank the heavens for small mercies.

"Watch her for me," Louis called down as a lank young man clasped manacles around his wrists. "Sabine?"

She did not react to her husband's voice.

Henri nudged her gently. No movement. Standing behind her, he could not see her face, but he suspected that her wide-eyed stare had returned. Not now, he thought. Not when his brother needed her more than ever.

But what of himself? Pulling from his own dumb stare and back to the present, Henri yelled, "This is a mistake! My brother has murdered no one!"

"Attempted murder," the guard curtly corrected Henri as he slapped the leather reins across the horses' backs.

"He will be proven innocent!"

"We shall see about that."

"Do not worry, Henri," Louis called over the rumble of turning wood wheels. "I've committed no crime. Go to l'Argent! He can help. Sabine! I love you," Louis called desperately.

When the carriage had turned off the Rue Buffon and Henri could no longer hear the sound of stones spitting up beneath the horses' hooves, he circled around to face Sabine. Her upper lip was pulled tight in a shivering line. Her eyes were wide. Come back, he thought.

A stale breeze swirled between them, feathering fragile strands of her hair across her eyes. Henri brushed them away. Sabine caught his wrist in her hand. Her eyes blinked.

"Christophe is still alive."

Gauging her firm grip to be a sign of lucidity, Henri nodded. "They are charging Louis with *attempted* murder."

"No!"

Her grip grew tight about Henri's wrist.

"Louis would not kill my brother. He could not," she insisted, the violence in her tone surprising Henri. Her eyes blazed lucid and bright. "We must discover the truth, Henri. They will hang Louis if we do not."

"We haven't much time. L'Argent's offices are but a half hour's walk from here."

"But it is late. Nearly morning."

"We must go and call him out, even if it means toppling him from his bed."

The pungence of the room knocked Henri back and to the doorframe. Sabine boldly entered and passed him by. He found a tinderbox on a shelf by the door and lit the single taper on the wall. Seeing the legs that protruded from behind the desk, Henri attempted to hasten Sabine out onto the street.

"He lies on the floor!" She wiggled from his grasp and darted to the other side of the desk. She didn't even jump. "So much blood!"

Henri gritted his teeth hard. Louis would admonish him for allowing her to see such a thing. But he hadn't time to worry for her sanity. What the devil had gone on in here?

Retrieving the taper, Henri returned to Sabine's side. Amid a foul mix of bodily fluids and darkening blood lay Ambroise l'Argent's stiff body. His eyes were wide, the fingers of one hand curled near the gaping hole in his throat. Almost digging. No color in his flesh, his lips more green than the proverbial blue. Dead perhaps a day? Not that Henri had seen many dead men to know, but he had been the first to find his father just hours after he'd succumbed to death in his sleep.

Sabine knelt and drew a finger across the man's throat. "A line of blood across his throat . . . almost as if it were slashed . . ."

Henri touched the black puddle of ink that had spilled across the mahogany desk and dribbled to the floor in scattered splats near l'Argent's left thumb.

Who could have done such a thing?

Scanning the dusky room, Henri's eyes traced across the single framed certificate on the wall, the clean front windows, the delicate porcelain figure of a young girl toting a basket of fresh flowers on the desk. Splinters powdered the floor before the desk. Henri knelt and discovered a pistol ball lodged in the pine floor. He almost touched it, but stopped.

Whatever, whoever, had done this, Henri had no intention of bringing it to the guard. Not when they held his brother for attempted murder of a man who was associated with l'Argent.

What the hell was going on?

Could Louis have . . . no . . .

What purpose would it serve Louis to dispose of l'Argent?

Unless his brother had become greedy. With l'Argent out of the way, well, no, that didn't make sense. If Louis wanted to kill anyone, it would be the castrato. He was the other heir, the only one who stood in Louis's way of inheriting riches.

No. Not Louis. Material possessions and money meant no more to Louis than a quiet little house in the country did to Cristoforo. Henri cursed himself for even allowing such thoughts. His brother was not a murderer!

He blew out the taper. Already the click of carriage wheels and vendors' calls echoed outside to greet the rising sun.

A quiet humming redirected Henri's focus. Sabine rocked gently over the corpse, her tune a gentle lullaby of nonsense syllables.

"No, not now." Henri dashed to her side. He touched Sabine's chin, the cruelty of his own treatment toward her over the past weeks hitting him hard in the heart. Such a fool he had been. "Sabine!"

His voice jarred her out of her trance. She placed a blood-soaked finger on his cheek. "Papa?"

"Huh? Oh, no." Pressing both hands over hers, Henri inwardly kicked himself for even allowing her to see such a sight. The glazed look had returned to her eyes. The devil, he'd done her so wrong!

She ripped her hand from his sandwiching grasp. Tucking both fists tight to her chest, Sabine rose and continued her rocking as anguished streams of words flowed from her lips.

"Papa and Mama. So cruel and hideous. It was not me, Christophe! Oh, so much blood . . . it stains the dirt a sticky black . . . on my dress . . . Mama's blood soaks my dress! Christophe, no, don't leave me!"

Guided only by his own breaking heart, Henri grabbed Sabine's wrists and struggled against her screams to try and get her to look into his eyes.

"Always the blood!" she wailed.

She garnered strength to match his own. He feared hurting her. So fragile and delicate. And so tormented, her mind. If only Louis were here!

"Release me!"

"No!" Quickly, he slipped his arms around her back and grasped her into a tight hug. Louis had done as much when she'd cried beneath the moonlight that horrendous night. "I'll not release you to the madness, Sabine. Tell me what I must do. Please, I cannot help you as my brother does. What must I do? Precious one, don't cry!"

"Bring them back!"

And the room fell silent as one strong kick from Sabine forced Henri to the floor. Her hands spread wide before her, she stepped away until her back hit the wall.

Henri winced and smoothed a hand over his aching knee.

Bring them back.

"If only I could," he said in the silence, "I would."

She turned and looked over the corpse, her fingers curling into claws as she did. Then Sabine raced to the door and ran outside.

"Shall I save my brother from the gallows to face a lifetime of this?" Henri murmured.

But the conviction in his brother's words as he'd pulled himself from his sickbed and vowed to find his wife would not allow Henri to return to his former disdain for her condition. When Louis looked at Sabine, he saw a beautiful and whole woman. A woman worthy of his love.

"And I shall see to it the two of you are together once again."

Sabine caught his glance as soon as Henri stepped outside. She stood by a hawker's cart overflowing with bright fruits and vegetables hugging herself in a steady back-and-forth rock. Henri's heart swallowed a breath.

He crossed the street, dodging a wayward child as she chased a mangy dog past him. Judging by Sabine's faraway look, Henri suddenly realized that she had been imprisoned for many days. Most likely she hadn't had anything of substance to eat. Perhaps that would bring her around.

He dug in his purse and paid the vendor for a red apple, and upon second thought picked one up for himself.

"Forgive me," he offered. "I haven't the compassion of my brother. My actions worked only to further frighten you."

Her hand was soft upon his. "Where is Louis?"

"The Conciergerie." Henri said.

As he crunched the sweet apple flesh between his teeth, he allowed his gaze to become fixed on the retreating cart. But his mind was far from this simple fruit cart. It lingered still outside the lawn of the institute. Louis had bravely stepped up and allowed himself to be manacled. Not so much as a fight.

Could he have known that it would be only a matter of time before his actions were discovered? Had he been surprised that Cristoforo lived?

What of l'Argent?

"This is not right."

"I need Louis," moaned Sabine.

"This whole situation," Henri said, overlooking the clinging woman at his side. "There are too many questions. But where lies the truth?"

Sabine gripped him by the shoulders, determination setting her jaw. "Christophe Bassange."

Your strength threatens to close us away forever.

"Perhaps."

How can you be so cruel, so vindictive, when it is we who have stood by you for years? Sheltered you in comforting darkness. Carefully guarded your wounds. Covered you with the madness that you need?

"Louis needs me," Sabine pleaded to the voices that screamed in her mind. "I need him. I haven't time for your silly fairy games."

Silly? How dare you! Know now, child, what it is like to experience the pain of your twin.

Struck deep inside by a gut-twisting pain, Sabine jerked to a halt, doubling over where she stood in the center of a stone-wall-lined street. No! she thought. *There is no time to waste. I must help Louis!* She took a careful step, her bare foot melding to the moist cobblestones. The pain was relentless, scorching through her abdomen and stemming out to her extremities in a burning red path. "Oh!"

Henri paused and rushed back to her. "Sabine!"

"Go on," she cried, gasping in a deep breath. "I will endure!"

"No, you are in pain." He embraced her from behind and pressed his cheek to hers. His hands smoothed gently over her hips and stomach, seeking the origin of her pain. "What is it? Did they hurt you inside Salpêtrière? Tell me, Sabine."

"It is only the bond," she whimpered, straining to control the sharp, jolting pains that echoed out to her fingertips and ankles and even to her brain. Henri's touch provided little relief. "Oh, Henri, he *is* still alive! Christophe . . . I can feel him. He is wounded . . . right here." She pressed her hand over Henri's, wincing at the pressure over her stomach. "We must hurry."

"I don't understand. Sabine, I cannot press you further when you obviously need medical assistance. We must find an apothecary. Someone—"

"No, Henri." It took all her inner reserve of willpower, but Sabine was able to right herself and smooth her palms across Louis's dirty frock coat. She turned in Henri's careful embrace, pressed a deep sigh out over her lips, and said fiercely, "It is not a real pain. I feel Christophe's pain."

Henri quirked one of his dark brows.

"We are bound by one soul, Henri. I cannot explain now. Trust me, I can do this."

"You are sure?"

Yes, she was. For the first time in her life, Sabine felt a reason to cling to the light. She no longer needed the darkness. Nor did she wish to retreat to the land of fairies and sprites

that amused and comforted her child's forgotten soul. No longer
did her mind crave the empty states of abandon she so often
entered as a means to escape the memories. She felt strength
encircle her with an invisible hug. A strength found and
increased by Louis de Lavarac's love. Memories of their wedding night, when Louis had lain with her and their bodies had
become one, fortified her willpower. She could draw upon
Louis's love for her, and use it to carry on.

It was not enough to mask the reverberations of her twin's
distant pain. But it mattered not. She could endure.

"You could never understand," she whispered in deep gasps.
"I need this pain. It will lead me to Christophe. Like a trail of
flower petals that takes one to the fairy treasure, this, too, will
bring me to the answers I seek."

With a sure nod, Henri turned and continued as the twosome
made way on foot down the filthy, narrow streets of Paris. It
was midafternoon. A time when the city took a welcome breath
from the bustle and rush. Hawkers sat roasting beneath the lazy
sun, eating fruits and bread with their fingers. Small children
were being corralled in for sustenance. A street cleaner worked
at the mucky gutters that ran down the center of the *rue,* jam-
ming his wooden pole repeatedly in attempt to loosen the hardened grime.

Henri figured that they would have taken Cristoforo to his
apartments. Surely the singer would not allow himself to be
carted to any hospital in Paris. A private surgeon would be
called in. Perhaps an Italian if one could be found.

As they gained the Rue St. Honoré, Sabine allowed Henri
to guide her back against the stone wall near him. Concentration
on the task at hand overshadowed the inner pain. But to keep
her mind focused would be the greatest challenge. Biting back
a scream, Sabine observed the commotion below Cristoforo's
window.

"So many people," she whispered.

"Adorers," Henri said dryly.

Yes. Like she. Sabine placed a hand on his shoulder. He could never understand. "He can sing the angels, Henri."

"Why do you try to convince me, when it is the castrato who may bring death to your husband?"

Sabine swallowed. Yes, why? Since leaving for Italy twelve years ago, Christophe Bassange had ceased to exist. He had been replaced by the vain and selfish Cristoforo. A man who would try to kill his own flesh and blood. Yet there had been a glint of compassion in his eyes when she had humbled herself before him in the darkness of her cell. Beneath all the glamour and prestige of the man he had become, there lurked the faintest hint of Christophe, her brother, her twin, the gentle young man whose only care had been for her happiness.

Sabine curled her fingers into a fist, imagining with the tenderest passion the feel of a thin, narrow stick coddled within. *Never farther than a heartbeat away.*

Henri tilted her chin up with the tip of his finger. He searched for comprehension, she knew, as his gaze darted from her left eye to the right.

"He is my brother," she finally said.

He closed his eyes and nodded. "But Louis is my brother. And I must do what is right for him. This time." He flashed his eyes open. "You know that it is what we both must do."

"Yes, I know."

"Agreed?"

She nodded.

The two looked over the crowd of dozens that had gathered below Cristoforo's window. Sprays of red rose petals burst above downswept heads. Moans of grief, whispered prayers, all in veneration of their idol, haunted the street. A double row of candles had been lit and set before the stone wall, the extravagance of lighting them at high noon bespeaking a great sacrifice of love. Shadows moved behind the lace curtain on the third-floor window. Cristoforo's window.

I have suffered your madness!

Agony engulfed Sabine's being. Was she somehow to blame for the man that Christophe Bassange had become? He'd told her that he had felt all her pain. All the madness that had become like a treasure to her had been a nightmare to her twin. She hadn't really known. Had never once thought that he could sense her so far away as he was.

But then she had felt him.

Like a sudden north wind that chills over your shoulders she would fall into the trance of music and song. Most likely during his performances, she thought now, those strange words that she sang were from his mouth, his mind. And the sudden odd sensations of desire and heat that curled deep within her groin. *My secret pleasure.* So much like the feelings she had for Louis when he touched her or kissed her. She now knew that it could have come only from Christophe. And the elation ... *mon Dieu*, she had felt his triumphs too.

"We'll go around back," Henri said. "Up through the tavern."

"Yes," she mumbled without even thinking.

The time had come to face her twin. One soul divided at birth. Two half-souls struggling for triumph, one over the other. Only one could win.

And she wasn't sure how she felt about that.

CHAPTER
TWENTY-SEVEN

"Who has made this insane accusation?" Louis knew the answer already, but he had to be sure. He stretched both fists apart, straining against the heavy weight of iron banded about his wrists. "I cannot believe that King Louis would have one of his own soldiers imprisoned—"

"Cristoforo, of course," the lackey said, and tried to close the cell door. "He's King Louis's guest. You harm the singer, you harm the king."

Louis stood firm. His back was pinched between the door's hinges, but as he pressed backward, he was able to force the door open.

"Get inside!" the lackey commanded. He raised the stiff black grip of a bullwhip before Louis's eyes.

The limp leather swung like a hangman's rope. He was far too weak to endure more pain. And if he were to survive this imprisonment, he must keep his wits about him. Escape would only have him wandering the streets in manacles. Not an easy thing to pass off in the streets of Paris.

"Fool," the lackey muttered before closing the iron-banded door and blocking out all light from Louis's cell.

Hunched over to avoid hitting his head on the ceiling, Louis took short steps about his cell. They'd removed his suede boots to manacle his ankles. Slimy, cold straw slipped between his toes. His cell was streetside, which only proved to filter in the sewer slop and animal droppings that had gathered during the day. Invisible mists of refuse rose from the Seine, delivering a punch to his nostrils. A virtual banquet of offensive smells.

He listened carefully. No evidence of rats. Yet.

Falling to his buttocks, he let equilibrium and exhaustion take over and pull his upper body to the floor as well. Closing his eyelids did not erase the image of Sabine's violet eyes fixed in her shocked gaze as he was carted away.

She hadn't uttered a single word to him. Hadn't even tried to pull him back or kiss him adieu, or protest. Had she retreated to the madness after all?

Louis buried his forehead in his palms, pushing hard. *No. Do not even allow yourself such nightmarish thoughts. You must remain strong to endure this imprisonment. The mistake will be discovered and soon you can return to your wife's loving arms.*

"Sabine," Louis moaned.

Without her he was lost. Like an explorer led into the jungle by a guide, only to turn suddenly and find no one there. So lost and alone. "Oh, my love."

"You have no weapons?"

Surprised at Sabine's practicality, Henri wished he did have a dagger or pistol. Even the rapier he'd lent Louis would have served him far better than his bare hands. But then again, he did not want to give the castrato reason to have yet another de Lavarac sent to the gallows this day.

"We won't need them," he whispered as the two huddled

beneath the stairwell of the second-floor apartment above the
Chat Precieux tavern. "There are but two up there that I can
hear."

Sabine glanced upward. They stood below the apartments
that Cristoforo occupied. Aging floorboards creaked intermit-
tently and soft footsteps brushed above their heads, signaling
an overweight person's tread. Another set of faster, lighter
footsteps scrambled back and forth.

"The boy." Henri looked at Sabine. "He is the singer's
valet. The other must be the surgeon. We must wait until he
leaves."

At Sabine's silent nod, Henri touched her chin and stared
for the longest time into her wide eyes. The shadows allowed
him little more than a partial view of her face, her tangled hair,
a smear of dirt streaked beneath her right eye. Her nervous
breaths hushed across the meat of his palm. Beneath the tattered
facade beat the heart of a strong and brave woman. A woman
capable of overcoming insurmountable odds. A survivor. Like
Louis.

She jerked her head suddenly at the crack of aging wood.

Indeed, it sounded by the descending creaks that started
above their head and gradually moved past them that the heavier
of the men was leaving.

Creak.

Henri stayed Sabine with a hand to her wrist. Her pulse
fluttered as quickly as his own. In the dim light that filtered
through the floorboards he could see her nod in agreement. The
footsteps had paused. Listening? Had they made noise? Silk
slithered across his brocade frock as Sabine adjusted her weight
from one foot to another. Henri pressed a cautioning finger to
her lips.

Minutes seemed like hours as the two listened. Blood pumped
in Henri's ears like celebration fireworks. Finally the creaks
began again and a deep voice echoed upward from the tavern

below. "He needs rest. Silence. Something must be done to quiet the crowd outside."

And with the sound of the tavern door swinging shut, Henri slipped his arm through Sabine's and they took the stairs upward.

"What is the meaning of—"

Pietro's nervous demands were quickly silenced by Henri's fist. The scrawny teenager wilted to a fuchsia-beribboned heap on the carpet at Sabine's feet. Henri quickly untied the lace jabot from the boy's neck and secured it around his mouth. Just to be sure.

He looked about in search of something to secure his hands. Pausing for a moment to take in the opulence of the room, Henri had to gasp. So this is what mere singing could bring? Gild and lace, silver and champagne. Seemed an easy way to make a living. But what a sacrifice . . . Testicles.

"Sabine." He turned around, but the room was bare of anyone save the boy. "Sabine?"

The sudden flood of candlelight within the adjoining room brought Henri to the open door. Sabine was placing a long white taper in the gold candelabrum near a bed. The castrato lay on the bed, his arm extended toward Sabine. Shadows grew from his outstretched fingers, crawling up the painted wall like the devil's claws. But he could not reach her.

No one else in the room. Henri stepped back. This was not his concern. He would stand watch.

The clatter of keys on an iron ring jarred Louis from his illusion of sleep. When he heard the door to his own cell crack open, he jerked up and scanned the darkness.

"Step out!"

It seemed he had been in the darkness for only a few hours.

But for all he knew, it could well have been days that he'd lain here. Louis crawled out on his knees and used the doorframe to pull himself up.

His voice was hoarse. "Am I to be marched to the gallows without so much as a trial? I never touched the capon. I am innocent."

"What of the *notaire?*" the lackey muttered, a mocking hint of mirth in his deep voice.

"The what?" Louis stumbled across his own feet as he was tugged out into the hallway by the guard.

"Monsieur Ambroise l'Argent was found shot dead in his own offices this very afternoon. Upon further consultation with Signore Cristoforo—who is near death himself—it has been determined that you have reason to see the man dead. Quite a spree you've been on in our lovely city of Paris. I must say you've some sick sort of gumption."

"I am being framed!" Louis shouted to no one but the narrow-walled hall that paralleled them and the deaf ears of the snickering guard. "I've killed no man—" Save the countless dozens of enemies on the battlefield. Ah! Was he finally being punished for his thoughtless deeds?

"And are you hastening your suspected murderer to the hangman's rope, is that where we are headed?"

"Justice will be served in due time." The lackey pushed Louis forward into a wide, empty room of whitewashed stone. Surprisingly cool, the air. "Until then, you've a visitor."

"Visitor? Who? Why did you not bring them to my cell?"

"She didn't wish to dirty her skirts. Be quick with you, I'm not your valet."

Skirts? Louis's heart lightened. Could it be? Had Sabine returned with evidence of his innocence?

No, no, it was an impossible hope. Just hours before she had been trapped in the darkness of her own soul. And where was Henri? Surely he would have accompanied her.

Louis stumbled about the main holding room, a simple, plain-walled enclosure that was brightened by the line of barred windows that rimmed the top of the walls. With his head down he saw the feet of a woman, clothed in fine shoes. As he drew his gaze up the smooth line of black skirts, a sudden hopeful glimmer burned in his heart. "Sabine?" he whispered, and drew his eyes up to look into his wife's smiling face.

But she did not smile. Nor did the dark-circled eyes and tightly drawn mouth belong to his fairy angel.

The sting of her open palm to Louis's cheek pushed him off balance, and tripping over his ankle chains, Louis fell to the floor. "What the hell? Who is this?" he demanded of the lackey.

"The widow Durant," the lackey announced.

Louis pushed up on his elbow. He licked away the coppery-tasting blood that trickled from the corner of his mouth. "Do I know you?"

She stepped closer, her body remaining as rigid as her mouth. "Madame Durant," she said. "I believe you know me by my Christian name, Evangeline."

"Wench," Cristoforo's hoarse gasps seeped from his throat. "Pietro has already called the guard!"

"If that is what you would like to believe." Spurred by an overwhelming burst of strength and self-confidence, Sabine was surprised that she felt more relief to find her brother alive than hate for his recent actions. She hadn't thought in advance what she would say to this man. Trusting her instincts seemed the only thing she could do.

She sat on the bed, spreading her foul-stained and torn skirts across the luxurious gold damask coverlet. Such elegance filled the entire room. It was as if they were tiny characters set inside a treasure box lined in gold, and ornamented with all the riches of the world.

She eased a hand over her gut. The pain had now dulled to

more like incessant stomach cramps. Nothing she could not easily overlook at the moment.

The invalid struggled to sit upright, but was able only to prop his head upon the mounds of fancily embroidered fringed pillows. "What are you doing here?" he spat out.

"I've come for the truth." Boldly, Sabine reached for the coverlet and pulled it back from her brother's stomach. His white lawn dressing gown was soaked through with ruby blood. He fidgeted and tried to grip the bedclothes, but she held firm. His fingers were long and fragile, circled by wide Belgian lace. Always graceful, she recalled.

He was so much taller than she, his chest wide and broad. To encompass his golden lungs, she knew. It was disconcerting to see how different in height and shape they were considering that they had always been identical when children.

Though everything else about them was as if she were gazing into a mirror. Christophe's hair was as hers, flowing past his shoulders in a lovely, soft buttery color. His eyes, shadowed by long lashes, were vivid and bright. Like wild violets, Sabine now knew after seeing her own eyes in the mirror at the hotel. Even the tiny red lines that scattered across the brilliant whites of her brother's eyes seemed somehow . . . decorative.

Sensing he was too weak to lunge at her or try to dissuade her from her actions, Sabine leaned across the bed and pressed her fingertip to the stain of blood over his gut. Warm and slippery. "Pretty color." *Like the lines in his eyes.* She felt a great thickness of bandages beneath the nightgown. Yet still the blood was abundant enough to pool through all the layers. He bled profusely. She was surprised he was not dead.

Surely a wound inflicted by a trained soldier would have brought instant death.

"Louis did not do this." She fixed her stare on Christophe Bassange's tearing violet eyes. "Did he?"

Watching his lip quiver, Sabine waited his confession. But it did not come. Instead, Cristoforo pushed Christophe away with a blink of his eyes. Violet changed to steel. "Of course he did. The man is a murderer—"

"Attempted murderer," Sabine quickly corrected her brother.

"I may be dead before the night is through!"

"True." She replaced the coverlet and sat up straight. It was easy to see through the lies. Christophe never lied to her. This man, though, did. She could feel the betrayal twist in her gut, far stronger than any physical pain he could ever transfer to her. "Tell me, was the pain sweeter when self-inflicted?"

He stared at her the longest time. She thought of the many cool days when the rains had blanketed the meadow, and they lay cozily inside on the trundle bed, defying the other with their fixed stares. The first to giggle or avert their gaze would be the loser. Sabine had been so much better at the game than her brother. But this time she feared the icy darkness that froze his gaze. Her eyes fell away, but she could still see a wicked grin draw across his fading countenance.

"The pain," he drawled out slowly. "Not quite as sweet as the rapture I receive when you've come in your lover's arms. Pity you've known that pleasure so little." Malevolence coated his words in silky syrup.

"Far better than the shudder I feel after you've debauched a woman. Pitifully short and insignificant."

"Damn you, Sabine . . ." A choking gasp stopped Cristoforo. He swallowed repeatedly, but a spittle of blood trickled over his lower lip. "I needed *Grand-père* so desperately." His clenched fist barely missed Sabine's jaw as it shivered before her. "I was too young. I needed protection, guidance . . ."

"I know, Christophe! And I am so sorry." *Grand-père* had chosen to stay with her. He'd asked many times if she would like to travel to Naples to visit Christophe, but she had merely turned a blank face away from the old man. Too trapped in her own horrors to hope, too afraid to leave her own meadow, too angry, initially, with her brother for leaving her alone. "I told *Grand-père* to go to you. But he would not leave me alone.''

Falling across the bed, Sabine pressed her cheek against her brother's chest. With each whimpering sob that spilled from his mouth, his chest expanded and deflated. He was so thin. Almost unhealthy. "Forgive me.''

The warmth of his body against hers brought about the most amazing thing.

The bond that had been snapped rejoined. A fusion of light rivaling the brightness of candleglow warmed her breast and spread throughout her body. A flicker of being—of finally knowing her place within this great and vast universe—sparked and secured itself to her soul. For this very moment their souls fused.

"Oooh.''

He felt it too. Sabine knew.

And the madness fizzled to a brilliant spark of light that dispersed and spread, thinning and disseminating, and finally . . . erased.

"Can you ever forgive me, Christophe? I needed *Grand-père* too. I had no one else. I was so frightened. I had nightmares. Always seeing Papa on his knees . . . the blood . . . it never stopped.''

"And Mama.'' Christophe's voice cracked and was coated with tears. "Did . . . did you bury them?''

"Out behind the castle,'' Sabine whispered with loving memory. "Beneath the silver willow where they used to lie on hot summer nights. *Grand-père* dug two graves side by side. I made him trench a wide tunnel between the two and joined Mama and Papa's hands before we covered them.''

"Fitting,'' he said.

Sabine felt a trace of blood spittle fall across her hand but she did not move. She feared severing this new bond. A bond that hung from a frail spindle of webbing.

"It was good that *Grand-père* stayed with you.'' The sudden pressure of her brother's hand slipped lazily down her head. "You needed him more. I . . . survived . . ." His voice grew weaker with each word. "I still had . . . you. Our bond. Tainted . . . as it was. But now . . . I fear . . . it will finally end."

"Never," she whispered into the folds of lawn and lilac-scented damask. Sabine squeezed her brother's inert body, not noticing that the harder she pressed, the more her brother gasped. "I will always have you in my heart, Christophe. Always."

"Yes . . . always."

He closed his eyes. Sabine raised her head and watched his chest rise and fall. Blood trickled steadily from his mouth. She could taste death in the air he breathed. It did not matter what she had come for. It couldn't . . . Christophe was her flesh and blood.

But she could not help but feel the battle had been lost.

Louis would hang as Christophe's last breaths died upon his lips.

It seemed the memory of her husband's kisses had already begun to fade into a permeable mist. As if the darkness sucked away his love for her as it retreated from her mind. Her heart reached out for a trace of his memory. It touched upon something. The vision of his gentle smile. A flicker of his dark eyes as they drank in her body. The haunting warmth of his body pressed next to hers as they shared their love with each other.

Fairy angel . . .

Sabine pressed her eyes tight. Yes, he was still there. Her heart would never release Louis de Lavarac.

Cristoforo's eyes flickered open. "He is a good man . . . Monsieur de Lavarac?"

Sabine whispered quietly, "My knight."

"I know . . . that he loves you. Takes . . . a strong . . . coura-geous man . . ."

"He has been imprisoned for the false claim of attempted

murder against you. Before the moon rises again, I fear I shall lose the only two men that I have ever loved.''

Cristoforo raised a hand and it landed on Sabine's hair. He twisted the dirty blond curls for a moment. ''Send for the guard. I must confess to my own death. Louis de Lavarac must live to love my Sabine.''

CHAPTER
TWENTY-EIGHT

His nightmare stood incarnate before his eyes. Fine-boned and dark, the paleness of her countenance only served to offset her height with a fragility that made Louis think she might shatter should he touch her.

But she wasn't weak. He knew that much from the smarting flesh on his cheek.

Swaying on his feet from lack of food, water, and the broken bones that had been joggled and bumped over the last few days, Louis reached out and caught himself against the cold stone wall at his side.

At Madame Durant's stern request, the lackey had left them alone. The rattle of keys and pacing boots they now heard outside the thick wood door most likely served to ease the woman's nerves. She was, after all, as the guard had reminded her, standing in a room with a man accused of two murders.

However, from what Louis could determine, she seemed calm. Quite unafraid to be locked alone in this cell with him. Proud, almost, to show her strength.

And her voice was controlled, steady, yet Louis could detect the barest hint of tension when she finally spoke. "I understand you are here because of two *other* murders, Monsieur de Lavarac."

Other? So she considered the death of her own husband a murder. And by all rights, it was. Though Louis had come to accept his own actions over the past few weeks. Yes, he was a soldier. And a soldier must kill.

If she only knew just how many his musket and dagger had claimed in battle. The death of her husband was no more than a sacrifice for his own country. At least that was how King Louis put it, and his regiment commander had stated very much the same. An honorable deed. Had the circumstances been reversed, and it had been Louis under the knife, Henri would have no claims to legal action.

He had killed for the king. He didn't have to like it though. And having overcome his regret, he knew that he would never raise a weapon to another living soul ever again.

"Attempted murder," he ground out, still clinging to the wall lest he should fall. "And I did not kill the lawyer. I don't know where that accusation came from. And they are not . . . *other* murders, as you so put them."

But of course, Louis could sympathize with the woman's loss. He knew her torment well enough.

She turned and granted him a long summation, her dark brows not even moving, the swish of her black skirts, perhaps flowing over fine linen petticoats, the only sound in the small room. It seemed pity pooled in her eyes. For some reason, Louis had always imagined she might have green eyes. But hers were of palest sky, almost colorless.

"The singer," Louis began. "He stabbed himself. He was soused beyond comprehension. True, I had gone in search of him fearing he would harm my wife, and yes, perhaps vengeance carried my footsteps swiftly, but I was too late." He pressed a hand to his forehead, then instantly dashed the same hand through the air. "He offered me his dagger! Wanted me to do the foul deed. I could not, Madame Durant." He stood before her, his soul bared. "Death is not the answer."

Her chin held firm, Evangeline replied, "I believe you."

Surprising calm held her still. Louis chuffed out a breath of mockery from his nose. "You needn't."

"But I do."

"You are a brave woman to come here, Madame Durant."

She cocked her head, the feathered gray hat she wore pointing westward toward the barred window.

"It was l'Argent that found you?"

She nodded.

"I wouldn't have believed it possible to find you with the little information I had. But how? If l'Argent has been murdered—"

"I was already in Paris," she cut him off. "I've been traveling with my aunt since my husband's death. We part ways in two days' time, I to return home, she for Spain. I spoke to Monsieur l'Argent just two days ago. But you are wrong, Monsieur de Lavarac, it is not bravery that brings me to the filthy gallows on this dreary day. While I must admit I was initially horrified to hear tell from Monsieur l'Argent that you sought me out, I've since recovered."

"Forgive me," Louis whispered. Perhaps this had been a foolish venture. What had he hoped to achieve by facing the nightmare of his soul? Salvation? Redemption?

He had already received both from Sabine. Whatever came of this meeting would serve only to help or hurt Evangeline. Most likely the latter.

The sing of her stiff skirts across the pounded dirt floor directed Louis's attention to her. She paced slowly toward the wall, her head bowed as if approaching confession in the dark stillness of a church.

"We had been married only six months," she suddenly said. She pressed a gloved hand to the cold wall, studying for a moment the deep ruts between the layered stones. And then ever so softly, so that Louis had to crane his neck to hear, she whispered. "I did love him."

"Well." She turned her head with a heavy sigh and glanced to Louis. "As much as one can when given such a short time together. It was an arranged marriage."

"I see," Louis said with an understanding nod. A loveless match agreed upon most likely by parents seeking a stable home for their daughter. But to marry her to a soldier? Such an unlikely choice.

"I'm quite sure you don't, monsieur."

Louis stepped back from her approach. He nearly stumbled over the chains at his ankles, but the wall was not far from his back. She stood so close, he could draw in the scent of garden lilies with barely a thought. Pureness surrounded her like a billowing silken sail. Had he walked past her on the street and she had been clothed in colors rather than widow's weeds, he surely would have paused to consider her beauty.

"You think to understand love?"

He nodded. "Yes." Of course he did! Now.

Love, the feeling that encompassed his heart with a brilliance comparable only to the sun's redeeming rays. Strong in its presence, and yet soft in its entry into his life. Nothing could match love. Nothing.

"But I shall not besmirch the memory of your love by daring to compare it to my own," he quietly offered. How could he? Love had to be so different from man to man, woman to woman. There were likely more forms of love than shades of color or species of plant and animal. Ah, but he blessed the moment it had chosen to enter his life.

"We loved with a passion that frightened others," Evangeline said in a husky voice.

Louis could immediately bring to mind the same such passion. Scent of persimmons and wine, the taste of orange juice in his lover's kisses. *Ah, Sabine.*

Michele Hauf

"I was warned by many to be cautious. We both knew that war would soon claim one half of our liaison, perhaps forever taint it with a distance that would be irrecoverable."

Yes, the distance between two hearts. *Never farther than a heartbeat away.*

"He never promised to return," she said, her voice growing quieter, blending into the shadows that chilled half the chamber in darkness. "Only that he would never forget our love. Never."

Evangeline fixed her gaze to Louis's. He caught words of apology in his throat, unable to release them. Instead, he remembered that night in the rain, the eve of his final destruction. The night he learned that there are no enemies, only a madness of the soul that blinds and taints and wreaks utter desolation in its path. A madness that each and every man holds locked within him.

A madness he knew all too well. A madness he had literally touched.

Evangeline sniffed away the first tear that Louis had noticed. She searched his eyes. "Monsieur?"

"Yes?"

"D-do you think he spoke the truth? That he would never forget our love?"

Finally the thread of loss and utter disbelief surfaced in her tearing eyes. Louis carefully reached for her hand. She didn't flinch when the chain attached to his manacles brushed across her fingers. Warm, soft, and sweet-smelling, just like Sabine.

"I held your husband in my arms as the rains washed over us and he breathed his dying words." Drawing in a great breath, Louis repressed his own burgeoning tears. "He said, 'Tell my wife I love her.' And then he spoke your name, 'Evangeline.' "

Louis allowed her hand to slip from his and feather across her skirts. He needn't tell her he'd been haunted by her screams for weeks. Had nearly gone insane himself with the heavy guilt that had cursed him.

Forever he would bear the scars of Evangeline's loss.

When he looked at her face, she struggled with tears, biting her lower lip fiercely. But in her eyes was a smile.

With one quick nod she stepped away and turned for the door. "Have you any more need for me, Monsieur de Lavarac?"

"No, I should never have requested your presence in the first place. I pray you can forgive my impracticalities. And even more, forgive that you should find me in such a situation."

" 'Tis well that I did come. It was good of you to save those words for my ears." She rapped on the door, signaling the lackey. "I'll go to the chapel and pray for your soul when I leave here. And your wife's."

The chamber door swung wide, and Louis expected Evangeline to step out, but instead she backed up to allow two people entrance. Squinting to adjust his tired eyes to the sudden flash of sunlight, Louis saw the tattered skirts of a woman's dress and beside her a man in dark breeches.

"Louis!"

Before even seeing her face, Louis knew that the woman who rushed into his arms held the missing piece of his own tormented soul. "Sabine. *Mon Dieu*, I thought I'd never see you again."

"You are a free man." Henri's voice. "Cristoforo signed a confession on his deathbed. He admitted to falsely accusing you. It was he himself who plunged the dagger through his lungs." Henri embraced Louis and Sabine both. "Free."

The threesome turned at the sound of a clearing throat. "Not so fast." The lackey jangled his keys. "Out with you two. This man is no more free than a field ox. He may have been cleared of the charges regarding Signore Cristoforo, but there is still Monsieur l'Argent's death. The trial has been set for Thursday. Come, pretty lady, you'll see your man on his way to the gallows."

"Louis would never," Sabine interjected. She smoothed a dirty hand against his cheek. Blessed heavens, he needed her touch! "I don't understand what is going on. Why has this been blamed on you? Who?"

"I'm not sure." Catching the guard's evil eye, Louis reluctantly pulled Sabine's arms from around his neck. He quickly kissed each of her hands, steeling himself against lingering upon the smoothness of her flesh. It would only make his confinement all the more unbearable. "But if Cristoforo is truly dead, as you say, I fear the answer may be buried forever. How did l'Argent die?" Louis asked Henri.

"A bullet."

"I never carry a pistol."

"Save it for the trial! Come! I've not all day to wait upon your guests like some British butler holding teas and cakes."

"I cannot seem to get a firm grasp on you, brother." Henri sighed. "There is a strange spell on the city for you to have been caught up in such a farce. I don't know what to do."

"Neither do I."

"I will not leave you here," Sabine cried.

"You will," the lackey growled.

Louis released his wife to his brother's arms. "Be brave, my love. I will not hang for a crime I did not commit. Two days' time, that's all you must wait. I'll be waiting with open arms."

"You promise?" she cried as Henri gently directed her toward the door.

Louis swallowed. How could he promise something when in truth he wasn't sure himself what would come of him? The only man who might have provided the truth was now dead.

Thunk!

The sound of metal against flesh reverberated through Louis's veins. He turned to find Evangeline standing in the doorway, the steel-bound prisoner log held in both slender hands. The merest hint of triumph curled her lips into a graceful arc.

"The devil!" Henri cried.

"Who is this?" Sabine returned to the safety of Louis's arms.

Evangeline dropped the ledger at her feet and drew up a firm chin. "I am the woman who has just bought your husband precious time. Use it well." And with that she shrugged her coat from her shoulders and unpinned her hat from a smooth hive of dark curls. "I've done this before . . . for my own brother. Here. You may need these to leave unawares."

"More trouble." Henri nudged the guard's inert body with his toe. "The devil has been riding our backs since the day you rode home with—"

Ignoring Henri's slip, Louis dove to the floor and pulled the ring of keys from under the guard's leg. "Trouble that never should have been mine, brother. Quick! Take the keys from his belt and unlock the manacles. I can't very well run the streets of Paris with chains."

"Yes, we must hurry!"

Henri worked quickly while Sabine slipped the heavy irons from Louis's wrists. He pressed a hard kiss to her lips and then rose, her hand in his. Evangeline placed her hat on his head and Sabine slipped the proffered coat up his arms. It would never fit properly, but its length flowed to his ankles.

"You think this will work?" Louis searched the English-woman's face as she studiously tucked his dirty hair up under her hat and fussed until it seemed she finally accepted her work. He knew he could never pass for a woman. He had a week's worth of beard started. No boots, nor a woman's narrow figure.

"It'll do. Keep your head down. If you remain on your brother's side, blind to the admissions guard, it should work. There is only the one who stands outside the door, for the other left to take a meal as I arrived."

"What of you?"

"I'll remain behind." Evangeline scanned the inert guard and pressed shaking fingers to her neck. "I'll have to claim you forced your way out."

"That will do." Louis gripped her gloved fingers and squeezed. "Thank you, Madame Durant. I'll prove your sacrifice worthy. I only wish—"

She stopped his words with a finger to his lips. "Say no more. For the moment we are allies. Run quickly. Avoid the right bank, for there is a hanging in the Place de Grève."

A decisive nod erased all regret from Louis's mind. Evangeline had forgiven in her own way. "We'll need only a few minutes. We've probably less than ten minutes before he wakes and has an entire battalion of guards on our trail."

"And just where do you intend to go?" Henri asked as he followed the two out.

"Certainly not the right bank," Louis answered.

A single desk sat empty, the missing ledger obvious for the rectangle of papers that formed an empty space on the desktop.

"The left it is, then," Henri decided for them.

The guard stationed near the entrance merely cocked a sleepy head their way as the threesome left the shadowed walls of the Conciergerie.

Much too easy, Louis thought.

Tears flowed from his eyes as they slowly adjusted to the light. It was blindingly white, and so he pulled the brim of the hat low and gripped Sabine's hand and allowed her to lead for a while.

"Say there!"

The threesome continued cautiously.

"Don't stop," Henri said, then turned. "Yes?"

"Good day to ye."

They slipped around the corner of the prison quickly. Henri eyed Louis's bare feet. "The man had to be talking in his sleep not to notice such a sight."

"It worked, Henri." Sabine beckoned him lead the way. "But not unless we keep moving."

They crossed the Boulevard du Palais. There were no tight alleyways or taverns to hide themselves away on the Ile de la

Cité. The streets were relatively calm. The aroma of cooking meat and spirits told Louis it was most likely mealtime. He hadn't the stomach to eat. His very life depended on how fast he could discover the truth.

How that would happen, he hadn't a clue.

The sky darkened to a dull gray almost as if a candle flame had been blown out. The first smatterings of raindrops stirred the dirt into mud between Louis's toes.

They crossed two more streets and filed down the Rue de la Cité past the Hôtel-Dieu. Henri directed them toward the bridge just ahead. "We must cross the Seine. The Latin Quarter is an easy place to lose oneself."

"Wait!" Louis stumbled to a halt and caught himself against Sabine's body. "What if what we need is not on the other side of the river?"

"And what is it we need?" Henri returned to his side. "Do you have any idea how to prove your innocence?"

Staring into his lover's eyes, Louis wished only that he could drown out the details of his present danger and dive deep into her soul.

"Are you listening to me! We cannot stand here in the middle of the city," Henri said with a jerk of his hand to direct the two into motion again. The bridge lay just ahead.

"The cathedral," Sabine said. To their left stood the gothic castle of saints and heaven. "We can take sanctuary inside Nôtre-Dame for a moment's respite. Come!"

The guard would not think twice about storming the church's doors in search of him. But Louis hadn't the heart to say as much to Sabine.

They entered Nôtre-Dame on the west porch through the Portal of the Virgin. The cold and expressionless eyes of saints and kings carved into the archway stared down upon him as though the label *murderer* had been roped around his neck.

Henri's boot steps echoed loudly as they crossed the stone floor and started down the outer aisle to the left of the nave.

At Henri's command they stopped and listened. Louis stood erect, holding Sabine close. Henri looked cautiously around. No one about.

They stood near the winding stairs that led to the tower. Red and blue and brilliant saffron painted across the floor, pouring down from the grand rose window just above and to the right of where they stood. The faint aroma of musky incense lingered, seemingly just out of hand's reach. Enticing and yet another warning that they tread cautiously.

"To the tower?"

"We may be trapping ourselves," Henri said.

"Yes, the tower!" Sabine pushed past both men and disappeared inside the column of spiraling stairs.

Ripping the felt hat from his head, Louis tucked it in his breeches before taking to the steps. The seams of Evangeline's coat had ripped during his flight. *Mon Dieu,* but the woman had done a brave thing. He would be forever indebted to her. The best way to repay her would be to prove his innocence.

He made to discard the coat as he groped blindly up the dark and twisting stairs, but then realized should they be followed, it would be too good a clue.

There had to be hundreds of steps, and the final third of the way was cramped and narrow.

All were breathless by the time they graced the upper tower. The sunlight slatted across the floor and cast narrow lines across the heavy iron bells. Opposite them rose the south tower, and between stretched a walkway open to the darkened skies. Rain blanketed the outer walls and open floors, washing over fancy openwork railings that bordered the apsis.

A few sparrows had taken refuge on the fretted stone that climbed above their heads. The grotesques that lined the circumference, keeping watch on all who passed below, gave Louis a small comfort.

Quiet in his arms, Sabine took in the small tower room while Henri walked to the balustraded edge to look down over their path. From their vantage point the entire Ile de la Cité could be seen and even a few of the major cathedrals and building on both banks.

Checking his own quick breathing, Louis realized his heart beat with a terror to match a night spent in enemy territory without a lamp or spark to guide one's way. He closed his eyes and pressed his cheek to Sabine's warm head. "Can you see the Conciergerie from here?"

"A thousand devils, they have begun to rally! I count . . ." Henri spoke as he observed. "Half a dozen guards already on horseback . . . another six on foot. All headed in this direction! We must get down before we are trapped. This was a fool idea!"

"Don't worry," Louis whispered as Sabine snuggled closer.

He wanted to hold her tight and never let go. To steal the innocent charm from her kisses and work it into a frenzy of desire. But Henri was right. They were on the run. No hiding spot would be that for more than minutes, a half hour at best. They had to use their time wisely.

"We must concoct a plan."

"Now he says this!" Henri threw up defeated arms and paced past the two into the tower, where the bells hung in silent anticipation of their duties.

"And you would have had me remain in the Conciergerie only to face a trial of that damned castrato's peers? You know I was as good as dead there."

"Watch your voice." Henri dashed to the open railing again to scan the city. "They'll search the entire city. I'd say twenty minutes at best before they gain the cathedral."

"He was not damned," came Sabine's soft denial.

Louis pressed a hand to Sabine's waist and lifted her up to spoon against his body. Just a hug. That was all he needed. A simple embrace to squelch the terror in his heart.

"Forgive me, fairy angel. You were privy to a man I have never known. It was not your brother who condemned me to the Conciergerie, nor was it he who sent the bravo to the vicomte's estate weeks ago.''

''But Christophe . . .''

''Yes, yes, never forget memories of that man. Brother of your blood. I can only imagine the times you might have shared. Oh, my Sabine.''

Crinkling petticoats snapped, almost as if paper as he pulled her close. Maybe?

''What is that noise?''

''Hmm? Oh, I nearly forgot.'' With a firm tug she pulled a crinkled roll of paper from the waist of her skirt. ''It is from Christophe. He gave it to me . . . when he . . . as he lay dying.'' She turned out of Louis's embrace and pressed the rolled paper against a wide column of stone.

He could hear her heavy swallow, the tiny sniff to hold back tears.

Louis cast a glance to Henri, who held sentry over the city, and then back to observe Sabine as she unrolled the paper carefully so that the crinkles would not make too much noise.

''I believe it is *Grand-père's* will,'' she said as she drew two fingers over the ink-riddled parchment. ''Oh . . .''

''What is it?'' Louis scanned the paper over her shoulder, though he recognized only a few words himself. He placed a reassuring hand on her shoulder.

''He signed it here. Christophe Alain Bassange.'' Louis pressed the side of his cheek to hers, wishing his very last ounce of bravery into her heart if only she would allow it. ''And here . . . this is my signature, Sabine Margot . . . Bassange.''

''Why do you falter?'' He smoothed a hand over hers, tracing one finger along the paper. ''What is wrong?''

''I signed no will. This is not even my handwriting.'' Henri stepped quickily to their sides.

''Let me see. You are sure you did not write this, Sabine?''

She nodded and pointed to one of the three signatures at the bottom. "I always make a large looping S. Like a flowing river."

"Do you think Cristoforo forged it?" Louis studied his brother's profile as his eyes darted across the document, his jaw pulsing, his fingers running in fast trails from one side to the other. He needn't give an answer, they both knew it was true.

"L'Argent has signed it also." The silence between the three of them felt tangibly heavy as only the raindrops beat a soft rhythm above and all around them. Henri's drawn-out sigh pulled Louis's hopes down at the same time. "Whatever the hell went on in that lawyer's office, we may never know. Damn the heavens! All who could have answered our questions are dead."

"But of course!"

Louis and Henri simultaneously shushed Sabine's outcry. But she burst away from the two of them and spun a gleeful circle. Watching her ragged skirts fly above the rubble-dusted floor, Louis felt his heart sink ever deeper. An abrupt return to madness? Had mention of Cristoforo pushed her back? Reopened the door to her darkness?

A final twirl deposited his fairy angel into his arms. The wideness of Sabine's smile and the clear glimmer in her eyes answered Louis's worries.

"The boy," she whispered.

CHAPTER
TWENTY-NINE

For everywhere Cristoforo went, the young man, Pietro, was not far behind. He must have witnessed l'Argent's death. Sabine prayed for that truth, for without Pietro, her Louis would be forever lost.

The rains had become heavy, clearing most people from the streets save those without a roof to flee to. It was decided that Henri was the only one who could run to Cristoforo's apartments on the Rue St. Honoré without notice. The guard had most likely dispersed throughout the city by now. And so the couple had a nervous wait before Henri returned with news.

Sabine's feet were cold and itchy and so was the rest of her body. She stood just beyond reach of the rain at the edge of the tower wall. Louis paced back in the shadows beneath the high-arching rafters. Occasionally he'd dash to the balustrade and scan the streets below, offering commentary she'd much rather not hear. No one from the guard had approached Nôtre-Dame. Yet.

Daring a chance, she slipped a few feet forward and pushed

her fingers up through her dirt-heavy hair. As the rains showered over her, the filth of many days past was washed away and Sabine was able to smile even though her heart overflowed with worry. Cool droplets spattered her flesh with stinging bites and gentler lashes. The coat that Louis had lent her became heavy, and so did her skirts. The material clung to her breasts, her arms, her thighs, like a snug wrapper of healing restoratives.

Opening her mouth wide, she drank in the crisp water.

"Come back inside," Louis called quietly.

"All will be well," she offered as she slipped back to the shadows of the tower. "I know it will." She snuggled tight to Louis's chest and gave him a soft, lingering kiss. His lips were dry beneath her rain-slippery mouth. "And when we are finally free to cherish each other, we will talk the hours endless. Of our future." She kissed him on the forehead. "The children we shall have." She sensed his gentle smile as she kissed him on the edge of his mustache. "The forever we will share."

"Forever will be soon." He circled her waist and tucked his face against her neck. His nose tickled her collarbone. "I hope."

She reminded herself not to hug him too hard, for he had explained his ribs were injured. Sabine could not begin to imagine the pain he had suffered to rescue her from the horrors of Salpêtrière. She had almost given in to the darkness, stepped over to the other side in hope that the vicious realities surrounding her would be forever erased. But she had been rescued.

It had actually been Cristoforo—no, that wasn't right, it had been *Christophe*—who had pulled her up from the depths. And then Cristoforo had reappeared, only to leave her alone when she thought he'd come to save her.

And the horrid men who came into her cell after her twin had fled . . .

You mustn't think of the horrors that have been, she reminded herself inwardly. *Think only of what can be.*

"Make love to me," came her urgent whisper into her lover's

rain-soaked hair. "Now. Quickly, before our worlds are shattered."

"I will not allow that to happen. Hold strong, my love." Louis dashed to the edge again, poised to run if need be, and when he seemed satisfied that they were still safe, he returned to her side. The look on his face was a confusion of tension and urgency and desire. He began to hike her skirts up in the front. "We've only the moment, but I cannot deny I want— no, need—you. I need to be inside you, my love. Together we are strong."

But for how long? She hated to think the words, but to look back on the way things had been going, it was impossible not to.

No! She mustn't allow her worries to cloud this moment. If forever were to be ripped from their hearts, then she planned to take with her the memory of her knight in all his glory.

Her fingers worked with their own will, quickly locating the half dozen buttons that secured her lover's breeches down each side in the front. Urgency made Louis's kisses across her neck and down her breasts hard and demanding. He fingered his frock coat, soaked and soiled to her very bones, and pulled, popping out two buttons. Her breasts rose in heavy breaths to meet his rough touch. His hands were cold. His intent focused.

They hadn't time for the intricacies of seduction, nor to play their passions until they were spent.

"My love—"

A throaty growl cut off his words as Sabine felt the hot spike of her lover's entry.

Reality offered its sweet moments.

Already Louis shuddered against her body, his teeth clenched as he rocked inside her and worked her own inner core to a frenzy.

"Do you think we should go look?" she gasped, wishing his answer to be a resounding no.

"Yes. But . . ." He closed his lips over her shoulder and nipped, though he did not use his teeth. "Soon."

Throwing back her head, Sabine gasped in cool rain that spattered from an outside column and misted to their inner hiding spot. As her body released its coiled desire, so, too, did Louis's. He spilled inside her, hot and heavy and forever and ever until her thighs dripped with more than just rain.

"I don't want to leave you." His deep growls filled her ear.

"Never farther than a heartbeat," she whispered.

Urgently, Louis tilted her head up to look into his dark eyes. "If anything should happen today to separate us—pray God that it does not—I will always be close. Right here."

She clasped the hand he placed against her heart, her breast pulsing madly beneath. "I feel you deep inside."

He slipped his other hand down beneath her skirts, where her body still throbbed with his presence. He touched upon the hot pearl that brought an uncontrollable shudder through her veins and up to flush her face.

"No more," she cried. "Or I shall never wish it to end."

"Please?"

"I'll cry out. You mustn't." Tears suddenly burst unbidden from her eyes. She could not control her own emotions. At this very moment everything was so right, and yet the situation they found themselves in could not be more wrong.

"Don't cry."

She snuggled her head against Louis's shoulder and received his hand in hers, rubbing the evidence of their passion between their palms. "I'm not sure this time if it is because of joy, or for the fear of losing the happiness I have gained." She sniffed and offered him a brave smile.

This new and tangible pain cut deeper than all the years of darkness she had suffered. To love a man and know love in return and then to have it threatened was surely the cruelest torment a woman could ever face.

"You should go check," she prompted with a lackluster gesture toward the sky.

Buttoning his breeches, Louis returned to his post. "Dammit!"

She didn't need to ask when he dashed to her side and grabbed her hand. She followed without question as he started across the bridge toward the south tower.

"Two guards have entered the west porch. They'll be on us soon!"

The walkway from tower to tower was no wider than the length of her arm. As they passed the corner pillars Louis slowed to squeeze through the tiny space. Her back to the wall as she eased her way behind Louis, Sabine let out a cry at the sudden view of the Seine. Way down there. "Louis!"

His hand gripped hers. "I'll not let you fall. Stay close, I'll lead you to safety."

She scuffled over loose bits of hay and slimy bird droppings as the entered the newer of the towers and Louis tugged her toward another dark and spiraling staircase.

"Stop!"

One guard had ascended the west tower.

"Can you run faster?"

The sound of the guard's voice on the other side of the cathedral worked wonders to move Sabine's legs swiftly. Her heart pounded in her throat. She feared she would slip. The stairs were narrow and short, twisting endlessly. Her throat hurt with every breath she took. The lack of windows forced her to fumble blindly. She stumbled, scraping her palm across the cold stone wall. Louis caught her.

"Go on!" she hastened out. "I'm not hurt. I can hear them above already."

They exited the south side of the church.

Only to be assaulted.

Grabbed from behind, one brute hand smothering her screams, Sabine kicked and beat at her captor's legs.

"Henri." She heard Louis's voice. And only when she looked up to see her husband's smiling face did she quit her struggles. Henri released her, but he immediately pushed her toward a waiting hay cart.

"Under the hay," he said as he followed her and Louis into the back of the cart. His next command was to order the cart owner to drive on.

The ramshackle thing started into a roll before they were completely covered. Sabine felt a hand glide down her leg and pull her skirts close, tucking them between her ankles.

"Now they will not see," whispered Louis's voice from somewhere amid a blur of hay. He slid his hand across hers. For the moment her heart was able to return to its rightful place in her breast.

"You timed that one well, brother. Any luck?"

"The room keeper told me that the boy left but an hour ago. They've taken the body to be prepared for the journey to Naples."

"No!" Sabine cried, only to have to spit out a wet strand of hay from her mouth. She could see nothing, only feel the rocking motion of the cart and hear the brothers' voices. "Not back to Italy. Christophe would never want that."

"We must get to the boy before he leaves," Louis said as he squeezed Sabine's hand. "Where have they taken him?"

"It's just at the end of the Porte Nôtre-Dame." Henri said. "I passed but two guards on my return here. They've spread thin, for the rains make the travel difficult. I believe we can make a run for it, and then slip inside before anyone notices."

Battling what had become a near-torrential flood of water, the cart slowed outside the coffinmaker's shop. Henri tossed the old man a few sous and beckoned him onward before they raised suspicion. Keeping close to the walls of a tall apartment building, Sabine stopped Louis before they entered the street-side shop. "I don't want to go in."

Louis could no longer judge whether the water streaming across her rosy cheeks was rain or tears. But he knew her reluctance as well as any.

She and the singer had been closer than he could ever imagine. Louis recalled Cristoforo's words. *One soul divided.*

"I've already bid him adieu," she said. "I kissed him and promised to lay his body next to Mama's and Papa's. Allow me to wait here under the awning. Just hurry."

He pressed a kiss to the soft flesh in front of her ear. "I won't be long. We'll find the boy and everything will be as it should." He glanced around. To the side of the shop was a narrow alley. "Stay in there and sit low. Please? There should be protection from the rains and . . . well . . ." They both knew the horrors he dared not verbalize should she be spotted.

With a brave smile Sabine nodded and backed toward the alley.

Louis followed Henri inside the shop. Leaving his wife for more than a second sent an icy chill through his already frigid veins. But he couldn't very well force her to look upon her dead twin.

Henri immediately gestured with a finger to his lips, then pointed across the room. Pietro sat upon a high stone table, his legs drawn up to his chest. His head was buried in his lace-encircled hands. His sobs were loud enough that he hadn't noticed the two brothers' entrance.

No one else stood in the room. A pile of fresh sawdust and a rusted saw lying on one end of the bench indicated the shopkeeper might have left momentarily.

"The stench." Henri turned to Louis and pressed his fingers over his nose.

Again, nothing he hadn't grown accustomed to in his military stint. But the small room served to enclose the unmistakable smell of human decay and breed it to a heavy cloud of pungency.

A quick scan found a few silver medical tools on a tray near the only window. A brown-glass jar half full of murky water seemed to harbor some *thing* that Louis didn't care to know about. Odd to find such a sight in a coffinmaker's shop. But then, one could never be sure what demented sort of people worked with dead bodies daily.

In the center of the room, lying on a granite dais and commanding notice with extravagant red velvet and sparkling diamonds laced around every hem and collar, was the body of the castrato. His face was green and violet, the plum of blood risen to the surface in each cheek like hideous stage makeup for some forest story.

Henri nudged Louis. "Let's get this over with before the smell does me in."

The boy still had not noticed their presence. Fearing he would flee at first sight of them, Louis carefully stalked the room. Had he worn boots, they might have sloshed and suctioned with each step across the well-swept floor. As it was, he could not be sure his own shivers wouldn't start his bones to a loud rattle and give him away.

When Louis stood close enough to touch the muddied red heels of the boy's damask shoes, Henri's boots cracked across an abandoned curl of wood shaving. Pietro's head shot up. He pushed back against the wall, heels slipping on the rain-soaked stone. Henri crossed the room, and the two formed a barricade to either side of the frightened young man.

"You dare to come here?" Pietro raged with wide, tear-streaked eyes. "Was causing his death not enough that you must further torment the man before his bones are even laid to rest?"

"Silence," Henri snapped.

"I've not come for any such thing," Louis began to explain. Each inhale drew in the putrid scent of death, which forced him to speak quickly. "And I did not kill this man, you know that! He confessed on his deathbed. I've been cleared of that crime.''

"You drove him to it," the boy spat out through yellowed teeth. He still cringed, his knees bent up to his chest, but his arms were splayed to each side in preparation for flight, his fingers clenched into tight, defensive fists. "Just as that evil woman did. She brought him to his knees. She worked her witchery on him daily! She killed him!"

"Your master plunged a dagger into his own heart," Louis blurted out. The boy knew this! Henri had told him he'd been present at the castrato's confession. "He knew himself that the torment worked both ways."

Pietro dashed to the right, but Henri was quick to blockade his exit.

Louis reached and grabbed hold of Pietro's arm. The boy's sky-damask frock coat closed about a thin arm as Louis tightened his fingers. "Do not struggle, or I shall break your arm!"

"And would you take as much joy as you did in breaking my master?"

The sound of Henri's palm connecting with the boy's cheek jarred them all to a stunned silence.

Louis released his arm. Henri raised a threatening hand, but Louis stayed him. The boy did not deserve this violence! There had to be a way to coerce him into speaking without hurting him.

"What do you want?" Pietro said meekly. He nursed his cheek with delicate fingers while his eyes darted to the door, over to his master, and between the two men.

The pounding of horse's hooves gaining the slick cobblestones outside alerted Louis. Many riders. And moving quickly. Only a fool would ride on such a day.

"The guard," Henri answered Louis's gut-twisting worries.

Louis gripped Pietro's frock coat and pulled him within a fist's width of his nose. "You were with Cristoforo when the will was signed? Answer me!"

"Yes."

"Who forged Sabine's signature?"

Silence.

Louis shook the boy so that his head flopped like a rag doll atop his shoulders.

"I did! At Cristoforo's command."

Henri stood just behind Louis, his breath heating the air in heavy anger. "And who killed l'Argent? Come on, boy, tell me your master pulled the trigger. My brother stands accused of a crime he did not commit and you are the only one who can free him."

Pietro spit into Henri's face.

Before the boy could suck another weapon into his cheek, Louis wrenched the skinny thing into a hold by the neck. "Take a look around, boy. You are in a most convenient place. Your dead body will be right at home if you don't talk."

"Go ahead," Pietro squeaked as he kicked and struggled against Louis's hold. "I'll take my knowledge to the grave!"

A woman's scream pushed through the storm. Louis froze, his eyes locked to Henri's.

"Sabine!"

Louis dropped Pietro and dashed to the door. Like a sprite released from a seed pod, Pietro followed close behind, Henri on his tail.

"Go on!" Henri called as he started after the teenager, who had dashed the opposite way Louis turned. "I'll get the boy!"

Louis did not have to go far. As he rounded the corner and thundered onto the street, six horsemen waited. Sabine's legs dangled above the mud-slick cobbles as she was clutched around the waist by one of the riders.

"Release her!"

The first rider chuckled. He wore the blue-and-silver colors of the guard and an insignia of rank. First Lieutenant of the King's Guard, from what Louis could make out through the blinding sheets of rain. The lieutenant drew his sword and pressed it to Louis's left shoulder, not threatening, but certainly easy enough to slash his throat if he made a move. "Louis de Lavarac, you are wanted for the murder of one Ambroise l'Argent. And for escape from the Conciergerie. Turn yourself over to the state of France"—the man cast a lazy glance over his shoulder to his cohort's struggles with Sabine—"and I shall release your wench."

"He did not do it!" Sabine cried. The man who held her jerked her head back and slapped a gloved hand over her mouth, sending water drops into the air like sparks in a fire. Her back bent at a painful angle over the horse's wide girth. Her struggles ceased.

Louis's body tensed, his legs ready to dash forward, his sword fingers curling about an invisible weapon. It had come down to the sacrifice of his freedom to save the only woman he loved.

An easy enough choice.

"Very well!" Louis held his hands, wrists up, to the lieutenant. "Shackle me if you will, but release her now. She's done no one harm. Now, I demand it!"

The lieutenant turned to the one who held Sabine and at a nod of his head, she dropped into the mucky puddle below the horse's belly.

Louis dashed to rescue her, but the guards on foot were much quicker. His ribs screamed as both arms were jerked behind his back and the heavy iron bracelets were returned to his wrists.

"Move quickly!" Louis was able to yell, and his wife took his direction just before her captor's horse stepped on her leg. Instead, one deadly black hoof tore the hem of her skirt as she struggled to distance herself from the huge beast.

The sight of his wife dragging herself up from the mud was more than Louis could bear. She searched his face and he locked gazes with her. So very different than the first time he'd looked into her violet eyes in the meadow. No flowers, no dancing, not even the elusive unicorn. Gone was the magic that had brightened her smile.

Only one thing could save the two of them. And that person was long gone by now.

"Move on!"

Jerked into motion, Louis stumbled backward to follow the crew of horses. They were going to march him to the Conciergerie, drag him through the mud before the innocent eyes of his wife. Oh, that things had come to such an end. The heartbreak in Sabine's eyes would remain forever imprinted in Louis's memory.

I believe in you! he wanted to yell. *I believe in fairy magic and love at first sight and the existence of forever.* "I will love you forever," he mouthed, knowing she could read his words.

"Halt!"

Louis slammed into the hindquarters of his captor's horse at the sound of Henri's voice. He still held Sabine's gaze, and the sudden openmouthed joy that changed her sadness made him turn quickly.

Henri held Pietro.

"You've the wrong man in chains!" His brother jerked the boy's right arm, causing the grieving child to moan and buck forward like a broken doll. "This man here will confess all. He was witness to the murder. It was the castrato!"

Louis caught the suspicious lifted brow of the lieutenant as he looked from each of his cohorts to the other and then finally to him. I've already found my prize, his steely look seemed to say. Why trade it for a dead man?

"He's just a boy," the lieutenant barked. "He knows nothing."

Pietro kicked out and managed to say in his own defense, "It is true! This man has threatened me with death if I do not say what he wishes!"

"Liar!"

The guards laughed as Henri's iron grasp choked a mousy

squeak out of Pietro. Louis's fate depended on a boy caught in the deceit and twisted lies of the castrato. He felt for Pietro while his own heart crushed under the weight of the dead man's evil legacy. Cristoforo surely laughed from the fires of hell at this very moment to know that he had ensured his twin would suffer the rest of her days.

"Please."

All turned to the soft, feminine voice that leapt from the quieting rains like a spark of crystal. Sabine had pulled herself up and pushed the saturated hair from her eyes. The rain had begun to slow, and as it did, it revealed the strength in her heart as she approached Henri and Pietro.

"Get her away from me!"

Henri held firm against Pietro's struggles. Even the lieutenant stayed his men with a placating hand as Sabine stood waiting Pietro's attention.

"She is a witch! My master would never have ended his life if not for her evil influence."

Louis gasped in a rib-cracking breath. He stood ready to defend his wife—be it through the sacrifice of his own life—when suddenly he held his words.

Sabine closed her eyes. Her hands rose, palms flattening heavenward as platforms to the lulling raindrops. She opened her mouth and began to sing. Pietro's accusations ceased. The rains even settled to a quiet hush. Her voice worked a rainbow through the eerie silence as soft strains of Italian opera fell from her lips.

"Vendinati siam dal cielo Porgi a me un ristòro . . ."

And it seemed to Louis that the spirit of her dead twin inhabited her body, or at least had taken control of her voice. Through Sabine's mouth spilled Cristoforo's golden voice. A sound that brought spilling tears from Pietro's eyes and threatened Louis's composure as well.

A redeeming sound of forgiveness and hope.

"I do believe in you," Louis whispered from the depths of his being.

Muddy water splashed the knees and thighs of Pietro's aquamarine breeches as he fell to his knees before Sabine. Louis felt the chains that bound his wrists go slack. Escape would come easily with all attention focused on his fairy angel. Did she do this just for that purpose?

No.

Louis held his ground.

"Diù non sperata di ritrovarlo . . ."

The boy nudged his head up into the cupping grace of Sabine's smoothing hand. Her music softened to a chastening whisper. Only Pietro could understand the foreign words.

Though Louis understood their power.

"He was so good to me," Pietro sobbed into Sabine's skirts. "I will be so alone without him."

"Ceder deve un fido amor . . ."

"I will confess!" the boy screamed.

The lieutenant's horse bristled and stomped the waters in great brown splashes at the sudden shout. "Is it not this man we have in chains who murdered Monsieur l'Argent?"

Pietro's dull nods captivated all. Sabine touched his shoulder, and he rose to match her stance. Downcast eyes, soaked dark hair, slumped shoulders, rose-pink lips. He was a mere child!

"Tell them," Sabine said softly.

"It was I."

"What?" Henri matched Louis's surprise.

"You needn't protect him anymore," Louis said reassuringly. "The man is dead. Nothing can change that. Tell them it was Cristoforo who murdered l'Argent, Pietro. Tell them!"

"No, it was I!" The boy fell again to his knees. He pushed mud-smeared hands over his closed eyelids and stretched awkward fingers up through his hair. "I pulled the trigger at my master's command! I killed the lawyer. It was I!"

"Shackle him!"

Everything happened too quickly. The manacles about Louis's wrists were removed and instead clamped upon the boy's fragile limbs. Sabine rushed to Louis's arms. The rains stopped, save the constant spattering of falling drops from the surrounding roofs and carts.

"He's too young," Sabine whispered into Louis's ear. "He'll hang for sure."

Pietro's pleas for mercy brought the bowlegged coffinmaker out onto the street. His confused expression mirrored the injustice that Louis felt in his heart.

"This man has just confessed to a crime that he was *forced* to commit." Henri spoke up. "Surely this will be taken into consideration when his sentence is given."

"Surely." The lieutenant hitched a heel into his mount's thigh and the group set off down the cobblestones.

Louis held Sabine close, blocking her view of the boy as he slipped and stumbled behind the horse. Mercy? He doubted the boy would live to see morning. Innocence corrupted by evil. But not even that. Innocence enthralled by a man who had been God in his faithful and workshiping eyes.

"He is in God's hands now." He gave Sabine's arm a reassuring squeeze, and her trembles echoed through his own body. "We must not look to the past. The past cannot be changed. What was then will always be. And I believe . . ." He couldn't help the smile that crept across his lips. A gesture of relief. Happiness. And finally joy. "The future will prove far better than the past."

"Does this mean forever?"

Louis hugged his wife's shivering body, smoothing his lips across her soaked hair as he did. "Yes," he said in a strong and sure voice. "The two of us, forever."

EPILOGUE

Spring washed the sky a crystalline blue and coaxed the sun to halt the misting sprinkles of rain. Storm-fed meadow grass grew ankle high, tickling her bare toes with each burdened step. Using her husband's hand as a guide, Sabine levered herself down to the graves that lay in the elusive shadows of the Castle Bassange.

Sabine panted a little finding that her tumescent girth would no longer allow for such movements with ease. But it did not trouble her. She hiked up her soft cotton skirts and spread them over the tall grasses.

The newest of the four graves was topped with a fine cross of turned iron, fashioned by a Parisian blacksmith especially for his singing idol. '' 'Tis I, Christophe.'' Sabine lay a delicate sprig of ivory lily-of-the-valley upon the grass and wild-violet-covered grave. She then pressed the fist-long oak branch into the earth next to the cross. ''Never farther than a heartbeat away.''

Sabine released an exhausted sigh. Well, that was no longer

true. It was more than a heartbeat now. It seemed a great ocean held her and her twin apart, the icy waves whipping high, quickly dashing away any faint hint of connection. She mourned the loss of her brother. Missed their special bond.

But it was as things should be.

Turning to *Grand-père's* grave, Sabine pressed her palm to the grass, squishing down the soft emerald blades. A mottled brown tree toad fled her nearness in three springing leaps. "I forgive you, *Grand-père*."

She'd known all along that the old man had killed her parents. Not Christophe's dreams. Not her lack of power. Only one man's blind greed could be blamed for the years of torment her mind had had to endure. And for the years that Christophe, too, had suffered. The Vicomte Bassange had not ordered her mother's and father's death. But they could have been prevented.

Settling upon the mounded hump of Christophe's grave, Sabine drew in the fresh meadow air. Swallows flitted by, their sprightly chirps brightening her disposition. The sun shone.

But she knew, deep within her heart, the darkness still lingered. Like a single dandelion kite caught upon a steady breeze, the madness hovered. She could control it. Like a breath blown beneath the dandelion seed, she could chase the images and uncontrollable thoughts away.

Most of the time.

Ah, but now it was time to return home. Henri had warned he wanted them both home before nightfall. He worried about them. He was her family now.

And the family was soon to be increased.

"Help me, Louis."

"Are you in pain?"

"No." She giggled. "I just cannot rise, silly man. I've the girth of an elephant and the clumsiness to match."

Louis lifted her beneath her arms and stepped around to stand before her. How she admired this man who would be her

husband forever. So handsome his face and gentle his dark
eyes. His gaze was never harsh or condescending. Always
loving. Always safe she felt in his arms. It mattered not to him
that she would sometimes become lost, temporarily pulled into
the swirl of memories that would forever haunt her.

She'd been rescued by this shining knight. And he in turn
found rescue in her arms. The desolation had left his deep
chocolate eyes. Louis was her sun and she his. And now he'd
given her a gift as precious as the stars.

"I can feel her moving," Louis whispered as he spread his
palms over Sabine's swollen belly.

"Her?"

"In one month's time our daughter will be born." He winked
and cocked a chivalrous smile at Sabine. "I know. She's feisty.
Just like her mother."

"And what if it should be a boy?"

Louis kissed her nose. "And what if?"

"Then he should be brave and handsome. A knight born to
rescue a needy damsel from despair."

For excerpts and information on Michele Hauf's current and upcoming romances, you can write to her at:

Michele Hauf
PO Box 23
Anoka, MN 55303.

You can also contact her via e-mail at: mihauf@aol.com. While on-line, check out her website at http://members.aol.com/mihauf/scarlet.html

ROMANCE FROM FERN MICHAELS

DEAR EMILY   (0-8217-4952-8, $5.99)

WISH LIST   (0-8217-5228-6, $6.99)

AND IN HARDCOVER:

VEGAS RICH   (1-57566-057-1, $25.00)